# ANTON DU BEKE

## We'll Meet Again

ZAFFRE

First published in the UK in 2021 by

ZAFFRE

An imprint of Bonnier Books UK

4th Floor, Victoria House, Bloomsbury Square, London, England, WC1B 4DA

Owned by Bonnier Books

Sveavägen 56, Stockholm, Sweden

A CIP catalogue record for this book is
available from the British Library.

ISBN: 978-1-83877-404-2

*Also available as an ebook and audiobook*

1 3 5 7 9 10 8 6 4 2

Typeset by IDSUK (Data Connection) Ltd
Printed and bound in Great Britain by Clays Ltd, Elcograf S.p.A.

Zaffre is an imprint of Bonnier Books UK
www.bonnierbooks.co.uk

With
love from

Antonia Beke +

# List of Characters

*At the Buckingham:*

**Raymond de Guise AKA Ray Cohen** – lead male demonstration dancer

**Nancy de Guise née Nettleton** – a chambermaid and Raymound's wife

**Frank Nettleton** – Nancy's brother

**Lord Bartholomew Edgerton** – director of the board of the Buckingham, Vivienne's stepfather

**Lady Madeleine Edgerton** – Lord Edgerton's wife, Vivienne's mother

**Maynard Charles** – former hotel director

**Walter Knave** – a hotel director

**Billy Brogan** – a hotel concierge

**Emmeline Moffatt** – the head of housekeeping

**Archie Adams** – the leader of the Buckingham's orchestra

**Louis Kildare** – a saxophone player in the Archie Adams Orchestra

**Rosa Bright** – a chambermaid

**Ruth Attercliffe** – a chambermaid

**Mary-Louise** – a chambermaid

**Gene Sheldon** – a demonstration dancer

**Mathilde Bourchier** – a demonstration dancer

**Karina Kainz** – a demonstration dancer

**Diego** – the head cocktail waiter
**Mrs Farrier** – head of the hotel post room
**Mrs Whitehead** – first floor mistress
**Mr Ashworth** – a police officer
**Clarence** – a page
**Dickie Fletcher** – hotel board member
**Francis Lloyd** – hotel board member
**Peter Merriweather** – hotel board member
**Uriah Bell** – hotel board member
**Adalbert Grice** – a guest at the Buckingham
**John Hastings Junior** – an American businessman

*Beyond the Buckingham:*
**Arthur 'Artie' Cohen** – Raymond's younger brother
**Vivienne Cohen née Edgerton** – Lord Edgerton's stepdaughter, Artie Cohen's wife
**Stanley 'Stan' Cohen** – son of Vivienne Edgerton and Artie Cohen
**Alma Cohen** – Raymond and Archie's mother
**Hélène Marchmont** – former female demonstration dancer
**Sybil Archer** –Hélène's daughter with late husband Sidney
**Noelle Archer** – Hélène's mother-in-law
**Maurice Archer** – Hélène's father-in-law
**Sir Derek Marchmont** – Hélène's late father
**Lucy Marchmont** – Hélène's aunt
**Mary Burdett** – the matron of the Daughters of Salvation
**Warren Peel** – a patron of the Daughters of Salvation
**Sir George Peel** – railway entrepreneur and Warren's father
**Malcolm Brody** – an Australian airman, son of Emmeline Moffatt
**Elliott Knave** – a banker, great nephew of Walter Knave
**Leah Elkamm** – refugee child fostered by the Cohen family
**The Brogan Family** – father William, mother Orla, siblings in order: Daniel, Annie, Roisin, Holly, Patrick, Conor, Gracie May

*For Hannah, George and Henrietta – the brightest of lights, the greatest of joys, my everything.*

# Prologue

## May, 1940

THE FIRST WAVE THAT CRASHES over him sends him sprawling. The second drives all the breath from his lungs. The third pitches him into the fisherman's son standing at his side, and the fourth nearly sweeps him over the stern, down into the depths of the English Channel. It isn't until the fifth and sixth times the sea nearly claims him that Frank Nettleton realises he can stand upright. Another hour has passed before he starts to think he might even be of some use out here after all. He has to tell himself to take ordinary breaths. He has to tell himself to be brave. It's what his friends have been doing, those out there on the other side of the water, those desperate to get back to the safety and sanctity of English shores. The least Frank can do for them is to pick himself up every time he gets smashed down. The least he can do is stay loyal and steadfast and true as this little fishing boat, the *Camber Queen*, ploughs through the dark water on its way to the beaches at Dunkirk. Frank has dancer's feet. He has balance and poise. The men he's with would tell him it's not the same thing as having sea legs, but Frank thinks it will do. He'll glide across the English Channel, just the same as he's spent the last few years gliding across dance halls and ballrooms in pursuit of his life's dream, and bring back the friends who matter to him most in the world.

Darkness creeps upon them. The other boats fanning out across the Channel begin to disappear into the encroaching night – but Frank knows they're out there. He knows he's not alone. Hundreds of other small vessels have answered the calling. Hundreds of fathers and grandfathers, rushing to their boats for the defence of the realm. Sometimes, he hears the guttering of engines up above – and, through the cloud, he can see planes turning overhead; it's English boys, he knows, going to harry the enemy, and the thought gives him cheer. The grizzled old captain of the *Camber Queen* roars out his approval every time a plane roars past. Pride like that fills Frank's heart. It helps him banish the fear he's trying hard not to show.

He hasn't told them his secret. They'd have thrown him back on to the jetty when he rushed down to volunteer if he had. Because Frank Nettleton cannot swim a stroke. He's a miner's son, who's spent his life between the Lancashire pit village where he was born and the gilded hallways of the Buckingham Hotel, that jewel in London's crown where he has latterly made his home. He's as far from home now as he's ever been, and he's scared, more scared than he could ever imagine.

'Captain!' comes a voice. Frank wheels around, to see the fisherman's son pointing across the dark, churning water. 'Survivors!'

Frank scrambles to the port-side railings. The captain sees it before Frank does, but soon he too can make out the flotsam being tossed around in the water: the wreckage of some vessel much greater than his, blown apart by fire from above or torpedo from below. So little of it is left: just driftwood, thrashed around by the waves.

And, clinging to it, the unmistakable shape of a human body.

'He's alive, Captain!' shouts one of the lads. 'Alive!'

'Bring her round,' says the captain, his meaty hand slapping Frank on the shoulder. 'We got ourselves a live one.'

Manoeuvring a small fishing boat in this inky black expanse of the unforgiving sea is not like dancing the waltz – though it seems to Frank that it is just as skilful, just as elemental, just as much a partnership as the boat and its crew work together to pull off a remarkable feat. Defying the wind, defying the waves, they bring the boat close to the thrashing flotsam.

Frank peers over the railings. His heart skips a beat. Then it skips another.

'I know him!' he gasps. 'Captain, I—'

'Step aside, young Frank,' comes the grizzled voice.

The captain is preparing to throw a rope down to the survivor – but Frank has found his courage and takes the rope in his own hands.

'It's on you then, boy!' the captain cries. 'Has he got a hold of it? Then heave!'

Frank watches as, down below, the survivor flails once, twice, three times for the loop of rope. Only when he wraps his hands around it – the roar of another plane puncturing the night sky above – does Frank start to heave. The other boat-hands are heaving, too. They're working together, just like the dance troupe back at the Buckingham Hotel, and, soon, the survivor – or what's left of him, because his leg is broken and bent, twisted round at an unnatural angle – is collapsing over the railing, on to the deck of the *Camber Queen*.

He's hawking up salt water, retching and retching again, when Frank drops to his side. Yes, he's certain of it now – he'd know this face anywhere. It's the face of his closest friend in the world. The friend who went off to war without him.

5

'Billy?' he whispers, wrapping his arms around the frozen young soldier while the others rush for blankets and whisky. 'Billy, can you hear me? It's me, Frank.'

The young soldier is a scarecrow, sodden through. Every part of him shakes as he lifts his head, as his eyes – with a cadaverous, faraway look in them – fix on Frank Nettleton.

'Frank,' says Billy Brogan, in a soft Irish brogue, 'what are you—'

'I had to come, Billy. I just had to. I'll tell you everything when we get you home. But Billy, your leg! Billy, what happened?'

There is a moment of perfect stillness. Even the sea, it seems, grants them a momentary respite. Billy's eyes, which have been black and empty, spark suddenly with life. They lock on to Frank Nettleton for the very first time.

'Frank,' he whispers, 'we have to go back. Turn the boat around. Back! Back towards Dunkirk!' He lifts himself, tries to stand, grapples with Frank and plunges back to the deck again. 'I left him, Frank. I *lost* him. I lost Mr de Guise.'

Nine Months Earlier

September 1939

# ~
# EVENING STANDARD
### 3rd September 1939
### ~

BRITAIN DECLARES WAR!

BRITAIN IS AT WAR WITH NAZI GERMANY, NO REPLY TO OUR ULTIMATUM HAVING BEEN RECEIVED BY 11am.

In a broadcast to the nation at 11.15am, Prime Minister Neville Chamberlain said: 'We are at war with Germany. You can imagine what a bitter blow it is to me that all my long struggle to win peace has failed. Yet I cannot believe that there is anything more or anything different that I could have done and that would have been more successful . . . Now may God bless you all. May we defend the right. It is evil things that we shall be fighting against: brute force, bad faith, injustice, oppression, and persecution – and against them I am certain that the right will prevail.'

Following Friday's invasion of Poland by Nazi Germany, the cities of Warsaw and Krakow, among other towns, continue to be bombed – and we can today report the annexation of the Free City of Danzig by Nazi forces.

In a surprise reshuffle of his cabinet, the Prime Minister has appointed the Rt Hon. Winston Churchill as First Lord of the Admiralty, in which capacity he has commanded the Royal Navy to be immediately mobilised.

In his address to the nation, Prime Minister Chamberlain declared that Hitlerism must be crushed and that it remains the duty of all of His Majesty's subjects to fight the good fight. The editors of this newspaper would like to add to this sentiment our deepest good wishes and solidarity with the peoples of the British Empire for what may inevitably be our darkest – and yet, perhaps, our finest – hours ahead . . .

~

# Chapter One

IT WAS A GOOD DAY for a wedding. Buttery sunlight spilled over the rolling red-brick terraces of Stepney Green; the faint smells of the end of a London summer – of smog and smoke and sweet cherry blossom – lingered long in the air; and, in the heart of the little register office just off the Bow Road, a curious, mismatched family had gathered to celebrate a new chapter in the unfolding saga of their lives.

Raymond de Guise had never imagined his brother Artie becoming a married man. There was a time when Artie was the one who slipped away in the dead of night, the kind of man who romanced a girl one week and then her sister the next, who didn't think of the future (or even the past) because the only place he belonged was right here in the present, and whatever borderline-illegal pursuit he'd got caught up in this month. A vagrant wolf, Raymond used to think. And, besides, what chance was there for Artie to settle down while he was rotting in a cell in Pentonville Prison, or spending every night racking up more gambling debts to the nefarious friends he met in the back rooms of boozers all across the East End?

And yet, there he was, standing at the front of the hall in the same suit he'd worn to Raymond's own wedding, only nine months before – his thick black hair slicked back with pomade, his face clean-shaven (courtesy of their overbearing, dogmatic mother Alma), and a flower in his lapel. You wouldn't exactly call Artie smart, no matter what he wore – there would still be something slightly feral about him if he was in Raymond's midnight blue evening suit, twirling across the dance floor of the Grand Ballroom at the Buckingham Hotel – but today he looked as debonair as Raymond had ever seen him.

It was the reflected glow, he supposed, of the woman whose hand he was already taking. Vivienne Edgerton – who in moments would adopt Artie's name and become Vivienne Cohen – was elfin compared to her husband-to-be. At twenty-one years old, she was younger than him by more than a decade, with rich auburn hair, now falling around her shoulders, and bewitching green eyes. Today she was dressed in a simple dress of soft satin; the silver locket around her neck was not an attempt at ostentatiousness, but a family heirloom passed down from Artie's mother, and her mother before her. It was a symbol, welcoming her to the Cohen family forever and all time. Surveying them now, Raymond had never felt closer to his family; he might not share the same name any longer – having adopted a stage name for the ballroom some years before – but, in his heart, he was a Cohen through and through.

The ceremony was about to begin. The registrar, a dour-looking gentleman whose appearance made him seem more fit for a funeral than a wedding, was organising himself at the desk where Artie and Vivienne stood. Across the room, a ceremonial hush descended. Raymond took his wife Nancy's hand; she squeezed it gently, caressing his fingers and remembering, fondly, their own wedding, when snow had tumbled across Marylebone and Mayfair, and the ballroom at the Buckingham Hotel, where they both worked, had been garlanded especially for them. The wedding they attended now might have been less extravagant, but it was no less filled with love. Alongside Nancy sat her – and soon to be Vivienne's – mother-in-law Alma; beside her were Ray and Artie's two aunts, May and Rebecca, and sandwiched between them the ten-year-old Leah, who had first set foot in England in the middle of last winter as a refugee child and, nine months later, considered herself at the very heart of the Cohen family who fostered her. Such was family in an age like this. To maintain some sense of propriety (for, though it might not have been important to the Cohens, it was crucial to the registrar), Vivienne and Artie's baby Stan was currently in the care of one of Vivienne's closest friends. And, if anybody there even thought about the absence of Vivienne's own blood relations at the service, not one of them gave two hoots about it. She was about to become a Cohen, and to hell with those who didn't want her.

The service was ready to begin.

The registrar gave a deliberate, and somehow officious, cough into a handkerchief and scoured the room with his eyes as if he was counting heads. Then he said, 'Well, we're a little pressed for time, today being what it is, so shall we begin?'

Raymond watched Artie smirk and was quite certain he could hear him whisper, 'That's a good omen, isn't it?' before Vivienne slapped the back of his hand.

'We are gathered – we *small few* of us are gathered – to join together in marriage the two people standing before us, Mr Arthur Cohen and Miss Vivienne Edgerton. As registrar, it is to be my honour to shepherd these two souls into the revered state of marriage, until death parts them.'

13

Raymond tightened his hold on Nancy's hand. It was probably only Artie's muttered comment that stirred the ill feeling in the pit of his stomach, but there always seemed something untoward about embracing death as part of a marriage ceremony. He remembered those words at his own service: 'as long as you both shall live'. The happiest day of his life, and it had to include some sort of deathly prophecy. At least Artie didn't seem to be thinking the same thing; he was still beaming, like the cat who'd just got the cream. It seemed to Raymond that he'd been wearing that same grin ever since he first took Vivienne's hand.

The registrar was still talking. 'And now we come to the declarations.'

Artie went first. He was a man who held good truck with tradition.

'I do solemnly declare,' he said with some gusto – he'd been practising the words for weeks and was determined to make them count – 'that I know not of any lawful impediment why I, Arthur Abraham Cohen, may not be joined in matrimony to Vivienne Rose Edgerton.' He breathed out. 'There, now it's your turn, love. See if you can do better than that.'

Evidently the registrar thought very little of Artie's improvisations; he turned, without comment – but with a severe expression – to Vivienne, in the hope that she might rescue the occasion.

This she duly did. Without hesitating a beat, she said, 'And I do solemnly declare that I know not of any lawful impediment why I, Vivienne Rose Edgerton –' she'd hardened the surname; she couldn't wait to be rid of it – 'may not be joined in matrimony to Arthur Abraham Cohen.'

'Then let us make it official,' the registrar announced. 'The parties are, I am given to understand, exchanging rings?'

This was Raymond's cue. Standing up, he approached the front of the room and presented two small ring boxes, out of which Vivienne and Artie each took a simple golden band. Then he retreated to his chair, feeling strangely proud of the entire occasion.

As Artie slipped the ring on to Vivienne's finger, and Vivienne slipped the ring on to Artie's, something changed in the world. It was not a thing anybody could see. But it was, without doubt, a thing that everyone in the room could *feel*. Something new had arrived. Something else – all the old feelings of loneliness and being lost in the world – had been sent into exile, never to return. Raymond listened as Artie and Vivienne made their vows, watched as the groom (his rapscallion younger brother, he had to remind himself) kissed the bride, and realised that this was what it felt like to make a family complete.

'Well,' the registrar declared, accepting their signatures in his book and snapping it shut, 'I very much hope yours will be a long and happy union. These are precarious times, and I fear they're about to become more precarious yet.' He tapped his watch. 'One hour, ladies and gentlemen. Let us hope and pray for what little time we may have left.'

Then he disappeared through a back door, out of the room.

'Well, he was a barrel of laughs,' said Artie as the wedding party emerged on to the Bow Road, which was curiously quiet. The only motor cars to be seen were the taxicabs idling by the pavement, waiting for them. 'It's only a radio broadcast. You'd think they'd spotted a meteor about to crash into Canning Town.'

'Well,' said Vivienne, halloing the cabs, 'let's not talk of that now. One hour, he said. Let's have one hour, at least, where we put it out of our minds. It mightn't be what we're all thinking. There's been "Peace for our time" once before, as I recall.'

'Yeah,' said Artie, 'and as long as there's some nice grub and a pint of ale in "our time" as well, I'll be a happy man. Come on, Raymond! A man only gets married once. He deserves a pint of best and a bowl of cockles. Lead on. We'll race you to the taproom!'

The landlord of the Oak Tree in Stepney Green had agreed to open the back room especially for the Cohen wedding reception, Artie having frequented his establishment – and practically paid rent on the table by the fire – for more than a decade. Artie considered the landlord, Derek Bower, a personal friend; you had to, when a man had lied to the police for you and seen things incriminating enough to send a man back to a prison cell. Artie had cleaned himself up in the past years, not least on account of the dazzling New Yorker he'd just taken as a wife, but he never forgot his friends, and they never forgot him. Consequently, the back room of the Oak Tree was festooned with bowls of eels and pies, cockles and winkles, and slabs of thick white bloomer sandwiched around lurid red salt beef. Just the kind of banquet a proper Cohen boy enjoyed. Artie was salivating the moment he stepped through the door.

The guests, those who weren't family and hadn't come to the service, leaped up to cheer as the bride and groom stepped into the room, closely followed by Raymond, Nancy and the rest of the wedding party. A couple of Artie's old friends waited in the corner. Warren Peel and his father, Sir George Peel, both business associates of the newly named Mrs Cohen, stood to attention by the bar. Billy Brogan, concierge at the Buckingham

Hotel – and friend to Vivienne in the days when she used to live in one of its suites – was already tucking into a helping of pie, mash and thick green liquor. He made sure to slurp the last of it up before he, too, rose to his feet, applauding.

'The bride and groom!' Raymond announced to the room – and, much to Vivienne's appalled amusement, Artie began making bows, taking every hand that was extended towards him, lapping up the congratulations like a dehydrated dog at a stream.

Hiding the smile on her face – Vivienne always made a show of barely tolerating Artie's shows of gregariousness, but she wouldn't have had it any other way – the new bride crossed the room to a table where a doughy, middle-aged woman was sitting, cradling a swaddled bundle on her lap. The moment Vivienne came within three feet of that bundle, it started squalling – as only a six-month-old baby can.

'He knows it's you,' said Mary Burdett, who looked extraordinarily unlike her usual self, dressed in such fine clothes. She was Vivienne's partner at the Daughters of Salvation, the charitable organisation that dominated both their lives – she was soon to become Vivienne's son's godmother to boot – and, until now, Vivienne had never seen her without the begrimed apron she wore at work. 'He's been a good lad. Hasn't given me a smidgen of bother – and me without the foggiest idea about babies an' all. He's gone easy on me, haven't you, Stan?'

Mary Burdett was lifting the bundle up to Vivienne when, out of nowhere, Artie swept in and swooped baby Stan – named after Artie's dearly departed father – into his own arms. Then he was off, waltzing around the room, showing off the babe whose parents had finally done the decent thing and made him legitimate. Not a soul in the room cared about that sort of thing, of

17

course. There wasn't a family among them that hadn't covered up some shame or another. But Artie seemed to enjoy the idea that he was, at last, a decent, honourable man. From the ribald comments his old friends were throwing at him, they seemed to be enjoying the idea, too.

As Artie put on his show, Nancy felt herself drawn towards Vivienne in the corner.

'Mrs Cohen,' she smiled.

Vivienne took Nancy's hand and squeezed it, gently.

'Sisters, then,' she said.

'Sisters,' replied Nancy, and there seemed such simplicity and beauty in the word. That tenderness spoke to the history between them – the way Nancy had once helped Vivienne at the lowest ebb of her life, and the deep, lasting friendship they'd built since. 'You look beautiful, Vivienne. I know you'll roll your eyes – I know it isn't what you *value* – but you do. So there it is.'

Nancy was right; Vivienne was hardly interested in beauty. There was too much made of it in life; she'd heard it whispered in her ear too many times by besotted suitors, who were really only interested in a good time – and, of course, her stepfather's millions. Vivienne, who had once been swept up in that gilded, moneyed world, had had to develop her own rules in life – and one of them was that true beauty came from within. Nancy, with her mop of dark curls and determined eyes, her sleeves rolled up – defiantly ignoring the limp that had dogged her since a childhood illness – typified real beauty to Vivienne. She was about to say as much when Raymond, whose eyes kept flashing meaningfully at the clock on the wall, crossed the room to join them.

The hands of that clock had inched to half past the hour, which meant that only a short window remained to make this celebration count.

'It seems a shame to cut them off,' said Raymond. 'Any other day, they might have indulged themselves all day.'

Nancy whispered, 'But it's not any other day, Raymond. And they deserve to hear what Artie's brother has to say. Listen, if it's to be their last memory of a world without war, oughtn't you to make it something to remember? Give yourself credit, Raymond. You're a showman. So *show* them something. What is it you always say about the ballroom?'

'You've got to give the guests what they want.'

'Well, go on,' grinned Nancy. 'Give it to them.'

So that was exactly what Raymond did.

It had been hanging over them for two days and two nights, this prospect of war to come. Or in truth, for much longer – twenty years, if you listened to the old men who'd survived the Great War and still woke in cold sweats, dreaming of that god-forsaken time. Raymond hadn't opened a newspaper in the last three years without some reporter or columnist opining the dark murmurings of discontent on the Continent. And there wasn't a good English soul who could look at the rise of the self-styled Third Reich and not envision conflict to come. But two days ago, when the armies of the Reich had marched into Poland, the world had held its breath. His Majesty's government had, long ago, made assurances that they would march to war on Poland's behalf, should that country ever be overrun. The clock had started ticking . . .

It was ticking now. Raymond could see its hands inching further and further towards 11 o'clock, when Prime Minister

19

Neville Chamberlain would address the nation. The sands of time, running through his fingers.

Raymond picked up a glass – not the finest champagne flutes he was used to from the Buckingham ballroom, but a big, frosted tankard that had, not long ago, been frothing with ale – and rung a knife along its rim until the room turned to face him.

'What can I say?' He beamed. 'Where to begin? Ten years ago, if you'd told me I'd be standing here today, speaking at my brother Artie's wedding as his best man, I'd have thought you a runaway from Bedlam. Three years ago, if you'd told me I'd be raising a glass to my valiant, stalwart – dare I say it, *heroic* – brother, toasting him on having married the love of his life, I'd have screwed up my eyes and told you to stop pulling my leg. And yet here I am – and the pride I'm feeling right now, at seeing Artie and Vivienne brought together like this, is like nothing else on earth.'

Raymond wasn't lying, and, though he wasn't going to rehash the details of their relationship here – how they'd not spoken for years, how Raymond had followed his dream into the grandest ballrooms and palaces of Europe as a champion dancer, while Artie had wound up in the same Pentonville cell to which their father had once paid an extended visit – almost everyone in the room already knew it. Artie had never made a secret of his bad choices, not like Raymond – whose life had once been full of so many secrets that he'd scarcely told a soul the truth about where he'd come from, even changing his name so as to disguise his past.

'In the past two years, I've seen my scallywag little brother become something enviable. Something to be cherished. You've all seen it, too. We, all of us, know about his exploits when the British Union of Fascists came marching through Cable Street.

All of us know the days and nights he's put into doggedly protecting the Daughters of Salvation, and helping his good lady wife save many a beleaguered soul through its good work. We've watched the journey he's come on together, but none of us are more proud of him than I am today. And I look back now, at all the scrapes and corners we got ourselves into – every last one of them Artie's design, I ought to add – and I can truly see that he had it in him all along. Scallywag you might have been, Artie, but you have never been less than loyal and true to the ones you love.'

Raymond stopped and turned to Vivienne.

'And Vivienne – my new sister,' he said, with a smile. 'What can I say about you that hasn't already been said?'

'Better not dig too deep, Raymond.' Vivienne grinned. 'Too many skeletons – just leave them in their closet.'

Raymond was silent, but only for a moment. There had been a time, not so very long ago, when Vivienne's drunkenness, her licentiousness, her addictions and hubris had been the gossip of every concierge and chambermaid at the Buckingham Hotel. Vivienne's stepfather, whom she had long ago disowned and been disowned by, was one of the hotel's significant shareholders, and had ensconced his stepdaughter there in a vain attempt to keep her out of his life. But the Vivienne who stood before Raymond now was hardly the girl he had known back then; the journey she had been on had been every bit as transformative as the one on which his ne'er-do-well brother had embarked. It was fitting that fate had brought them together. It was perfect that, today, they were as one – and that the symbol of it, not just the rings on their fingers, but the baby wriggling in Artie's arms, was here with them.

'Vivienne Cohen,' he said. 'I couldn't have chosen a kinder, better, more well-suited soul to accompany my brother through the rest of his life.' He lifted his glass. 'To the bride and groom, everybody! To Mr and Mrs Cohen!'

As a group of Artie's old friends launched into an impromptu, and entirely off-key, version of 'For He's a Jolly Good Fellow', Raymond threw a look at the clock on the wall. The hour hand was creeping closer to eleven, but it was not there yet. 'Shall we?' he said to the landlord, who had returned to the bar – and the old man couldn't help but crack a smile. Moments later, he had fired up the gramophone above the counter and one of Noël Coward's latest recordings was soaring out.

Across the room, the dancing began. Raymond took Nancy in hold. Artie swept up Vivienne, depositing little Stan back into the arms of Mary Burdett – who herself was promptly taken in to the arms of one of Artie's ne'er-do-well friends, and quickly had to pass the baby to Alma and Leah to protect. There was so little space for dancing in the back room of the Oak Tree, but what space there was quickly became a hurricane of kicks and turns and glides. Nancy, whose left leg still pained her when she danced, gave in to it. Raymond lifted her up and, as he turned her, she caught sight of Artie turning Vivienne the opposite way. The girls' eyes met, each smile a perfect mirror of the other. Then they danced on.

But the dancing could not last forever. The music had soared, the dancing erupted, the joy in the room had turned incandescent – and was perfectly summed up in Stan's gurgling laugh from the corner of the room – when, suddenly, it came to a halt. At the bar, the Oak Tree's landlord lifted the needle from the record. Now it spun silently on, as he lifted the wireless onto the bar and turned the knob.

Raymond's eyes darted at the clock. The hour had come too soon. Bad news always did.

For a time, as the happiness and excitement of a new marriage filled everybody's thoughts, it had been possible to forget the declarations of two days ago, and the headlines of every newspaper since. But now, as the silence of expectation settled – as even baby Stan fell quiet in solemnity, waiting for the prime minister's voice to crackle over the radio waves – all those thoughts came rushing back. Raymond put his arm around Nancy as the pompous, rounded tones of the newsreader took them through the prelude to Mr Chamberlain's speech, with the gravity that only a BBC broadcaster could.

'It might not be what we're thinking,' Nancy whispered into Raymond's ear, with a tone that suggested she was trying to convince herself as much as her husband. 'We don't know yet.'

But as Raymond looked at every face in the room – at his brother and Billy Brogan, at his mother and new sister-in-law, at the refugee girl, Leah, who had already lost her home and whose homeland had, two days ago, been invaded – he had the sinking feeling of finality. He loved Nancy for her faith, and the flame of optimism she always tried to kindle. But there was a moment when hope ran out.

He feared that moment was here.

At last, the prime minister was introduced. Raymond let the words cascade over him.

'I am speaking to you from the cabinet room at 10 Downing Street. This morning, the British ambassador in Berlin handed the German government a final note stating that, unless we heard from them by eleven o'clock that they were prepared at once to withdraw their troops from Poland, a state of war would exist between us.'

Raymond held Nancy so tightly it was almost fierce.

'I have to tell you now that no such undertaking has been received, and that consequently this country is at war with Germany.'

There was more to be said – so much more, it turned out – but, although Raymond listened to it intently, he could scarcely take it in. He looked at his brother, whose eyes had lifted to meet his own; he looked at Billy Brogan, who'd already been spending his weekends with the Territorial Army since the first dawn of summer; he looked at Artie's backstreet friends, at Vivienne's upper-crust colleague Warren Peel; and he looked, at last, into the eyes of Nancy, his wife.

'This man,' Chamberlain concluded, 'will never give up his practice of using force to gain his will. He can only be stopped by force . . . And now that we have resolved to finish it, I know that you will all play your part with calmness and courage.'

*Calmness and courage*, thought Raymond. *Well, there's calmness and courage enough, right here in this room.*

As the prime minister's address ended and the newsreader returned, soon fading into background static as Derek Bower silenced the wireless, the wedding party breathed as one.

'Well,' grinned Artie, all of a sudden, 'this isn't a day we're likely to forget!'

'I think it deserves a drink,' Bower said. He was already lining up glasses at the bar. 'I think the good Lord will forgive us our trespasses if we raise a glass together this Sunday.'

'That's right,' said one of Artie's friends, 'this here's my church! If I'm off to fight, I'll do it with a pint of best in my belly, and no mistake.'

The drinks were being poured, the glasses being raised – Artie and Viv's wedding party turned into a send-off to war – when

Raymond noticed the young concierge Billy Brogan buttoning up his overcoat, slinging a pack over his shoulder, and heading for the door. He hadn't so much as touched a tipple.

Nancy had seen it, too. 'Go to him,' she whispered, and with a squeeze of her hand, Raymond was off.

Billy hadn't said goodbye to a soul, so when Raymond caught him at the pub door, it was a startled Irish lad who turned to face him. Brogan had matured in the last year; his features had hardened, his freckles grown darker, his red hair had a richer, almost nut-brown tinge. He was still as gangly as he had been when Raymond first met him, a fourteen-year-old page at the Buckingham Hotel, but he held himself more confidently now. He'd built muscle during the long months of summer. Attending to the rarefied guests of the Buckingham Hotel did little to encourage a man's physique, but long weekends spent marching in the hills with the army reserve certainly could change a man.

Raymond saw an unfamiliar look in Billy's eyes. Billy was known, at the Buckingham, for his ability to spin a tall tale out of almost every situation, to find diamonds in the dust; now, he looked as if he wasn't quite in the same room as the rest of them, as if he'd left already.

'You don't have time for a drink, Billy?'

'You know me, Mr de Guise. Eager to be getting on with it. Well, if there's a war to fight, sir, you can bet they'll need me out there. They'll be batting it back and forth right now. "Where's Bill?" they'll all be saying. That's what they call me in the reserve. *Bill*. Not Billy. They'll need me, Mr de Guise.'

Raymond said, 'They will, Billy . . . *Bill*. But let me stand you a drink first.'

Billy faltered. 'It's funny, isn't it, Mr de Guise? We've all known it's been coming. Seems we've talked of nothing else this year. And me, I've known it more than most, what with being called up for the reserve and all that, but somehow, you still don't think it'll ever come. I remember when my ma was waiting for all of her babies to arrive. You knew she had one cooking in there, and you knew one day it'd come out crying and making a mess and keeping you up all night. But until it happened, well, it was like it wasn't real. Like it wouldn't happen for another few months. Some time next year. Somewhere down the road . . .' He paused. 'This war's the same. But now it's here, and off we go. I've got to head for camp, Mr de Guise. It's what the rest'll be doing. I can't let them down.'

'All those boys, Bill, they'll be taking the time to see their sweethearts first. Their mothers and fathers. The ones they're going to miss—'

'Well, I figured I might have time to get myself down to Lambeth before I make for a train. Give the Brogan brood a proper goodbye. The little ones are off to Waterloo in the morning. Swept out of London with this evacuation order, like the rest of them. I ought to see them all, before I go. I mean to say – I *want* to see them.'

They called it Operation Pied Piper, and it had been announced mere days before: all the hundreds of thousands of children from London's streets, off to a future not one of them could envisage. Billy's parents had agonised about sending theirs; it was fear that had made their decision, in the end.

Raymond looked over his shoulder, back into the room where the toasts were still being made.

'What about your friends?'

Billy dwelt on this for more than a moment, and Raymond watched as whatever it was – the fear, the expectation, the *need* to just get on with it – that had been propelling him out of the doors faded away.

'I reckon I could have a tipple with my friends as well.'

Raymond slung his arm around Billy's shoulder in an unaccustomed gesture, and the lad didn't shake it off as the older man turned him around. Together, they made to go back to the wedding party.

'I'm going to sign up too, Bill.'

Raymond's words had a dignified air about them, as if they had been in his mind for a long, long time – and only now got their release.

'I always knew that, if the hour came, I'd do it. I'll go to the War Office tomorrow. Oh, Nancy knows it. She's known it all summer long. Married less than a year, and now we'll be parted. But that's the way of the world.' He stopped, before they crossed the threshold back into the room. 'The thing is, we're all coming up behind you. We'll be there, at your side, just as soon as they ship us out. I say we finish this thing before it has a chance to get going. Before the whole Continent gets entrenched again. Before things get out of control. They've never been stood up to, these Nazi thugs. It might be they don't have the thirst for the fight either. It might be, as soon as somebody bloodies their noses, things get resolved. But we'll do it together, Bill, every one of us. And then we can get back to the Buckingham, and the proper business of life . . .'

At this, Raymond shepherded Billy into the back room, where a dozen faces rounded to meet them.

'Let's stand our lad Bill Brogan a drink,' said Raymond, 'and raise our glasses to him, and all the other brave lads about to answer the call-up.'

'Hear, hear!' came a dozen shouts.

Even baby Stan – tucked happily under his father Artie's arm – added his voice to that chorus.

But not one of them got to raise a glass – because, in that very moment, a strange new sound was heard in the skies of London. Nancy put down her drink and rushed to join Vivienne at the windows. Artie held Stan tight and, catching his brother's eye, dashed for the taproom door. Alma Cohen hid Leah under her arm and tried to bury her from the noise while, at once, the landlord began to bark, 'There's a shelter, three roads over, and the church vault's not five minutes away. Down your drinks, lads, hell's a-coming!'

Half an hour since war was declared, in the skies across London, the air-raid sirens had started to sound.

# Chapter Two

THE BUCKINGHAM HOTEL: A PROUD sentinel overlooking Berkeley Square, a hallowed hall in the middle of Mayfair, a playground for generations of the rich, the famous, the rarefied and esteemed. At summer's end, the great copper crown at the hotel's summit looked down across the verdant green of the square itself, where the late summer flowers were in full blossom – and the only signs that the world was suddenly at war were the empty streets, the shuttered windows, the last sound of the air-raid siren that was fading into the air. In Berkeley Square, the birds were still singing. The September butterflies still flew. Life, in all its infinite mysteries, went on.

Inside the hotel, the indomitable Emmeline Moffatt – for over thirty years a stalwart of the Buckingham, and Head of Housekeeping for half that time – was bustling her girls up from the new shelters in the hotel's cavernous cellars, through the Housekeeping Lounge and on towards the Grand Ballroom.

'All hands,' she kept saying, picking up stragglers on the way. 'Everyone to attend!'

Mrs Whitehead, the First Floor Mistress, had apparently snoozed through the sirens by the warming oven in the House-keeping Lounge, and the less said about that particular situation the better; Mrs Moffatt woke her, surreptitiously, as the rest of the chambermaids flocked on.

'You're fortunate it was a false alarm, Mrs Whitehead,' she said, with matronly concern and not a little hint of admonishment. 'Next time, we might not be so lucky.'

By the time the girls from Housekeeping were shepherded around the sleek reception hall and into the Grand Ballroom, through the empty dressing rooms where the hotel's dancers and musicians primed themselves for their performances each night, the rest of the hotel had already assembled. The concierges and pages would be late to the 'all hands' meeting, because they had been appointed custodians for the guests, leading them to and from the air-raid shelters constructed this summer. But the kitchen hands, the porters, the restaurant staff and accountants, the chauffeurs and desk clerks, the members of the Archie Adams Orchestra and the hotel's famous dance troupe, had all taken their places upon the glistening dance floor: the hotel's own army, ready to face whatever was coming their way.

Mrs Moffatt straightened her white curls and apron, gathered her girls and, across the sea of faces, caught the eyes of Archie Adams, perhaps her closest friend – perhaps even more than that – at the Buckingham. There was a resolute calmness about the veteran bandleader. There always was, even in the heat of one of his orchestra's fiercest numbers. That clenched Mrs Moffatt's heart. She had wanted to go to him in the hotel cellars, when the sirens were still wailing, but duty and propriety had meant she had to stay with her girls – with Rosa and Ruth, both excellent chambermaids, and the newer girls who were just joining the Buckingham – and see them through the ordeal. They had, she believed, coped admirably, Rosa in particular. But how they might cope when it came to the real thing, Mrs Moffatt was not sure. It hadn't been like this during the last war, she remembered. The last war had happened somewhere else. If this one truly did take place in the skies above London, Mrs Moffatt wasn't sure how she herself would manage.

The hubbub in the Grand Ballroom was rising to a pitch, all the good souls of the hotel finally finding some release after the panic of the sirens. This place was the beating heart of the Buckingham. It was the place that gave the hotel its reputation, that drew in kings and queens and crown princes from near and far. *Yes*, thought Mrs Moffatt, *this place has seen some dramas*. But the drama it would see in the coming years would make a mockery of all others – of that there was no doubt.

'Girls,' said Mrs Moffatt; she had seen the great arched doors that led to the reception hall fluttering and knew the moment was here. 'Girls, calm down. He's here.'

Rosa and Ruth, who had been bickering over some insignificant detail, straightened themselves out. Silence spread from them to the surrounding girls, and from there across the dance floor. Two hundred faces turned to the ballroom doors.

They opened.

And in their frame there appeared a lean beanpole of a boy, nineteen years old, with curly hazel hair and a startled expression.

'It's only your sweetheart, Frank,' Ruth chided Rosa, with a snort of laughter. 'Frank Nettleton!' she cried out, and soon other pockets of laughter had broken out across the Grand Ballroom. 'Late as always!'

'Get over here, Frank!' Rosa exclaimed.

Her cheeks, like Frank's, were burning the deepest shade of crimson, and it seemed to set her chestnut hair aflame. But

Frank, upon hearing her, had started to scuttle her way. He moved with much more grace than his rabbit-in-headlights appearance allowed. He had dancer's feet – and, if you could look beyond his often dishevelled appearance, he was beginning to have the long, lithe physique of a dancer as well. A summer of hard training could do that to a man.

Frank crashed through various porters on his way to the group of chambermaids, who wrapped themselves around him as if he was their little brother. Rosa – to whom Frank was something more than a brother – threw her arms over his shoulders, and the only thing that stopped her covering him in kisses was when Mrs Moffatt gave her a scolding look. After that, Rosa stood back and dusted Frank down; it was only now that she saw he was covered in bits of dirt, and that his trousers were scuffed at the knees.

'I was hardly off the train from Rye when the sirens started. Rosa, I didn't know where to go—'

'Where did you take shelter, Frankie?'

'There was a shopkeeper. He let us into his basement.' He looked at his knees. 'I'm afraid I tripped and fell on the stairs.'

'Frankie,' Rosa laughed, 'you'd hardly think you're training as a dancer.'

'Well, maybe not for much longer,' he said.

It was only a matter of months since Frank had taken part in his first demonstration dance, those afternoon fixtures where the hotel dance troupe performed for the pleasure of the guests to whom they'd be hired out that evening. It had been a moment he'd been dreaming of ever since he turned up at the Buckingham Hotel, a simple Lancashire lad coming down to join his sister Nancy in the big city. Now, after two years working hard as a page, he'd been afforded his chance at proving himself a dancer on the hotel stage, perhaps one day rising up to become a dedicated member of its troupe. He'd spent yesterday training, long into the night, at the home of one of the Buckingham's retired dancers, Hélène Marchmont, who had taken it upon herself to help Frank sharpen his act with occasional lessons. Now, however, it seemed as if dancing would be a thing of the past; it would be the soldier's life for him. His best friend at the hotel, Billy Brogan, had already been enlisted. Frank supposed it was only a matter of time – days, hours even – before he himself got the call.

Rosa flashed him a look of concern. 'You all right, Frank? You look shaken up.'

'Maybe a little,' said Frank. 'Aren't we all? I mean, there've been air-raid tests before, but . . .' It had felt different, knowing that war was truly declared. 'There were planes in the sky, Rosa.'

'Must have been ours,' chipped in Rosa. She dazzled Frank with a look, as if to tell him that everything was OK, that all of this foolishness would be over in a few days. She could be like that – Rosa Bright, determined to see the up-side to everything. Frank needed someone like that in his life. 'Look at us, we're making air raids against ourselves, and the war's not yet one hour old—' She stopped. 'Eyes front, girls. The door's opening again.'

Mrs Moffatt hustled her girls back into formation, as all eyes in the Grand Ballroom turned back to the front. Slowly, inch by inch, the doors drew back.

'Here he comes, girls. Keep your hands folded and backs straight. You know what our director likes to see.'

In the open doorway stood the hotel director, Walter Knave.

The pages called him Methuselah, which was a joke one of them from a particularly devout family had concocted. Methuselah: the ancient man. Walter Knave did not have all of the Biblical character's 969 years, but he had a good number of them. Variously, reports put him at 79 and 86 years of age. He had shrunk with the years and, never having been a particularly hefty chap, now looked positively childlike as he stepped through the doors. Childlike, that is, if it wasn't for his wisps of grey hair, his face like a wrinkled-up bed sheet, and his eyes that loomed, comically large, behind gold-rimmed spectacles. Frank sometimes thought of him as a tortoise in human form. The clothes he was wearing had fitted him once upon a time, but, unlike him, they had not shrunk with the years. Evidently, nobody had thought to provide the director of one of London's most prestigious fine hotels with a new wardrobe for his role. Because, as old as Walter Knave was, the fact was that this was his first year back in charge of the Buckingham Hotel – the first summer, after a twenty-year hiatus, when he had marshalled the hotel's staff and taken charge of its every detail. 'A safe pair of hands' the board had called him, when it became apparent, last Christmas, that a new hotel director would be needed to replace the outgoing old. 'Somebody who knows the hotel inside and out. Somebody to steady the ship as we sail into choppy waters. No, we can't take a chance on some young upstart. Better we look to tradition. Better we look to somebody who knows their onions. Somebody who's been here before.'

Walter tottered into the ballroom, leaning heavily upon his walking stick, scoured the assembled staff with eyes that seemed barely able to make out a face, and ventured down towards the dance floor. The space between the doors and the balustrade surrounding the dance floor was not vast, but it took him an aeon to cross it. There he propped himself, took a few laboured breaths and began:

'Well, one air raid in and we're all on our feet. That's a good sign.' Then he started hawing with laughter. It was a most uncomfortable sound; it sounded, to Mrs Moffatt's ears, like a donkey being repeatedly kicked in the kidneys. 'Another good sign – no panic in the halls. No headless chickening around. We got our guests down to shelter and up again with a minimum of fuss. That's to be applauded. We did a good job.'

Walter wiped his lips with the back of his hand. Mrs Moffatt remembered that gesture well; it was the gesture he used to make, during his first tenure at the Buckingham, to disguise the traces of the hotel's best Merlot that were perennially on his lips. Walter Knave had always enjoyed a drink – and, apparently, in his dotage the habit was even worse. Well, men often succumbed to the bottle when their darling wives departed the earth. Walter had been married for forty years before his sweetheart Blythe passed away. She must have been the one to keep him in check – Mrs Moffatt remembered her as beautiful but austere – because, now that she was gone, his lips were permanently the colour of a livid bruise.

'Look, we've been expecting this. I didn't get where I am today without expecting and preparing for the worst. But you're –' he hiccuped dramatically; it seemed to shake his whole body – 'in the best possible hands. Some of you were here with me, during the Great War. We saw the hotel through a dark time, then. We'll see it through a dark time now – or my name's not –' he hiccuped again, more dramatically than the last – 'Walter Knave. The news today isn't what any of us wanted. It will dent our business. It will close our borders. It will, I'm sure, mean a tightening of purse strings and suites sitting empty. But we've a duty – a duty to one another – to keep this hotel running. Business goes on. Guests are still here – to be cherished and served. Now, I know things are going to change. If the whispers are true, some of you won't be here for very much longer. You'll be in uniforms and going out there to bloody this Hun's nose and stand up for your king. And that's only right. Those of us left behind will be soldiering on in your absence. And make no mistake about it – we will all be soldiers, now, soldiers in the service of this fine hotel. And I, Walter Knave will be your . . .' He faltered, but it wasn't because of a hiccup this time; evidently something he'd eaten was giving him some gripe, because he suddenly cupped a hand to his belly. '. . . general,' he finally said. 'There's still this winter ball of ours on the horizon. The Midwinter Serenade. There are still meals to be prepared and beds to be changed. So let's not break stride, everyone. Let's stick together. Let's . . .' Walter Knave couldn't find the final word; he waved it away airily. 'Back to your posts, everybody. I'll be in my office until evening. Those of you thinking of attending the War Office directly, I'd ask you to report in to me first. We all have to be prepared. Let's march on!'

Then, showing in no uncertain terms exactly what he meant by 'marching' – tottering in a zigzag back to the ballroom door, and lurching off towards reception – Walter Knave departed the throng.

For a time, there was silence in the ballroom. Mystified faces looked at mystified faces. It wasn't that Walter Knave hadn't said the right things; it wasn't that he hadn't meant to inspire; it was that there was a peculiar mismatch between the things he'd said and the feeling behind them. He might as well have been reading from a script. He was, thought Mrs Moffatt, like the engineer who often came to tinker with and fix the hotel's various boilers – moving steadily through his checklist of things to inspect and boxes to tick, so that he could get away with a minimum of fuss.

Some of the gathered parties were starting to disperse. The hotel dance troupe – what elements of it were there – were gravitating with the musicians towards the back doors. The chef of the Queen Mary, the Buckingham's finest restaurant, was marshalling his kitchen hands and waiting staff back to their tasks. Mrs Moffatt rallied her girls, too.

'You heard Mr Knave. Still beds to be changed. Let's keep our hands busy and not get distracted. It's seismic news, but there'll be more of it to come. And, as for you, Frank Nettleton ...' She looked him up and down and warmly added, 'Get yourself sorted, Frank. The guests will have a hundred errands they need running on a day like this.'

The chambermaids seemed only too happy enough to rush back to their duties, though Mrs Moffatt had little doubt they'd be distracted all through the long day. Everybody had a brother, a father, a lover or husband whose life was about to change. She stood in the emptying ballroom, remembering vividly the last time war had come and how, back then, she herself had been one of those chattering chambermaids, about to learn some hard lessons about the world.

She was so lost in those thoughts that she didn't, at first, realise that Archie Adams, with his immaculate near-white hair and spotless dinner jacket, was approaching her through the dispersing crowd. The first moment she knew he was there was when she heard her name, 'Emmeline,' being whispered with a tenderness she was still unused to.

'Feeling inspired, Emmeline?'

Mrs Moffatt gave a rueful smile. 'I think we have to find our own inspirations, Mr Adams.' She still called him 'Mr Adams', even though their friendship sometimes seemed to promise much more; but Mrs Moffatt – with her wise blue eyes and inner calm – had always believed that the best things in life matured slowly. Like Stilton cheese and Christmas pudding. 'I'm not sure my girls are truly taking it to heart – not quite yet. Good Lord, if Mr Charles was still here . . .'

Maynard Charles, the director who'd left the Buckingham at the start of the year, would have inspired them. Mrs Moffatt didn't doubt that. They'd have rallied to him: the porters and the pages, the musicians and dancers, the high-born and low – everyone who had pledged their services to the Buckingham Hotel. But rallying around Walter Knave would be like dancing around a flaccid maypole.

She said, 'I don't know what to say to them, Archie. We're going to lose so many staff. This hotel's going to feel empty. Your orchestra—'

'Some of us are far too old for fighting,' said Archie.

He was referring, of course, to himself. 'And some of us are very glad to hear it. There are some advantages, after all, that come with age. But, Archie, what happens to Malcolm?'

Mrs Moffatt's son, Malcolm, an airman by trade, would soon be flying sorties over the Continent; soon, she imagined, he would be turning spirals over London's skies to repel any attack. She had given Malcolm up for adoption when she was little more than a child herself, and found him again only recently. She'd missed out on so much about being a mother, but the one thing she hadn't missed out on was the aching fear that something terrible might happen; that – the most unnatural thing – a mother might somehow outlive her son.

'We needed a better man than Knave,' she whispered, careful not to be overheard. 'Why the board entrusted the hotel to him, in this moment, I'll never know.'

Archie hadn't been around when Knave last ran the Buckingham; back then, the ballroom didn't exist, and the idea of music and dance being at the heart of everything the Buckingham did was strange and fanciful.

'But *I* remember,' said Mrs Moffatt. 'He was weak then, and he's weaker now.'

'They say he got the hotel through the Great War.'

'No,' said Mrs Moffatt. '*We* got the hotel through the Great War. Every last one of us, rolling up our sleeves and pushing ourselves to our limits. Mr Knave sailed through with all the credit for it – and what little he did do was down to his late wife, Blythe. Now *there* was an engine room of a woman. *There* was a leader. I admired Mrs Knave – for her character, if not her choice of men. But . . .'

Mrs Moffatt faltered, and into the silence, Archie said, 'We'll simply have to dig deep again.'

'I just wonder if my girls have it in them.'

'Knave's in Lord Edgerton's pocket, of course. That's why he's here, Emmeline.'

Words like that were close to treachery in the Buckingham Hotel this past year. Bartholomew Edgerton: the imperious member of the Hotel Board, the man whose capital had once rescued the hotel, and the man who was determined to control it. He'd been frustrated in his ambition to control the board two years ago, by the appearance of the American industrialist

John Hastings; the last hotel director had forged a strong bond of trust and friendship with Hastings, but there was little doubt that Knave was Lord Edgerton's man.

'Politics and puppets,' whispered Mrs Moffatt. 'Rich men and their need to control. You'd have thought we could put aside rivalries like that, in a time like this. You'd have thought we could work together, with everything we had.' She paused, uncertain if she should say what was on the tip of her tongue. 'Mr Knave's been taking that fascist newspaper, *Action*. I've seen it on his desk.' Mrs Moffatt lifted her hand to her mouth; both were trembling. 'He always had his ideas. Even during the last war, he wasn't shy about saying things, not when he was drinking. And . . . Oh, I don't suppose he's a member of the union like Lord Edgerton and the rest – but he's still friends with the nasty little fascists. To have one of *them*,' whispered Mrs Moffatt, 'at the head of our hotel. In a time like this. I'd understand it, if he were even *capable*. People make deals with the Devil all the time, don't they? Appoint a man like that, if you must, but at least make sure he can run things properly. The staff need inspiration, Archie. They need togetherness. Mr Knave doesn't have what it takes.'

Archie had stepped a little closer to her as she spoke. He was so close, now, that she could smell his aftershave, the talcum powder around the collar of his shirt.

'Maybe not,' he said, 'but *we* do, don't we, Emmeline? All of us, here, in the Buckingham?'

'We'll have to,' said Mrs Moffatt – and their eyes met tenderly across the ballroom floor.

# Chapter Three

NANCY DE GUISE HAD SPENT the year of 1939 fashioning the empty rooms at number 18 Blomfield Road into a home she and Raymond could be proud of. They had lived, separately, in the Buckingham Hotel for so many years that moving out to establish a home of their own had, at first, felt unnatural and strange. It was in the ballroom that they'd first met; in the ballroom where they'd danced for the first time; in the hotel's hallowed halls that they'd fallen in love, lost each other, and found each other again. They'd been anchored in the Buckingham; but with marriage, life changed, and now they were anchored in each other instead.

Number 18 Blomfield Road sat in the heart of Maida Vale. One year ago, it had been an empty house – cherished in days gone by, but now as bare as a life before love. Then came the furniture they'd chosen together, the wedding gifts from family and friends, the new portraits that hung on the wall, of the day they were joined and their lives before that. In the sitting room, above the fire, sat a portrait of Nancy's mother and father, long gone from this world, on the day they, too, were wed. There was a picture of Frank, as an eight-year-old boy with his sixteen-year-old sister – as good as a mother to him – with her arm draped around his shoulder. All of Raymond's trophies gleamed on one of the shelves set into the alcove, and so, too, did the framed portraits of him in the Imperial Hall in Würzburg, or the Schönbrunn Palace in Vienna – the famous and feted ballrooms he'd visited in those whirlwind years when he'd criss-crossed the Continent, answering the call of dance. Two lives, condensed into the seven rooms of number 18 Blomfield Road.

And now, all of this was to be torn apart by war.

Dinner tonight was Lancashire hotpot – the meal of Nancy's youth, the meal over which Raymond had first proposed marriage, and now the meal over which their lives would change again. She served it in the white china Mrs Moffatt had given them on their wedding day, and poured them each glasses of the hotel's best Bordeaux; well, there were yet perks to working in one of London's finest hotels, and this was one of them.

The war was not an elephant in the room. Nancy and Raymond did not conduct their marriage like that. There had been too many secrets in their pasts, so secrets had long ago been abandoned in favour of bold, open conversation. Nancy could conduct her life no other way, and it was one of the very many things Raymond loved about her. She broke the top of her hotpot, releasing a geyser of steam and the rich, meaty scent of slow-cooked mutton, and said, 'Will you do it straight away?'

The idea had not left Raymond's mind all day long. Ever since he'd stood with Billy at the doors to the Oak Tree, and learned where the young lad was destined, the thought had been preying on him.

'If I'm right, they wouldn't come for me straight away. I'm 33 years old. An old man, by their standards. It might be a year,

42

even more, before I got the call-up. Who knows what might have happened by then?'

'The war might be over,' Nancy interjected.

Raymond was still. Neither of them had been old enough to fight the last time war came around, but both had grown up in its shadow; not a man alive could escape the touch of those dark days, and all the false promises that had been made. They'd said it would be over by Christmas. Well, nobody was making those assertions this time round. When Raymond thought about it, all that he saw were long years of war stretching ahead.

'I have to do my duty, Nancy. I can't leave it all to lads like Billy. Lads like –' his eyes roved across the portraits sitting on the mantel – 'Frank.'

A ghostly look washed across Nancy's face. 'He's too young, Ray.'

*Ray.* She only used that name – the name by which he used to be known, long before he came to the Buckingham Hotel and took on the moniker 'de Guise' – when she was at her most naked, her most vulnerable.

'He's 19 years of age,' said Raymond.

'He's a boy.'

*He* was *a boy*, thought Raymond. Sometimes a boy became a man at the age of eleven; other times, his youth followed him deep into his twenties. Until he'd come to join Nancy in London, Frank had worked in the pit in the village they'd called home – but not even that environment had really stopped him seeming like a lost, motherless child. *It was dance*, thought Raymond, *that was really helping him mature.* There was nothing like discovering a talent to define who you were. And now it would be

43

rifles and bayonets; forced marches and fatigues. His heart sank but, at the same time, it hardened his resolve.

'It's why I have to sign up. For King and country, yes. But . . . for Billy, and Frank, and all the countless thousands like them. I've known Billy Brogan since he was 14 years old. A plucky little scamp, making himself useful at the Buckingham. I couldn't look myself in the mirror each morning, knowing that the likes of him were out there, fighting this menace and I was . . . waltzing in the arms of some crown princess. It just wouldn't do, Nancy. I just wouldn't be me.'

She reached for him, across the table. 'I know, and I wouldn't want it. Raymond – *Ray* – you and Frank, you're all I have left. I'm . . .'

She faltered, and Raymond knew that this was one of those very rare occasions when Nancy was harking back to her mother, who had died giving birth to Frank; and her father, who, after years of punishing his lungs in the pits – and becoming in thrall to opiates along the way – had passed away four years before.

'I need you,' she said. She folded her hands over his. 'Give them a bloody nose, Ray. Put them back where they belong, so that the rest of us can get on with this business of being alive. There are enough bad things in the world without wars. So bloody them, Ray, but come back home. And bring my Frank back with you, won't you?'

Raymond did not like making promises he was not sure he could keep, but he saw the look in Nancy's eyes and knew that – strong and defiant as she had always been – there was a crack here. It broke his heart that it was not a crack he could fill in; not a wound he could hope to heal – not when the world was calling him to action.

'I'll do everything in my power to come home and live my life with you, Nancy. I'll do everything I can to have Frank with me when it's over – when there's peace.'

*In the circumstances*, thought Raymond, *it was the very best I could do.*

He kissed her across the table, and felt her melt into him. She needed this tonight. And Raymond, in the confusion of fears that suddenly rushed through him, needed it too.

That conversation was replayed in a hundred thousand different homes, in a hundred thousand different combinations. Across Sunday dinners and Sunday prayers, in quiet, thoughtful perambulations along the riverside, in homes and in clubs, in restaurants and on street corners – hundred thousand lives being written and unwritten, hundred thousand different futures beginning to be made.

In the two-up, two-down house they'd moved into in Whitechapel, Artie Cohen sat with his arm around his wife Vivienne's shoulder, baby Stan in his basket by the hearth. It was a balmy summer evening – Artie had not lit the fire in days, except to make hot water for his pre-wedding bath – and, through the open window, there came the occasional rumble of an omnibus as it guttered along the high road. The curtains fluttered, letting in the night. There was no Luftwaffe in the skies over London. There were only stars.

'But what about Stan?' Vivienne said, lounging into Artie's shoulder. 'He needs his father.'

Vivienne's own father had passed away some time before – but he'd been absent for so long, in thrall to his business interests, that she hadn't known him as a true father. The stepfather who'd been imposed upon her after that was so much worse. But it was meant to be different for her new family. She was meant to be setting things straight.

'I'll say he does, but he needs a father who stands up for what's right. What good's a father who doesn't?'

Vivienne was silent. She thought of all she knew about Artie. She pictured all the endless nights he'd stood outside the disused chapel where the Daughters of Salvation was first founded, warding off unsavoury guests, standing sentry to them all.

'It isn't the wedding night I imagined,' she snorted, with the air of a joke she was not, in truth, finding very funny.

'I can still sort that out,' a wolfish Artie grinned, with the air of a joke he wasn't sure would be well received.

'Oh, Artie,' she said, slapping his hand away, 'it's never far from your thoughts.'

After a little silence, Artie said, 'I'll be OK, you know. Those fascist bastards didn't kill me at Cable Street. I can't tell you how many scrapes I got into in Pentonville. It's all just *stuff* that happens, isn't it? I've got through everything else, so I'll get through this. Stands to reason. By God, back then I didn't have anything to live for – not really, not when you count it all up. But now there's you and there's Stan and . . . well, that's why I know it – Viv, my dear, I'm coming back home.' He faltered. 'You know I've got to do it, don't you?'

Vivienne said, 'I do,' though she wished it was a lie.

'Besides,' Artie went on, 'I can't let Ray suck up all the glory. Bloody de Guise has been doing that all his life, ever since we was kids. Can't let Ray get all the adulation, not this time. You can bet your life savings, he'll be down at the War Office by dawn, telling them all what an incredible leader he'll be – what with him leading all those dancers, of course.'

Vivienne knew that Artie was joking – but the love between the brothers was a complicated, many-sided thing, replete with splinters and scars and old wounds that, though they had healed, were still visible every so often, so she knew there was truth in it as well.

'Just promise me you won't do anything stupid, Artie.'

Artie reeled back in mock horror. 'But when have I ever?'

*Too many times to mention*, thought Vivienne, *and hundreds more than that.*

But it was still her wedding night, she decided. They were at war, but there had still been a wedding.

And Stan was soundly sleeping, so she led her new husband upstairs.


The news, which had reverberated up and down the Buckingham halls since the prime minister's broadcast, had settled, by evening, like snowfall across the hotel's many nooks, niches and hideaways. The talk in the Queen Mary restaurant was muted and respectful; those taking cocktails in the Candlelight Club – where the terrace had been closed for fear of light spilling out – spoke in low whispers, barely daring to betray their true feelings at what was about to unfold; in the ballroom, where no dances were scheduled for a summer Sunday night, the troupe's new female principal, Karina Kainz, practised with her counterpart's understudy, Gene Sheldon, longing to imagine a world where dance and war did not have to intermingle; while, in the uppermost reaches of the hotel, where the chambermaids all lived, the chatter exploded and died away, nobody quite knowing what to conclude.

In the middle of it all, Frank Nettleton sat – as he did most evenings, before he went back to his lodgings at the Brogan house, just south of the river – with his sweetheart Rosa, being plied with the teacakes, scones, clotted cream and butter that had been discarded from the room service trolleys that afternoon. Rosa liked to feed him up – she joked that he was skin and bone, and it gave her such pleasure to spread a crumpet with green-gage compote for him – but tonight it seemed more important than ever. She hadn't dared ask him the question she needed to yet; though she scarcely dared admit it to herself, she was afraid of what the answer might be. Rosa had been drawn to Frank because of his dreaming, his innocence, his wonder – and, yes, the bravery he'd shown in leaving his Lancashire pit village and founding a new life in London. She knew he'd want to be brave now, too – she just wasn't sure she wanted him to be; it would be better if this war just didn't exist. Rosa had always been an unstoppable optimist – that, she thought, was what Frank liked about her – so she slathered a scone with butter, a slab of toast with damson preserve, peeled him an orange and laced his tea with the special Royal Gardens honey, whose apiarists existed, it seemed, to serve the clientele of the Buckingham Hotel alone. Then, while the other chambermaids chattered on, she took him to the window and peeled back the blackout blinds.

'Rosa, you can't—'

'Oh, Frankie, it'll be all right. There's no siren, is there? It was all a mistake this afternoon. They're not coming for us. Not yet.'

Frank still didn't like the idea of it. The lights had gone out across the country on Friday, but they'd been out in London since the middle of August. Three weeks ago, Frank and Rosa had been out on Regent Street to watch as the blackout came into force. One by one, the street lamps had died. They'd taken a stroll down to Piccadilly Circus and seen nothing but darkness – all of the illuminations snuffed out, for the first time in a generation. Workmen had been painting the kerbs with white marks for weeks already, little things to help motorists when the world went dark – though, of course, the government had already started broadcasting that everybody should stay indoors. When Frank left, later that night, and picked his way back to Lambeth, he'd have to find his way by the stars. He'd walked the route hundreds of times before, but it was strange how the city was a different place, robbed of its light.

'You're a dancer, Frankie. You're not a soldier.'

Frank shrugged. 'I think I have to be what the world wants me to be, Rosa. I don't think I got a choice.'

'Doesn't mean you have to march to the War Office tomorrow, does it?'

Frank thought there was some kind of pleading in Rosa's voice, and he wasn't surprised. They'd been together – Frankie and Rosa, Rosa and Frank – for nearly two years; this summer, he'd even been down to sunny Southend to meet her mother, Mrs Abigail Bright, who cleaned houses there. He hadn't met Rosa's father, because Alf Bright had died from injuries sustained at the Battle of Passchendaele in 1917 – and the only time Rosa herself had met him was when she was a baby. Perhaps that, he wondered, was why she was so fearful of him signing up.

'What else can I do, Rosa?'

'Hold out, Frankie. You're needed right here.'

Frank, who didn't think this was actually true, said, 'Bill didn't get a choice, did he? He's been in the Territorials since summer. I'd have been there, too, if I was just twelve months

older. They're coming for me, Rosa. There's no stopping that.'
He paused. 'I wish Nancy was here.'

This kitchenette – a crowded little place, with three hot plates,
two kettles, and raggedy sofas (no longer fit for the guests)
arrayed around a little table where old copies of *Woman's Own*
and *Woman's Illustrated* were piled up – had once been Nancy's
world. It was the place that had welcomed her to the Buckingham Hotel and, after that, it had welcomed Frank, too. The hotel
felt empty, now that she was living out with Raymond de Guise.
He'd need to go to her, soon. He'd need to find out what she
thought, find out what she wanted. Frank didn't like listening to
the whisperings of his own heart, not unless he had his big sister
Nancy to listen with him.

'I'm scared, Rosa.'

She put her arms around him. 'I think it's normal to be afraid,
isn't it?'

'I don't want to kill anybody.'

That was just like Frank. Other people would be afraid of
being killed; Frank Nettleton was afraid he'd be the one doing
the killing.

'Hey, Frankie,' came a voice from the other side of the kitchenette. Ruth Attercliffe, who had recently cut her mousey hair short
and started wearing reading spectacles, was quite the fiercest of
the chambermaids and, Frank always suspected, a good bit more
intelligent than most of them as well. Sometimes she put him in
mind of Mrs Moffatt; though she was much younger, and hadn't
yet developed the full matronly air of the Head of Housekeeping,
Ruth didn't suffer fools gladly. 'Aren't you glad it's here at last?'

'Glad?' snapped Rosa. 'Ruth Attercliffe, that's just like you
to—'

'Oh, put a sock in it, Rosa. It wasn't meant like that. Me, I'm glad it's here because at least we *know* now. It's been coming down the line for months and months. Why, you can hardly turn on the wireless without some old toff chuntering on about it. It's Nazis this, and Hitler that. Chamberlain and Churchill and about a thousand other voices in between. Well, at least now it's here, we can do something about it. The sooner it starts, the sooner it's gone – and now we can all roll our sleeves up and get on with the job of finishing it.'

Frank was surprised to see that Rosa's cheeks had started purpling. He'd rarely seen her angry before; it bunched her features, narrowed her eyes, turned her lips the colour of a bruise.

'Well, it's not down to you to *finish*, is it, Ruth? It's down to poor sods like my Frankie, about to be rounded up and turned into soldiers when—'

'Who said I was talking about Frank?' scoffed Ruth, with just as much calmness as Rosa had irritation.

'Then what on earth are you gabbing on about?'

'I'm talking about me, Rosa. *Me. I'm* going to make a difference.'

Ruth marched to the other side of the kitchenette, took her overcoat off a hook, and stomped out into the hallway. Mere moments later, she had returned with her tattered old suitcase, which she put down in the doorway.

'I've been wanting a way out of this hotel all summer long,' she declared, as a dozen faces, locked in consternation, turned to consider her. 'I've had it up to here with thinking I'm making an ounce of difference by changing some old dowager princess's bedlinen, or collecting crusts from some dainty little lord's breakfast trolley. And if any of you girls have got any sense, you'll start thinking the same soon enough. Goodnight, girls!'

And with that, she was off.

For a time, there was silence in the kitchenette. Then Rosa picked herself up and cantered after Ruth – until, at the top of the service stairs, she reached out and caught her by the sleeve.

'Ruth,' she said. 'Ruthie. You're not ... serious, are you? You can't just leave.'

Ruth looked about to say something waspish – it was just her usual way – but then she softened and took Rosa's hand.

'I've never been more serious, Rosa. What use am I here? What's to stay for? Look at you – you have your Frank, and I've got—'

'*Me*,' said Rosa. 'You've got *me*. This war's going to go away, Ruth. I'd stake my life on it.'

Ruth whispered, 'You might have to.'

'But, Ruth, this place – the Buckingham ... it won't be the same without you. We *need* you. This war ... It can't change *everything*, can it?'

Ruth considered Rosa closely. She was about to say something when Rosa blathered on, 'It's only politicians. Politicians sizing each other up, like any old boxers in a ring. It's all getting out of hand, that's all it is. You can't go, Ruth. And my Frank, he can't—'

Ruth, who was not given to spontaneous acts of affection, seized Rosa by the shoulders, leaned in and kissed her on the cheek.

'I hope you're right,' she whispered.

'I am,' Rosa said, as Ruth disappeared down the stairs. 'Aren't I?'

And then Ruth was gone.

Back in the kitchenette, Rosa flopped back at Frank's side and seized his arm.

'Ruth Attercliffe, off to do her bit. It beggars belief,' she declared – and Frank wondered if, by the tone of her voice, she was being so forceful because she needed to convince herself. 'She'll be back, won't she?' Rosa seemed fretful all of a sudden, fretful in a way Frank had not seen her before. Frank could sense a nervous energy in her, quite at odds with her usual larger-than-life gregarious self. 'We'll keep her seat warm, girls. Keep it warm for when this silly war just blows over. Because it'll have to. It *will*. These men in high places can't keep threatening to destroy us all. They'll just have to sort themselves out.' At last, she seemed to have talked herself back into calmness. She cuddled up to Frank. 'Ruth, off to do her bit! Off to win a war! Yes, quite reckless. But what are you thinking, Frankie?'

But Frank couldn't bring himself to answer.

By the time Ruth got to the bottom of the service stairs, she was quite out of breath – but not yet out of pluck. Grasping her suitcase in one hand and a letter in the other, she marched through the back passages until she came to the Housekeeping Lounge.

There were still lights on within. There always were, long into the night, because this was when Mrs Moffatt worked on her orders and rotas, totting up the ledgers and service sheets she had to turn into the hotel director at every month's end. Ruth knocked on the door, waited until Mrs Moffatt's warm voice invited her through, and then stepped into the Housekeeping Lounge – for, she alone knew, the very last time.

It was harder telling Mrs Moffatt than declaring it to the girls. The truth was, Ruth hadn't felt as if she fitted in in the chambermaids' kitchenette for some time. Nancy's absence only made it worse; there were new girls now, the kitchenette was fast becoming Rosa's little fiefdom, and Ruth had known, since Christmas, that her days at the Buckingham were numbered. Sometimes, she reckoned, jobs were like relationships: they came to a natural end, but circumstances could make you linger in them until they turned quite rotten. But, just like relationships, you always needed somewhere to go. You couldn't just flounce out. You needed somewhere to flounce off to. The war had arrived – but, to Ruth Attercliffe, the war presented opportunities.

She waited patiently as Mrs Moffatt read her letter. Then the matronly woman, with her doughy face and kind glassy eyes, looked up at her from underneath her tight white curls and smiled, sadly.

'Are you sure, dear?'

'Yes,' said Ruth. 'I've known I would, for a long time. All summer – maybe even before. I'll go to the War Office tomorrow morning and ask for a recommendation, but I want to do my part.'

Mrs Moffatt invited her to sit down and reached into the drawer of her desk for a handful of the barley sugars she doled out to her girls, every time they came to her with some problem or another. Mrs Moffatt had often said that there wasn't a problem she hadn't heard; that there wasn't a life situation – a death, a pregnancy, a runaway lover – that she hadn't confronted with one of her girls, here in this little office. But today that old maxim failed her. She'd never stood up to a war before, not quite like this.

'Ruth, the world is changing – more rapidly than any of us can quite imagine. Sometimes, in times like this, it's good to have some solidity. Some ground beneath our feet. The hotel could provide that for you. It's a steady wage. It's a roof over your head. And – mark my words, my girl – there'll be opportunities a-coming. You're a smart girl. You always have been. The complexion of this hotel is going to change, just like it did the last time a war came crashing down around us. When the Great War started, I was a chambermaid, just like you. By the war's end, I was a floor mistress – and, shortly after that, the Head of Housekeeping. Now, Ruth, I don't intend to go anywhere myself – but a place like the Buckingham, in a time like this, well, it could be the making of you. I expect that it will be.'

Ruth paused, considering her words, before she said, 'Mrs Moffatt, it isn't my home.'

'Oh.'

'They reformed the Women's Land Army this summer. I was thinking . . . a place like that, I could find my own feet. I could make my own path. I'd be out of London and –' Mrs Moffatt nodded; this part of Ruth's plan seemed to make sense, at least – 'I'd be doing something to help.'

'You'd be helping here, Ruth. The Buckingham is too big to fall. Too many lives depend on it. It isn't just the lords and ladies we serve. I might run away myself if it were. It's people like you and me. It's their families. Hundreds of families that this war will throw into poverty, if the Buckingham falls . . .'

Ruth stood. She had helped herself to a barley sugar, just for old times' sake.

'I'm sorry, Mrs Moffatt. My mind's made up.'

Ruth was already at the door when Mrs Moffatt lifted herself from behind her desk and bustled across the room.

'Ruth, dear.'

'I'm sorry, Mrs Moffatt, please don't try and . . .'

But Mrs Moffatt hadn't come to dissuade her. She had come to wrap her arms around her, for one last time.

'Where will you go this evening, my dear?'

'I was going to go and see my mother, up in Finchley. I thought, under the circumstances, the hotel might understand if I didn't serve notice.'

Mrs Moffatt, who ordinarily might have fretted over her schedules said, 'There'll always be a home for you here, Ruth.'

'Thank you, Mrs Moffatt,' said Ruth, 'but I mean to find one of my own.'

Then, with one last embrace (and one last barley sugar), Ruth was gone.

She made directly for the tradesman's entrance, meaning to disappear along Michaelmas Mews, and would have been out into the balmy blackout directly, if only she hadn't seen Billy Brogan entering there. Billy looked older, somehow – it was as if he'd aged a year in a day – but, when he saw Ruth, he broke into the awkward grin he always wore, and doffed his cap in the familiar ostentatious way. *Still the old Billy Brogan, then*, thought Ruth, *even if he is Bill Brogan in uniform.*

'You all right, Bill?'

Billy said, 'You know me, Ruth. I'm bright as a button. Ready to be up and at 'em. Going to stick one in their eye, then come home for Christmas and enjoy the party down in the House-keeping Lounge. I'll grab a dance off you then, of course. Just like old times!'

It was Billy's joke. There were, of course, no 'old times' – well, not in any romantic sense, despite Billy's previous intentions. But there was a friendship here, deep and lasting – and Ruth hadn't appreciated, until this very moment, what an ordeal it

could be to say goodbye. The farewells had been so straightfor-
ward until now.

'I won't be here at Christmas, Bill. I'm off. Off like you are –
off to do my bit.'

'Oh,' said Billy, and, 'Oh,' he said again, while he tried to rustle up some more inventive words.

'You'll stay in touch, won't you, Bill? Here, look, I'll give you
my mother's address. You can write to me there. She loves being
a postmistress for me. Always has.' Ruth was grinning as she
scrabbled in her suitcase for a pencil, wrote down her mother's
Finchley address on the back of an envelope, and handed it over.
'Well, you go steady now, won't you, Bill?'

Billy was still struck dumb as she brushed past him. He
caught her scent of coal tar and carbolic, and reached suddenly
for her arm.

'Stay safe, won't you, Ruth?'

'You don't need to worry about me.' She leaned up and, quite
out of character, placed her lips upon his cheek. 'I'll be seeing
you, Mr Brogan.'

Then she stepped out into Michaelmas Mews.

Still reeling, Billy ventured deeper into the hotel and took
to the service stairs. He'd come to make his goodbyes – it was
just that he hadn't been prepared to be making them the very
moment he stepped through the doors.

He was quite breathless (not good for a soon-to-be soldier) by
the time he reached the chambermaids' quarters and hovered in
the doorway of the kitchenette. He'd heard their voices from the
end of the passageway and it had almost filled him with tears –
which was ridiculous because, as everybody in the Buckingham
knew, Billy Brogan wasn't the sort of character to be overcome

with emotion. He was somebody who got things done. Somebody who confronted problems face-on. Somebody who was always ready with a smile and a solution.

He'd snorted those tears back in by the time he reached the kitchenette. And he realised, then, that they had been tears of happiness anyway – because he loved it here, he truly did.

'Frank Nettleton!' he cried out. 'Get over here!'

Some of the newer girls didn't know Billy, but Frank and Rosa were quickly at his side, dragging him in and filling him with crumpets, scones and hot, over-brewed tea. Billy didn't mind. It still tasted of the Buckingham.

'When you off, Bill?'

'I'm reporting in tomorrow,' said Billy, showering crumbs from his lips. 'Just thought I'd check in and make my goodbyes first. I been home, Frank. I been to see my parents. They're in a pickle. Me off to France, and all the youngsters off to the country – and God knows where.' Billy only hoped the war didn't last so long that Daniel, the eldest of his plethora of brothers and sisters, might be devoured as well. 'Ma thinks they'll be separating them. Not going to find a place for all of them together, so she's fretting they'll be tearing them apart. Pa's got it in his head he can fix it – but I don't know if he can.' Billy paused. 'You'll be there for them, won't you, Frank? Help Ma herd them wherever they've got to be herded. Just stand with her, won't you, if Pa can't be there and . . . put an arm round her for me?'

Bill had said it with the air of a solemn promise – as if he was charging Frank with a holy duty.

'You know I will. Only, Bill, I—'

'He's going to the War Office in the morning,' interjected Rosa. 'My Frank Nettleton, off to war!'

She was near hysterical with the idea of it. Frank had to take her by the hand and draw her near.

'Look at you two,' she said, eyes darting between Billy and Frank. 'Answering the king's calling. It's enough to make you . . .' Her words came apart. Frank was about to remonstrate with her, to tell her it wasn't his choice, that he'd do anything to stay with her – that it was the world dragging him into it, and he'd stay if only he could, when suddenly she found the resolve herself and said, '. . . proud! It's enough to make you proud! Oh, come here, you two!' She threw her arms around them both, in quite the most ungainly hug either of them had ever experienced. 'Where one goes, there goes the other. It's always been like that with the pair of you. You look after each other out there. When he gets out to you, Bill, you make sure he knows his way around. And each of you, bloody well make sure the other comes back. That's a promise you've made each other, right? So now it's a promise you're making to me.'

She was holding them so tight that there didn't seem any other choice but for each of them to say, 'We promise.'

And, after that, they had as much leftover teacake, scone and crumpet as their stomachs would allow.

# Chapter Four

THE MEN FACING WALTER KNAVE were not like officers of the Metropolitan Police used to be. In the hotel director's day, the Metropolitan Police were *friends* to the Buckingham. You might slip them a nice bottle of sherry, or a bouquet of pristine blooms for whichever sweetheart they were trying to romance – or even, if the mood was right, offer them the use of one of the vacant suites for the evening. Tricks like these were so commonplace as to be almost mundane. So it was with a startled expression that he saw the lead officer, a man who called himself Murray, shaking his head with stoicism and pointing his fat finger at the paper he'd just deposited on the hotel director's desk.

'Gentlemen, this is outrageous. Unconscionable. Out of order!'

'That's a discussion for His Majesty's government, Mr Knave. We're just here to enact the orders we've been given.'

'Lily-livered cowardice,' stammered Knave.

The lead officer stiffened. 'Sir, this country is at war.'

A week had passed since Mr Chamberlain's proclamation. The French had joined the hullabaloo as well. So had the Canadians, which only went to prove that the British Empire still counted for something.

'I'd already spotted that for myself,' said Walter. 'But, gentlemen, you have to understand my position. You've no idea the expense this hotel has gone to to make this appointment. Authorising it was one of my first acts as returning director. Last year we lost our principal dancer – a lady you fellows might know as Hélène Marchmont. We had to fill that void, and in Karina Kainz we had somebody ready and willing to take on the mantle. A *supreme* dancer, gentlemen. *Superlative.*'

'And . . . Austrian,' concluded the lead officer.

Walter Knave spluttered, 'The lead dancer in a feted Viennese troupe, and she came to us! Karina is a beauty. She's brightened our ballroom this summer, and we have the Winter Serenade to think of. You'll have heard of our Winter Serenade, gentlemen. Our grand winter ball.' At this, the police officers were mysteriously silent. 'Gentlemen, the board will not stand for this—'

'Well,' said the lead officer, 'perhaps your board ought to have thought of that before they started inviting potential saboteurs into your midst.'

Walter exhaled sharply. His round spectacles immediately fogged up.

'Saboteurs! But she's not a saboteur. She's a . . . dancer!'

'Nevertheless,' the lead officer said, unmoved by Walter's feeble remonstrations, 'she is a citizen of Vienna – and, therefore, by the terms of their *Anschluss*, a citizen of the Third Reich. Dancer or not, Mr Knave, she is subject to the same laws as everybody else. The hotel can have her back, should the tribunal decide she poses no threat. But understand, Mr Knave, that the British government takes potential saboteurs very seriously indeed – and, until it is proven otherwise, she is going to have to come with us.'

For a moment, there was silence in the hotel director's office. Then, with trembling hand, Walter Knave lifted his telephone receiver and spoke to the reception hall.

'Bring me Frank Nettleton.'

A voice buzzed back: 'He's in the dance studio, sir. He's due in a demonstration.'

'Then he's perfectly poised for the matter at hand!' Walter spat, showering the telephone receiver with spittle. 'The boy is still a page. He isn't paid for his prize fandango. So send word for him and do it at once.'

An uncomfortable silence reigned in the office until, some minutes later, there came a tentative knock at the door, and Frank stuck his head, with its mop of hazel curls, into the chamber.

'Frank,' Walter began, ignoring the way the boy's eyes bugged out at seeing the Metropolitan Police officers standing there, 'have the demonstrations yet begun?'

'N-no, sir, w-we're just preparing.'

'Good,' Knave said. 'Then you can escort these gentlemen to the studio and direct them to Miss Kainz.'

Frank had opened his mouth to ask a question, perhaps disbelieving the evidence of his own eyes, but thought better of it when he saw the grim rictus that was Walter Knave's face. Meekly, he muttered, 'This way, sirs,' and hurried off up the corridor, nervous to have the police officers so close on his heels.

The dancers were still gathered in the studio when Frank opened the doors. Raymond de Guise was guiding Karina Kainz across the practice floor, while Gene Sheldon and Mathilde Bourchier – twenty years old and possessed of a devilish beauty – kept time from the sidelines.

*A week*, thought Frank, *and the world is still ticking.*

A week of war. Billy was, no doubt, already somewhere on the Continent; Raymond and Frank himself, who'd both been to the War Office to put their names on the paper, would no doubt be following soon enough. A week in which the world had changed.

It was about to change again.

The dancing stopped, but the music went on. The gramophone in the corner was playing one of Archie Adams' own recordings, 'Kiss Me Goodnight'; it was one of his faster, feel-good numbers, perfect for the quicksteps the troupe was due to demonstrate in a little less than an hour. But the good feelings had suddenly evaporated out of the room. The eyes of Raymond, Karina, Gene and Mathilde, as well as the other dancers in the troupe, all tried to comprehend the meaning of the figures who had just stepped through the doors.

'Miss Karina Kainz?' said the lead officer.

On the practice dance floor, Karina Kainz stiffened. She was still in Raymond's arms, so his arm stiffened around her as well.

'Yes?' she began. Then her eyes drifted from the police officers to Frank. 'Frankie?'

'I'm sorry, Miss Kainz. They were with Mr Knave. I don't know what they're here for.'

'Oh,' said Karina, her beautiful Viennese accent suddenly pronounced, 'but I do.'

The officers straightened. 'You'll have to come with us.'

Frank saw a look of fear ghosting across Karina's face – but it was in Raymond that he saw the lack of understanding turn, first to disbelief, and then to anger.

'What's the meaning of this?' he demanded. 'You can't just waltz in here and—'

63

'I'm afraid we can, Mr de Guise.' They were already crossing the dance floor. Mathilde and Gene reeled backwards to let them pass. Some of the other dancers scattered, while others stood their ground. 'Miss Kainz, we are here to take you into custody, pending such a time that a tribunal can be convened to determine what threat, if any, you pose to the United Kingdom. As an enemy alien, I'm sure you understand and I'm doubly sure you will co-operate fully with the process about to be enacted.' He stopped. One of the other officers was reaching to his belt. 'I'm afraid we'll have to handcuff you, Miss Kainz.'

Karina Kainz had been but six months at the hotel. Statuesque and blonde, she had brought some otherworldliness to the dance floor this summer season. She'd first come to the Buckingham as part of a Viennese dance troupe touring the United Kingdom, off to compete in Brighton and Blackpool and adopting the Buckingham as their home away from home; but, when the opportunity to remain was presented to her, she'd leaped at it with open arms. What better a place was there for sanctuary from the war that had swallowed up her homeland? What better way to escape than through music and dance?

Now she looked at the approaching officers with mute horror. A piece of her had wondered if it might happen. She had heard the whispers of the Italian restaurateurs slung into the back of a wagon, the Bavarian railway man who'd turned up for work at Oxford Circus and never gone home, and dared to question when they might turn up for her. But she'd thought, at least, that there might be a warning. An afternoon, an evening, to pack a bag and set in order everything she was going to have to leave behind.

'I'd have turned myself in, if you'd only sent word,' she said, softly but with a hint of defiance. Raymond and Frank both recognised this from the dance floor – the magnificent way she could seem both strong and vulnerable at once; the perfect combination in so many of her dances.

'People run if they know we're coming,' said one of the officers. 'I'm sorry, Miss Kainz. This is the easy way. You've time to pack a bag. Our understanding is you have quarters right here, in the hotel?'

She did. The same small suite vacated by her predecessor, Hélène Marchmont. She'd slept there for scarcely a season, but the thought of leaving it was unmooring her.

She said, 'Do you really have to use the handcuffs?'

'We're only doing our jobs, ma'am.'

Karina looked at the other faces in the dance troupe. She locked eyes with Raymond, with Frank and Gene. Mathilde herself, who had always harboured such jealousies at Karina's appointment – believing truly, she should have been made principal – turned her face away, unable to watch.

'Then let us do it with dignity, gentlemen,' Karina announced.

She was about to go with them when Raymond said, 'Now, wait here! She's no enemy. She's no spy. She's one of us. She's family. This is our ballroom, and we have a say in what—'

'I'm afraid you don't, sir,' said one of the officers. 'That's for the tribunal to decide. If your friend Miss Kainz is as innocent as you say she is, well, she'll be back among you soon. Then you can dance to your hearts' content.' He looked the dance troupe up and down. 'Those who aren't loyal enough to be fighting for His Majesty, of course.'

Raymond had opened his mouth again when Karina said, 'Hush, Raymond.'

'How can you be so calm?' he protested.

Karina simply shrugged. 'Because I'm the only one here who really knows the truth. That I have absolutely nothing to hide.' Her lips turned upwards; it truly was an entrancing smile. 'Let their tribunal see me for what I am, Raymond. Just a dancer, through and through. I'll be coming back home.'

Raymond watched her go, but his incredulity and fury hardly abated, not even as the gramophone finally reached its end and silence fell over the studio.

'Frank,' he finally said, 'keep practising. I'll be back shortly.'

'B-but M-Mr de Guise,' Frank stammered. 'The demonstration – it's almost here. What are we going to—?'

'Just keep dancing,' Raymond said through gritted teeth, 'as always.'

The police officers were already shepherding Karina Kainz to the service lift when Raymond reached the reception hall, with its myriad of black-and-white chequered tiles and the famous obelisk in its centre, streaming with water from the fountain hidden underneath. *Some of the guests must have seen her*, thought Raymond as he hurried through. That would have been forbidden in the old days – the scandal of the Metropolitan Police marching so brazenly into the hotel and, without any shame, apprehending one of their own. It was this thought that bubbled in him as he strode down the back corridor towards the hotel director's office.

The door was ajar, so he marched through.

There was Walter Knave, reclining in the director's chair with his eyes half-closed and a crystal brandy decanter open on the desk. The glass he was drinking from had already been drained. So, it seemed, had the decanter.

Raymond slammed the door. 'Mr Knave!'

His eyes flashed around the room. A half-written letter, addressed to one of the hotel financiers, lolled out of the old Olympia Elite typewriter; one of the desk drawers hung open, with its key dangling down – and, behind Walter Knave, the hotel safe sat exposed. Raymond bristled with a fury he knew he could not allow himself to set free; however useless, careless and half-cut Walter Knave was, he was still the hotel director – he still had the faith and trust of the board.

The old man was only just coming to his senses. Raymond tried not to think about what might have happened if a less upstanding person had marched into the office and found him like this.

'Mr de Guise,' Walter Knave began. 'Have you ever heard of knocking?'

'I believe you didn't hear me, sir,' said Raymond through gritted teeth.

'Staff are not permitted in the director's office without invitation, Mr de Guise. You know that.'

Walter was still fumbling his spectacles back on to his face when Raymond said, 'They're taking Miss Kainz. Arresting her, sir, for the crime of not being British. Did you know about it? Were you warned?'

'I believe I may have had a few minutes' foreknowledge. But what would you have me do? Defy the Metropolitan Police? Defy the direct order of Parliament? I am your superior, Mr de Guise, but not some spinner of miracles. Now, if you would kindly leave me alone, I am in the middle of composing a most difficult communication and . . .'

*Draining a decanter*, thought Raymond – though he had sense enough not to say it.

'Sir, the ballroom—'

'What of it, Mr de Guise?'

'Karina was at the heart of it. A new addition to the troupe, yes, but its shining star. You needed her, Mr Knave. We were fortunate in hiring her. The chance that somebody of her renown and calibre might make the Grand her home does not come around very often. And now . . .' Raymond despaired. 'The Grand was already going to feel different. Frank and I, we're awaiting our medical assessments to declare us fit for the war. Gene, too, I shouldn't wonder.'

Walter waved his hand dismissively. 'You don't need to worry about Mr Sheldon. If his report to me is correct, he won't be leaving us until it's absolutely necessary. It's this grandmother of his – the one who raised him. The old dear doesn't have anybody else, so he's sworn to stay until the War Office sends for him. He hasn't signed up.'

Something knotted and unknotted itself repeatedly in Raymond's stomach. As the principal dancer, and leader of the troupe, he might have expected Gene to confide such information to him – but the thought of war, of bravery and cowardice and all the infinite shades in between, did funny things to a man. He would speak with Gene later.

'The fact remains, Mr Knave, that the troupe is going to be decimated – and war hasn't truly begun.' Raymond was right: the declarations were made; the first transports had rolled out, but no shots had been fired in anger, not yet; no bombs had been dropped; no sea battles had been convened. 'You needed Karina to steady the ship. Somebody as experienced as her comes along but once in a lifetime. I know the ballroom means little to you, Mr Knave. I know there wasn't song and dance at the Buckingham, the last time you were here—'

'When you were in short trousers, boy, and don't forget it.'

'. . . but it's the firmament now, Mr Knave. It's the very stars. You have to protect it. You *have* to.'

Walter Knave rose to his feet. Standing, he was still a foot shorter than Raymond. He beetled his eyebrows, his hands unsteady.

'I'm not unsympathetic, Raymond.'

Raymond realised that all the waspishness had drained away from him. He was not a spiteful man; just a little insipid, perhaps, and far too many fathoms out of his depth. It was hard to believe that Walter Knave had ever had the gravitas and authority to steady a ship like the Buckingham Hotel. In this, he was as far away from his predecessor, Maynard Charles, as it was possible to be.

'The hotel board, especially our American champion Mr Hastings, has been very forthright with me about the importance of your ballroom and keeping that flame alive through the war. But we cannot stand in the way of His Majesty's parliament. I did my best – I told those officers they'd have to go through me first, that they wouldn't lay a finger on one of the Buckingham family without laying me out cold . . . but I am but one man, Raymond. We'll simply have to survive. There'll be Gene, for a time. And there is Mathilde – a rare beauty, and home-grown, too, so we won't have to worry about any nasty insinuations.'

'Mathilde is a fine dancer. A champion, one day. But she isn't Karina Kainz. She doesn't have the presence. She doesn't have the experience—'

'We may have to hire, Raymond. Find an older gentleman, one who won't be rushing off to battle, to court our guests. And I dare say the clientele will understand.'

'The clientele are fickle. If they think there's more magic, more spectacle, at the Imperial, or the Savoy—'

'I'm quite aware who our competitors are, boy! They were our competitors in 1914, and they'll be our competitors into the future.' The flurry of waspishness evaporated again. 'I'll do my job, and you do yours. Oh, and Raymond? Please don't come into my office again, berating me like I'm one of your dancing boys. I'm not. I'm your hotel director and –' he hiccuped and clutched at his chest, as if pantomiming somebody about to have a heart attack – 'I deserve your absolute respect.'

Raymond was still fuming as he left the office, flushing red with rage as he reached the reception hall and saw the Metropolitan Police officers escorting Karina Kainz across the black-and-white chequers and out through the hotel's revolving brass doors. They hadn't even used the tradesman's entrance, and somehow this smacked of basic indecency. The porters and concierges were just watching them go.

*She won't be the last*, thought Raymond. As soon as word got round, there'd be Italian pot-washers eager to make a run for it – if only there was anywhere to run to. Thank God the French were allies again because, without its stellar French chefs, the Queen Mary would have to close its doors.

He reached the dance studio to find the troupe still standing there stunned, the gramophone spinning out its silence.

'Raymond?' Frank whispered.

He shook his head, and in that simple motion was everything everybody there needed to know. Karina Kainz was gone, but the show had to go on.

'Mathilde,' he announced, 'congratulations. You've just become the principal female dancer at the Buckingham Hotel.'

Mathilde Bourchier was petite and elfin; she did not have the same presence as Karina Kainz, but there was an enchanting beauty about her nonetheless. Her eyes were cerulean blue. She'd so long coveted the principal dancer role – been tutored for it, even, back when Hélène Marchmont was in the ballroom – that she could not help but smile.

The smile brought a look like daggers from Gene Sheldon, who wheeled around and said, 'Raymond, she can't possibly be gone?'

'She is,' said Raymond, 'until this tribunal sends her back. And who knows when that might be?' He looked at the clock, up on the wall. 'The demonstrations are due, people. Let's get ourselves in order.' He shook his head, wearily. 'Mathilde, it looks as if you're dancing with each of us in turn. Let's make it count.'

At Raymond's instruction, the troupe gathered and passed through the studio doors, into the dressing area directly behind the Grand Ballroom. There, Archie Adams and some of the orchestra were already waiting; though the demonstrations were rarely played with a full orchestra, the dances always had a live accompaniment – no expense was ever spared in the Buckingham Hotel. Louis Kildare, who played the saxophone, gave Raymond a nod as the troupe sailed through; Louis, Raymond knew, had visited the recruiting station on the same day as him and Frank. It wasn't only the ballroom floor that was about to be denuded; the orchestra would be cleaved apart as well.

It was the orchestra that filed out first. As they struck up the opening number on the ballroom stage, Raymond gathered the dancers together and prepared to lead them out. He'd been leading them for years. The thought that he would not be here to do so through their most difficult hour was preying on him, now;

then he thought of Billy Brogan, already somewhere over the English Channel, and knew he was doing the right thing.

Gene was at his side. Raymond whispered, 'You didn't tell me that you hadn't signed up.'

For a moment, Gene was silent. Then he said, 'I've been in torment about it, Raymond. But it's my grandmother. She lost my father, you see, in the Great War. I made her a promise. I'll do my duty, when the time comes. But I have another duty, a duty to her. You understand, don't you?'

Raymond clasped him by the shoulder. 'You're a good man, Gene. Don't ever think otherwise. And it's not just your grand-mother who needs you. This ballroom will need you as well. You've stood in for me before. But now—'

'I'll do my best, Raymond. You have my word. Until they call for me, I'll keep this ballroom alive.'

'Then let's dance.'

The doors opened and, one after another, the dancers of the Buckingham Hotel – depleted, dejected, but determined to dem-onstrate the beauties of the ballroom at their very best – soared out to meet their public, dancers in the very eye of the storm.

# Chapter Five

ONE WEEK AFTER BILLY BROGAN bade his farewells to
family and friends, two letters landed on the doorstep
of number 62 Albert Yard, Lambeth. Frank, who had
been up before dawn, was the one who picked them up from the
doormat. He sat with them at the kitchen table until he heard
William Brogan senior stirring upstairs, his footsteps echoing
through the empty house. The house seemed so much bigger
without all the children flocking its halls. They'd been gone for
mere days, but it might as well have been an ice age.

When Mr Brogan appeared, Frank handed him the letters.
His eyes opened wide, as if he was breathing in a victory.

'Orla!' he called up the stairs, and very quickly Frank heard
Mrs Brogan moving above. 'Orla, they've come!'

Mrs Brogan's voice drifted down the stairs. 'What's come?'

'Letters from the children!' he called up. 'They've sent word!'

The days since the evacuation had stretched out interminably, with no knowledge nor indication of where the Brogan
children might have been sent. The morning of their departure
was emblazoned clearly on Frank's mind. He'd barely slept that
night. Long past the midnight hour, he'd lain awake, listening
to the tossing and turning and fidgeting through the walls of the

bedroom he rented in the Brogan house. It had once been Billy's room – Billy's bed as well – and Frank supposed that, once upon a time, Billy, too, had lain here listening to his brothers and sisters padding around, unable to sleep, jostling and stirring one another in the bedrooms to either side. But Billy had never listened to the whispered conversations Frank had heard. Billy had never been awoken by a line of anxious, sorrowful faces appearing at his bedside, asking, 'Are they really going to split us up, Frank?' and, 'Can I stay? I want to stay . . .'

'Just until Christmas,' Mrs Brogan had said as she clucked around the kitchen, when Frank trod downstairs, still in his pyjamas. Seemingly, she'd been up half the night, raiding her larder to make the children the best farewell breakfast she could spirit up. Billy's job of bringing leftovers home from the Buckingham – things the lords and ladies left behind, but which were treasures beyond compare to a family like the Brogans – had been taken over by Frank in the two years he'd been living here, and consequently this was to be an extra-special breakfast; crumpets and scones, elderberry preserve, kippers warmed on the stove and even a pot of the kedgeree they served in the Queen Mary restaurant. There were oranges and strawberries, candied apple pieces and segments of sugared lemon. If Mrs Brogan was being compelled to let her children go, she was going to do it with as much love as she could muster.

Mr Brogan, who had excused himself from Billingsgate that morning, was drinking tea by the embers of last night's fire, his pipe in hand.

'Are they still sleeping, young Frank?'

'Daniel's awake,' said Frank. He'd heard the eldest of Billy's brothers and sisters prowling up and down when he awoke.

There were seven Brogan children, excepting Billy – Daniel, who, at 14 years of age was plucky enough to believe he, too, ought to have been fighting alongside Billy; then Annie, the twins Roisin and Holly, Patrick (the spitting image of Billy), Conor and little Gracie May. 'Gracie May was in his bed all night. He promised her he'd go where she goes and look after her – but they won't get the option, will they?'

'William, dear, do you think we should let them sleep?'

William Brogan Sr stood up and said, 'I think we should rouse them all, shouldn't we? For one last Brogan party?'

Mrs Brogan dropped her wooden spoon. It clattered against the rim of the porridge pan, then cartwheeled to the kitchen floor.

'Less of the *last*, if you don't mind. There isn't a *last* anything. It isn't the last time we'll see Billy and, as long as I've still got a heart, it isn't the last time I'll see the rest of my babies either.'

Realising his mistake, Mr Brogan put down his pipe and marched across the kitchen to embrace his wife. With Mrs Brogan buried in his shoulder, he looked at Frank and said, 'Hop to it, Nettleton. The sooner they're up, getting their bellies filled, the more time we've got to savour them.'

Frank had tried not to think about Mrs Brogan's tears as he hurried back upstairs and roused the children. As it happened, Daniel had already woken the younger ones. Annie, who was 13 years old, was dressing Gracie May, while Daniel tried to whip some sense into unruly Patrick and Conor.

'Ma's upset down there, and you can bet your life I'll make this year even more of a misery for you if we ruin it for her. She's bad enough as it is.'

Frank had hovered on the landing, soaking up the hubbub going on in the rooms around him: the sounds of brotherly spats, the sounds of sisterly support, the whole wonderful chaos of the Brogan house when it was at its fullest, just brimming with love. He was going to miss this.

'Hop to it, you lot,' he finally grinned – forgetting, for a second, that he was using Mr Brogan's own words. 'There are still three hours until we're due at the station. Time for a fine old breakfast, and to make this the best send-off you can imagine.'

But Frank's heart had been hammering as they all scrambled past him, down the stairs and into the waiting arms of their parents. It had been hammering, still, as breakfast plates were piled up and devoured and, as they sometimes did, the children started singing en masse. That was something he and Billy had brought home from the Buckingham for them. A gramophone would play and, in one unruly chorus, they'd caterwaul out one of Archie Adams's numbers.

He quite understood, then, why Mrs Brogan was so full of emotion. The silence in the house was going to be deathly.

And deathly was exactly what it was. Frank hadn't experienced silence like it. It wasn't just quiet. It was an absolute absence of cheer.

Now, he waited as Mr and Mrs Brogan together opened the letters by the embers of last night's fire.

'They've been sent to two different houses,' said Mr Brogan, with an air of relief. 'That's better than it might have been, Orla. Annie's with the girls, and Daniel the boys. That's a system, at least.'

'Two different villages,' Mrs Brogan added. She sounded more despondent than her husband, but there was light in her as well. 'Oh, Frank,' she said, looking around, 'they're safe. They're not all together, but no one's alone . . . and they really did make it.' She paused. She had sensed a silence in Frank that didn't seem right. 'Is everything all right, Frankie? Not feeling too peaky, are you?'

*Peaky*, thought Frank. *Honestly – sometimes, it's like people think I ought to have been evacuated, too. Billy's out there fighting, and the other Brogans are banished from their home – and I'm going to do my bit as well.*

'It's just going to be a long day,' he said, 'so I thought I'd get it started. Demonstrations at two o'clock – and . . . a-and, I-I've . . . got my m-medical.'

Mr Brogan put the letter down and strode across the room to face Frank across the kitchen table.

'Good for you, son.'

A sudden thought struck Frank. 'I didn't want to leave you in the lurch. I know you'll be short of rent. But with the children not here, I thought maybe you could manage. And, if you can't, there are a dozen pages at the hotel – some of them young enough not to be heading off. Any one of them would love a place like this. I'm sure they could rustle you some leftovers from the hotel as well.'

Mrs Brogan smiled one of the soft, motherly smiles that Frank had come to know. Something melted inside him whenever a mother smiled at him like that; some little piece of him, the piece that would forever be a motherless boy, seemed to cry out for it.

'You've been a good boy, Frank. William and I, we'll be sad to see you go.' She reached out and folded her hand over Frank's. 'But you give them hell, son. Give them hell with our Billy, and then get back here. There's too much time being lost already. We've got to end the fighting, once and for all.'

Frank kept those words in his head as he set out with the first light of day. London, today, was grey and overcast. The city was changing. The evidence of it was all along the riverbank, as Frank weaved his way between the shopkeepers and city clerks, over the river at Westminster and up through all the shops and public houses of Piccadilly. Gas masks in every hand. New posters on the walls. When he looked upwards, he could see the shapes of the huge barrage balloons lounging in the clouds, tethered by great cables to docking stations in the city's very heart. They'd been a part of the London skyline for a year already, but in the past weeks they seemed to have proliferated. His own gas mask was hung by a strap over his shoulder. He studied its face. He'd heard of gas attacks, of course. He knew the feeling of choking in a cloud of dust – he'd done it so many times, himself, back in the pit village where he'd been born. Something about the idea of the mask frightened him, though. It seemed to be staring straight into his soul.

Some of the theatres, as he picked his way through the West End, had announced closures. One of the cinemas had converted its basements into a shelter where a working projector might still display a picture, even if the city was being turned to rubble overhead. Frank took a detour, up through Soho and past the dark archway that led into the Midnight Rooms, the little underground club where he and Rosa often came dancing. Well, perhaps a place like that might carry on, blackout or not. Perhaps there were worse ways to endure an aerial bombardment than dancing to big band numbers in the arms of someone you loved.

He was early to the London Combined Recruiting Centre, which nestled just behind St Pancras New Church, just south of the Euston Road. He was not the only one. Two dozen eager faces looked into his when he arrived, and yet more had lined up before they started admitting people within. Raymond, Frank knew, was to be called before the Medical Board later in the week; a part of him hoped they might, somehow, get to serve together. The world was vast and unknowable, and to have Raymond at his side would be a very good thing.

The recruiting centre was housed in what had once been a conference hall. Hasty partitions had been erected and now it hummed with activity from a dozen different cubicles and rooms. Directly through the door, the waiting area was quickly packed with men – most Frank's age, some a little older – and together they jostled, spoke nervously, rustled newspapers and made idle chit-chat about the services in which they wanted to enlist. Frank himself had very few preferences. One of the boys was talking about working for his father, fixing motorcycles and other various engines – and how he, surely, could be put to use in the belly of an aeroplane, fixing it up for another sortie over the Channel. Two brothers were discussing the Royal Air Force as if they were born to it, another how his father's father had been of great import in the Royal Navy. But Frank Nettleton hardly cared. He'd told them, at registration, that he had experience underground, and this seemed to be noteworthy; everything else he'd told them, about the Buckingham Hotel, hadn't even seemed worth the ink. But he was diligent and hard-working and, more than anything else, he truly *wanted* to do the best he could. Whatever it was, he'd jump to it and give it everything he had.

He was nervous when his name was called, along with half a dozen others, and a stern-looking man with a patched tweed jacket and a patrician air escorted them into a cubicle where each attendee was asked to stand up against a wall for measurement, then to strip down to their vests and undergarments to be weighed. If any of the other recruits seemed uncomfortable with the idea, none of them showed it; one was positively eager to take off his shirt and kick off his trousers – and beamed at the other boys as the medical doctor asked him to step onto the scales. Frank, who had once bunked in a Lancashire boarding house, was not unused to the company of men, nor the ribald kind of jokes they liked to tell, but he still cringed when he stepped out of his clothes and permitted the doctor to weigh him. He was not as boyish and scrawny as he used to be; he'd always been strong – you had to be, to work in the pit – and the last year of dance tuition had given his body a kind of litheness as well. But he still feared looking anyone in the eye. He felt himself flush crimson when the doctor started taking measurements. But there'd be a lot of this in the barracks, he supposed, so he'd have to get used to it soon.

Once he was fully dressed and the group's measurements all complete, Frank and the others lined up against the wall until, one by one, they were taken through to a further cubicle where a second doctor sat, his table laid out with clipboards, stethoscopes, a cuff for measuring blood pressure and all the various other articles of his trade.

'Frank Nettleton?' this new doctor began, his eyes on his notes; he hadn't yet looked up to appraise the boy who'd marched in.

'Y-yes, sir.'

Now, the doctor looked up. Younger than the first, he had a kinder expression; his face was rounded and he had a faintly piggy appearance – which, to Frank, made him seem much less threatening. He had the look of somebody who might work at the Buckingham rather than frequent its highest quality suites, and this put Frank's mind at ease.

If only he could say the same for his heart; it seemed to be beating wildly as the doctor instructed him to disappear behind a curtain and fill a small glass phial.

'F-fill it, sir?'

'Why, yes, young man. To the brim, if you could.'

Frank hesitated.

'With the passing of water, young man.'

Frank nodded, as understanding dawned. 'Of . . . Of course.'

It was wretched how stage fright hit him now – when, no matter how much he danced, whether in the demonstrations in the Grand Ballroom or in the clubs across town, it had never hit him before. In the end, it took him minutes of pushing and straining like a much older man before the phial was even half full. This, he supposed, would have to do.

After that, the doctor began, 'This shouldn't take long. A fit young chap like you ought to sail through. Eyes, ears, heart and lungs. I see your physique is in decent order. So let's get started.'

The eyesight test hardly took a moment; so, too, the test for his hearing. After that, the doctor made him sit down on a bench so that he could strike each knee with a small wooden mallet, the better to test his reflexes.

'Exemplary, young man!' the doctor said – and this further calmed Frank.

'It's because of dancing, sir.'

'Mmmm?'

'I dance. I think it hones the reflexes, somewhat. Well, that's what my tutor tells me.'

The doctor smirked. 'There's a little bit more to His Majesty's armed forces than dancing, Mr Nettleton. Now, let's listen to your chest. Cough, would you?'

With the cold stethoscope pressed against him, Frank did as the doctor instructed. First one cough, then another; then, when the stethoscope was repositioned, he coughed yet again.

The silence that came from the doctor, this time, had a different air about it.

'If you'll excuse me a moment, Mr Nettleton.'

The man was on his feet and heading out of the cubicle when Frank said, 'Doctor, is there a problem? Did I do something wrong?'

'Just one moment,' the doctor interjected, and then he was gone.

Frank had to wait alone for some minutes before the doctor returned, trailing a second, more senior-looking official, with him. As the first doctor watched, the second pressed a stethoscope to Frank's chest and instructed him to cough once more. Then he looked up, with a furrowed brow.

'You didn't list asthma on your registration form?'

Frank said, 'I don't suffer from it, sir.'

'Cough again, boy.'

Frank coughed again.

'Hay fever then, is it? Something of that order?'

Frank shook his head. 'No, sir.'

'Come on, boy, we're on the same side here. There's no use us sending you off to basic training if the body isn't up to it. History of lung conditions, is it?'

Frank said, 'My lungs are fine, sir. I'm a dancer.'

The doctors shared a look. 'Dancing again,' said the first, with a roll of his eyes. 'Son, these lungs have been affected – bronchitis, I should say, in infancy.'

The second doctor stood up, instructed Frank to tuck in his shirt and sharpen up, and said, 'Come this way, Mr Nettleton.

There are further tests we can do. But we'll have to file the paper-work first.'

It was a dazed, discombobulated Frank Nettleton who wended his way into Mayfair, early that afternoon. His head, his heart, his whole body felt empty – and not only because he hadn't been able to stomach a thing since he left the London Combined Recruiting Centre. Now, with his thoughts somewhere far away, he slipped along Michaelmas Mews, entering the great halls of the Buckingham Hotel by the tradesman's entrance. It was sup-posed to feel different, today. He was supposed to come here, bursting with pride, eager to tell Rosa and Nancy that he'd done it, that he was going to serve, that it wasn't just Billy and the Brogans whose lives were being irrevocably changed by the declaration of war – that he, too, was to fight for his country.

Instead, with a small manila envelope crushed in his fist, he picked his way by the back passages to the Housekeeping Lounge, where the chambermaids were all convening for lunch. He tapped tentatively on the door, until it drew back to reveal Mrs Moffatt.

'Young Master Nettleton,' she smiled. 'Which one are you after? Sister or sweetheart?'

Some of the girls, who were seated at the great horseshoe table, restoring themselves with tea and hot scones before they went back to their rounds, tittered. One of them dared some applause.

'It's a b-bad time,' said Frank, suddenly chastened. 'I'll come back.'

It was not like Frank to beat such a hasty retreat, no mat-ter how many chambermaids clucked and cooed around him (honestly, sometimes he felt as if he was their *pet*). He'd scarcely retreated halfway along the corridor when Nancy hurried after him, wheeling him around by the shoulder.

'Frank, what's happened?'

Seeing Nancy always did this to him. He felt as if he was eight years old again, running home with a grazed knee, or having been dunked in the village pond by the boys from the bottom of the lane. He found that he couldn't speak – not without letting his stammer carry him away – so instead he handed her the envelope. There was only a single sheet of paper inside it, a form filled out by the recruiting doctor's hand.

'Grade 4,' said Nancy. 'But what does Grade 4 mean?'

Between breaths, Frank tried to explain. 'Unfit for service. Nancy, they won't send me to training. They won't enlist me at all. They had me huffing and puffing into all sorts of instruments. They say . . .' He stopped. 'Did I ever have bronchitis, Nance, back when I was small?'

'Three years running, Frank, but that never stopped you . . .' She was still staring at the paper, as if trying to make sense of something unfathomable. 'Frank,' she whispered. 'Oh, Frankie.'

It hung unspoken in the air between them: only three years before, their father's lungs had given in to years of disrepair, and ushered him off to his end. But that was a lifetime in the pit, wasn't it? Pneumoconiosis, the doctors had called it. Decades of breathing in the choking dust underground – and Frank, he'd barely spent more than a couple of seasons down there.

Nancy was about to take Frank in her arms when Rosa appeared in the corridor behind her.

'Frankie?' she asked.

In moments, and to Nancy's chagrin, Rosa had bustled her aside and put her arms around Frank.

'What is it?' she kept asking. 'What's happened?'

Then she, too, read the letter.

'But . . . but it's . . . the best news! Isn't it, Frank? You're not to go off with the others! You're to stay in the hotel, stay in the ballroom, stay with . . . me.' She stopped, because something did not seem right; her jubilation was unmatched by anyone around. 'Frank, you oughtn't to be upset. There isn't a thing you can do, not when they don't want you. You turned up, you did your bit, you were first in line – but . . . now you get to stay, and do what you want with your life, and not have to risk it all for this war. We don't have to think about losing you. Frankie, *I* don't have to think about losing you.'

She tried to wrap her arms around him again – but there was something a bit abrupt about her Frank today, something she could not understand.

He stepped out of her embrace, his eyes darting around. 'The demonstrations are due,' he said. 'I'm meant to be dancing.'

*Dancing*, he thought. *Dancing, while the world turned towards flames.*

He retreated further, along the corridor.

'Come to the kitchenette after you're done,' Rosa called after him. 'I'll be finished at three.'

Frank nodded. Then he turned on his heel and slipped along the passages, images of the recruiting centre and the ballroom circling each other through his mind.

That was the first day since the one he dared step into the ballroom that Frank Nettleton couldn't lose himself in the dance.

October 1939

# Chapter Six

MRS MOFFATT HAD SETTLED INTO the big, soft armchair in the Housekeeping Lounge. This place could either be a hive of activity, or a sanctuary from the whirlwind of the Buckingham Hotel, entirely depending on the hour of day. The lounge itself was dominated by a big breakfasting table, and around its edges, above the higgledy-piggledy sideboards and old kitchen units, were portraits of the hotel from times long past. At one end of the lounge a semicircle of big, comfortable armchairs were arrayed around a small table, where a wireless sat – and, at the other, a door opened into the office where Mrs Moffatt trudged through her daily paperwork. It was in this little den that she was relaxing, a pot of tea on one side and a plate of shortbread on the other, when the knock came at the door. Putting down her paperwork, she waddled over to the door and opened it up.

There was Nancy de Guise. At the end of a long day, first in the suites and then in the store cupboards, she looked a little more dishevelled than Mrs Moffatt ordinarily saw her. Her cheeks were flushed and her brown bun looked to be escaping its hairpins.

'Sore feet?' smiled Mrs Moffatt.

'Rather,' said Nancy.

'You got my message, then?'

Nancy nodded. 'I meant to come earlier, but we've been so busy.'

Mrs Moffatt stepped back and invited her within. 'I'll say. I was just settling down with the rotas for next month. We're seven chambermaids down now, and only three new staff on the way. At this rate, we'll be working double shifts every day by Christmas, and we still won't keep on top of things. Did you see Vera today?'

'She was with Rosa, up on the third storey.'

Mrs Moffatt tottered over to her desk and produced a letter, which she waved at Nancy.

'At least she'll work until this month's end. She's number eight. Off to be a teacher, I'm told. There's a lack of them, for those children who got left behind. Half-empty classrooms, right here in London. Vera has experience nannying for some wealthy family out west, so apparently that qualifies her.'

Ruth had been only the first to leave the Buckingham in the weeks since war had been declared. The first letter she'd sent them had been read out at last week's breakfast service and was now pinned up on the Housekeeping noticeboard: she'd found work out on a farm near a place called Pillerton Priors, in Warwickshire. When Nancy's eyes were drawn to it now, she noticed that a strip had been torn off the bottom of the letter before it had been pinned in place.

'Well,' said Mrs Moffatt, when she caught Nancy's eye, 'she seemed to be suggesting there were places for more girls, any who wanted to get out of London and do their bit. It's a noble thing our Ruth's doing, don't get me wrong, but my attention is on things a little closer to home – like how we keep this hotel running when we're losing staff every week. I've petitioned Mr Knave, of course, for more hirelings – but it's all moving too slowly.' Her eyes opened fractionally, as if she was about to spill some secret and take Nancy into her confidence. 'Nancy, it's rather why I wanted to see you. Come on – there's tea enough for two. And I know you won't say no to a piece of shortbread.'

Nancy was grateful for the opportunity to take the weight off her feet. There was no reason that Mrs Moffatt needed to know this – not when the responsibilities of the hotel only seemed to be growing heavier with every passing week – but she'd long ago earmarked this evening to journey out east, to visit Vivienne and the Daughters of Salvation. Nancy, who had been instrumental in helping Vivienne's investment in the Daughters, had once been a fixture in the old red-brick chapel where the charity was housed; since marriage, and moving out – and especially since the arrival of the new hotel director, when suddenly there seemed so much more to do at the hotel – she'd been there less often. Tonight was her opportunity to set that straight – if only she could get there before the blackout came into true effect.

She'd worked a double shift today – in the hotel by 6 a.m., readying the girls for their rounds, then straight through lunch and into the long afternoon. The shortbread was very welcome. The crumpets at lunchtime seemed like an ice age ago.

'Nancy, you've been with the Buckingham Hotel for three years. A lot's changed in that time. You're no longer a Nettleton, for starters. It isn't often we have a married woman working in these halls. Now, let me first say, I'm glad that we do. Times are forever changing, and we all have to change with them. But there's no denying the fact that it's changed your relationship with the girls. Without you in the kitchenette every night, sleeping on the same hall – with that ring on your finger, and your three years of service, and all of these new girls coming through . . . you're not one of them anymore, Nancy. Do you understand what I'm saying?'

She did – though it came as a barb to hear Mrs Moffatt articulating it in quite this way. It hadn't been the same since she moved into number 18 Blomfield Road with Raymond. Without the long nights gossiping in the kitchenette, without being at every single breakfast service and pot of tea at the end of a tiring shift, she was as removed from Rosa and the others as she'd ever been. Nancy had been diligent in learning the names of all the new girls, befriending each as they worked the floors together, but there was no pretending it was the same as gathering together to listen to the wireless and gossip and gripe at the end of each day.

'It's going to change even further, Nancy, if you agree to this thing I'm about to propose. You don't have to give me an answer now. It's right that you should go away and think about it – discuss it, of course, with your Raymond, and see what he thinks, too. But, should you agree, I am quite certain it will put you in a stronger stead to cope with Raymond's absence in the months to come.'

'Mrs Moffatt, you're making me nervous.'

Mrs Moffatt's face opened in a smile. 'You've no reason to be, my girl. I'm asking if you might consider becoming a floor mistress. Second and third storeys. Now, the job isn't easy – there'll be girls to marshal, and orders to oversee, and about a thousand other details to keep on top of. About a thousand little problems to contend with, too, and I can hardly predict what one of them might be. But it would be an extra something in your pay packet each week, and the girls look up to you – you're already a step removed, and this would be a way of making it official. The hotel could use somebody like you, stepping up in a time like this. We'll lose more girls before the year is out. Those who come will need somebody to guide them.' She paused. 'Nancy, what are you thinking?'

'Mrs Moffatt, I really don't know what to say.'

'You could start by saying . . . yes.' Mrs Moffatt smiled, once more. 'It's time, Nancy. The Buckingham needs us all to stand up and do our bit. And I'm going to need more help than I have, if we're to make it through this war unscathed. I don't know what's coming. The world isn't on fire quite yet. But, with all the talk of bombing and evacuation . . . well, it's the sort of moment in history when we all have to ask ourselves – what more can we do?'

After that, Mrs Moffatt let the silence linger a little while longer in the Housekeeping Lounge. Then, at last, she said, 'I haven't proposed this to Mr Knave yet. He'll need to sign off something like this. But you should know, dear, that he takes a dimmer view than his predecessor did of married women working in his hotel. He ought to remember, of course, that women – married or not – were what guided this hotel through the Great War, and they'll be what guides us through the next. So he'll come to the right decision in the end. It will make that ring on your finger make a little more sense to him. Think about it, won't you, Nancy?'

Nancy stood. 'I don't need to think about it, Mrs Moffatt. I should be honoured.'

Mrs Moffatt nodded. 'The honour is mine, Mrs de Guise. We'll get the paperwork in order, we'll make sure Mr Knave adopts the correct position, and then we'll get on with marshalling this Housekeeping department together – you and I. Nancy, my girl, it's going to be a long road ahead.'

Crossing the city in the blackout was no small endeavour, but Nancy had already resolved to make the journey – so soon she was boarding a car of the Central Line and rattling her way by Underground into the east.

It was a chill October night by the time she reached the Whitechapel Road, then veered off the main thoroughfare to pick her way to the red-brick chapel where the Daughters of Salvation lay. The taprooms along the way had already shuttered up and, in every window along the row, the blackout blinds were in place.

*Thank God it's a cloudless night*, thought Nancy; she picked her way by the light of the stars to the steps of the disused chapel building, and found Artie Cohen standing outside.

The chapel seemed dead but, when she looked carefully, she could see the slivers of light coming from behind its own blackouts.

'We're strictly candlelight only,' said Artie, as he ushered Nancy into the darkened porch, closed the heavy oak door behind them, and then led her deeper in, where the partitioned former chapel was lit up by a multitude of lanterns and candles.

There was something sad about seeing the Daughters in such a way. Founded to help the addicts and alcoholics of London's East End, for two years its doors had been flung open every evening, the courtyard at the rear of the chapel strung up with lights to coax in the hungry and the needy, anybody who sought its help. Artie was employed to stand sentry at the gates – because wherever recovering addicts went, so, too, did the men who made fortunes by luring them back into the opium dens. But now there was no hive of activity – only whispers coming from behind the partitions. The smells of steaming soups and stews that ordinarily filled the rooms were only faint memories in the air. The back doors were locked, the hall becalmed.

Vivienne was waiting for them in the back office, looking as harassed as Nancy had ever seen her. She was tidying papers when Artie showed Nancy through, but now she froze, as if caught in the middle of some unconscionable act.

'I wasn't sure you'd make it.'

'I wasn't either,' said Nancy, 'but here I am. Are you ready?'

Vivienne was already wearing her coat – a simple felt thing, quite unlike the ostentatious Regent Street garments she would have worn, once upon a time. Not for the first time, Nancy thought back to what Mrs Moffatt had said – how much could change in three years. Three years ago, she'd barely known Raymond de Guise. Three years ago, Vivienne was a spoilt little rich girl, with an opiate addiction of her own. Three years ago, the birth of Stan – who was happily being watched over by Alma at the old Cohen house – would have been impossible to imagine.

Three years ago, there hadn't been a war on.

'Artie's going to lead us there,' said Vivienne. 'It isn't far. Let's just hope the sirens don't start, shall we?'

Leaving the Daughters of Salvation in the charge of Mary Burdett, they set off in the blacked-out night. Artie himself had no need to navigate by the stars, because he had spent too many long nights prowling these neighbourhoods in the darkest hours – and, no matter how much the city had changed since then, he would never lose his feel for it. Consequently, he roamed three, four yards ahead of them as they picked their way closer to the river, with all its ripe, salty smells.

'Artie got his call-up papers,' said Vivienne. 'They landed yesterday morning. In three weeks, he goes to Salisbury Plain.'

'Raymond, too,' said Nancy. 'It feels real now, doesn't it? It's in the headlines every day, the newspaper boys are crying it from the corner every time I head to the Underground each morning – but it's been so quiet. All those hospitals preparing for the wounded. The air-raid drills. And then – nothing. But now that Raymond's going, it feels like it's started. In *here*.' She clasped a hand over her heart. 'I'm telling him he's doing the right thing. Every night, we talk about the duty of it. But . . . is it such a terrible thing to admit I don't want him to go?'

Vivienne snorted. 'You're so dainty, Nancy – worrying about a thing like that. By God, I tell Artie it every night. Not that it could ever change his mind. He's set on it.' Vivienne hadn't known Artie, the day he stood at the Cable Street barricades and last looked a fascist in the eye. He'd been beaten and bloodied that day, but evidently he hadn't been broken. 'It's like he can't wait to get at them. And him with a baby son waiting at home . . . Says it's for him, of course. To build him a better future. Artie thinks he can set the world straight by one punch to a Nazi's nose. Me, I think the world's a little more complicated than that.' She paused. 'How's your Frank?'

Nancy was hushed. 'He'll scarcely talk about it. Not to me, and not to Rosa. He's got the shame of it, just like your Artie's got the pride. But it isn't his fault. It isn't a choice he made. If only he could see that! Raymond told him it's part of his duty now, to keep the ballroom alive. That there ought to be light and joy, if everything's going to teeter into darkness. But . . . Frank needs to see it for himself. He's like your Artie in that as well – he just won't be told.'

'That ballroom's his home.'

'And it needs him more than ever. They got word about Karina Kainz this morning. She's in a camp, somewhere near Liverpool – thousands like her, interned and waiting for their tribunals. Might be she doesn't come back at all. Frank could weave some magic in that ballroom, but I need him to get the shame out of his head.

He's letting it taint him. He's been like that, ever since he was small – he thinks everything's his fault, even the things out of his control. He just needs to find a way.'

They were almost at the river now, and Artie led them along a wide, cobbled row that ran parallel to the embankment.

'Well, at least there'll be some good men left in London. Your Frank and . . . Look, he's here now. Warren!'

The lean figure of Warren Peel, swallowed up by a fur-lined coat, was waiting on the corner. He hallooed to Artie as they approached, beckoning them onwards.

'Warren failed his medical, too,' whispered Vivienne, 'though I don't think he vests much shame in it. It's his history – all the opiates, the bad years, the ruin it made of his body. Oh, he looks well now – a picture of health! But it's inside him still. They saw it in a second. It doesn't matter that he turned himself around – not to them. To them he'll always be the mistakes he made. They just couldn't let a man like that fight for Great Britain, no matter the good he's done.'

'It's this way,' said Warren, when they reached him on the corner. 'Father's waiting. He wanted me to warn you – it might not seem right, not at first. But he's got a vision. It's got such potential.'

The H. J. Packer Chocolate Company, though based in Bristol, had kept a manufactory here in the late-nineteenth century, a facility which had been repurposed as the site of various production lines and storage houses ever since. In the last three years, the grand brick structure into whose dark and cavernous interior Warren led them had remained largely empty, passed from one vendor to another in a succession of stalled, and largely fruitless, sales.

'But now it's up for auction again, and Father has his beady eye on it,' said Warren.

His esteemed father, Sir George Peel – whose family had once owned the blacking factories in Charing Cross – was a relatively new investor in the Daughters of Salvation, and first came to the concern because it was they who had rescued his errant son from a life in the gutter. Now, his investment in them was soaring to new heights. He'd promised them new premises a season ago, and at last was making his promise real.

'Mrs Cohen.' The towering figure of Sir George Peel, lean of frame but jowly, invited them on to the barren factory floor. He stroked his significant moustache as he declared, 'Welcome home.'

Vivienne heard her footsteps echoing as she, Nancy and Artie reached the middle of the great, dusty expanse. Without light, it was difficult to perceive the edges of the place, but she had the distinct feeling she was standing inside a vast cathedral.

'You picked an unfortunate moment for a guided tour, Sir George,' Vivienne joked. 'We might have come in the morning.'

'Yes, but I have the keys for this evening alone. A favour from an old associate of mine. Well, it always pays to have associates in the trade. The auction is tomorrow, ladies. If I'm to make an offer on a place like this, I have to know it's the right one. So – shall we explore?'

Nancy reached out and squeezed Vivienne by the hand, suddenly aware that Artie was squeezing her on the other side as well. In a chain of disbelief, they followed Sir George around the factory floor, through a succession of back offices, and into a stairwell that climbed to yet more storage rooms and offices above.

'Of course, it's the potential of the building you have to think about,' said Sir George. 'Think of what your little chapel was like when you first set up there. Mary Burdett, a few pots and pans, and some beds lined up against the wall. Few people would have envisaged that as the beginning of an empire. And yet . . .'

In the gloom, they continued to explore. Nancy saw Vivienne picking out the crannies and corners, committing a picture of it to her memory. Nancy tried to do the same, overlaying that image with ideas of what it might one day look like, if the Daughters of Salvation really could thrive in a place like this. There would never be a return on Sir George's investment, not in financial terms; but it was joyful to learn that there were wealthy men who wanted their spiritual returns here on earth. You couldn't buy your way into Heaven, but you could certainly use money to pave the way to a better world.

'Here,' said Artie, from somewhere in the darkness. He'd broken away from Nancy and Vivienne as they walked their circuit around the factory floor, and now he stood at the head of a silhouetted staircase that seemed to plunge into a basement level beneath their feet. 'Shall we take a peek?'

'I'm afraid the gates are locked,' said Sir George, 'and not without reason. I'm told there may be structural work to complete in the cellars. Nothing that undermines the property, or so says the surveyors' report. But money would need to be expended. And . . . there are rats.'

Artie shrugged. 'Rats in London? Who'd have thought?'

Nancy felt Vivienne straining on her hand. Together, they reached the head of the staircase.

'What are you thinking, Vivienne?' Nancy whispered. She could sense some dawning of understanding in her friend.

'I'm thinking . . . it got so much more serious, this thing I've been trying to build. It started with addicts, just like me. Well, you were there, Nancy. You know the depths of it all. And it got bigger – bigger than I'd thought. We're ready to leave the chapel. We have been since Christmas, and even before. But I didn't count on war. I didn't count on the air raids they say are going to happen. I always wanted to help the needy, Nancy. Those who couldn't help themselves. But . . . how many needy are there going to be in London, when the Luftwaffe come? How much can we do, in the face of all that?'

Nancy considered it in silence, then said, 'I should think we can do exactly what we have been doing – our very best. Nothing less, but nothing more. You can't save the world, Vivienne. But you can save as many souls as a place like this might allow. And I think that should be enough, for one lifetime.'

Vivienne ruminated further.

'It seems so vast, now that I'm here. The thought of it, filled with people in want – it's exactly what I'd envisaged. But, Nancy – I'm a mother now. And I'm to be a mother alone.' She cast her eyes across at Artie, who had occupied himself with some other caved-in corner of the masonry. 'Alma says I should go and live with them. All the Cohen women, under one roof.'

'Then you won't be alone, Vivienne. And I'll be . . .'

It was the first time Nancy had thought about the true feeling of loneliness as well. If she was no longer a part of the chamber-maids' circle, nor waiting for Raymond to return at the end of each night, number 18 Blomfield Road was going to feel pecu-liarly empty as well.

'There's something else, isn't there, Miss . . .' Nancy caught herself. She was about to say 'Miss Edgerton', the name by which she'd always deferred to Vivienne. But they were sisters now, related in marriage – equals, in all but name. Sometimes, old habits die hard. 'What is it?'

Vivienne stared into the portal of blackness at the bottom of the stairs.

'I was thinking about cellars. Nancy, we're going to need cellars, aren't we? Our patrons are going to need somewhere to go when the sirens start sounding.' She turned on her heel, located Sir George standing in the shadowy interior of the factory floor. 'Sir George, I should very much like you to make a bid to acquire this place for the Daughters of Salvation.'

Nancy watched the silhouetted figure incline his head, thoughtfully, towards her.

'I was hoping you'd say that, Mrs Cohen. Then let us see what tomorrow might bring.'

Outside, as the Peels returned to their idling motor car, and the chauffeur who had waited patiently in the dark, Artie, Nancy and Vivienne returned to the alleys and terraces leading north.

'Warren's getting himself re-examined,' says Artie. 'Reckons they'll pass him as fit for home service, if he puts it to them. He might not make it to France, but there's every chance he'll end up stationed somewhere after all. Has your Frank dug into it?'

Nancy said, 'Dr Moore doesn't think a decision like his is so easy to overturn.'

'There'll be a way,' muttered Artie, and stalked ahead.

'It's coming for us all,' said Nancy, 'this war. It's changing everything.'

'Not all of us,' said Vivienne. 'There'll be plenty who get away with it. My stepfather wheedled his way out of the Great War – vital war work at home, that's what he claimed. Of course, sitting in a gentlemen's club, playing backgammon and drinking fine wine *does* seem vital to the war effort, doesn't it?'

Nancy snorted with laughter.

'So they lock up dancers, just in case they're dissidents, and let men who openly courted these Nazis sit in Boodle's all war long. Yes, the British do a nice line in hypocrisy when it suits them.'

Nancy tucked her arm inside Vivienne's own. She looked, hesitatingly, at the vast, open skies above London. Only stars twinkled between the barrage balloons tonight; she saw no conical searchlights sweeping over the city.

'Don't let the Metropolitan Police hear you saying such things! Vivienne, it's practically sedition.'

'I'm just glad I'll never look my stepfather in the eye again.'

'Well, I'm seeing him more and more often.'

Vivienne froze, then continued marching on.

'Oh?'

'Ever since they brought Walter Knave in as director, Lord Edgerton's been back at the hotel – two, three times every week. It just wasn't like that when Maynard Charles was in charge – not towards the end. But now? Now, he's in the Candlelight Club every Thursday. He brings your mother to the Queen Mary most Saturday evenings. I've seen the rest of the board flitting around, although John Hastings seems swept up in war work of his own – well, you never quite know what the Americans are going to do – and Lord Edgerton seems happy to be using the hotel again. I dare say he doesn't need a gentlemen's club. Why spend money in Boodle's, when you could get everything on the house at the Buckingham? He's got all sorts coming through. There's a man, name of Adalbert Grice, who's taken suites regularly this year – and all on your stepfather's account, if Bill Brogan's to be believed.'

'Grice?' murmured Vivienne. 'I know that name.' She fell into silence as she tried to place it. 'You ought to steer clear of him, Nancy. Grice is one of Mosley's old friends. You know – the Right Honourable Sir Oswald Mosley. My stepfather's been toadying up to that crowd for too long. And, look, I know Mosley's told every damn man in that fascist union of his to sign up and fight for His Majesty . . . but a leopard doesn't change his spots, does he? All that cosying up my stepfather's crowd did to Mr Hitler and his cronies – it hasn't just gone away, has it?'

They'd reached Artie again, who had been waiting on a darkened corner.

'Bah!' he snorted. 'You'll hardly find a man alive who admits to being part of that lot now. But they're still out there – you'd better believe it. Taking the king's shilling.'

'Adalbert Grice is one of the worst of them. He writes for *Action* – that's the paper the fascist union set up. Mark my words, Nancy, if Maynard Charles was still hotel director, he'd be watching that man like a hawk. Spying on him, if what they say about Mr Charles is true.'

'But now that Mr Knave's director?'

'Well, it's open season for my stepfather to turn the Buckingham back into his own little fascist club.'

'It might be you should tell Knave all this,' said Artie. 'A dent in the Buckingham's reputation at a time like this? I wouldn't want my Ray coming home to find his beloved ballroom all shuttered up.'

But Vivienne snorted once again. 'I wouldn't trouble yourself, Nancy. Walter Knave might not be a Blackshirt himself, but he's been in my stepfather's back pocket for half a generation. Something tied those two together, long ago. Why else do you think

Lord Edgerton would force through the appointment of a man so decrepit at such a precarious point in the life of the hotel?'

'They say he shepherded the Buckingham through one war – so he can shepherd us through another.'

'I'd be surprised if Walter Knave could shepherd his own posterior onto the lavatory seat without a helping hand.'

Artie's guffaw was so loud that it alone could have triggered the air-raid sirens.

'The Edgertons have known the Knaves for a lifetime,' said Vivienne as they returned to the Whitechapel Road. 'It's probably one of the reasons my stepfather first invested in the Buckingham. He treated that place as his playground, back in the twenties. Of course, back then, my mother and I, we weren't part of his world. He was a man about town, courting who he wanted to court, and the Buckingham was where he did business. Look, Knave's nothing more than my stepfather's puppet – he'll twist him round his little finger, whichever way he can, and use him for his own ends. The man's a weakling. A pushover. If my stepfather's taking men like Adalbert Grice for cocktails in the Candlelight Club, it seems to me he's doing it with the full knowledge, even the help, of Walter Knave.' Vivienne looked up. The old chapel that housed the Daughters of Salvation was looming on top of them now – the symbol of all the good she hoped to do in the world. 'There's no point running to Walter Knave and telling him a thing, Nancy. He already knows. Yes, with Knave at the helm, the Buckingham isn't a bastion of light on a dark night anymore. It's a torrid little pit, and all you poor souls are just flailing around inside of it.'

# Chapter Seven

FRANK WAS SITTING IN THE bedroom at the empty Brogan house, perched on the end of Billy's old bed with a pen and paper in his hand. He wanted to write to Billy, wanted to explain, but the words just wouldn't come. When the words failed him – yet again – he looked up, to see the bedroom floor strewn with all the other letters he'd tried to write, then screwed up. At least Billy had something to write about. His first letters had landed last week – one to his parents, one to Frank, and another to be sent on to the village where the Brogan children had found themselves washed up – and, ever since then, Frank had been trying to find a way to transform his feelings into words. The problem was: those words didn't exist. They slipped away every time he tried to commit them to paper.

It was even worse to talk about it. Rosa thought it was the very best news: her Frank, staying right where he ought to be, right at her side. She wanted to talk about the things they'd do this Christmas. She wanted to talk about next spring, next summer – as if there wasn't even a war to be frightened of. It was true that, nearly two months since its declaration, the bombs hadn't rained on London. It was true that Billy and his lads hadn't been swept up in some conflagration on the Continent. (As far as his letters were concerned, they just seemed to be running the same kinds of exercises and drills as they'd done in training, then laying in fortifications for some fictitious war to come.) But it was also true that Frank had started to feel an emptiness inside him – something that not even dance could fill.

And that was why he was sitting here – in his dancing shoes and his smartest clothes – trying desperately to write to Billy, instead of jumping aboard the Underground from the corner and hurrying into Soho, where Rosa, Nancy, Gene Sheldon, Mathilde Bourchier, and even Raymond de Guise, were waiting.

They must have got tired of waiting and already gone down the dark stairs into the Midnight Rooms by the time he arrived – because, when Frank hurtled up through the blacked-out streets of Soho, not a soul was there on the corner of Berwick Street as they'd arranged. London was different after dark. There was a time when Frank had come down and seen the lights blazing from the public house on the corner. Drinkers spilled out in merriment from the old John Snow, just down the cobbled row. But here, where the market traders would stand at first light, there was only the blackness. If you cocked your head, you could still hear sounds of revelry from behind shuttered windows and doors – but, up here, there was only the night.

The Midnight Rooms lay down a narrow staircase, beneath a shopfront where the window glass had been taped up in criss-cross patterns in anticipation of the deluge they said would come. Frank, who had diligently brought his gas mask slung over his shoulder, approached the top of the stairs warily, loosening up only when he heard the sounds of a big band stomp coming from far below. The doorman who lingered at the bottom of the stairs recognised him well enough; the Midnight Rooms was Frank's first training ground as a dancer, and it was here that he'd learned to throw himself wholeheartedly into jitterbugs and foxtrots.

'She's already in there, Frank.' The doorman nodded at the barricaded doorway. 'You ought to be more punctual, son. A bright girl like that'll slip through your fingers if you let somebody else whisk in.'

Frank wasn't sure he found the remark funny, no matter how wide the grin on the man's face. But, unable to muster a single word in reply, he smiled vaguely and waited as the hulk of a man opened the door a fraction so that Frank could slip inside. Moments later, he found himself entangled in the black curtains keeping the light of the stage and dance floor within. Then he was through, into the swarming, sweaty throng of the Midnight Rooms.

They said the nightlife in London was going to be devastated by even the merest whisper of war. Theatres would close, they said. Restaurants and public houses would have to shut up shop at the first touch of twilight. But human beings – and Londoners in particular, thought Frank – were ever-resourceful creatures, and what Frank saw in the Midnight Rooms tonight bore very few differences from what he'd seen this summer, or in the summers past. The club existed in a single subterranean cellar, with a stage dug into the bedrock at the rear and, in front of that, a dance floor excavated in the earth. A bar at the back was served by two young women and a middle-aged man with an appearance that was both grizzled and debonair – as if a cave bear had been buttoned up inside a midnight blue evening suit. This was Mr Knight – or, as he sometimes joked, 'Mr Midnight' – and the

Midnight Rooms belonged to him. He wasn't a dancer himself – an old war wound had stopped him in his prime – but, if there was a thing to know about the music and dance of London's dance halls and clubs, Owen Knight knew it.

The walls around the dance floor were pitted with cubbyholes where candles flickered over tables, and dancers took cocktails to recuperate from their exertions. Frank's eyes gravitated towards one particular cubbyhole, and there he saw Nancy and Rosa, locked in conversation while Raymond gazed out at the dance floor itself. The band was playing a wild Coleman Hawkins number and, in the middle of the floor, Gene and Mathilde were lost in a wild jive – so different, so much more exuberant, than the stately dances in the Grand Ballroom.

Frank had often longed to demonstrate something just like this in the Buckingham Hotel. It might be that the day would come when ballrooms across the world embraced the wild emotion of such dances – but, right now, he was simply grateful to be *seeing* it. It felt a little like he'd been holding his breath for hours, pent up and dissatisfied. Now he breathed out and, for a fleeting moment, everything made sense.

He picked his way across the dance floor to reach Nancy, Rosa and Raymond. It was Nancy who saw him first, and she crossed the club to walk with him. Giving him a motherly look, she said, 'You're late. I was worried about you.'

'I'm sorry.' Frank slipped into the booth beside them. 'I was writing to Bill. He sends his love. He's doing all right. Of course, it *could* just be Bill's bluster. Might be he's a prisoner in a camp somewhere – he'd still write back like it was sunshine and roses, and all lads chipping in together. But, well, I reckon he's getting by.'

'How about you, Frankie?'

'I don't know, Nance.' It was only Nancy he didn't feel shy around when he was spilling his heart. 'It's like when Dad died, you know? I don't know how I'm supposed to feel. I just know it doesn't feel *right*.'

Nancy wondered if anything could feel right, in a year like this. She drew Frank near, putting her arm around him.

'You've got a good heart, Frank. You do know that, don't you? Don't forget it.'

They'd almost reached the cubbyhole where Raymond and Rosa were waiting. Frank stopped, suddenly, and said, 'Is *she* all right?'

'Who? Rosa?'

'She hasn't been acting herself. You know what Rosa's like – so full of vim, so full of life. And, yes, she's been like that – but it's like she's forcing it sometimes, you know? Putting on a show. You don't think, down inside, she's *ashamed* of me, do you?'

'Oh, Frank.' Nancy was half-motherly, half-stern now. 'You've got to get that thought out of your head. *Nobody* is ashamed of you.'

'I think maybe I am.'

'That's the devil in you, telling you lies,' Nancy said. 'Frankie, I love you.'

He'd needed to hear that. He nodded, and said it in return.

No sooner had they reached the cubbyhole than the band came to the end of their Coleman Hawkins number and broke into something a little more stately, a number to calm the passions being poured out on the dance floor. Raymond got to his feet.

'Shall we?' he said to Nancy – and when she hesitated, he added, 'Leave the lovebirds to it?'

Soon it was only Frank and Rosa in the cubbyhole. A rum cocktail – perfect for Frank's sweet tooth – had been sitting waiting for him all night, and now Rosa pushed it into his hands.

'You've got a little catching up to do, Frankie. Then we can dance.'

Part of Frank yearned to. The familiar fluttering sensation had washed over him almost as soon as he stepped through the curtains – it was almost like falling in love. And yet his feet weren't tapping. Only his fingers were drumming out any kind of rhythm at all – and that was only because he was so nervous. He couldn't sit still.

'I don't want to talk about the war tonight, Frank,' said Rosa, draining her gin rickey. 'I've had it up to *here* with talking about it. Last dances and last kisses. There's half the boys in here tonight shipping out next month, just like Raymond and the rest. They've come out for one last party before they put on their marching caps. Well, that's not why we came, all right? We came because it's what we do. Because it's what we love. And it doesn't matter what's happening today or tomorrow. I just want to dance with you and not talk about the bloody war.'

Frank said, more darkly than he'd meant to, 'You picked the right man, Rosa, if you don't want to hear about the war—'

'Oh, Frank!' Rosa spluttered. 'You know what Billy's said. There's nothing going on anyway. Nearly two months of war, and what's happened? A few ships out at sea. Even when the French did attack something, they quickly thought better of it. You wouldn't be doing anything out there. You'd be sitting twiddling your thumbs, and playing cards with Billy Brogan. You're beating yourself up for nothing. There's scarcely any war to fight.'

Frank stammered, 'I know, b-but—'

'No buts, Frankie. You're attacking yourself more than any British soldiers are attacking Jerries right now.'

'I've put in a request for a new medical examination.'

Rosa's lip trembled. 'What's so wrong with staying right here with me?'

'It isn't like that. It's a . . . feeling I have. I don't want to be –' he looked out over the dance floor, at the turning bodies and the bobbing heads – 'a disappointment.'

'Well,' said Rosa suddenly, 'you'll be disappointing me right now, if you don't get up and dance. I've been sitting around waiting all night. Come on, Frank! We only live once! I'm sick of this war talk already. I'm sick of carrying a gas mask and blacking out the windows at night. It's . . . against common decency, that's what it is. It's all just scare stories. Bombs falling out of the sky? Over *London*? You'd think we weren't the most civilised country on earth.' She was being fierce, but she was grinning as well. She leaped to her feet and extended her hand – it was an instruction, not an invitation. 'Oh, come on, Frank!' she pleaded, with all the urgency of a six-year-old being denied her plum pudding. 'Isn't it just typical that a war would come along when I'm twenty-one and ready to get on with my life? Well, we have that chance! Let's not ruin it by being miserable. Listen to that music! Who could be miserable with a band playing?'

*She's right*, thought Frank. *Of course she is. It's just so difficult to feel it.*

Nevertheless, he took her hand – and, together, they sashayed down to the dance floor.

The band had struck up one of Frank's favourites – Cab Calloway's '(Hep-Hep) The Jumping Jive', a number that made him picture all of the underground jitterbug joints Raymond de

Guise had once seen on a voyage to New York City. *The music of another world*, thought Frank, and he tried to open himself up to it as he took Rosa in hold, spun her out of it again, and threw himself into the dancing.

The dance floor was a whirling pandemonium – but, as he always did, Frank shut all of that out and tried to simply exist here, in a small little bubble – just him, Rosa, and the music enveloping them. He kicked and he bobbed; he weaved and he swung. He took Rosa by the hand and together they turned around, shuffling in unison, scissoring apart and then coming back together again. In the corner of his eye he saw Raymond lifting Nancy – his own Nancy, who had once been so shy she wouldn't dream of stepping on to a dance floor – up high, while Gene Sheldon and Mathilde Bourchier swapped partners with some strangers. The stab of trumpets, the long, slow glide of the saxophone – the drums like a determined, insistent thunderstorm. Frank felt it cascading all around him. But something was wrong. Something had changed. The last time he'd been here, he'd felt the music swimming through his very soul – as if he himself was one of the waves. But now its waters just lapped around him, touching him but never flooding his veins.

The music came to its titanic conclusion – but, somehow, Frank's dance had faded out some time before.

Rosa was still straining on his hand, desperate for the next number to begin.

'Oh, Frankie,' she said, but Frank was drawing to the edge of the dance floor.

'Perhaps another drink,' he said. 'I need to loosen up, Rosa.' He faltered. 'I don't mind if you dance. I'm sure everyone would want to dance with you tonight. *They're* all packing up, of course. *They've* all got their marching orders.'

Frank was climbing the steps away from the dance floor when Rosa rushed after him.

'You fool, Frank Nettleton,' she chided him, not unkindly. 'I'd much rather sit and drink another gin rickey with you than dance with one of that lot – even if they *are* packing up. You're thinking about it too much. It isn't your fault. Why worry about it if it isn't your fault?'

What was certainly Frank's fault was that he'd left his wallet on the dresser in Billy Brogan's bedroom, so that Rosa had to venture to the bar for him. When she came back – empty-handed, because 'Mr Midnight himself's bringing them over' – she took Frank's hand and said, 'It doesn't make you any less, Frank. Not in my eyes.'

Frank believed her. But it was what it meant in his own eyes that mattered.

'I could understand it if I had half a heart. If I was bow-legged or blind. It just . . . doesn't seem real, Rosa. I might be dancing in the Buckingham and all those faces looking at me thinking – if he can dance like that, well, why can't he march off to war?'

'But that's exactly it, Frankie. The Buckingham! You might get your chance in the Grand. I'm not talking about the afternoon demonstrations, as wonderful as they are. I'm talking about the big time – the evening. The Buckingham ballroom! The Christmas and Summer balls! With Raymond away, and what happened to Miss Kainz – why, even Gene's going to be off to war eventually. It will only take a few months before he gets his papers. Then the ballroom's going to be empty. Mr Knave will have to hire new dancers. He won't be able to go poaching from the Savoy and the Imperial – they'll be stripped bare, too. So . . . Frank Nettleton, star of the Grand!'

For a fleeting moment, he could see it. He watched, in his mind's eye, as the backstage doors of the Grand opened up – and out of them spiralled all of the dancers, led not by Raymond de Guise, but by Frank Nettleton: the youngest star of the ballroom.

Now, if only he could dismiss all those other insidious thoughts – about what everybody thought of him, about weakness, about (he barely dared think it) *cowardice* – he might have had the freedom to revel in the idea.

He was just opening his mouth to reply when the hulking form of Mr Midnight, coils of grizzled beard spilling down over the starched collar of his shirt and the midnight blue lapels of his dinner jacket, appeared at the booth, carrying two gin rickey cocktails. These he put down – his enormous hands dwarfing the minuscule glasses – as he opened his mouth in a beam.

'Why aren't you down on the dance floor, Nettleton? I don't give free drinks so you can sit in a booth swooning over your sweetheart, charming as she is.' He nodded, with a wink, at Rosa. 'You light this place up, boy. Get your drink down you and get out there.'

Frank nodded, meekly. 'I'm just not in the mood tonight, Mr Knight. I'm—'

'It's all this war talk,' sighed Rosa, with a roll of her eyes. 'Too much talk, talk, talk. I've had it with the talking. I just want to dance.'

'You'd better talk to your gentleman friend here then,' said Mr Knight.

'Frank's failed his medical,' Rosa declared.

Frank opened his eyes in horror. The very idea that she'd say it so brazenly had shocked him.

'Well, you have,' said Rosa, 'and it's not your fault – and the sooner you start believing it the better.' She looked up at

Mr Knight. 'He's worried people will think less of him. He's worried he's not brave.' Now she turned her eyes back at Frank. 'Well, *I* know you, Frank – and I know you'd have been the first in line, if they'd let you. And maybe, maybe I can see why you'd feel so rotten about it. It's hurting you in your heart. But you can heal that heart, can't you? You want to help in this war, well, there's got to be other ways. And maybe the first one of them is not being so distraught and despairing that you get to stay behind, and . . . and look after the people who love you!'

Rosa stood, drank her gin rickey in one swift motion, and marched on to the dance floor.

Frank Nettleton was left reeling.

'Rosa,' he stumbled, but she was already gone. And he felt wretched inside, then – wretched that all she wanted was for him to stay, and all he wanted was to do his bit and go. He'd so rarely seen Rosa flustered and upset. He didn't know what to do. She'd been like it for weeks – his spontaneous, fun-loving Rosa, jittery and wild.

He looked up at Mr Knight. The great man seemed to hover there for a second, before sinking into the chair Rosa had just left behind. He barely fitted in it, but he shuffled close to the edge of the table and peered at Frank over the steeple of his hands.

'They told you you couldn't go?'

Frank nodded.

'And it's bothering you, right?'

Frank nodded again.

'Look here, Nettleton.'

Mr Knight stuck his leg out from under the table, proceeded to roll up his midnight blue trousers and reveal what lay underneath.

But no pink flesh appeared in the Midnight Rooms' subterranean light. The leg that Mr Knight revealed was nothing but solid oak, smoothed and varnished to a shine. It ended somewhere around Mr Knight's knee joint, where a metallic cup was strapped into place with knotted bands.

'Think they'd send me off to the Somme with this, do you? I was seventeen when it happened. Dancing in the local halls. Fancied myself a bit of a star, as a matter of fact. I figured I had a chance in the competitions. Then – *bang!* – life changed. I took a fall, got an infection – and there was nothing for it, but to take me to the old sawbones and have it dealt with. I was like you, Frank. I thought it was over. There wasn't a woman who'd want me. There wasn't a place I could dance. And, when the Great War came, there wasn't a regiment in the land who'd take a peg-leg – not even for marching over the top, straight into the Kaiser's bullets.'

'I didn't know,' whispered Frank.

'Of course you didn't. Why would you? The point is, it doesn't matter. Oh, it did back then. Once upon a time, it was the end of my world. I watched my neighbours and friends get swallowed up by that war. The shame of not being there with them weighed me down. But then . . . Well, then it hit me – I wasn't doing the world a service, lost in my own anger. I wasn't the only one who couldn't go. I didn't get a say in it, one way or another. But the one thing I did get a say in was how I used the time I had. So do you know what I did?'

Frank just looked at him.

'I found a different way,' he said.

'What do you mean?'

'Well, it could be anything. Me, I volunteered at St Thomas', down on the river. There were countless soldiers coming back, and too many of them looked like me. I started to help them learn again – how to walk, how to get fitter, stronger, how to cope with one leg or none. Suddenly, me being a peg-leg didn't seem such a terrible thing. I'd found a way to take part. It was,' he said proudly, 'how I won the war.' He beamed. 'Not on my own, of course. But I damn well mean it when I say I helped. I've never been prouder. What I'm trying to say, Frank, is this – I didn't have to stay on the sidelines. Do you understand me?'

Mr Knight didn't wait for a reply. Taking Rosa's empty glass, he stood and drifted out of the cubbyhole, back to his duties at the bar.

Moments later Rosa, about to step into hold with a stranger down on the dance floor, felt a tap on her shoulder and turned to see Frank Nettleton standing there, asking if he could cut in. As the disgruntled dancer drifted away, Frank spun Rosa around and smiled.

'I'm being a fool,' he said.

'Yes,' said Rosa, 'but you're my fool.'

The band launched into another number. Nancy and Raymond flurried by, catching Frank's eye as they danced.

'It really is stuff and nonsense, this war,' said Rosa. 'It'll be all right, Frank.'

Frank felt quite sure that, of all the things this war would be, 'nonsense' was not one of them. But Rosa seemed to be clinging to the idea with some strange urgency, so he didn't breathe a word in reply. He just spun her round, spun her again, then lifted her as high as his head as they turned a final time.

Nonsense or not, he was going to find a way. Frank Nettleton was down – but he wasn't out yet.

November 1939

# Chapter Eight

Remember, remember, the Fifth of November, Gunpowder Treason and Plot . . .

THE DAYS HAD NEVER SEEMED longer to Nancy de Guise. This morning, she'd arrived at the Buckingham before dawn to get the girls ready in the Housekeeping Lounge. At lunchtime, after interviewing three new potential chambermaids alongside Mrs Moffatt, she had briefed the girls on the changes to the rota that inevitably came with every change of staff (another girl had left last month, off to serve as a housekeeper in a provincial manor – as far away from London as she could find). Then she had worked a full afternoon in the uppermost suites, and returned to the Housekeeping Lounge for an evening debrief with Mrs Moffatt. Only when that was done, and the guest list cross-checked for the following day, did she set off to leave. As she passed the reception hall, she saw the imperious figure of Lord Edgerton striding in through the hotel's revolving doors. He lingered by the obelisk, shaking the hand of a weaselly figure with lank hair dripping in pomade, before together they marched towards the guest lift, setting out for the Candlelight Club above.

*Adalbert Grice*, Nancy thought.

He wasn't staying at the Buckingham this month – yet he still used it as a home away from home. Not for the first time, she remembered what Vivienne had told her – and, not for the first time, she tried to put it out of her mind. There were manifold worlds inside the hotel. Her duty was to allow those worlds to co-exist, to flit between them, neither seen nor heard. *The lot of any good chambermaid*, she told herself – and she was one of the best.

So she set aside all her ill feeling and left by the tradesman's entrance, off into the blacked-out night.

Nancy remembered the Fifth of Novembers of her childhood well: the bonfire in the village, Frank excitedly collecting pennies for the Guy to be tossed on top of the pyre. That burning face had always frightened Nancy, but to Frank it had seemed somehow wondrous. She could still recall it now: leading him back from the flames, his face sticky with cinder toffee, then sponging him down in the tin bath at home. Family, in its truest sense. But this year, there was to be no Guy Fawkes celebration. She'd seen the advertisements up on the billboards and in magazines for 'indoor fireworks' – Rosa had wondered if Mr Knave might organise a show in the Grand – but London was silent this evening. Even the roads seemed deserted as she bustled to the Underground and made her way to Maida Vale.

Raymond was already at home, laying out the things he'd be taking with him. The Lancashire hotpot she'd made the evening before was ready to be put in the oven – and, as they waited, she helped him fold and pack his shirts and undergarments, as well as the trinkets of good fortune that would offer him comfort. Nancy had bought him a St Christopher medallion, to slip into his pocket and bring him good luck. He wore his wedding band with pride, and turned it on his finger.

'You're tired,' he said to her, as they settled down to eat. 'I've never seen you work as hard.'

Raymond did not say it lightly, because he'd seen Nancy throw herself into her work too often in the past years – not only at the hotel, but at the Daughters of Salvation as well. But tonight he could see it in the shadows under her eyes.

'I'm getting into the stride of it,' Nancy said, heaping hot-pot onto his plate. 'When we've got new girls coming through, things might ease off. Until then, it's all hands to the pumps at the Buckingham.'

'Don't let Mrs Moffatt run you ragged, though, Nance.'

Nancy gave him a look. 'I don't think it's you who ought to be worrying about me. Not tonight.'

Tomorrow morning, at 8 a.m. sharp, Raymond de Guise would join his brother Artie on the platform at Paddington Station – and, along with hundreds of other men, they would board the trains that would take them to Salisbury Plain, and their basic training.

Raymond said, 'I know I've left you before. That year I went to California and New York. I know how hard it was for us. I wouldn't leave again, Nancy, if it wasn't the right thing.'

Nancy folded her hands over his. 'I know it. I'm proud of you. When I see what this thing's doing to my Frank, it near breaks my heart – but at least I'll have him. I just . . .' Words were use-less at moments like these. 'I'll miss you in the evenings. I'll miss you in the mornings. I'll miss you, Raymond. That's all. And I want you to come home.'

There: she'd said it – this thing which had been eating at her throughout the last weeks and months. One day soon, she would say goodbye to him, not knowing if it was the last goodbye. The brutal fact of life was that, at some point, every living soul made their final farewells. Nancy just didn't want it to be for another sixty years. The 1990s. The year 2000. How strange and peculiar that might be . . .

'Don't be a hero, Raymond.'

She'd just blurted it out.

'A hero?'

'I *know* you,' she smiled. 'The King of the Ballroom. The lord of the dance. Well, you don't have to be that man out there. The world isn't asking for heroes. Just for everybody to do their ordinary, little acts of heroism – thousands of people ending this war, one footstep at a time. Just promise me, Raymond. Do what you can to come home.'

Raymond laid down his knife and fork, stood and walked to her side. There he kneeled down, took her hand as if proposing the marriage of which they were already a part, and looked into her eyes.

'I'll promise to do everything I can,' he said. 'But Nancy, the war's coming here, too. Promise me you'll stay safe, here, when it does.'

Nancy bent down to press her brow against his.

'Let's hope Rosa's right. Stuff and nonsense, she keeps saying – as if . . . as if she'd rather pretend there wasn't a war at all.'

Raymond knew others like it. They thought that, because it wasn't happening right now, it wouldn't happen at all.

'Maybe she just wants to make Frank feel better,' said Nancy.

*Or maybe she's scared*, thought Raymond, *and covering it in denial.* 'Home by Christmas' – well, they'd all heard that one before. Some people's emotions ran riot when all the certainties in their lives were suddenly gone.

After they'd eaten, Raymond cleared the table and set the gramophone to play one of his favourite records – not the faster jives he'd been listening to of late, but a slower, older waltz tune. He took Nancy in his arms and box-stepped with her around the sitting room, with only their long shadows on the wall to watch them.

'The Buckingham isn't going to be the same without you, Raymond.'

She stepped closer to him, so that they danced almost as a soloist, turning around the room.

'It will still be the Buckingham,' said Raymond. 'You'll still have those same halls.'

Nancy wasn't so sure. 'Do you ever feel like . . . it isn't the *safe* haven it used to be?' She didn't know if she should say more; it sounded so foolish, when you gave it a voice. 'I feel like we're sailing blind. Mr Knave's locked away in his office all the time. Mrs Moffatt thinks he just sleeps the days away. And that's what it's like for all of us. Like we're sleepwalking into something terrible.'

'Maybe that's just the feeling of war.'

'It's more than that,' said Nancy. 'I can't put my finger on it. Maybe it's how many people are leaving us. Or the new faces I'm starting to see in every corner. But . . . Lord Edgerton was there again tonight. He's hosting one of his soirées in the Candlelight Club. It's like . . . with Mr Knave asleep at the wheel, the hotel's different. It's . . . changing.'

Raymond tried to console her. 'Lord Edgerton's part of the board, Nancy. I don't like the man any more than you do. The man has less than half a heart. But it's his hotel.'

'He wouldn't have dreamed of bringing men like Grice to the hotel in the old days. Open fascists. They're pariahs, now, because of all the things they said about Mr Hitler and his type – but, somehow, the Buckingham's their playground.' She paused. 'Vivienne says Mr Knave's in his pocket. The only reason Mr Knave's at the Buckingham at all is so that Lord Edgerton can do with it as he wishes. I'm thinking . . . I'm thinking of telling the rest of the board. John Hastings wouldn't stand for it – Lord Edgerton bringing fascists into the hotel, when the whole country's at war to bring them down. It's topsy-turvy, Raymond. You're going off to war to fight them, while I'm changing their bed sheets.'

Raymond stepped out of the dance. He crossed the room, lifted the needle from the gramophone and invited the silence back in.

'Nancy,' he said, with a hint of concern, 'I've made my promises to you. Now, please, you make one to me.'

'Raymond?'

'Look after yourself. Whatever's going on at the hotel – maybe this time it isn't your battle. If Lord Edgerton really does have some control over Mr Knave – if that's how he's wresting back control of the board from John Hastings – well, I'd want to end that as well. But we're on the precipice of something here. You've just been given a promotion – you're becoming part of the fixtures and fittings there. Don't endanger that. It might be that work's going to be hard to come by, or that money's about to be scarce. I don't know what's going to happen on the Continent – but I do know you have to look out for yourself, Nancy. You just told me not to be a hero. Well, listen to me – I'm laying the same promise on you. Whatever shenanigans there are at the hotel, whatever battles are going on in the board, whatever the reasons Walter Knave was really brought back to run the place when he's clearly unfit – don't get caught in the crossfire. Look after your-self, and look after your girls. Do you hear me?'

There was silence as Nancy took it all in. There was a time when the thought of not standing up for what was right would have gnawed away at her, day and night. Now, however, she fancied she could see the sense in what Raymond was saying.

She marched to the gramophone, lifted out the slow waltz record, and slipped in another one of Raymond's favourites.

'I don't want the slow numbers, not tonight.'

Cab Calloway had started playing.

'Are you sure?' grinned Raymond.

'It's just all too sombre,' laughed Nancy. 'I don't want to be sombre. I want to be . . . joyous. I want to feel alive. You're going, Raymond,' she declared, 'but you're coming back – and there's going to come a day, after this war, when we look back on this night and know it was the beginning of something, not the end.'

'Then let's dance.'

And, long into the night, that was exactly what they did.

On the other side of London, Artie Cohen was dancing as well – not with his own good wife, but with his baby son Stan. Nor was it a joyous, unbridled dance in which Artie was engaged – for, without a single note of music, he was dancing around the room, trying to stop the baby from caterwauling at the top of his voice while Vivienne changed the cot sheets.

'Come on, boy,' Artie was warbling, 'it's your old man here! Chin up, soldier – worse things happen. I've wet the bed myself on more than one occasion . . .' He looked down at Vivienne, who was giving him a look like daggers. 'In my old days, of course. Back when I liked a few bitters on a cold winter's night.'

'It isn't funny, Artie,' Vivienne snapped. An hour ago, she'd been dozing in the sitting room, happy to be resting her head upon her husband's shoulder on his last night at home.

'Come on, Viv, you've got to see the light.'

In silence, Vivienne slipped the new sheets over the mattress in the cot, plumped the pillow, lifted out the teddy Nancy had sent (it would dry out nicely, hung by the fire) and then wrestled Stan back out of Artie's arms.

'He's teething,' she said as she laid him back down.

*Teething*, thought Artie, with a wolfish grin. Every time a baby cried, it was *teething*.

'Come on, Viv. The pot's still warm.'

Artie was trying to put his arms around her as they slipped out of the room, but Vivienne shook him off and marched into their small, cramped kitchen, muttering, 'I need to wash my hands.'

After she was done, she found Artie back in the sitting room, his face lit by the fire while he pored over the racing results in the local newspaper. 'I'll miss this,' he said. 'You'll let me know, won't you, how Prince Regent does? And Somerset Sam? I expect I'll be home by the Grand National. We'll have put them back in their own backyard by then.'

Vivienne couldn't help herself. She ripped the newspaper out of his hands, screwed it up and tossed it in the fire. In mere moments it was cinders and ash.

Artie's eyes goggled. 'What on earth—?'

Then he saw the way she was holding herself, arms wrapped around her breast as if she had to keep herself from falling apart – a broken puppet, patched together with string and glue.

'Viv?'

He went to her, his arms open wide in perfect opposition to her own.

'Oh, get off me, Artie,' she said – and her voice cracked with a great sob. 'You can't make it better with a kiss and a cuddle. I can't . . . I can't . . .'

Artie was silent. It was the first time in his life.

'You can't what?' he finally asked, softly.

'I can't . . . do it,' she sobbed. Her arms came apart, and she fell against him. It was good to be folded in his arms – and with this realisation there came another: that it hadn't been very long since the idea of being propped up by a man – *any* man – would have filled Vivienne with disgust. She wasn't supposed to need anybody. Ever since her mother had gone off with Lord Edgerton and left Vivienne to fend for herself, she'd told herself that. But now she was the polar opposite. How strange the world could seem. 'What's it going to be like, when you're gone, Artie? And Stan's in there, and I'm his only person in all of the world. Every day and every night. Every morning and afternoon. What if I can't cope on my own? How am I going to—?'

Artie led her back to the settee and compelled her to sit down.

'You're Vivienne Cohen,' he said. 'Look at what you've done. You can do *anything*.'

She dried her tears.

'It's going to be all right.' Artie's grins were infectious, and he was grateful to see that they hadn't lost their power; Vivienne had softened in his arms. 'Do you know what's going to happen? This time, you Yanks won't wait three years before turning up. This time, your lot'll see the worth in fighting the good fight. You mark my words – you Yanks will come and save the lot of us.' He paused. 'Just like this Yank did for me,' he said, lifting her chin and kissing her lips.

'I'm scared, Artie,' she said.

'And that's why.'

'Why what?'

'Why I'm going,' said Artie, and in his voice there was some new resolve. 'I have to do this, Viv. And it isn't for the sake of the world, it's for you – and for Stan in there. You're the reason I'm going . . . and you're the reason I'm coming back. Hell, I've been through worse scrapes than this. There was more fighting on Cable Street than there's been in France in two months of war. I got my nose bloodied in Pentonville Prison so many times I lost count. It's what gave me my rugged good looks. And that lot in there are far nastier than any of this Nazi lot over the water. Vivienne, I've been standing guard at your door for two years now. Stopping the worst of the world getting in. Look into my eyes.' She did so. They held each other's gaze. 'Let me do it one more time. I got a voice inside me, telling me it's the right thing to do. I haven't always listened to that voice, Viv. But it's the same voice telling me to break a few jaws when they marched down Cable Street. Or to walk three steps ahead of you when we're out on a dark night, just in case somebody jumps out of the shadows. That voice is telling me to get out there, get the job done – then come home, and give you and Stan the life you deserve. You see that, don't you?'

There was a faltering hesitation before she nodded. 'You are coming back, though, aren't you, Artie?'

'You've got my absolute word on it. Me and Ray, we'll do what we got to do, and then we'll come home together – to a better world.' He grinned, like an idiotic old fool. 'And you can bet your last farthing I'll come home more decorated than Ray as well. That man might dance a damn sight better than me, but let's see who's King of the Ballroom when we're at war! A year from now, two years or three, we'll be up at Ma's – me and you, and Stan belting around with whatever little sprogs Ray and Nancy have managed to pop out – and we'll be looking back on all this like it was a dream. It's going to be all right.'

There was such certainty in his voice that Vivienne believed it, too. And, of course, all across London it was the same. From the tables of the Queen Mary restaurant at the Buckingham Hotel, to the lowest terraces in Whitechapel; from the private members' clubs of Soho and Park Lane, to the flophouses in Lambeth and homes beside the railway in Streatham Hill, the same panics, the same prides, the same anxieties and fears and celebrations of young men's courage were being played out. The same conversations, coloured in a thousand differ-ent hues, wherever a husband said to his wife or a son said to his mother that, of course, he was coming back home; that, of course, he wouldn't be one of the unlucky ones, the ordinary, everyday casualties of war. Death was a thing that happened to other people.

So in Maida Vale, Raymond and Nancy danced; and, in Whitechapel, Vivienne and Artie danced as well – both couples in their little bubbles, waiting for the morning to come.

# Chapter Nine

THERE WERE A HUNDRED SILK poppies on show in the Grand Ballroom this November evening. Mr Chamberlain's government had, some time ago, decreed that Armistice Day would not be celebrated this year – perhaps, thought Frank Nettleton as he scurried around backstage, nobody had an appetite for talk of peace and remembrance, not when so many men had already been marched to the Continent, and the wars they'd once said would never come again. Now, as he helped what remained of the dance troupe ready themselves for the evening ahead, his mind wandered to Billy, already entrenched somewhere in France, and Raymond de Guise, learning the rudiments of war out on Salisbury Plain. Nancy said he was bound to join up with the 5th Infantry Division once they reached France, which had brought Frank some modicum of joy along with the guilt still nipping at his heels. The 5th Infantry was where Bill was as well; the Buckingham boys were to be reunited on foreign soil.

No Armistice Day this year, but tomorrow had been prescribed a national day of dedication. Frank wasn't sure what form that might take, back at the Brogan house – where, two nights before, Mr Brogan had returned home from Billingsgate with the news that he and some of the older hands were going to sign up with one of the new Home Defence battalions everybody was talking about. 'Too old to take the king's shilling,' Mr Brogan had said, taking a deep draught from his pipe before dinner, 'but I'm young enough to give Jerry a bloody nose if he drops out of the sky. You could join, too, young Frank' – which made Frank feel hopeful and *silly* in equal measure. The wags were already calling the home battalions the 'King's Elderly Infantry' or the 'Royal Geriatrics'. As far as Frank was aware, they were almost entirely to be made up of the proud veterans of the Great War, refusing to sit out the fight this time round. It gave him a thrill to think of joining a unit in the defence of his home – but he was nineteen years old, in the prime of his life, and felt certain there had to be a better way.

Mathilde Bourchier looked nervous. *She's overzealous as well*, thought Frank, as she flung instructions at one of the other girls and fixed her hair in front of the dressing-room mirrors. Gene Sheldon was doing a good impersonation of Raymond de Guise, sashaying among the dancers, checking that they knew which guests they'd been promised to that evening, running through the moves for the first dance to come. He'd understudied for Raymond once before, but somehow this time felt different – for nobody truly knew when Raymond was coming back. *If* he was coming back at all. You didn't talk about 'if', of course, though in the back of your head you knew it was a possibility. The newspapers were so devoid of stories of battles and devastation that it was easy to pretend, even, that there wasn't truly a war going on. But, even so, the thought of it was here, in the air, all around them. Death, or the prospect of it, was creating vacuums all over the hotel.

'Nancy's a floor mistress,' Rosa had said last night when, with the blackout due, they had taken a long walk, down through St James's and along the river. 'She's going up in the world. You can too, Frank. You have to talk to Gene. Get him to talk to Mr Knave. You're ready. You could be dancing at the Winter Serenade.'

The dream of it hadn't left Frank, not even in his darkest moments, but in his heart he knew he wasn't ready – not quite. He hadn't been to train with Miss Marchmont in a month, now, but there was something she'd said to him that always stuck in his mind.

'There's a difference between good dancing and good *ballroom* dancing. If you want to dance for the joy of it, well, the world's already yours. There'll always be music. But if you want to step out into the Grand Ballroom on an evening and take some beautiful crown princess on your arm . . . well, Frank, we're going to have do something about your poise. About your bearing. You dance like you were born to it, but it's *elegance* we're after.'

What Miss Marchmont meant, but was too genial to say, was that he was still a Lancashire pit boy at heart – a promising dancer, yes, but there was still the look of a mine rat about him. That was why, when he looked at Gene Sheldon taking the arm of Mathilde Bourchier and lining up at the Grand Ballroom doors, he knew he couldn't truly stand among them. Not yet – but one day . . . if he could only get this damn guilt out of his mind.

Out in the ballroom, the first number struck up. Louis Kildare was gone from the orchestra, along with two others as well, but Archie Adams had talents Frank couldn't begin to comprehend and, in mere days, he'd refashioned his arrangements to accommodate their loss. Perhaps there'd be a new saxophonist soon. Perhaps a new trumpeter or two. But it still sounded good to

Frank's ears. As the doors to the ballroom opened, the music rushed through and he let it wash over him.

The ballroom was full. He could hear the applause that always greeted the appearance of the dancers. As they whirled out, arm in arm, to signal the start of another Saturday night, Frank felt the same, familiar thrill from when he first came to the Buckingham. The wonder. The longing. Rosa said that could be his contribution: to keep the magic alive, to help keep the Grand Ballroom alive until its heroes returned. There were moments when Frank could even believe it – but, in his heart, *he* wanted to be a hero, too.

There waltzed Gene Sheldon. There waltzed Mathilde Bourchier.

There, one day, Frank Nettleton.

He'd just have to solve this crisis in his heart first.

It was like Mr Midnight had said: he just had to find his way.

Walter Knave had to admit that the spectacle was inspiring. From his table above the dance floor – where he sat, dwarfed by Lord Edgerton, Uriah Bell, John Hastings and all the various other members of the hotel board – he watched as the dancers pivoted around one another, speeding up and slowing down according to the movements of the song. Yes, this ballroom had certainly proved its worth in the years since he had last been director here. Who would have thought that music and dance were so valuable? *Times*, he thought, *really are changing*.

So was the hotel.

The Grand Ballroom had once lit up the nights across Berkeley Square. Now, its tall glass windows, and the doors which had opened on to the square all summer long, were painted a deep matt black and shrouded in curtains just as dark.

The chandeliers and spotlights which ordinarily lit up the ball-room had been angled and repositioned so that the fringes of the room remained in shadow – making the ballroom's very heart, the dance floor itself, appear like an oasis of starlight on a vast, impenetrable night. The preparations had the effect of making the ballroom seem smaller and more intimate, somehow – perhaps it didn't have quite the spectacle of years gone by, but where something was lost, something else was gained. The Grand Ballroom seemed to be more daring. Its light might not have spilled out into the London night, but in here the dancing went on. There seemed some small victory in that.

'Of course, all this capital expended,' intoned Lord Edgerton, with the solemnity of an undertaker, 'and what have we to show for it?'

He didn't just mean the refurbishment of the Grand Ball-room. Before the first dances had begun, Walter Knave had led the board on a tour. They'd taken a drink in the Candle-light Club, where the terrace was similarly blacked out and new lighting arrangements gave each table a private, secluded feeling. Then it was down to the hotel basements, from which Mrs Farrier's post room had been relocated and where the old laundries – which, for years, had served as a meeting place for the hotel's pages – had been transformed into shelters of opulent design.

'Quite as lovely as any suite,' Mr Knave had croaked – and, while there might have been some embellishment in the state-ment, there was no doubting the attention and expense that had gone into creating something which would both soothe and comfort the hotel's guests during the dark nights ahead. Down there, beds were separated by thick velvet curtains;

private rooms had been constructed for the hotel's most discerning (and wealthy) patrons, and there was even a bar where cocktails and champagne could be relied upon to steady the nerves.

The hotel staff, of course, had to be provided for, too. Their air-raid accommodation was not nearly as opulent, though it had still taken much expense to excavate and repurpose the wine cellars beneath the Queen Mary restaurant (and the Queen Mary itself had had to undergo month-long renovations to protect it from any blast out on Berkeley Square). Along with the blackout blinds in the rooms and suites, and the refitting of the chambermaids' staircase, the costs associated with preparing the Buckingham for war had been astronomical.

'And that's before we start factoring the cancellations into our calculations,' John Hastings interjected.

The youngest member of the Buckingham board, Hastings was a native of New York City, the scion of a family that had made its fortune ten times over and come looking to Europe for new countries to conquer. For two years, Hastings's family firm had been a significant shareholder in the Buckingham Hotel. Of the men gathered at the table, only Lord Edgerton's stake rivalled Hastings's own.

Yet the two men could not have been more different. Lord Bartholomew Edgerton was barely able to shroud his contempt for Hastings – who, scarcely into his thirties, was half Edgerton's age (and, by virtue of his family holdings, wildly more wealthy). With the single exception of his second wife, Edgerton had always hated the Americans; not one of them respected the rights of hereditary wealth. And this John Hastings was one of the worst. Bespectacled and unassuming, the younger man barely had the dignity to *act* as if he had money. By God, he'd come to the Grand

Ballroom tonight in nothing but a smart suit and tie, as if he was attending some common shareholders' meeting.

'A hundred and fifty thousand pounds lost in cancelled banquets alone,' Hastings was saying, with a weary shake of the head. 'Hotel rooms sitting empty. Gentlemen, I've been saying since I arrived that the Buckingham Hotel has relied, for far too long and far too deeply, on the patronage of our European neighbours.'

'Reputation, Mr Hastings!' Uriah Bell, the bird-like financier of the Limehouse Docks, chipped in. Bell had been doing nicely out of the run-up to war, but his shipping interests had taken an inevitable dive since the actual declaration. Since that moment, he'd been skittish and drunk, and he was in precisely the same mood tonight. 'Reputation, reputation, reputation! You weren't here when the old King Edward made this ballroom his playground – but you've seen enough foreign dignitaries, enough European princes and counts floating through here, to understand what that means. *Reputation*, sir, is where the wealth of this hotel lies.'

Hastings removed his glasses and rubbed them wearily. As he did so, he caught a glance of Walter Knave, whose eyes were firmly focused on his lap, as if he neither played no part, nor wanted one, in a conversation of this gravitas. Yes, a fine hotel director they'd chosen. *They*, he thought – as if he hadn't been strong-armed into it by majority decision, and that majority strong-armed into it by whatever secrets and lies Lord Edgerton held over them. John Hastings was a man of business, which meant he'd lain down with vipers before – but there was never a viper as poisonous and sly as an aristocratic English one.

'Reputation won't balance the books this winter, gentlemen. Listen to me – none of us knows the way this war will go. Let us pray it is short and swift. But the evidence of our lifetimes would point to a longer, more gruelling affair, and we would be remiss not to take that into our forecasts. We've already petitioned the government for tax relief.' The Savoy, the Imperial, the Ritz – they'd all come together for this petition: sworn enemies in business, now united as one. 'But a prolonged drop in income, such as we've seen this autumn, will sink this hotel, gentlemen. Which among us has deep enough pockets to keep it afloat?'

*Quite probably all of us*, thought Hastings, *but we would each see more profit by burning the place to the ground – and that's what I'm frightened of.*

'There are twelve hundred employees at this hotel, gentlemen. Let us not forget our duty to them.'

Lord Edgerton's eyes opened in disbelief, but Hastings continued before he could interject. Edgerton and the rest of the board understood 'duty' as a one-way road; it could not possibly have occurred to them that there were lives and livelihoods beyond their own.

'There must be opportunity here, gentlemen. And we must be ready for it – because you can be certain the boards at the Savoy and the Imperial have their eyes on the very same prize.'

Lord Edgerton directed his gaze over the ballroom. On the opposite side of the dance floor, near the blacked-out windows and half-hidden in shadow, a table was thronged with older men.

'I am doing what I can, gentlemen, to bring new patrons to this hotel.'

'Indeed,' said Hastings, 'I believe Sir Oswald Mosley himself took dinner here last week and, unless my eyes mistake me, that is Lord Rothermere and his coterie?'

Viscount Rothermere: the former publishing baron at the head of Associated Newspapers. The man indirectly responsible for the hundreds and thousands of words devoured, each day, over breakfast tables and pots of tea. He was an elderly man now, in his early seventies, his face dominated by a thick, silvery moustache, but he still radiated power. Sitting among his crowd was Adalbert Grice, which shocked Hastings; Grice was a journeyman in the newspaper world, not somebody to sidle up to Lord Rothermere and his ilk. Grice's words were read by thousands; Lord Rothermere's had been read by millions.

'Lord Rothermere is a patron the hotel can be proud of.'

'And Sir Oswald Mosley?'

'A politician – and, in lieu of our European dignitaries, politicians will surely do. Mr Hastings, I fail to see the dilemma. We are in want of patrons. And . . . here they are.'

Hastings lifted his eyes from Lord Edgerton and moved them to Walter Knave – who was studying the mottled spots on the backs of his hands.

'You speak of reputation, gentlemen – and yet we are populating our restaurants and suites with the kind of men who actively opposed this war. Men who would have had Great Britain cosy up with Mr Hitler and permit him to do what he wanted with the peoples of Europe. "Hurrah for the Blackshirts," Lord Rothermere wrote. His words, gentlemen. Not *mine*. When I joined the board at this hotel, it was not to transform it into some kind of sanctuary for—'

Lord Edgerton seethed, 'Watch your tongue, Mr Hastings. Lord Rothermere is an old family friend. He lost two of his own sons fighting for this country in the Great War. Is it any wonder that he would try to propel us towards peace? Good God, man, the world is not so simple as "good" and "bad", as "dark" and "light". You, a man of money, must understand that. There are countless dignitaries in this country who wanted the same peace as Lord Rothermere did. As *I* did as well. Now they find themselves on the wrong side of public opinion, and scrabbling to make sense of a world gone mad. Is there any reason they shouldn't be permitted a place to call their own? Is there any reason society should oust them? I say no, gentlemen.' He paused. 'Any thoughts, Mr Knave?'

Walter Knave, who had been content studying the dirt beneath his fingernails, promptly looked up. He had the look of a rabbit trapped in headlights.

'Well, gentlemen, far be it from me to inveigle my own thoughts into such weighty matters, but . . .'

His obsequiousness was almost painful to watch. Hastings started wringing his hands underneath the table.

'Traditions matter,' Walter stammered. 'We built this hotel on traditions, once upon a time. Traditions can see us through.'

'I think what Mr Knave is trying to say,' said Lord Edgerton, 'is that we must simply hold on until this war comes to its inevitable conclusion. Don't be alarmed, Mr Hastings. There *will* be peace. Mr Chamberlain has devoted his life to it. Don't believe he has given up. And our good friend Lord Rothermere over there – he would have peace as well. It is a very powerful weapon, public opinion, and he is its wielder. Mark my words – when the fighting truly begins, people will very quickly press their politicians for a negotiated peace. It does not have to be a peace won on the battlefield. Then we may have the borders open, and prosperity once more. We must simply bide our time, and welcome whatever new patrons we can in the meantime.'

Lord Edgerton had caught Lord Rothermere's eye across the dance floor. The two men nodded, in silent greeting, and then returned to their private conversations.

'I can agree with you on one thing, my lord. We must bring new patrons to this hotel. We must see war as an opportunity and, in it, the means to thrive. Gentlemen, London is already filling with refugees. Not all of them are penniless. Polish aristocrats are flocking to make London their home. The Czechoslovakian princes. There is money flowing from Romania and the Transvaal – almost everywhere the Nazis are planting their flags. They come to London, gentlemen. More will inevitably follow. Dethroned royals. Governments in exiles. The further Mr Hitler extends his hand, the more will escape to our very own sceptred isle. But let us strive to make their destination a little more specific than simply "Old London Town". Let us make it, clearly and boldly, the Buckingham Hotel.' John Hastings drew a breath. At least he'd drawn the eyes of the rest of the board, even if Lord Edgerton was dismissive – and even if Walter Knave had shrunk so far into his chair that he had almost disappeared. 'Gentlemen, I propose that we make this Winter Serenade a celebration of the new worlds coming into London. Let us open the ballroom doors to those who have lost their homes. Let us show the world that London stands in solidarity with all of Europe's fallen peoples. Let *that* be the reputation of this hotel, gentlemen. Rich or poor, titled or not, let us make a statement that the Buckingham Hotel and its feted Grand Ballroom are the champions of light in what might be a long, dark winter.'

There was silence at the table, echoed by silence on the dance floor as the Archie Adams Orchestra came to the first number's climactic end.

In imperious silence, Lord Edgerton looked down on the dance floor, where Gene Sheldon and Mathilde Bourchier had come apart and were welcoming the evening's guests into their arms.

'Hardly Raymond de Guise, is he?' he said. 'I suggest, Mr Knave, that you begin making preparations to hire a gentleman dancer. Somebody of breeding, if we may. And somebody war will not be taking from us. Can you manage this, Walter?'

Walter Knave didn't seem to recognise that Lord Edgerton had dropped any pretence at formality. He nodded and kept his eyes turned away.

'Gentlemen,' Hastings began, determined that Lord Edgerton could not brazen him back into silence, 'my proposition is clear and has only positive repercussions for our hotel. Are we open for business, or do our doors remain closed, serving a dwindling clientele . . . and whatever else we can dredge up?'

Lord Edgerton bristled, but said nothing.

'I need but one of you for a majority decision, gentlemen. Do we want the Buckingham to succeed or fail? To thrive in spite of war, or surrender?'

Lord Edgerton would not meet his eyes. Neither would Uriah Bell. So, at last, John Hastings looked at the most minor members of the hotel board. Dickie Fletcher controlled but a fraction of the power in the hotel – but he would be enough.

'Dickie, now's the moment. A vote, now, is a vote for the prosperity of this hotel. It's a vote for your own prosperity as well.'

Fletcher, who scarcely ever had a word to say that wasn't immediately smothered by Lord Edgerton, nodded.

'I should like to think we made runaways and refugees feel welcome.'

'Then it's decided.' Hastings got to his feet, just as the orchestra began their next number with a riot of trombone. 'The Winter Serenade will be a symbol of British defiance. A shining light to show the world that we won't be cowed. And that dethroned princes, runaway royals and exiled ministers can dance among the refugee peoples of Europe, right here in our ballroom. Gentlemen, I'll bid you goodnight.'

After he was gone, Lord Edgerton let out a long, vengeful breath. *Power*, he thought, *is the only thing that matters*. It was power that they fought over in Europe. It was power that forged nations and won wars. And it was power that that upstart American was trying to wrest from him tonight.

'Paupers in our ballroom,' he snorted. 'Peasant folk in the arms of our dancers? The man's gone mad.' Now he, too, was on his feet. 'Walter, with me,' he snapped, and Mr Knave rose, obediently, to his feet. 'As for the rest of you,' he said, with an especially withering look for Dickie Fletcher, 'I believe it may be time to decide where your loyalties in this board truly lie.'

December 1939

# Chapter Ten

'HERE IT IS, MRS DE Guise, mind your head!'

The arrival of the traditional Norwegian fir tree that dominated the hotel reception from the start of December until Twelfth Night had always been a highlight in Nancy's year. That first Christmas in London, it had symbolised all the promise and hope she'd felt on coming to the Buckingham, reinventing her life and blazing a path that Frank would be able to follow. Now, it represented hopes of a different nature. She stood by the concierge desks, the night still thick and vast across Berkeley Square, and watched as the men from the Forestry Commission manoeuvred the enormous tree up from the tradesman's entrance, along the narrow passageway, and into the reception hall. Bound up in netting and twine, it hardly looked as majestic and grand as it would in a few hours' time, when the guests would come down for breakfast to discover it bedecked in lights and garlands, scattered with stars. But to Nancy it was still a reminder: the world, with all its infinite intricacies, rolled on.

At half past three in the morning, Nancy left the workmen levering the tree into place with a complex combination of ropes, pulleys and some good old-fashioned grit, to ride the service lift upwards, into the Buckingham's highest reaches. There, she stole along the passageway towards the chambermaids' kitchenette, with the strange pull of nostalgia that she always felt upon knowing that this place was no longer hers. She passed Rosa's door, the door behind which Ruth used to sleep – and, finally, came to the room where she'd spent two and a half years of her own life. Those were the years in which she'd done most of her *living* as well. It was strange, coming back here. It had felt peculiar ever since she married Raymond and moved into a home of her own. But there was something infinitely stranger today – because she was not coming back as one of *them*, but as their manager instead.

She hadn't expected it to feel the same, but nor had she expected this heavy feeling in her heart.

She'd arrived, expecting that she'd have to rouse them all – but they were already awake, fortifying themselves with milky tea and honey in the kitchenette. Rosa was clucking around the new girls like it was her personal fiefdom.

It looked so different, without Ruth sitting in the old armchair, without all the other familiar faces.

Nancy lingered in the doorway, the horrible thought that she was a ghost at the feast niggling away at her, and gently coughed to announce her appearance.

The girls' faces all turned to her.

'Well?' Rosa grinned. 'Is it here?'

'Come on, girls,' beamed Nancy; she had to fake the smile at first, to cover her awkwardness, but soon it blossomed for real. 'It's only one day a year you get to wake up to this, instead of some lordling's dirty sheets. It's going to be a good one.'

*It* is *a good one*, thought Nancy, *but it isn't quite as grand as it has been in years gone by.*

The Norwegian fir – which was filling the reception hall with its fresh pine scent when she led the troop of excitable chambermaids out of the service lift – did not stand *quite* as tall as it had done last year, or the year before that. Its boughs were not quite as heavy and something in it seemed lacklustre, somehow; its branches did not have the span, its pine needles were not as rich and dark – and Nancy was quite certain that one of the boughs had snapped in the transportation. She would have to hide that with baubles and garlands.

The girls didn't seem to notice. For many of them, it was their first Christmas in the Buckingham – and compared to the little trees their families put up in front of their hearths, this was a tree of wonder and grandeur. Before they had arrived, Nancy had already unearthed the chests of decorations from the House-keeping stores, and soon Rosa was leading the girls in opening each box up, taking out tangles of tinsel and sacks of baubles – and the cloth angel, with her hands perfectly folded, who would sit sentry on the top of the tree.

'You'll have to help each other, girls. There are stepladders by the desks. Short straws for the angel,' Nancy instructed (she'd thought of it the prior evening, determined that everybody should get a fair chance), 'and remember – symmetry! Rosa will tell you about the year before last, and what we did with the baubles. By the time we'd set it straight, the guests were already waking.'

She paused. There was no point saying more, because the girls had already taken to the task with the kind of urgency she'd not seen in them all year. *If they took to the guest rooms like that,* she thought with a wry smile, *they'd hardly need half of them on the team.*

Nancy looked down. The chests had been emptied in such a hurry that lengths of gold and silver tinsel were pooled around her feet. It seemed clear, too, that the girls weren't yet thinking of order and design – they'd just scrambled for the brightest, most enchanting baubles they could find, and left behind many of the garlands that would need to be carefully woven through the branches. She grinned. She remembered decorating Christmas trees like this with Frank – no thought, just the joyful abandon of creation. Imagination doing its best, messiest work. She'd have to bring some order to it herself, if Mrs Moffatt was going to approve – let alone Walter Knave and the rest of the hotel management – but that, she supposed, was as it should be.

She heaved a sigh. She wasn't one of the girls any longer.

Down on her hands and knees, she started sorting through the chests, lifting out the garlands and assembling them in rows. She had just about got to the bottom of the second chest, the girls still clamouring and chirruping around the tree behind her, when her fingertips brushed something cold and silver, buried at the box's bottom, too big to be a decoration for any Christmas tree. She reached in – and realised that here, in her hands, was a photograph in an ornate silver frame.

She lifted it out.

She recognised the scene at once, of course – because she was standing in the exact place it had been taken. In the black and white image, the reception hall was dominated by a tree taller than the one being decorated behind her – and, standing in front of it, were ranks made up from the staff and prized guests of the Buckingham Hotel. A board in front of them had been propped up to read: CHRISTMAS 1912, THE BUCKINGHAM REJOICES.

Nancy looked over her shoulder. The girls seemed to have organised themselves now. Rosa was running around the circumference of the tree, weaving a silver garland through its lowest boughs, while two of the tradesmen cheered her on.

She looked into the faces in the picture. *Yes*, she thought, *that is Walter Knave – no spring chicken, but much younger than he is now. And there –* that *was surely Mrs Emmeline Moffatt.*

She turned the picture over and, by good fortune, somebody had recorded the names of the staff and guests for posterity's sake. *Walter Knave and his wife Blythe; Lord Edgar Edgerton* (Lord Edgerton's father? Nancy thought); *Emmeline Ellis; Clementine Carruthers; Elliott Knave* . . .

'Hey, girls, look at this!' she called out.

Soon, the girls were gathered around, cooing at how young Mrs Moffatt looked. There was something, Nancy decided, almost inspiring about seeing this picture.

'They got through the Great War together, girls,' she said, as they passed the photograph around. 'Four long years, and the Buckingham survived. Well, we can do that, can't we? One day at a time!'

Nancy was proud of the observation. She hoped the others would see the light in it, too.

'Their tree's a bit grander than ours,' Rosa remarked, with a roll of the eyes. Trust Rosa to see the cracks in things – even though she did it with a grin. 'Things weren't quite so perilous for them that they had to be saving money on two feet of Christmas tree. Their baubles look *new*, as well.'

Now some of the other girls had started chirping too.

'Well, we've got to make sacrifices,' one of the new girls said. Mary-Louise was seventeen years old, a South Londoner by the sound of her voice. She had the brash confidence of somebody who'd been here for years as she dusted her hands down and reached for another bauble. 'They reckon there'll be rationing by January. They'll let us get fattened up at Christmas, and then make us start spreading our butter too thin.'

'Of course,' one of the other girls chipped in, 'they won't be rationing in the Queen Mary. They'll be eating all the foie gras and king's venison they can find. Quail eggs!' She laughed.

Rosa, who had drifted away from the photograph to gaze up at the tree, said, 'All poppycock. There'll no more be rationing than there will be air raids. It's like this blackout and these bloody gas masks we're dragging around with us all the time. Just –' Nancy heard it before Rosa even mouthed the words – 'stuff and nonsense! Have you ever heard the like of it? Telling us to stay indoors. Telling us we're all going to be bombed out of our houses. Telling us we're going to . . . starve! It's all just so bloody . . .'

All the colour had drained out of Rosa's face. Nancy was not sure if it was because she was outraged or terrified. Suddenly, she was holding herself rigidly.

Then, as if internalising some thought, she shook it off, dabbed at her eye, and continued, in silence, to hang baubles on the tree.

'Rosa,' Nancy ventured, 'are you all right? Is something bothering—'

But she didn't get a chance to finish that question, because Mary-Louise suddenly piped up, 'You're just saying that because your Frank's found a way to get out of it, Rosa. Just because *he's* dodged the bullet, doesn't mean there's no war to—'

Rosa swung her hand back and brought it down, in one firm slap across Mary-Louise's face.

For a second, there was absolute stillness in the hotel reception. Then, the tradesmen who'd been watching exchanged startled looks and quickly backed away.

The silence continued.

Mary-Louise had reeled backwards, clinging to her stinging cheek. When she lifted her hands away from the place she'd been struck, Nancy could see the livid red discolouration. One of the other girls rushed to her. The others turned their scowls on Rosa.

'You nasty, viperous little—'

Nancy had a sinking feeling, deep inside, but in that same moment she understood: this was her responsibility; this was her task. She took a step forwards, planting herself firmly between Rosa and Mary-Louise and yelled, 'That's quite enough!'

All of the chambermaids looked at her.

Nancy wasn't quite sure what to say next. The last time she'd given anybody a scolding it was Frank, and that was years and years ago, back when he was a boy. It was only when an image of Mrs Moffatt popped into her mind that she found the faith to carry on.

'You girls ought to be ashamed of yourselves,' she said, in her best impersonation of a draconian old schoolteacher she'd once had. 'Standing here, in the reception of the grandest hotel in the whole of Mayfair, and acting like children! Good Lord, girls, remember where you are! It's fortunate Mrs Moffatt isn't here. It's fortunate Mr Knave hasn't just wandered through. If we can't respect each other, we can at least respect the hotel! Rosa.' She turned on her heel, and looked Rosa square in the face. It was only now that she faltered at all – because this wasn't just Rosa the chambermaid. This was Rosa, her friend; one day, God willing, her sister-in-law as well. 'Go back to your room.'

She had to force herself to hold Rosa's eye. 'I don't know what's got into you, but something's not right.'

'You heard what she said, Nance! She was maligning our Frank.'

Nancy gritted her teeth. She knew what she had to do, but felt as if she was plunging a knife into someone she loved.

'It's Mrs de Guise to you, Rosa,' she said, trying to hide her sadness at having to say it, 'not Nance, not while we're on duty. To your room, please. I'll see you in the Housekeeping Lounge for breakfast at seven, prompt.'

Rosa stood squarely, unable to believe what she was hearing. There she remained, Nancy's eyes boring into her, until something inside her caved in. Unable to marshal any of her remaining resolve to hide the tears, she turned and fled for the service stairs.

Nancy rounded on the other girls.

'Mary-Louise,' she said, 'you're to return to your room, too.'

'But, Nancy—' She caught herself. 'Mrs de Guise, you saw what she did. That was uncalled for! Can't I just keep—'

'You can do exactly what you're told, Mary-Louise – not one thing more and not one thing less. Do you hear me? You girls have been given a privilege this morning. Decorating this tree has always been the highlight of our year. But you've turned it into a rabble – you and Rosa between you. There was no call for what you said to her. No call whatsoever.'

'She's been chirping about the war for weeks, Mrs de Guise. It's like it doesn't even matter to her.'

Nancy had the inalienable feeling it was something much more than this – but that particular mystery could be kept for another day.

She said, 'Calling my brother's courage into question was a slanderous, hurtful thing to do. But I'm dismissing you back to your quarters not because he's my brother, but because you pointedly provoked one of your fellow chambermaids and have thrown the unity of our department into chaos. Mary-Louise, you're on thin ice. I'm telling you to leave the reception hall *now*. I expect you to do it.'

Nancy wasn't sure how much more resolve she had. Nor was she sure what else she could say or do, if Mary-Louise remained exactly where she was.

One second turned into two. Two turned into three. Each second lengthened and strained.

Then, struggling to hold in the tears, Mary-Louise turned and fled the reception hall.

For another second, Nancy was still. The tension rushed out of her, and she turned to the remaining girls.

'You've got a job to do,' she said. 'Don't let the Buckingham Hotel down.'

When Nancy returned to the reception hall after breakfast in the Housekeeping Lounge – a shamefaced Rosa sitting at one end of the table, and a shamefaced Mary-Louise at the other – the Norwegian fir tree looked as grand and resplendent as it had in years gone by. The girls, she judged, had indeed done the Buckingham proud in the end, and none of the guests who stopped to gaze at the stars sparkling among the branches, or to point at the beautiful angel glimmering on top, would ever know of the nastiness and spite of that morning.

Nancy knew, though. It niggled at her all day. It bored into her, whenever she issued an instruction on the third storey, or dismissed the girls at the end of their shifts. By the time afternoon turned into evening, she was sick to the stomach with it.

She stood there, staring at the tree.

*Hope and promise*, she told herself.

Christmas was coming. The Winter Serenade. And she remembered, vividly, how she had stood here with Raymond last December, mere days before their marriage. How full of hope and promise life had seemed.

*He'll be home soon*, she told herself. His letter from camp had arrived only two mornings ago: ten days' leave over Christmas, before they shipped out for France in the New Year. How strange it had been without him – and how strange, now, it seemed that he would soon be coming back.

It wasn't only exhaustion – the need for a pot of tea and shortbread, and perhaps a few barley sugars on the side – that took her back to the Housekeeping Lounge after all the girls' shifts had come to their end. It was deeper, more fundamental.

She needed somebody to tell her she was doing a good job.

Mrs Moffatt was happy to rise to this particular challenge, and to provide shortbread, tea and barley sugars as well. With paperwork arrayed around them, she and Nancy settled down in the Housekeeping Office and pored over the events of the day.

'You did the right thing, Nancy,' Mrs Moffatt began, once Nancy had unburdened herself of that morning's altercation. 'Fair and hard, just as I would have been.' She paused. 'It's plaguing you, though, isn't it?'

Plaguing was exactly the right word. Nancy had spent all day trying to work out why – though she was certain that she'd done the right thing.

'I don't know who I am to the girls anymore,' she finally admitted. 'When I go to the kitchenette, it doesn't feel right. There isn't a space for me there. I don't mean my old armchair, Mrs Moffatt. I mean—'

'You can call me Emmeline. And, Nancy,' she said, with a twinkle in her eye, 'I think I might have just an *inkling* of the way you've been feeling. It's how we all feel, when we take that next step. Things change. They shift underneath you, like sand. You're not one of the chambermaids anymore. What you did this morning was exactly right. It must have been hard, to reprimand Rosa like that. But it *mattered*. And you may have done yourself a great favour as well.'

'How so, Mrs— How so, Emmeline?'

It seemed significant, somehow, that Mrs Moffatt had asked Nancy to use her Christian name. *Not one of the chambermaids*, she thought – but she *did* belong somewhere else.

'The girls will see fairness in you. They'll see even-handedness and lack of favouritism. It's because of that that they'll trust you. They'll know where they stand. Had you punished one or the other of them, they'd have sensed weakness. Oh, perhaps they wouldn't have expressed it or even thought of it like that. But, inwardly, they'd have known you were open to argument. Open to persuasion. And that, Nancy, can never work with a leader.' She paused. 'Your Raymond understood that with his dance troupe. I dare say he's receiving another reminder of it in camp this winter. It must be strange for him, not to be at the head of the troop anymore.'

*While here I am*, thought Nancy, *learning how to lead from the front.*

'You're doing the right thing, my girl. And one day, when this war is done, you'll see it clearly – how your actions, and your fairness, and your clarity with the girls helped them to weather something unimaginable in their lives. That's what it was like for me during the Great War. That's how it will be again.'

'I found an old photograph,' Nancy said, suddenly reminded, 'of the Buckingham at Christmas 1912. You were there, Emmeline. Walter Knave and his family, too – his wife, Blythe, and somebody named Elliott.'

'Oh, Elliott Knave.' Mrs Moffatt smirked. 'I remember him well.'

'I said to the girls that your generation pulled the hotel through the Great War, and that we had to do the same.' Nancy faltered. 'I'm not sure they believed me. Were things *better* back then, Emmeline? In the picture, Mr Knave looked . . . well, perhaps not *heroic*, but at least like he really was leading the hotel. I wondered – his wife, Blythe, and his son, Elliott—'

'Elliott was Mr Knave's nephew, Nancy. Or . . . his great-nephew.'

Nancy nodded. 'I wondered if he had more fight in him, back then – when he was a younger man?'

'I think that's fair to say. Men do tend to have more about them when they've something to care about. Or *someone*, I should say. Mr Knave isn't the sort of man who's married to his job. He never was – which was a shame, because that's the way it ought to be with a position like his. But when Mrs Knave was still with us . . . well, she kept him in order. He was loyal to his wife in a way you wouldn't believe to look at him now. He was in love, and I don't believe the love he held for her had faded from the day they were married until the Great War was through and they were entering their dotage together. So, yes, Nancy, he had a little more fire in him, in the old days. Blythe Knave made certain of it. She lit the fire underneath him every morning.'

'And Elliott Knave?'

'Well, *that's* a different story. The last I heard of Elliott Knave, he'd found his fortune in the City of London. A power broker, they say. A money man. One of those that can spirit thousands of pounds out of nowhere, at the drop of a hat. The wonder of mathematics. Well, he wasn't like that when I knew him – I'll tell you that for nothing. He was lucky to get his start in the audit office, here at the hotel. You see, the Knave family always thought Elliott was a little . . . useless, I suppose, is the word. The black sheep! But Walter had a soft spot for him. He brought him here, put him in the audit office, had him learn the ropes. And, to his credit, he took that learning as far as he could go.' Mrs Moffatt smiled. 'There's a lesson in that for you, Nancy. You can make what you want of yourself in the Buckingham Hotel. You can take what you're learning and reach for the stars.'

'Well, I'd like to think Mr Knave might rediscover some of his old fire soon. The hotel needs it.' Nancy hesitated before going on. 'The girls noticed the tree in the old photograph dwarfed the one we have this year. The pennies are being counted, aren't they, Emmeline?'

'Well, that's a product of the times as well, I'm afraid. That Christmas tree isn't the only corner that's been cut this year, I can tell you. I found out last month why the Buckingham's bedlinen has felt so stiff since autumn – Mr Knave switched us to an industrial laundry outside of the city. Anything to save a few farthings.'

'Is it so very bad, Emmeline?'

Mrs Moffatt heaved a great sigh. 'I'm not privy to the talk of the board, Nancy. I'm barely privy to the talk of management anymore, not now Mr Knave's back at the helm. It was different

when Mr Charles was the director. He trusted me. We were ...
friends. But Mr Knave, I suspect, still sees me as the scurrying
little chambermaid I was back when he last worked here.' She
paused. 'It's a perilous moment, Nancy. There isn't any denying it. But one rather suspects that a shorter Christmas tree
and some cheaper soap is hardly enough to recompense for all
that we've lost. I have to admit, I've found myself wondering if
Mr Knave might be back to his old ways.'

There was something about the way she said the last two
words that gave Nancy pause.

'What do you mean?'

'I shouldn't say this, Nancy – but, seeing as you're part of the
Housekeeping management now, I know it won't go any further
than these four walls. You see, back when Mr Knave used to run
the hotel, there were always ... whispers, shall we say? Rumours –
that he liked a flutter on the horses a little bit more than a regular
gentleman might. Well, of course, that's no crime. But the other
managers used to joke that Mr Knave didn't need his account at
Lloyds, because the Buckingham Hotel was his bank.' Mrs Moffatt
shook her head, wearily. 'There, I've said it. But you know what a
place like this is like for rumours and lies. I'm sure there's nothing more untoward going on in this hotel, now, than Mr Knave
cutting back costs because of the war. It just seems a shame – with
Christmas on the way.'

'And rationing in the New Year.'

'You get the sense that what people truly want is one last
Christmas, one last day of indulgence and cheer, before the pri-
vation really begins. A night we can all remember, if there are
dark days to come. Well ...' Mrs Moffatt sighed. 'We have our
Winter Serenade – and you have your Raymond coming back

from camp. There has to be some cheer in that, doesn't there?' She paused. 'I'm glad you came to me tonight. That door's always been open to my girls – now more than ever. And it's never going to be closed to you. You might not feel like you have a natural place with the girls anymore, but you have one right here – at my side. We've a war to get through, Nancy – and, if we have to carry each other through the deeps, we'll do it together, you and I.'

# Chapter Eleven

A WEEK INTO DECEMBER, THE first snows fell across London. By then, the newspapers were already full of the stories pouring out of Finland, where Russian soldiers had rolled across the border in their tanks and endless infantry lines – but to the staff of the Buckingham Hotel that was all happening in a different world. The snow that fell on them was light and enchanting. It changed the city but it did not smother out life. Fires still burned in hearths of the town houses of Berkeley Square; the radios still played; restaurants still served the finest caviar – while, in Hyde Park, ice skaters pirouetted across the Serpentine's frozen waters. A winter wonderland in London, but a winter war one thousand miles in the east.

Preparations for the Grand Ballroom's Winter Serenade had been going on since the end of summer – but, as the first weeks of December rolled by, they reached a new intensity. In the studio behind the Grand Ballroom, Mathilde Bourchier and Gene Sheldon took the rest of the troupe through their paces, while Frank Nettleton and the other part-time demonstration dancers looked on. In the hotel director's office, the last preparations were made for looking after the Serenade's 'Honoured Guests', and Nancy de Guise had twice seen representatives from the

Polish and Czechoslovakian embassies passing through to take meetings with Mr Knave. Seventy-five invitations to London's refugees had been issued for the night of the Winter Serenade, and the staff of the audit office had been diverted from their monetary tasks to vet the intended guests for their suitability for the Buckingham. Nancy rather suspected this was a special directive issued by Lord Edgerton – the rumour was that he'd roundly condemned the idea of 'riff-raff in the ballroom', and that he was seeking to nullify Mr Hastings's decision by any means at his disposal. But the feeling up and down the Buckingham was that times were changing. In the Housekeeping Lounge, the very idea that the 'riff-raff' would be enjoying the spectacle of the Grand Ballroom this Christmas was a cause of great celebration (and not a little envy). The kitchen porters, the cocktail waiters, the concierges and pages – every one of them rejoiced that, this year, the winter ball would not be the preserve of princes and dukes, European dignitaries and Right Honourable Members of Parliament. 'We mightn't be fighting, except at sea,' said Mrs Moffatt in the Housekeeping Lounge, 'but there are folks right here, in our very city, whose countries went up in flames. Why not give them something to revel in this Christmas? If it were up to me, I'd clear out the Continental and Grand Colonial suites as well. Give them the lot, for a night they'll always remember.'

Winter balls at the Buckingham Hotel had always been very special things. This year, it seemed, there would be even more to remember.

Midwinter's night had come and gone. The evening of the Winter Serenade was hoving into view. The air in the Buckingham was throbbing with expectation. And on a train wending

163

its way across the snowbound Wessex downs, the expectation was running high as well. For eight long hours the train had laboured from one lonely country station to another, sitting in the sidings while the railwaymen and the more willing passengers worked together to shovel snow from the tracks ahead. As the day had paled towards evening, the train had lumbered on, snow tumbling in hypnotic waves past its windows – while, in the last carriage, two brothers, dressed in standard issue infantry uniforms, rubbed their hands together for warmth and watched their breath pluming in the air.

'I shovelled much more snow than you that time, Ray,' said the first brother as the train ground forwards.

'Counting were you, Artie?'

Artie Cohen let loose a cackle. 'You can bet I was. Well, somebody's got to!'

Raymond de Guise was not the only new infantryman on the train bound back for London. Some of the carriages were overflowing with new recruits heading home for Christmas, a short reprieve granted before the transports took them into France and the Low Countries in the New Year. Nor was he the only one turning the wedding band on his finger and dreaming of seeing his beloved once again. Eight weeks was a long time to be away from Nancy and, in many ways, it felt much longer. The wad of letters she'd written was stowed neatly in his pack. He meant to place them in his bedside drawer as a promise that he'd one day return and read them, over and over, into his old age. Right now, though, it was not the dread of leaving her again that was plaguing him; it was, he had to admit, a strange nervousness at seeing her again. These eight weeks had changed him. He'd gone to Salisbury as Raymond de Guise, King of the Ballroom, champion dancer; he was returning as Private de Guise – and, opposite him, chewing on the dog-end of a cigarette, was his brother, Private Cohen. The world had turned.

He wished the train would speed up, too. He'd thought to be in London before the blackout. Now he'd be lucky if he didn't have to sleep in some hedgerow with the snow tumbling down.

'You want a smoke?' Artie asked.

Raymond waved it away.

He'd been forewarned what camp would be like, but it had been difficult to fully visualise until he was there, standing outside the quartermaster's store and being kitted out in uniform, before being marched off to barracks. Four blankets, a mattress and a pillow – these were the sum total of each new recruit's possessions while in camp, and God forbid they weren't folded in the dictated fashion at 7 a.m. each morning. For Raymond, who was used to late nights in the ballroom and more leisurely mornings, it was the sudden change in how his days were arranged that hit hardest. Artie was more comfortable with the lack of sleep – and never more so now that Stan was caterwauling at all hours – and took pains to remind Raymond of it on every possible occasion. He took pride, too, in the fact that his assigned identification number – 7520975 – was three hundred higher than Raymond's own, 7520675.'They see me as more crucial to the war effort, Ray. Three hundred steps closer to the top brass.'

Raymond remembered Artie's jocular bragging well. Sometimes it grated, but he had been grateful to have his brother in the same barracks, even when, two weeks into training, Artie was found to have burned the edge of his beret on a cigarette end, and subjected to seven days' punitive measures for his slovenliness. But that was just Artie. At least by the end of that week he'd learned the emphasis the regiment placed on order and attention to detail. And Artie was never a man who lacked a work ethic. Yes, in times gone by he'd put that work ethic to use stealing from railway yards (and scrubbing pans in the kitchens at Pentonville Prison) but, after long weeks of marching, training with bayonets, parading and being put through rigorous drills by the camp's physical education instructors, Artie was leaner and more focused than Raymond could remember. Raymond, too, was leaner and stronger; the ballroom equipped a man with strength and poise, but it seemed that a whole extra set of muscles were being brought to life in training. Raymond ached and burned just like all the rest.

Artie, he had to admit, was more natural with the .303 Lee–Enfield rifles with which they'd been issued. He was more eager to train with the light machine guns, too.

'But you'll never look as good in uniform as me, Artie,' Raymond laughed as the train ground onwards.

'Yeah?' Artie grinned. 'Well, we'll see what my Viv thinks about that.'

A dozen false starts later, the train reached Paddington Station under the cover of darkness, and Artie and Raymond tramped out into the unseen city. As the rest of the returning soldiers fanned out around them, Raymond and Artie lingered in the falling snow to make their farewells – Artie to travel by Underground to Whitechapel, Raymond on the slow march into Mayfair.

'A parting of the ways,' Artie grinned again.

'Only for two days, though. I'll see you for the Peels' banquet on Christmas Day. Stan's first Christmas, of course. He'll be glad to have his father home.'

Artie was about to light up a cigarette, when Raymond snatched the matchbook out of his hands.

'Relax, Ray,' Artie said, 'there's no Luftwaffe up there tonight.' Then he clapped his brother on the shoulder. 'Christmas Day, Ray. Don't you dare be late. Ma will carve *you* up if you are.'

After Artie had gone, Raymond slowly made his way across the empty expanse of Hyde Park – where the snow lit up the world so much he felt quite certain any invading Junkers would be able to see him from far above – and across the opulent Park Lane. It felt strange to be in Mayfair again, and not for the first time he marvelled that it had only been eight weeks. *Eight weeks would be nothing*, he thought, *compared to whatever came next.* Billy Brogan had already been away for months, and no doubt he'd remain there for many months longer.

Raymond paused on the edge of Berkeley Square, and wondered what the world might look like when he next came here. What *his* world might look like. *No ballrooms*, he thought. *Just bombed-out Berkeley Square.*

And Nancy . . .

His thoughts were leading him to the dark, troubled places he'd done so well at keeping at bay, so he tried to shake them off and looked up at the Buckingham's blacked-out face. Looming above the snow on the square, the white façade of the hotel looked like a fairytale palace, sculpted from ice.

*Or*, he thought grimly, *a giant's uprooted tooth.*

It was one of the saddest sights he'd seen – this place that ordinarily radiated such magnificence and hope, now sealed up like a dilapidated mansion. The only thing that brought him cheer was the thought of what was happening inside. It might have been boxed up from the world – but, through the hotel's revolving brass doors, the splendour surely went on.

It would not do to go through those doors, not even in his uniform, so he entered by the tradesman's entrance – where one of the hotel pages, standing guard in the frigid air, was startled at his appearance. Then, onwards he marched. He could hear the music already. He could feel the prickling heat of the hotel. And he began thinking, as he wended his way through the hallways to reach the Housekeeping Lounge, how it had been for all those veterans of the Great War who'd returned here after four years in the mud of Flanders. How alien these halls must have seemed to the concierges and porters who'd gone off to fight and been lucky enough to return. It was going to feel otherworldly when he finally put his dancing shoes back on and took his place in the ballroom.

*If* he ever did.

The door to the Housekeeping Lounge was open. He stole through. The lounge itself was empty, and on its other side the door to the office stood ajar. He glanced inside. There she was, with her head in her books: the perfect vision of Nancy. He knocked.

She looked up.

The papers cascaded around her as she rushed into his arms.

'You're late,' she chastised him, gently, with her head pressed against his shoulder.

'But I got here in the end.'

They remained that way for some time, in the perfect intimacy of silence. Then, as they came apart, he said, 'I could hear the music, ringing through the halls.'

'The Winter Serenade,' she told him. 'Raymond, you wouldn't believe it. Mr Hastings held the board to their promise. Lord Edgerton might not have liked it, but he made it happen – and the ballroom's . . .' She faltered. What was the use in talking about it, when he could simply see it for himself? 'Come on.'

She gestured wildly at all of the paperwork through which she'd been working. 'All of this can wait.'

They had to go by the back entrance, weaving around the reception hall and into the network of dressing rooms behind the ballroom. Here, the music was muffled only gently by the walls. The Archie Adams Orchestra were in the middle of one of their biggest numbers, the fast and energetic 'Burgundy Waltz'.

'Go on,' Nancy told him. 'Go and see.'

'I came back for you, Nancy,' he said. 'Not the ballroom.'

Nancy raised a taunting eyebrow. She knew that one thing did not preclude the other.

'You'll have me all the way until New Year. But the Winter Serenade happens only one night of the year. The Christmas Ball, Raymond – it's not like any you'll ever have seen.' She stopped. 'Well, go on! While they're still dancing!'

Nancy took Raymond's hand and cajoled him to the dance floor doors. When she pushed them apart, just a crack, a riot of grand piano and trumpets sallied towards them with the power of a wild electric storm.

Raymond looked out upon the winter wonderland of the Grand Ballroom. It seemed smaller tonight, for the blackout curtains that kept the light from spilling into Berkeley Square cocooned the whole ballroom, and the edges were fringed in shadow. *But somehow*, thought Raymond, *that only makes it seem more bewitching*. The chandeliers were hung low, turned into wreaths thick with holly and plump red berries. The balustrade around the dance floor was entwined with white paper roses. Clusters of crystalline decorations dangled from the rafters and railings, catching the ballroom's spotlights so that they shimmered like snowfall.

And there, on the dance floor, being pirouetted and turned by Gene Sheldon, Mathilde Bourchier and all the other dancers he'd left behind, was a collection of men and women who, though dressed in their finest garments, were clearly not the ladies and lords who ordinarily frequented the Buckingham balls. They were not wearing the finest confections Regent Street had to offer, but hand-me-down gowns stitched together by loving hands; threadbare, perhaps, and worn a hundred times before, but still holding some of the glamour they must once have had. Nor were their wrists and necks adorned with silver, gold and gemstones precious enough to be kept in safes all year long and insured at Lloyd's of London; no, these dancers were wearing heirloom jewellery, things passed down from grandmother to grandchild through the generations. Compared to the members of the hotel board who stood above the dance floor – compared to the dukes and duchesses who were still in attendance – these dancers were commoners, music hall grubbers at best.

*But their joy*, thought Raymond, *is just the same.*

Nancy explained, 'John Hastings turned the Winter Serenade into a charity ball to honour London's refugees. The Buckingham won't make a penny from this evening – oh, but the reputation . . .'

Raymond looked back through the door. He tried to pick out Lord Edgerton in the shadowy edges of the room. He was standing apart from the rest of the board, flanked by figures Raymond did not recognise.

'Arnold Leese,' said Nancy.

'I know that name,' Raymond whispered.

'You'll wish you didn't,' Nancy sighed. 'He's the publisher of *The Fascist*. The director of the Imperial Fascist League – or he was, until he dissolved it this year. Now he's for King and

answer, he looked to his side and saw that Walter had scuttled away. Now, he was standing in the shadow of Lord Edgerton and his reprehensible guests, head bowed as Lord Edgerton muttered some instruction into his ears.

On any other night, perhaps it would have troubled John Hastings – but tonight he chose to breathe through the irritation, and returned his eyes to the dance floor instead. To think, there had once been a day when he himself did not see the merits of music and dance. Well, here was the proof that the world needed music much more than it needed war. It needed dance floors much more than it needed parade grounds and army camps. If everyone in the world could feel the togetherness he was feeling right now, as landed gentry stood with refugees, as Poles and Czechs stood with Englishmen and Englishwomen, then there would not be wars. Better to dance than to bury bayonets in each other's breasts.

'Enjoy it, Mr Hastings, while you can,' came a baritone voice to his rear.

Hastings turned again, to see that Lord Edgerton, still flanked by his own honoured guests, was approaching.

'It won't come as easily again.' Lord Edgerton looked imperiously upon the dance floor. 'The founders of this hotel would be turning in their graves this evening – to think of foreign pickpockets and thieves, invited into the halls of princes. Wait until the first thefts begin, Mr Hastings. Wait until one of your common friends out there decides he takes a fancy to some lord's daughter. *Then* we'll see what the Society pages have to say. Do you think they'll trust us then, Mr Hastings? Is that how the Buckingham survives?'

John Hastings could not meet Lord Edgerton's eyes, not for long. A certain black magic always affected him when he looked into those dark, pitiless orbs. John Hastings was not a man who hated very easily, but Lord Edgerton could conjure it out of him in a mere moment.

'We, too, are part of the world, Bartholomew,' he said, pointedly pronouncing Lord Edgerton's Christian name. 'For one night only, let's acknowledge that. By Christmas Day, we'll be back to roasting geese these folk can barely dream about. While they're eating stews, we'll be serving rare venison and charging our diners more for one meal than these people can muster between them. It's a mere moment in time for us – but let's read the Society pages this Christmas. Let's see how they speak of us then. Because I believe, Bartholomew, that you and your friends here have misread the mood of this country more than you know. Leave aside the humanity of it, if you must. But at least consider the commerce. We're about to be toasted—'

'To be toasted by men without means is scarcely to be toasted at all,' intoned Lord Edgerton, 'and as for the mood of the country . . .' He shared sidelong looks at his compatriots. 'Well, let us just say that not all Englishmen think alike.'

He was about to say more when John Hastings interjected, 'Perhaps we can agree to simply enjoy the spectacle tonight, gentlemen?'

His eyes snapped back to the dance floor. While the music swelled and rolled around them, nobody had noticed the backstage doors fluttering open and two new dancers joining the throng. But John Hastings would recognise that midnight blue anywhere. He saw it glide, effortlessly, between two other pairs of dancers – and in its arms was a beauty in ivory chiffon and simple, elegant lace. The man's black hair shone as he turned with his partner in his arms. The space around him seemed to open up, like the Red Sea – so that, though no exodus of dancers left the dance floor, somehow there was space for him to dance and glide and lift his partner from the ground.

'I didn't know he'd returned,' said John Hastings.

'Nor I,' said Walter Knave, who had sidled close again, still in Lord Edgerton's shadow.

The Archie Adams Orchestra was playing their Christmas number, 'That Time of Year', which somehow seemed to have turned 'God Rest Ye Merry Gentlemen' into a fast, frenetic swing. John Hastings sank against the balustrade and focused his eyes on Raymond de Guise. Fascists to the left of him, cowards and cronies to the right, but if he looked straight ahead – if he kept his eyes focused on only that which he could see, and the future in front of him – he remembered there was still hope. And that was the lesson of the evening: in a country at war, with uncertainties building on every front, you simply had to keep your focus. There was a way through the most unnavigable channels, if only you picked the right route.

But for now, it was enough to gaze down on the dance floor and know that, for one more Christmas, the King of the Ballroom was here to light the way. He didn't think there was a soul in the ballroom – even, perhaps, the seething Lord Edgerton – who would not agree with that.

# Chapter Twelve

THERE WERE NO CHRISTMAS LIGHTS strung up in the shop awnings this year, no glittering Christmas trees dominating every shop window, but that had not diminished the mounting feeling of joy coursing through Mrs Moffatt as, directly after dismissing her girls back to their quarters on Christmas Eve, she hailed a taxicab out on Regent Street and directed the driver to take her to King's Cross Station.

The roads might not have been choked by traffic, but the platforms at King's Cross were thronged with the last Londoners leaving the city to spend the Christmas season with their loved ones. The main concourse was filled with families as well, huddled in their overcoats and woolly scarves and waiting for the next carriage to disgorge its passengers. Everywhere Mrs Moffatt looked, there was some other family welcoming its children back into their arms. According to yesterday's papers – Mrs Moffatt often liked to sit with a pot of tea, poring over the newspapers the guests had left behind – the influx of evacuees back into London in the last two weeks had been considerable. That would just give Rosa more evidence for her 'stuff and nonsense', she thought – though the young chambermaid had been quiet of late. Perhaps her dressing-down by Nancy had done her some good after all.

Mrs Moffatt was wondering, idly, if the Brogan children had made their way back into London – the hotel had seemed just a little bit emptier without Billy Brogan prancing up and down its passages – when she looked up and saw a group of airmen, dressed in their navy-blue uniforms, tramping off one of the platforms. Her eyes searched through the faces for one she knew well.

She saw him long before he saw her. There he was, all six foot seven of him, roaring with laughter as one of his fellow airmen told a ribald joke, their hullabaloo echoing even in the crowded station. With his big round face and his hair the colour of sun-burnished sand, it was not immediately apparent that he was Mrs Moffatt's son – but that was who he was.

As he and his fellow airmen left the platform, Malcolm Brody looked up and saw Mrs Moffatt standing there. It had been some months since they last met. The height of summer, when war was just a rumour in the halls of Westminster and the folk in the Buckingham Hotel were trying to push it out of their minds, even while the construction work went on in the hotel cellars. She had quite forgotten how diminutive she felt when she saw Malcolm – not just physically, but in her heart and mind as well. She wanted to shrink from him every time they met. This time, she tried to meet him eye to eye.

'Boys,' Malcolm began, in the soft Western Australian accent that would always speak of his true history, 'I'd like you to meet my English mother, Emmeline.'

*English mother* – because Malcolm had been taken from Mrs Moffatt's arms mere moments after his birth; and, one tear-stained signature later, he was making his way to the new parents who would ultimately take him to the other side of the world. He'd found her again last year, now that he was stationed in Great Britain with the Royal Australian Air Force and determined to find out from where he'd come. The shock of it was still subsiding for Mrs Moffatt. It washed over her every time she saw him again. And yet . . . *English mother*, he'd said, with a smile. There was a place for her in that. She would continue to embrace it.

'Malcolm,' Mrs Moffatt said, 'I didn't know you'd be bringing guests.'

'Three days leave, Emmeline,' Malcolm replied, 'and my boys here had nowhere to go. Well, you can't leave stray dogs out in the cold at Christmas.'

Mrs Moffatt had arranged a room for him at the Buckingham. Nothing fancy – just staff quarters, vacated when some of her girls had gone home for the season.

'But I'm not sure there are enough beds, Malcolm. I'm just—'

'Oh, any corner will do, ma'am,' one of the other Australians said. He had the same kind of charm, Mrs Moffatt decided, as some of the more syrupy guests at the Buckingham – though, at least with him, it was a jocular affectation. 'We'll be no bother. And Malcolm here reckons you throw the best Christmas shindig in the whole of London town.'

Mrs Moffatt was quite sure that the best Christmas 'shindig' in the whole of London town had already been held in the Grand Ballroom last night – but she had always been proud of the festivities the chambermaids, porters, concierges and pages threw in the Housekeeping Lounge every Christmas Day. She was quite certain that the addition of a few burly airmen wouldn't do anything to diminish the proceedings. It might even *enliven* things. Just wait until her girls found out.

'Taxicabs are this way, boys.' She turned to the front of the station, where the snow was still flurrying down. 'We might have to take two.'

Christmas morning dawned.

At number 18 Blomfield Road, Maida Vale, Nancy de Guise turned in bed, to see the long, lithe figure of Raymond lying there. She reached out for him and, by instinct, he turned so that he cocooned her body. And there they lay, in the crystalline beauty before dawn, until Nancy's alarm started trilling and she picked herself out of bed.

Raymond rolled over. 'Happy Christmas, darling,' he said.

'Stay where you are,' she told him. She was already getting dressed in front of the mirror, fastening her hair and rubbing the sleep from her eyes. 'I'll see you soon.'

Raymond picked himself up. It was still dark in Maida Vale, but the snowdrifts in the street outside had captured the moonlight and made it seem as if dawn had already arrived.

'I wish you didn't have to work,' he said.

She wished it, too. But, 'Needs must,' she said, and returned to kiss him one last time. Then, opening her bedside drawer, she removed a small package tied in scarlet ribbon, placed it at his side and said, 'Wait for me, Raymond,' before she hurried out of the door.

*Wait for me.* Three simple words. He'd be saying them to her soon enough. Ten days and counting, before Private de Guise embarked on his military career. He crashed back to the pillow, and held the package close to his heart.

Nancy had crossed the ethereal, early morning London every day in December, but this one seemed the most frozen. By the time she was crossing Berkeley Square, she could hardly feel the tips of her toes.

At least the fires were roaring in the Housekeeping Lounge. There were always fewer girls working on a Christmas morning, but the table was still bedecked with hot toast and crumpets, scones and a multitude of different candied fruits and preserves. Because it was Christmas morning, there was a plate of kippers dripping in butter, and chestnuts that Mrs Moffatt had been roasting in the pan over the Housekeeping fire. The air was filled with the scent of the gingerbread one of the porters had just brought down from the Queen Mary restaurant, whose under-lings had been toiling since midnight in service of the banquets to come.

'Rationing in January?' Rosa scoffed. 'Well, not at the Buck-ingham. Dig in, girls!'

Some of the girls laughed at that, but when Rosa caught Nancy's eyes, she looked shamefacedly away. They'd often come across each other in the halls since that early December morn-ing, but their exchanges had been few and far between. Frank had scarcely mentioned it either. Rosa's indiscretion, it seemed, had been swept under the carpet – and perhaps that was the best way to deal with it. Except, whenever Rosa made a joke like that, Nancy thought that there was something more to this story than the chambermaid was telling – something buried that, if it wasn't excavated soon, would surely explode.

But thoughts like this, she decided, could wait for another day.

The girls always worked eagerly on Christmas morning. Nancy worked eagerly, too. By mid-morning most of the guests had vacated their suites to indulge in the lavish breakfasts the Queen Mary was serving. By lunchtime, if past years were any barometer, many of them would already be merry, and certain others so high on the season that they ought to go back to bed. So Nancy and the girls marched ardently through the suites and storeys, and by the time mid-afternoon came – the smells of buttery roast goose billowing up from the Queen Mary – they were ready for some festivities of their own.

Nancy was late to the Housekeeping Lounge. By the time she'd run an inspection of the suites in which her girls had been working, the annual party was already in full swing, and she entered to a cavalcade of music. Some of the trumpeters from the Archie Adams Orchestra had made an early appearance, and the tables were already separated so that the girls could dance. To her astonishment, she saw three airmen in navy-blue uniforms twirling the chambermaids around while the other girls clapped and cheered them on. The countertops were bedecked with glass bowls, jugs of mulled wine and spiced punch – and, by the startled look on Frank's face, he wasn't quite prepared for the festivities exploding around him.

'Frankie,' she said, and presented him with a brown paper parcel she'd decorated herself.

It was a Nettleton family tradition, which stretched back to Frank's earliest years. There hadn't been much money after Nancy and Frank's mother died, so they'd saved the wrapping paper and used it again each and every year. This paper was the same as she'd used when he was scarcely as tall as her knee.

He opened it up, to reveal a thick knitted jumper, perfect for a winter's day. When Nancy opened hers in return, she unearthed a thick knitted cardigan – perfect, presumably, for the very same winter.

'Great minds think alike, Nance,' said Frank.

Together, they looked at the makeshift dance floor. Nancy's eyes might have been deceiving her, for she was certain she saw Mrs Moffatt herself dancing with one of the airmen. Then her eyes gravitated to Rosa, who was on the other side of the room, dunking a glass into the punchbowl.

'Keep an eye on her, Frankie. Don't let her drink too much of that punch. If it's anything like last year . . .'

Frank's cheeks started flushing. Nancy had barely spoken about that morning she'd sent Rosa back to her room; Rosa herself had hardly mentioned it. The only reason Frank knew anything at all was because some of the other girls had been chattering.

'Just ask her to go for a walk or something, Frankie. That cold air will sober her up if she takes it too far.'

'Rosa's not like that, Nancy, I promise. She just wants to have a good time. And it *is* Christmas.'

*Christmas or not*, thought Nancy, *Rosa couldn't afford another moment like the first of December.*

She kissed Frank on the cheek, whispered, 'Happy Christmas, Frankie. Next year – at my house!'

Then, after depositing the paperwork she'd been carrying on Mrs Moffatt's desk in the office, she slipped quietly out.

She'd enjoyed Christmases in the Housekeeping Lounge once upon a time, but this year was going to be different.

Nancy hurried out of the hotel by Michaelmas Mews, then tramped through the drifting snow into Berkeley Square. As she crossed the undulating white expanse, a convoy of taxicabs drew to a halt outside the hotel's marble colonnade, and out of the carriages stepped Lord Edgerton, with his diminutive wife on his arm, and the others she'd seen in the Grand Ballroom at the Winter Serenade. Arnold Leese ignored the doorman and hurried up the sweeping marble steps. The Right Honourable Archibald Ramsey followed swiftly after. Then, out of the final taxicab, a lean figure with the lined face of a sixty-year-old and wearing full Royal Navy regalia, allowed himself – and his good lady wife – to be guided up the steps. Nancy had seen him at the hotel before and knew him as Admiral Sir Barry Domvile, once one of the Royal Navy's most feted senior officers. Now, it seemed, his interests lay in other directions. He was grasping Lord Edgerton by the hand in greeting as Nancy hurried away.

Nancy reached the old Cohen house in the falling snow. Inside, Raymond was waiting, bedecked in his midnight blue, along with his mother Alma and the refugee girl Leah. But no table had been set here this Christmas Day. The house was not filled with the smells of turkey and sage as it had been in years gone by. Nancy saw that Raymond was still holding the present she'd left him that morning.

'I wondered if you'd wait,' she grinned, as he took her hand and led her back into the snow.

After stopping to collect Artie and Vivienne – a picture of frazzled beauty, thought Nancy – the family picked their way south, through the streets of Stepney Green and Whitechapel, until they could almost smell the salt from the Limehouse Docks. There, hidden behind ornate iron gates, stood the mansion house that belonged to Sir George Peel, benefactor of the Daughters of Salvation.

'Christmas Day with the toffs.' Artie was laughing as they reached the frozen gates, dripping with icicles. 'Well, it's a new one on me, but as long as there's grub, I'll take what I can get.'

The gates were locked.

The invitation had been extended some weeks ago. Sir George had lived alone in his mansion house since his wife's death some years before, attended to only by the servants and nursemaids who had raised his son Warren. Warren's previous fall from grace, arrested by the efforts of the Daughters of Salvation, had turned Sir George away from his plentiful business interests in the past year – though he would never leave them entirely, for the game suited him too well – and he had decided that now was the time to properly begin celebrating Christmas again. Too many had been lost along the way. Consequently, Sir George had invited Vivienne and her extended family to the Peel mansion for the occasion.

But now the manor was locked – and, by the frost riming the railings, it appeared to have been locked for some time. There were no lights on in the mansion frontage. Neither did any smoke curl from its manifold chimneys.

'A note,' Raymond ventured, his eyes drawn to the bolts that locked the gate.

There, tied to a rail with a length of frozen string, was a little envelope, hidden by the falling snow. He opened it up and read out loud, '"Come to the H. J. Packer Chocolate manufactory. Post haste. Yours in Yuletide, Warren Peel."'

'What does it mean?' asked Artie.

Raymond gave him a withering look. 'Precisely as it says, Artie. Well, Nancy, you'd better lead on!'

The old signs for the H. J. Packer Chocolate manufactory had been retained during the reconstruction and refurbishment of its former premises. As Nancy led the snowbound group in their final approach, she was staggered at how much progress had been made since she'd visited the site with Vivienne in October. The once-crumbling brick edifices had scaffolds erected around them but, even so, she could tell how quickly the reconstruction had commenced. Much of the masonry had been torn down and built again. New timbers framed the windows and entrances. Above the main door, half-obscured by scaffolds and snow, a sign read THE DAUGHTERS OF SALVATION in statuesque scarlet letters – and, on the storeys above, the windows (though boarded and blacked out) had all been replaced.

She was staggered, too, to see the line of people trailing out of its new entrance. They stretched back, five deep, along the icy row.

The noises coming from inside were full of cheer as well. Nancy took Raymond's hand and, with the rest of the family following close behind, picked her way through the line of people in rags, and into the entrance way.

The first face she saw belonged to Warren Peel.

'You made it!' he laughed.

Stepping aside, he revealed that the inside of the factory was even more transformed than the outside. New walls were in the process of being erected, doors branching off from a central entrance hall whose floor had been tiled in chequered black and white, just like the Buckingham Hotel. As was one side of the

185

reception hall, opening out into what Nancy could only describe as a restaurant area. Several thousand shades shabbier than the Queen Mary, it was nevertheless a hive of activity. Dozens of people sat around long trestle tables decorated with sprigs of holly and mistletoe. In front of them, bowls were heaped high with stew with dumplings, stew with potatoes, stewed apple with raisins and honey. Between the tables a host of familiar faces waltzed with jugs and trays in hand – all of the volunteers Nancy knew from her nights at the Daughters of Salvation. Among them was the round, ruddy face of Mary Burdett. She seemed to be in her element – the queen of this new, buzzing domain.

Fires were burning and dishes were being filled.

Before Warren could explain, his father materialised out of the crowd. Nancy had only ever seen Sir George dressed in his finery before. He did not look slovenly today – something about his bearing would never permit it – but, without his smart suit and top hat, he did look *ordinary*. And on a Christmas Day, this seemed the most extraordinary thing of all.

'I see you've become apprised of our change of plans,' said Sir George, wryly. 'I'm afraid I've perpetuated the lie, but it was all Warren's idea. You see, we were making preparations to host you all back home, when the thought struck Warren that . . . well, it mightn't be right.'

'I've been wrestling with it since September,' Warren said, 'when they told me they won't send me to fight. And suddenly it was Christmas and we were talking about roast goose and figgy pudding at the mansion – and how everyone would be there to join us. It seemed such a delightful thing – until I started think-ing that . . . well, it wouldn't be *everyone*, would it? It would be us, dining and getting fat, while there are people out here without any

Christmas dinner at all. That was when the thought struck me. That was when I knew what I could do. Oh, maybe it doesn't make up for me not going off to fight, but it's *something*, and that's what matters.' He turned, directing everyone's gaze to the makeshift restaurant. 'Christmas for everyone – while we still can.'

Mary Burdett had spotted them and laboured across the factory floor to greet them.

'There's food enough for everyone,' she said. 'It mightn't be roast goose, like in your Buckingham, but it's thick and hearty and there's cobs of bread to go with it.' She gave Vivienne a wink. 'It's taken days to put together, but I think we've done them proud. I'd have told you, my girl, but I thought ... Well, what with your Artie coming home, that maybe you had better things on your mind.'

Vivienne took it all in with wonder.

'We'll have opened up the premises for good by spring,' said Mary, 'but it's nice to give it a good airing, don't you think? Now, who's up for some dumplings?'

It wasn't a Christmas like anybody remembered, but it was a Christmas they'd treasure for as long as they lived. After filling their stomachs with stew (the meat was an indeterminate mixture of butcher's offcuts, but Nancy felt certain there was turkey in there somewhere) and hot baked potatoes, the extended Cohen and de Guise clan set about serving and cleaning and talking to their guests. The news that the Daughters of Salvation were providing hot Christmas dinners had spread far and wide and, by the time afternoon was paling towards evening, new families and stragglers were still turning up, wondering if there was any left to spare. There was plenty. Sir George's pockets ran deep, and his desire to outdo himself ran even deeper. *To think*, thought Vivienne, *that there was once a time when I'd sought to propagate the charity using only the allowance my odious stepfather gave me each month.* But acorns grew into oak trees. And the Daughters of Salvation was something more now.

'Look at us,' Vivienne said to Nancy as they worked together at a big tin sink, scrubbing bowls and plates for whoever came next. 'There's you climbing the ladder at the Buckingham Hotel – and me and the Daughters on the rise as well.'

'And those two off to fight for King and country,' Nancy observed. Raymond and Artie had spent the day trying to better each other at their serving skills, hurtling around the tables, spooning out extra helpings of stew and spiriting dirty dishes away. 'That is, if they can stop acting like children.' Unlike Leah, who ten years old, had the maturity of both of them combined. 'I should tell Frank,' Nancy mused. 'A thing like this might inspire him. He should meet Warren. He's looking for a way to make a contribution, too.' She stopped, because a new thought had suddenly occurred to her. 'I'm glad it went like this today, Vivienne. I really am. When I left the hotel, I saw your stepfather heading in to dine with your mother and his associates. Christmas dinner in the Buckingham Hotel, with Arnold Leese and Adalbert Grice. With Mr Ramsay and Sir Barry Domvile—'

'Domvile?' Vivienne shook her head wearily. 'I remember him.'

'You do?'

'He used to visit my stepfather regularly. Styled himself a thinker and a writer – being a lauded admiral wasn't enough for him. My stepfather used to read draft chapters from his book. I think he called it . . .' Vivienne had to think hard. '*The Case for Germany*,' she finally remembered. 'Lord knows if he ever published it. Nancy, he's one of those who was at Nuremberg – the rallies – at the personal invitation of *you know who*.'

'Mr Hitler,' said Nancy. 'And he's eating Christmas goose in my hotel. Oh, Vivienne, I know where I'd rather be this Christmas. Stew and dumplings here, or fat, buttery goose in the Queen Mary? There's scarcely any choice.' She faltered. 'Listen, Viv, there's something else—'

Nancy was cut off – for suddenly, on the other side of the manufactory floor, Warren Peel was leading a chorus of 'Good King Wenceslas' with some of the guests. Nancy dearly wished he wouldn't; Warren had a good heart, but he had absolutely no sense of melody.

'What is it?' Vivienne asked.

Nancy drew closer to her. Instinct told her this ought to be private.

'It's something Mrs Moffatt told me,' she said, 'about Walter Knave. A little while ago, I dug out an old portrait of them all – from back before the Great War. Mr Knave, who was the hotel director back then, and his wife Blythe. They were all standing around the Christmas tree, in the hotel reception – and there was Lord Edgerton, the old Lord Edgerton. Edgar, it said.'

'He's my stepfather's father. He passed on long before my mother and I came to London. But that's the old connection. The Edgertons have always used the Buckingham like a home away from home, long before my stepfather invested and joined the board. The Knaves became their personal friends.'

'Mrs Moffatt said there were rumours, in the old days . . . that Mr Knave used to like the horses, just a little too much. That he built up debts. That the only way he could manage them was . . .' She almost felt ashamed to say it, even though she was merely

189

repeating the information she'd been told. 'Was by using the hotel like his own bank account. The staff used to joke he barely even needed his account at Lloyd's. The Buckingham was his bank.'

'Nancy, you're wading into things that could—'

'I know. *Cause me trouble*. It seems the Buckingham was different, once upon a time. The Knaves were an institution. Mr Knave even had his great-nephew Elliott working there – the audit office showed him the ropes, then sent him off into the City for a career in the banks.' She stopped. 'Did you ever know Elliott Knave?'

Vivienne was silent as she rummaged through her memories.

'There was a New Year, just before you came to the Buckingham. I'd been dragged out to my stepfather's Suffolk mansion for a party. Well, they sometimes liked to indulge me like that – if only to mollify me for another year. The Knaves were there – though I've every reason to think they didn't want to be. Walter Knave used to admire Edgar Edgerton, but as for my stepfather . . .' Vivienne choked back a laugh.

'If there's no love lost between them, then why is he even at the Buckingham?' Nancy sighed. 'It's to do with those men he brings to fraternise there,' she concluded. 'It has to be.'

'My mother told me to stay away from Elliott Knave. More than twice my age, she said, but it wouldn't stop a man like that trying to romance me. But, when I did meet him, he hardly seemed interested at all. For a man they say wields proper power in the City, he was meek as a dormouse that New Year. His great-uncle Walter was as well. Until . . .'

'Until what?'

'Mr Knave – Walter, that is – always liked a drink.' Nancy could vouch for this herself. 'But that night he'd taken one brandy too many. I remember Elliott had to take him away in the end. The old drunk amused my stepfather. I wondered if that's why he was invited – the entertainment for the evening. I was the one who found him, wandering in the garden. He'd gone, he said, to take the air, then lost his way and wound up sheltered in the gazebo. I told him I'd come to take him back inside and . . . and . . .'

She remembered it, now, as vividly as day. The way Walter Knave had resisted her. The way he'd wanted to stay there, though the night was chilling him to the bone. The way he'd ripped his hand away when she'd tried to take it and said, 'You poor girl, you're in the wrong family. You've got to get out.' Then the way he'd slurred, when she'd asked what he meant, 'Don't ever let him find you wanting. Don't ever show him how you're weak. We're all weak, girl. Every human being who has ever lived has a chink in their armour. But don't let him find it. He'll use it against you for the rest of his days. Just like he did my boy.'

'His boy?' whispered Nancy. 'Meaning Elliott Knave? His . . . great-nephew?'

Vivienne pondered. 'Nancy, I know everyone's saying the same thing – but you will be careful, won't you? My stepfather isn't a man you ought to cross. Trust me on this. You know the kind of man he is.'

Nancy thought: *I know the kind of man he's fraternising with, too. I know the kind of reputation he's bringing to the Buckingham. If he has his way, he'll turn it into an embassy – the haven for any fascist hiding out in Britain, the vocal ones and the secret ones; the men who stood at Hitler's side at Nuremberg; the ones who still think that an alliance is better than war, that a negotiated peace is better than victory; that, like Archibald Ramsay says, the Jews are in charge of His Majesty's government and ought to be eradicated, one by one.*

'Where's Elliott Knave now?' she asked.

'Nancy, I told you—'

'But if it's the reason Mr Knave was brought back ... If it's the chokehold Lord Edgerton has over the hotel ... If the Buckingham doesn't stand for what's good and right anymore, if we're readying ourselves to welcome them in, Mr Hitler and the others ... If this alliance they're dreaming of comes off ... well, oughtn't the rest of the board to know? How could we just stand back and let it happen?'

She turned across the makeshift restaurant floor. Warren Peel was still leading his chorus of Christmas carols now, but other – more melodic – voices had joined in. Nancy was surprised to hear Raymond among them. His voice had a beautiful cadence; it always had. Artie's was rougher round the edges, but it had a certain Whitechapel charm. And, what was more, the two voices dovetailed together in a perfect harmony. Among all the others, they soared.

'They're going off to fight this evil, Vivienne. But if there's something rotten in the heart of the Buckingham and we don't do everything in our power to carve it out ... well, what are they fighting for? How can we let them do that and just sit back and watch this happen?'

Vivienne was silent, trapped in her thoughts.

Then, fighting some ominous sense of inevitability, she nodded, and continued to scrub, while a hundred voices wassailed around them: the strains of 'Silent Night' filled up the cavernous factory floor.

# January 1940

# Chapter Thirteen

I T WAS THE FIRST NEW YEAR that Raymond hadn't danced in
the Grand Ballroom in eight long years. The first New Year
that he hadn't stepped out to take some foreign dignitary or
crown princess on his arm, and waltz her on the journey from
one year into the next. This New Year, he watched from afar as
he waited for Nancy to finish her day's work, bustling the girls
up and down the Buckingham halls. Then he waltzed her, alone,
back home – and on their last few nights together.

On the morning of the 4th of January, as the winter sun
rose high above the city's frosted streets, he and Nancy were
standing on a platform in Paddington Station – just two lovers
among hundreds making their farewells. Paddington was a sea
of green, the carriages bustling with soldiers about to set out,
the platform awash with the wives and mothers who'd come to
say goodbye. This Raymond did, almost without words. As the
other soldiers streamed past them, he took Nancy in his arms,
kissed her on the hand, kissed her on the lips, and looked into
her eyes.

Then, with the certainty of love in his eyes, he said, 'We'll
dance again, Mrs de Guise,' and his fingers slipped from hers as
he boarded the train.

Nancy was not a woman of excess. She had meant to allow herself only a little time to linger there, thinking of the journey he was going on, the journey from which – it hit her now, like a train – he might never return. She merely meant to watch him slip on board, before she slipped from view herself. But, in the end, she waited until, in a shrill explosion of steam, the train was pulling along the platform. She held herself together, and tried not to cry the tears that were in her eyes, as the carriages dwindled into the distance, then rounded a bend in the track and disappeared. Then she waited some more, as the station emptied around her, leaving only the regular travellers.

It was cold in Paddington. Nancy felt the chill for the first time that day.

From somewhere, the station clock started striking. She waited until the twelfth chime had sounded; then she stepped back into the city. The year yawned open in front of her. With every breath that she took, Raymond's train was taking him further away.

But there was still the Buckingham. There always would be. And, some time later, when she stood in Berkeley Square, she understood it was the Buckingham that would see her through.

She slipped in through Michaelmas Mews and went to find her girls.

At precisely the same moment that Raymond de Guise was boarding the train that would take him to war, Frank Nettleton was sitting in a train carriage of his own, clasping Rosa by the hand and staring out over the rolling green fields outside Stratford-upon-Avon.

It had been dawn when, hurrying up from Lambeth, he had met Rosa at the Buckingham. Rosa herself had been up for an hour already. Though she wasn't on shift today, she'd breakfasted with the girls in the Housekeeping Lounge and then waited, filled with nerves, at the tradesman's entrance. By the time Frank arrived, she was almost bursting with anticipation.

'What are we doing, Frankie?' she asked him – and he handed her two paper train tickets.

'Stratford-upon-Avon?' she gasped. 'But what's in Stratford-upon-Avon?'

'It's not *what*,' said Frank, 'it's *who* . . . and it's a little way from Stratford-upon-Avon. We might have a bit of a tramp. Or maybe there's a country bus. But it would do us some good to get out of London, wouldn't it, Rosa?'

He'd been thinking of it for some time. He'd been thinking of it for himself – because, truly, there was nothing Frank thought would restore him quite like some country air – but, ever since Christmas, he'd been wondering if a change of scenery might put Rosa back on her feet. When Frank looked back at it now, she hadn't been the same since summer – and that business with the Christmas tree . . . well, that had been the strangest of all. Stranger still had been how quickly Rosa seemed to forget about it, blundering on through the Yuletide season as if nothing had ever happened. But he'd noticed her skittishness coming back since New Year paled away. He'd noticed how she'd started scoffing about the new ration books the girls' families had all been issued – 'a fuss over nothing, there's enough blackberries in the hedgerows to feed us all, they've a mountain of butter just sitting there going to waste' – and the advertisements for new Anderson shelters in the magazines in the chambermaids' kitchenette. He was noticing it, even now, as they crossed London in the eerie light just after dawn and saw the billboard hoardings with their new proclamations that everybody should DIG FOR VICTORY. She still laughed and she still joked, but there was something almost manic about Rosa these days – something that didn't fit well alongside her old, carefree ways.

But today he put that all from his mind, and instead led Rosa north to Marylebone Station.

By mid-morning, they had disembarked at the little station in Stratford-upon-Avon. Frank soon persuaded one of the local tradesmen to give them a lift in the back of his wagon, who put them down on the main road some miles out of Stratford. As Frank helped Rosa down from the back of the wagon, giving the joiner a cheery wave as he took one of the lesser roads, he couldn't help but see the look of mock disgruntlement on Rosa's face.

'You know how to give a girl a good time,' she grinned.

Then she stepped aside. The milestone was half-hidden by hawthorn and rhododendron. It read: PILLERTON PRIORS, 4 MILES.

'Pillerton Priors,' Rosa mused. 'Why do I know that . . .?' Then it hit her, a memory triumphantly resurfacing. '*Ruth*,' she grinned. 'You're taking us to see Ruth . . . at Pillerton Priors.' Her bottom lip trembled, in a jocular pout. 'Four miles, Frank. Four . . . miles?'

Frank had already started walking. 'Actually, it's five. Pillerton Priors is only the nearest town. Ruth's farm is some way yonder.' He looked over his shoulder. Rosa was still standing at the roadside sign, the pout suddenly quite real. 'I brought sandwiches.' He shrugged. In the knapsack over his shoulder there was a heel of bread stuffed with cold roast beef and onions. He'd brought apples and candied lemon from the Buckingham stores, too. He even had an iced currant bun. 'You do five miles every morning, Rosa, in and out of the hotel suites. Come on, the sun's almost shining!'

Rosa hurried to catch him up. 'But Ruth, Frankie . . . Why Ruth?'

'Well, I reckoned you might enjoy seeing an old friend.'

Rosa was suddenly wordless. The silence of it was almost unnerving to Frank. Then she quietly said, 'I reckon.'

'A-and—'

'Frankie, you always stammer when you're nervous. What is it?'

'W-well, I thought . . .' He marched on a little, elongating his stride as if that might make him find his confidence. 'I thought it would be good, you know, to see what Ruth's made of herself. To see what folks are doing, even though they're not all boarding trains and heading off to France like Billy and Raymond.'

'Frank Nettleton!' Rosa laughed, gambolling to catch him up. 'You can't seriously be thinking about joining the Land Army?'

Frank just kept on marching.

'Frankie, it's the *Women's* Land Army!'

Frank shrugged. 'I just wanted to see, that's all. And if you can see Ruth again, too, well, maybe that's the best thing for both of us.'

Rosa linked her arm through his. For a little while, they walked together, in contented silence, along the road.

'So what do we do, Frank? Follow this road all the way?'

'Oh no.' Frank grinned – and, leading Rosa by the arm, he stepped off the track, through a gap in the hawthorn hedging, and on to the outskirts of some farmer's field, where Rosa tramped immediately into a frosted heap of manure. 'It'll be much quicker if we take a short cut like this.'

After a mile of circumnavigating the farmer's winter wheat, Rosa demanded a break, so she and Frank took elevenses together beneath the branches of a storm-damaged rowan tree. Frank had made the tea sweet, just like Rosa liked it, and the flask had kept it warm all the way from London. It was just the restorative she needed. She helped herself to most of the currant bun as well. It was while rummaging in Frank's knapsack looking for it that she found the box of treacle toffees and jar of barley sugars tucked into the bottom.

'We can't break into those, Rosa,' Frank said as they set off again. 'They're for Ruth, a present from Mrs Moffatt.'

'Just one, for the road?'

Frank couldn't resist Rosa when she grinned at him like that. Knowing it was wrong made the barley sugars seem sweeter somehow as they trod along, Frank explaining how the trip had come about along the way.

'It's Bill she'd been writing to, you see. They've kept up quite a correspondence since he took off. They're writing every couple of weeks. So it's Billy's fault really. He's the one who put the idea in my head. He said Ruth's never seemed happier. Never seemed more *alive*. And isn't that a funny word to use about Ruth?'

*Ruth Attercliffe*, thought Frank, *who never even used to dance.* He remembered her fondly, but mostly her sitting in the kitchenette with her magazines, quietly bemused by the gossiping of the other girls.

'I'll bet Billy's still sweet on her,' Rosa said as they came through another hedgerow by a wooden stile and saw, some distance ahead of them, a succession of barns scattered around an old stone farmhouse.

Frank wasn't sure. 'I reckon they're just kindred spirits. They've got more in common than me and Bill do now . . . Well, they're both doing their bit, aren't they?'

Rosa cocked her head to one side; then, deciding this wasn't quite fierce enough, she jabbed him in the ribs.

'When the right moment comes, you'll do your bit, too, Frank. You're as good and brave as any of them. You'll see.'

Frank dearly hoped so.

'Come on.' He looked at the sun and tried to judge the passage of time by its arc across the endless blue sky. 'She said she'd meet us in the yard.'

'You're late.'

It wasn't Ruth Attercliffe standing by the farm gate when Frank and Rosa finally approached, but another one of the farm girls, dressed in the regulation tan dust coat and dark brown dungarees of the Women's Land Army. After introducing herself as Margaret ('the girls call me Marge, but you can call me Margaret'), she told them, 'Ruth waited as long as she could, but she couldn't slack off for long. She's up the other side of the beetroot fields, gone collecting.'

'Collecting?' asked Rosa, as Margaret begrudgingly admitted them through the gate.

'Oh, aye,' Margaret said, 'our Ruth's the best rat-catcher we've got. She's in charge of the defence.'

They had plodded a little distance into the farmyard when Rosa, having considered this closely, stopped short and said, 'Defence?'

'Well, there's no barrage balloons to defend against invasion by rat – and this farm's seen its worst winter yet, as far as those vermin are concerned. Ruth's our own Expeditionary Force – battling them out there in the fields, day and night.'

There was so much that was surreal about this image that when Rosa said, 'I'll bet she's doing a lot more fighting than our boys in France as well,' Frank hardly noticed it.

Margaret did, though. She glowered and said, 'Brave lot of boys, over there. They've got my respect. They've got all our respect out here.'

The forcefulness of it caught Rosa off guard.

'Of course,' she said, 'I meant to say that—'

But Margaret was already leading them on. The farmyard was a vast horseshoe of mud surrounding a stone farmhouse that, by Frank's reckoning, was several hundred years old. He'd known some like it, back up north. Around the old house were stone barns just as old – but many of the wooden buildings had the look of much more recent construction.

'Some of the girls are in digs in Pillerton,' Margaret explained, 'but some of us are bunking here. There was Land Army here during the Great War, too. That there –' she indicated one of the new barns – 'is where we sleep now. Well, Ruth will show you around. I'll take you to her.'

'Is it far?' Rosa was distinctly aware of the mud (and possibly manure) already smeared up her leg.

'A couple of miles. I'm sure your lovely little city legs will carry you. Come on.'

'Well, there you go, Frank,' whispered Rosa with a wink, as they set off. 'You're getting a taste of what it might be like to be in the army anyway.'

'What do you mean?'

Rosa shook her head wryly. 'Forced marching.' She grinned – and then they set off.

Frank's first sighting of Ruth was of a small figure, working among three others on their hands and knees at a hedgerow on the field's furthest side. By the time Margaret had led them across half the field, he had begun to marvel at everything he saw. Three years ago, he'd come to London, following Nancy on her dream of building a new, better, safer life for them in the city. But now the sights and smells of the countryside rolled all around him. He'd gone trapping for moles with one of his father's friends when he was a lad. The old mole-catcher would string them up as a grisly deterrent, as if to ward off other underground revellers – and succeeding only in inviting down ravens and crows and other carrion birds. Ruth and her girls looked to be doing something of a similar job. For them, though, there was no grisly gallows on which to announce their kills – just a couple of wheelbarrows, already heaped high with dead rats.

'Attercliffe!' Margaret shouted, hailing the girls from halfway along the field. 'You've got visitors!'

One of the girls, who had been re-laying a trap at the bottom of the hedgerow, looked up. Frank reeled. Yes, this surely was Ruth – Ruth of the Buckingham Hotel! – but not quite like he used to see her, in and out of the bedrooms of the feted guests. Her dark hair had grown longer – and, no longer subject to the Buckingham's strict 'neat and tidy, never a hair out of place' rules, it had collapsed into its wild, natural curls. Her complexion was different too – darker, perhaps, from the sun;

weathered, by the wind. She had more colour in her cheeks, that was for certain. And Frank saw, now, that what Billy had said was true: her eyes sparkled with more vitality than he could ever remember.

'Rosa,' she said, 'Frank!'

And, with her hands begrimed in hedgerow dirt, she rushed up to embrace them.

'Rats, Ruth?' gasped Rosa. '*Rats?*'

Ruth had a brace of dead ones in her hand. She tossed them, airily, into a barrow with the others.

'Oh, it isn't just rats,' she said. 'There's foxes and rabbits and moles. Almost anything can be a danger to these crops.' She stopped when she saw Rosa's agitated face. The more horrified Rosa looked, the more it seemed to tickle Ruth; she started to beam. 'Anything that might get at the crops, we'll stop them. It's like bailing out a sinking ship, but it's got to be done.'

'But, Ruth . . .' Rosa said. 'Just look at you, Ruth!'

Ruth stood back and gave them a twirl. 'Well, it's what they'd do in the Grand, isn't it?' she laughed. One of the other girls had whistled at her, like any old farm labourer, from the hedgerow. Then she looked to Margaret. 'It must be about time for some grub, isn't it?'

'Grub's up in half an hour,' said Margaret. 'That's half an hour's more rats to set traps for.'

Ruth shrugged, amiably. 'Half an hour,' she said to Rosa. 'You want to help?'

There were twelve girls working across Southall Farm – and, if Mr Yardley, whose family had worked this land for generations, had his way, there'd be twelve more by harvest time.

'Well,' said Ruth, as she led them into one of the barns, where a long trestle table was dressed up (if you ignored the scattered hay and the occasional farm dog scurrying through, looking for scraps) much like the one in the Housekeeping Lounge, 'he can pay us less, can't he?'

This, evidently, was something not to be spoken about, because some of the other girls rolled their eyes. *Not very much has changed then*, thought Frank. Ruth always used to speak her mind – and to hell with who it affronted – back at the Buckingham as well.

'His farm boys could have stayed, of course. Reserved occupation, isn't it? You can't stop the farms from farming. There's going to be precious little food as there is. But most of the labourers here, they were the first to sign up. "Up and at 'em", they said. And off they went.' Ruth marched around the table, filling two plates with apples, bread rolls and wedges of cheese. The milk in the jugs was alabaster-white with a head of thick, luscious cream. She sat her guests down at the foot of the table and pulled up a chair to join them. 'So here we are. What do you think?'

Rosa hardly knew what to say. It was half like being in the Housekeeping Lounge, and half like being stuck in the back of beyond – only with the best tasting milk she'd ever drunk.

'But *rats*, Ruth. *Rats*—'

'Enemy of the people, aren't they? Put two rats in a field, unchecked, and in a year there'll be a million of them. We've got to stop 'em. Otherwise, there won't be enough ration books in the world to feed the country.'

Rosa bristled. 'Come on, Ruth, look at this place – it might not be the Queen Mary, but there's enough here to feed an army.

And in the Buckingham, too! All this ration book stuff, it's just to frighten us. Well, I'm not going to be frightened.'

Some of the girls at the table, who had been chirruping among themselves, looked sidelong at Rosa, then averted their eyes once again.

'Rosa, if you heard the whispers around here, you wouldn't think that. Mr Yardley gets it all from the Ministry. The shipping's barely getting into Britain. Might be you don't see it, not in the Buckingham – well, money always finds a way, doesn't it? – but there's already shortages. Butter, bacon, ham, sugar . . . well, you don't think it all comes from Blighty, do you? Show me a good old English sugar cane farm! You can't, because there isn't one. Stands to reason.'

'We'll win the war at sea, Ruth,' Rosa said, obliviously munching on an apple. 'We'll have whatever supplies we want. By golly, didn't they sink that battleship, the *Graf Spee*, before Christmas? And even that was on the other side of the world, Ruth. It hardly matters to us. In fact, if you don't mind, I'll have another knob of butter on this bread. Yes, I'll bet you farm girls won't be losing weight this war. I've a mind to move here myself!'

'It'll be hard work.'

Rosa laughed. 'Maybe I'll stick to changing some stuck-up toff's bed sheets after all!'

Throughout this exchange, Frank had been feeling increasingly uncomfortable. He reached for Rosa's hand under the table and squeezed it tight. As his fingers intertwined with hers, he realised she was trembling. It wasn't like her. It wasn't like her at all. It was only when she was talking, Frank realised, that she was keeping the tremors at bay. He moved closer, as if to bring her some comfort – and, though he dared not ask her what was wrong, not in front of the rest, he was glad to feel her trembling subside.

Though it wasn't cold in the barn, he poured her another hot, sweet tea – and decided a change of subject was probably in order.

'Bill written to you since Christmas, Ruth? His ma and pa got his card, with ones to send on to the rest of them. We thought the kids might be back for Christmas, but they didn't make it. Mrs Brogan wants them back. Mr Brogan isn't so sure.'

'They should never have gone in the first place,' Rosa muttered, darkly.

Frank shot her a look.

'What?' she said, as if she'd said the most innocent thing in the world.

But Ruth ploughed on. 'I've got it somewhere, Frank. I'll go and find it. Billy writes the most fabulous letters. He can't say much, of course, because there's someone reading everything they send. But it's his turn of phrase. It always makes me laugh.'

After Ruth had hurried off to dig the letters out of the boarding barn, Frank whispered, 'Rosa, what's wrong?'

'Nothing,' she said, pouring more cream into her tea.

'There *is*. Rosa, you're shaking. And all the—'

'The *what*, Frank?'

'The . . . arguing.' It seemed useless, but there was no other word for it. 'I thought it would be a good trip.'

'It *is*,' Rosa said, with the forcefulness of a mother convincing her unruly children to give her five minutes' peace and quiet. 'Ruth's *thriving*, isn't she? She hardly seems like Ruth at all!' She paused. 'What are you thinking, Frank? Now, I hardly think "farm labourer" suits you – and there's not much farm labouring to be done in London ... but, you never know, they might start planting potatoes in Berkeley Square before all this is done. *Dig for Victory*, Frank!'

Rosa had started laughing. Frank, though, didn't seem to think it was very funny at all. He was about to say as much when Ruth returned, clasping her latest letter from Billy in her hands.

'Here it is,' she said, her eyes roaming the page. '*The boys have started calling me Brigadier Bill, on account of I'm the one they know will rise to the top. Last night, in our billet, we were playing cards, when I caught our staff sergeant sticking the ace of spades up his sleeve to slip it out later. Well, I had to stand up to that barefaced cheek, so now they call me Brigadier Bill the Bold – on account of the fact that you really oughtn't to stand up to your superiors. Life in the army is much like life in the Buckingham Hotel . . .*'

Frank grinned. 'That's Billy, all right. That's the stuff he never writes home with.'

'He even met a nice girl, just before Christmas. A Red Cross girl. Name of Aggie, if I remember right. Now, the way Billy tells it, Aggie's quite sweet on him as well. So it seems, for all the upheaval, this war's good for something.'

'The whole world at war, so that Billy Brogan can get himself a girl!' Rosa hooted. 'Oh, Ruthie, you ought to have given him a go when you had the chance.'

Ruth stiffened, but said nothing. 'Come on,' she said, 'finish up. I'll take you on a walk around the farm—'

'Oh, I've seen quite enough already,' said Rosa. 'I'm happy enough here with my tea and these crumpets.'

Frank and Ruth shared a quizzical look, but said no more. A few moments later, they were out in the farmyard together, one of Mr Yardley's Old English sheepdogs turning circles around their heels.

The farm stretched to every horizon – rolling fields of beans, and others where the land was yet to be seeded. The hulks of machinery lurked on the edges of the farmyard. In a paddock, Mrs Yardley's two roan horses watched as Frank and Ruth steadily marched past.

*It's quiet in the countryside*, thought Frank, and he'd missed that. Blackbirds arced overhead. A rabbit darted into a hedge.

'You're . . . happy, Ruth, aren't you?'

'As I've ever been, Frank. You know, it always niggled at me, back in the Buckingham – that feeling of what my life was meant to be about. I can't say I had great dreams growing up. I wasn't one of those who thought they'd fly in aeroplanes or change the world. And I was happy enough, when I got to the Buckingham, just to have left home and be earning my way like my mother had to do. But it started gnawing at me, some time after that. That maybe I could do something other than change bed sheets. Frank, I'm not like you. There isn't a thing in the world I'm good at – not like you and your dancing. But out here? Out here it feels like I'm changing things, one bit at a time. I suppose what I'm saying is – it's good, to be doing something that matters.'

They'd reached the edge of one of the pastures and stood, looking over the hedgerow, into the field beyond.

'You know they won't let me sign up. I'd be in France right now, otherwise. Raymond shipped out this morning. Louis Kildare's been gone since before Christmas. Up and down the Buckingham, you're starting to see how it's changing. Nancy's like Mrs Moffatt's shadow now. And in the Candlelight Club, the young cocktail waiters are all gone. Now it's old men – veterans, they call themselves, drafted back into service to mix Martinis and gin rickeys all night long. Everywhere you look, there are holes. It won't be long before even Gene's gone from the Grand. And still ... there's me, flitting around, doing all the odd jobs, running all the guest errands. I'm the oldest page there now. The rest are barely old enough to fight.'

'You're being too hard on yourself, Frank. It wasn't your decision.'

'No, but the next one *is*.'

'The next what?'

'The big decision – what I do with the next years of my life. Nancy says it's enough to dance. Maybe she's right. There's joy in that, and the world deserves to be reminded that there's still such a thing as joy, doesn't it? But I tell myself that for just a few days – and then ...'

Ruth picked up that sentence for him. 'The old feelings resurface?' She had a little inkling of what denial felt like, how a person's mind could play tricks and trap itself, though she didn't mean to talk about that – not now, and not with Frank. 'What does Rosa think?'

Frank looked back, over the pastures, at the farmyard. From where they were standing, he could just about make out the top of the barn where they'd taken lunch. 'Oh, Ruth, I hardly know anymore.'

The words hung heavily between them. Neither one of them looked at the other, directing their gazes back to the fields instead.

'She isn't herself, is she, Frank?'

'You don't know half of it. There was a moment, before Christmas, when Nancy had to discipline her. She slapped one of the new girls, when they were decorating the tree. She'll hardly speak of it since. Says she was defending my honour. But—'

'You think it's more?'

Frank nodded. 'You know Rosa – she's always been one who likes to talk. It's probably what I've loved about her the most. There's me, stammering my way through my words – and there's Rosa, with enough words for both of us, and more besides. But she keeps saying the wrong thing. She's riling the other girls. She's riling Nancy – and you know what Nancy's like. I can count on one hand the times she got cross with me while I was growing up – and there's not many who can say that.' Frank breathed, deeply. 'She says she doesn't believe. All the air raids and the blackouts, and now the ration books. She's sick to the teeth of it – like none of it's real.'

'She's not the only one who thinks like that, Frank.'

'But there's Raymond, gone off this morning – and my Nancy not sure if she'll ever get him home. There's Brigadier Billy, already not seen his family for months – and them wondering, every day, if this is the day the real war starts, if the next letter they get won't be from him, but from the Ministry, telling them he's lost.'

Ruth moved closer to him. 'Did you ever think she's just . . . scared?'

'Scared?'

'You know how people get. So scared that part of them doesn't really know it.'

Frank whispered, 'I'm scared, too.'

'It just shows you're listening, Frank.'

'Oh, I don't mean I'm scared for me,' said Frank, as they turned back across the pasture towards the farmyard and the barn, 'though I reckon that's in me as well. I'm scared for *her*, Ruth.'

They reached the doors of the barn – and Frank saw that, in their absence, Rosa had whipped the other girls into a sudden party. With hands tied behind their back by lengths of baler twine, the girls were lining up at the table and taking turns to dip their faces into big bowls of water, in which all the plump, crisp apples had been tossed. As they watched, Rosa plunged her head into an ice-cold trough, and came up victorious with a Cox's Orange Pippin in her teeth. Through the water that streamed down her face, she caught Frank's eye. She beamed – and out dropped the apple, with a huge bite taken out of its side. The other girls roared in approval.

'You see,' said Frank, 'it's either this or it's the other. And she won't talk to me about it anymore. She won't even acknowledge anything's wrong. I'm worried that, if she slips up again, she won't even have the Buckingham to fall back on, Ruth. And then . . . then where will she be?

'Your turn, Frank Nettleton!' cried Rosa, charging over to bustle him to the bowls. 'See what my Frank can do! Go on, Frank, show them! He's got poise, girls. He'll whip those apples up in a second. My hero, Frank Nettleton!'

So Frank found himself marched to the table – and, as he dunked his head for the first time, he looked up and saw Ruth looking sadly back. *Yes*, he thought, *she can see it, too.*

He snatched an apple on his very first turn.

February 1940

# Chapter Fourteen

I
N THE SHADOWY INTERIOR OF the hotel director's office,
Walter Knave shuffled his papers awkwardly and tried not
to catch the piercing blue eyes of the imposing gentleman
sitting on the other side of the desk. Walter Knave had never
enjoyed interviewing candidates for posts at the Buckingham
Hotel – in the old days, Blythe had taken care of much of that –
and this particular appointment was more problematic still.
Principal Dancer; Champion of the Grand. There hadn't even
been a ballroom, back when Walter Knave last ran the Buckingham Hotel. He'd have scoffed at the idea, and so would have
the old board. Now, it seemed, the Grand was the epicentre
of everything. The strangeness of this made itself apparent to
him every evening. Stranger still was the letter lying on top
of the papers on his desk. His eyes kept being drawn, inexorably, back to it, no matter what the fine gentleman across the
table – wearing a black evening suit and burgundy cravat –
had to say.

*Walter, it is imperative that the new appointment be a man of the
appropriate measure. Make it so. Yours, with trust, Lord B. Edgerton.*

A nondescript little note it might have been – but to Walter Knave, who had opened the letter twelve mornings ago, it was loaded with meaning. Damn near saturated with the stuff. He'd tried getting rid of it, of course, but something – his old cowardice, he supposed – stopped him from tearing it to shreds.

It didn't matter. Whether he kept the paper or not, it was the words that mattered. *A man of the appropriate measure.* Walter Knave knew what that meant. Somebody Lord Edgerton could manipulate and control.

Power on the board; power in the Buckingham; power in the ballroom itself: Lord Edgerton had been refashioning the hotel since the start of last year. Now, with half the dancers already gone, he would tighten his hold on the Grand.

And Walter Knave would be his vessel.

The gentleman sitting opposite him was named Marcus Arbuthnot – and Walter had already convinced himself that he was the man for the job. The first test was that he hadn't balked at seeing the copy of *Action* sitting on the director's desk. Walter Knave himself did not care for the newspaper, but ever since Lord Edgerton's crowd had started frequenting the Candlelight Club with such regularity, the paper had been left lying on the tables there – and Knave had felt it his duty to quietly tidy it away. When Marcus's eyes had landed on it, his eyebrows had risen, but he had said not a word. Either that meant the man knew the value of keeping his own counsel, or he was sympathetic to the cause behind the British Union of Fascists' magazine. Either way, he hoped it would satisfy Lord Edgerton's requirement for 'a man of our measure'.

It didn't matter that the thought made him sick. Walter knew his place better than any.

The dance troupe – or what was left of it – had been gathered here since the end of the afternoon demonstrations. In the studio's heart, on its practice floor, Gene Sheldon and Mathilde Bourchier were turning to the strains of one of Archie Adams' recordings, while the rest of the troupe – six of them remained, as well as Frank Nettleton and the two part-time porters who took part in the demonstrations – watched from the sides. The dancing couple didn't miss a step as Walter and Marcus entered. They just waltzed on.

'Work's already begun on our Summer Ball,' Walter Knave explained. 'You can imagine the effort we put into these things. To capture the heart of the city. To be splashed across Society's pages . . .'

'Indeed,' said Marcus, 'as you were this Christmas.'

The Society pages had covered the event with unnatural vigour; yes, there had been the occasional dissenting voice, but most of the editorials had rhapsodised over the event as a Christmas celebration quite unlike any other. But Lord Edgerton's view had not changed: the Grand was devalued, he said; it had set a delinquent expectation.

'We need a new principal to restore the old world honour,' he'd declared. 'A man we can trust. A man of our own minds.'

*A man I can own*, thought Walter, with silent venom. Well, Arbuthnot seemed vain enough that a little flattery ought to control him; and, if he was grateful to Lord Edgerton for the chance to re-enter the world of ballroom dance, so much the better.

'This Summer Ball will be the high society event of the season,' Walter explained. 'A clarion call to the great and good an announcement that Society still flourishes, even while great swathes of London are being closed around us. By then, as I've said, we won't merely be without Mr de Guise – but Mr Sheldon, here, will have been taken from us. That's why we need a man of your . . . calibre.'

Marcus Arbuthnot had the pride of a peacock as he sashayed on to the dance floor.

Though the music hadn't come to an end, every eye in the studio turned to face him. Mathilde slipped out of Gene's hold. Frank Nettleton rose to the tips of his toes; the lad was no dwarf, but compared to Marcus he was diminutive.

'Ladies and gentlemen,' Walter Knave said, with an awkward shuffle, 'I should like you to meet the newest star of the Grand Ballroom, Mr Marcus Arbuthnot.'

The gentleman dancer gave a slight bow, as if to an adoring public.

It was Gene Sheldon who came, first, to shake Marcus's hand.

'I saw you dance in Brighton, back when I was a boy. It's a pleasure, sir.'

'Always a delight to meet a fellow craftsman, Mr Sheldon. I shall do the Grand proud in your absence.' Even as he was speaking, his eyes had already moved on; now they landed on Mathilde. 'And I look forward, immensely, to working together, Miss Bourchier. I've seen you dance in the ballroom twice already. I'm sure that, together, you and I will achieve great things.'

Mathilde had not yet offered her hand, but Marcus took it all the same, planting a rubbery kiss on the backs of her fingers.

'Of course, Miss Bourchier remains the understudy to our principal, Karina Kainz,' Walter Knave began, 'who may be back with us before long.'

Mathilde's face wrinkled with displeasure; it seemed that Karina's absence, and the circumstances of her own elevation, had been conveniently forgotten in the Grand Ballroom this season.

Marcus had heard the stories.

'Well, let me tell you, many a young dancer has seized her opportunity in circumstances like this. A sudden injury, a family bereavement – they rob the ballroom of their champions for fleeting moments, and in their absence, new heroes must rise.'

Mathilde's anxious face softened, turning finally to satisfaction. She lifted her hand again – this time unprompted – for Marcus to hold.

'You must all be filled with uncertainties,' he said, warming again to the sound of his own voice, 'with your champion Mr de Guise gone off to war, and so much change all around you. Well, I've seen troupes labour under the burdens of too much change and fall apart – but I've seen them rise triumphant, as well. My friends, *we* will rise triumphant.'

He marched around the room, shaking the hand of each of the other dancers (Frank felt the handshake ricochet up and down his body), before returning to the head of the studio.

'Mr Knave, if it suits you, I should like to begin straight away.'

Walter Knave was caught quite off guard.

'But, of course, there are formalities we should—'

'Renounce the formalities!' Marcus declared, with a theatrical flourish. 'Seize the moment! I've taught dancers who have conquered the ballroom world – and that has always been my edict – *you must live now*. You must *dance now*. Happy the man, and happy he alone, he who can call today his own! He who, secure within, can say – tomorrow, do thy worst, for I have lived today!' He gazed around at the astounded room. 'The words of no less than John Donne, my brothers and sisters – and let them be an inspiration to us all. A new day is dawning in the Grand Ballroom – and we will be there at sunrise, to welcome it in!'

*Well*, thought Walter Knave, *it wasn't* quite *what I had expected, but it would do.*

The dancers seemed to be captivated by the man who'd suddenly been thrust upon them. It helped, of course, that Gene Sheldon's days in the ballroom were numbered; it helped, too, that there was no natural successor among the lesser members of the troupe.

*All in all*, he decided, *it has been a good day's work.*

Retiring to his office, he made certain the door was sealed shut and picked up the telephone receiver, dialling a number that – to his chagrin – he knew by heart. When a maidservant answered, he politely requested the presence of the lord of the manor and waited, with his heart beating a syncopated rhythm, for the deep, gravelly voice to erupt.

'Mr Knave?'

'My lord,' Knave sniffled, 'we have made an appointment.'

The silence humming down the line begged further explanation.

'Marcus Arbuthnot,' Walter Knave went on. 'You saw his portfolio, sir. I believe him to be a man who would be delighted to make your acquaintance. I've already seen him dominating the ballroom. The man has leadership qualities we have been lacking.'

'I'm pleased to hear this, Walter.'

'He's from old money, sir. He isn't titled, but you don't have to reach far into his ancestry to find those who were. He'll bring the old world charm back. I'm quite certain he won't tolerate any of these newer dances the likes of the Nettleton lad are cultivating. No jitterbugs, sir. No jives. Just classic ballroom dance.'

'Yes, yes, yes,' said Lord Edgerton, to whom this was but a fringe concern. 'Walter, I'll want to meet this fellow directly. Issue an invitation. I shall take dinner with him in the Queen Mary. No – cancel that. Invite him to the manor. I should like the opportunity to get under this fellow's skin. To extend him a little friendship, as it were – before John Hastings can do the same. I never did like the way it was Mr de Guise who introduced Hastings to our hotel. I never did like the special relationship those two had. So let us restore the balance. This Sunday evening. I'll send a car. Make it quite clear to this Arbuthnot which side his bread is buttered.'

'As you like it, my lord.'

But before Walter Knave could put the telephone receiver down, Lord Edgerton continued, 'You're to come too, Walter. It's been too long since you and I sat down, in private, away from the Buckingham Hotel.'

Walter froze. This, he supposed, was the feeling an antelope got on being invited into the lion's den.

'Sir, I feel my responsibilities at the Buckingham are consuming at present. Perhaps it is better if you and Mr Arbuthnot dine alone—'

Lord Edgerton's voice came back, clear and insistent. 'At whose sufferance do you serve, Walter?'

Walter Knave felt the familiar sinking feeling in his stomach. 'Yours, Lord Edgerton.'

'And I should like you to be there. Is that too much to ask? That you should come and sample the exquisite food my kitchen prepares? One night away from the Buckingham won't harm you, good fellow. It will do you some good to perpetuate the friendship we have.'

Walter heaved a sigh before he said, 'Sunday evening, then, sir. I'll look forward to seeing you then.'

Only when the telephone receiver was put down did he sink back into his chair and let the shaking subside.

*Secrets devour you*, he thought. *One tiny mistake echoes through a life.*

But he was old and spent, and his part in it would surely be finished with soon.

It was the others he was fearful for – because, after he was gone, who would be left to protect them then?

# Chapter Fifteen

HMS *EXETER* VICTORY PARADE
A Parade is Announced in Celebration of the
HMS *Exeter* and HMS *Ajax's* Triumphant
Return from the Battle of the River Plate
21st February 1940
Waterloo to Whitehall

T
HE NOTICE, TORN FROM THE pages of an *Evening Standard*, had been pinned to the board in the chambermaids'
kitchenette since the start of the month. Once or twice,
Rosa had passed it by and rolled her eyes – but, the closer the day
had come, the more tantalising the prospect had started to seem.

'Well, it's a reason for a party, isn't it?' she said to the other
girls as they gathered around the wireless the evening before.
'Six months of war, and one battle – but we won it. We might as
well have a dance for that. What do you think?'

The BBC news said that the crews of the *Exeter* and the *Ajax*
were safely back home. In a few days, they would march all the
way from Waterloo to Whitehall – where they would be honoured with medals and garlands on the Horse Guards Parade –
and all of London would pour out to see it.

'The brightest news for a weary public,' somebody was intoning, 'and a day to give us faith that His Majesty will be victorious in the battles to come.'

'Well, never mind about the battles to come,' chirped Rosa, pouring the tea. 'If it stays fine, if the sun's shining and spring's just about in the air . . . well, that's enough for me. Who's with me? You're coming, of course, Frank?'

Frank, who often came to the kitchenette before heading back to the Brogans' house – he still took leftovers from the hotel kitchens, even though the house was empty without the Brogan brood – faltered before he said, 'Mr Arbuthnot wants us all in the studio tomorrow afternoon.'

'Well, that's perfect. The parade's at 11. You'll be back, Frank.'

Frank looked doubtful, but said nothing as Rosa dashed over to kiss him, twice on each cheek.

'I'll come to the studio and find you. We just need to convince your Nancy that we can get out of here early.'

This, it turned out, was easier said than done. By the time Nancy arrived in the Housekeeping Lounge for breakfast service the following morning, it seemed apparent that every last one of the chambermaids had their hearts set on attending the parade – and the chorus of voices that met her, as she walked in, was like a tidal wave. By now, Nancy had developed a distinct motherly stare that said 'patience, girls', and she duly delivered this as she walked through the lounge to the Housekeeping Office, where Mrs Moffatt was waiting.

'You've some hearts to break today, Nancy,' Mrs Moffatt smiled, knowingly, as Nancy looked through the rotas.

'I've had it worked through for weeks,' she smiled. Then, with the rota in hand, she walked back out to meet the banks of anticipatory faces. 'Girls,' she began – and Rosa strained, from the back, to catch Nancy's eye. Nancy wasn't oblivious to it, but she'd long ago decided that there would be no favours between friends, not now that she was a floor mistress. 'We've been through this already. If you're on shift today, there are no exceptions. To visit the parade would be a fine thing – but the success of the Buckingham comes first. You girls know that.'

A dozen disgruntled faces returned to their crumpets.

'Nance,' Rosa called out – and Nancy worked hard to disguise her irritation that Rosa was being so informal, 'I had an idea . . .'

Nancy said, 'Yes, Rosa?'

'Well, it seems to me that going to this parade will be a boost to all us girls. You know, something that'll make us think there's an end to all this nonsense. Light at the end of the tunnel, if you see what I mean?'

Evidently Rosa had prepared this speech.

'And, well, I was thinking – the Horse Guards Parade is only a fifteen-minute dash from here, isn't it? What if – just this once – we were allowed to nip out and see it? Work until it's almost started, dash off down there, and dash straight back? A bit of excitement for the day, Nancy? What do you think?'

Nancy was aware that Mrs Moffatt had appeared in the doorway behind her. Now she wasn't merely *listening* to every word; her eyes were boring into her as well. She thought back to what Mrs Moffatt had said, on that cold December night: 'Fair and hard, just as I would have been.'

'Girls, I know this is a disappointment, but the Buckingham—'

'Can bend the rules, every now and again,' came Mrs Moffatt's voice from behind. 'Girls, Mrs de Guise and I have discussed this at length and we're both decided ... If, and *only* if, your allocated rooms are in order by mid-morning, we will, today, permit a change in working hours so that you can each visit the parade. It will come in lieu of a lunch break, of course – so make sure that you have some sustenance, somewhere along the way, to get you through the rest of the day. Mrs de Guise and I will run a spot check at 10.30 sharp. Any falling standards will be noticed, girls.'

The girls' faces had turned from disappointment to delight in a second, but Nancy's own had furrowed with confusion – and a burning hint of humiliation, which she tried to keep at bay. She followed Mrs Moffatt into the Housekeeping Office and said, 'Emmeline, I—'

'Nancy, I'm sorry – you must feel, and quite rightly so, that I've undermined you.'

'You said – fairness, and hardness, all at once. If they saw me open to persuasion, they'd sense a weakness. So ... why?' She looked back, over her shoulder – where, through a crack in the door, she could see the celebrating girls.

Mrs Moffatt invited her to sit down. 'It's a balancing act, Nancy. We're walking tightropes, all the time. Never, ever let them see you change your mind when it matters. A disciplinary matter, or a matter of standards – or even some hard lesson you need them to learn, to better themselves at this hotel. They must see you as principled and strong – and you're both of those things. But if we're saying no all the time, that's when the discontent settles in. I saw it, back when I was a chambermaid here. Old Mrs Luckraft, the Head of Housekeeping, was a dragon – and she took pleasure in it. We grew to hate her for it. Oh, it bonded us together, but the feeling gnawed away at us all – girls often came and went, back in those days. Nancy, what I'm trying to say is – every now and then, throw them a delight. Don't do it so frequently that they ever expect it – but let them see some sunshine, here and there. It will keep them singing.'

Nancy thought she understood. 'When Frank was tiny, we didn't have much money. But there was a boy in town whose father owned shares in the pit. He had all the best things. I had to tell Frank, time and time again, that he couldn't have those things. But, every now and again, when my father and I scraped enough together, there'd be a present at the end of his bed. I think those moments made up for the long months he had so little.'

'But now imagine you had two dozen Franks, and how they'd darken and turn against you if you kept them bottled up all year round, with never a treat to make life worth living. Our girls don't have much. The Buckingham gives them a roof over their heads and a pay packet at the end of each week, but it doesn't go far – not when set against the likes of the people we serve. A treat like today costs us nothing, but it wins us so much.'

Nancy thought for a time. 'You've got to be a politician in a place like this, haven't you, Emmeline?'

Mrs Moffatt reached into the drawer of her desk and brought out two sweets wrapped in wax paper. It was never too early for a barley sugar.

'Nancy, if they put the likes of us in Westminster and Berlin and all the other seats of power in the world, why, there'd hardly be a war at all.'

Once Mrs Moffatt had cast a discerning eye over the suites on the hotel's fifth storey and pronounced them satisfactory, Rosa

229

rushed down to the dance studio behind the Grand, knocked on the door – and, without waiting for an answer, tumbled in. There was Frank, waltzing with one of the other dancers in his arms, as they mirrored the movements of Gene Sheldon and Mathilde Bourchier. The gargantuan new figure, Marcus Arbuthnot, was conducting them from the edge of the dance floor, swaying in time to the music.

'Remember,' he declared, with a voice that could have filled the Royal Albert Hall, 'it's summer! What did Mr Gershwin teach us? It's the time when the living is easy! Let's feel that in the dance! Let's be the spirit of summer. We're soaring. We're bright. The world might be staggering and reeling, but for a brief, glorious moment of respite, it's just us – you, and me – and we're sailing on the sunlight itself. The cherry blossoms are falling over us. It's summer, it's summer, and we're alive!'

'Pssst! Frank!'

The glacial blue eyes of the Herculean dance instructor found Rosa in the doorway. Then they found Frank.

The moment was lost. Frank slipped out of hold and, flushing red, cantered across the studio to meet Rosa while Gene and Mathilde danced on.

'Are you ready?' Rosa asked, with a thrill.

Frank's eyes darted back into the studio. 'Ready?' he whispered.

'Your Nance let us out after all. Come on, we've not got much time. It's medals at eleven. We'll already have lost the good spots.'

Frank shifted uneasily. His shoulders dropped. 'I'm not coming, Rosa. I'm—'

Now, Rosa's face fell. 'Frankie, don't be like that. It's our chance...'

Frank could feel the pull of her. He always felt the pull, when she looked at him like that – with eyes that half pleaded with him, and half cajoled him along. He could see the wicked glint in them. It was the same devil-may-care glint that twinkled in her every night they stepped out to dance. The 'just one more gin rickey' look she gave him in the Midnight Rooms.

He shook his head.

Now her face changed. 'I know what you're thinking, Frank. You're thinking you don't deserve to be there, at a parade where men are getting medals for going off to fight. Well, I'm . . . I'm telling you, Frank – you've got to stop thinking like it. You've—'

It would be a lie to say that that thought had not entered Frank's head. But it would also be a lie to say it was the only thing directing him.

'We're rehearsing, Rosa. Look, with Mr Arbuthnot here, and Gene on the edge of having to go . . . I might get to dance in the Summer Ball. Imagine it, Rosa. That'd be something, wouldn't it? Something in the thick of this horrible year.'

Rosa remained silent for a second too long. Frank saw her face start to crease, as she took in what he was saying.

'Well, that's good for you, Frank – but I thought . . . I thought we could get out of this stinking hotel again and go and *have a good time!*'

Frank could scarcely believe what he was hearing. He'd never heard Rosa so viperous before. She turned from him, and Frank became distinctly aware that the other dancers in the studio had heard her, too. Though their dancing continued, they were all trying hard not to look.

'Rosa, I never said I was going to go to—'

'Well, you do as you please, Frank Nettleton,' Rosa said, with the tremor of tears in her voice, 'and I'll do what I please, too. I'm going to have a good time – for one stinking hour – and *pretend* everything's . . . pretend everything's . . . Oh, forget it, Frank!' she snapped – and then she was gone.

Behind Frank, the music had finally come to its end.

'Is everything well, young Nettleton?' intoned Marcus Arbuthnot.

*No*, thought Frank. *Everything's not well at all. Rosa* . . . *Rosa's not well.*

But Marcus's arm was around him, guiding him back to the studio floor.

'The course of true love, Mr Nettleton – it never did run smooth. Let's see how that might become the body of our dance, shall we? Let's see how that might look and feel . . .'

The *Exeter* and *Ajax* Victory Parade was already thronged when Rosa and the other chambermaids arrived, picking their way through the heaving pavements of Trafalgar Square. The traffic had been stopped from passing up and down Whitehall, but the unseasonable sunshine had emptied London's households of their inhabitants – and everywhere Rosa looked, the roads stood ten deep with spectators, eagerly awaiting the arrival of the parade.

'We'll never get to the front,' said Rosa.

They had arrived at the head of Whitehall, where the crowd was at its thickest – and, though no signs of the parade could be seen, the air was already alive with chattering and cheering. She fancied she could hear the real roars of approval; the procession was somewhere close – of that she was certain.

'Here, try and get through, Mary-Lou – there's no point us coming at all, if we can't catch a sight of them.'

Suddenly, the cheering intensified. Up and down the line, people were whipping out handkerchiefs and scarves to flutter them in the air.

'It's them,' said Rosa. A man by her side had hoisted his daughter onto his shoulders, so that she might see the heroes marching towards Horse Guards Parade. 'It's a shame our Frank wouldn't come. He'd have given me a leg up.'

'In need of assistance, madam?'

Rosa turned. Mary-Louise and the other chambermaids had forced a gap to open in the spectators – but it wouldn't take them far. However, looming above her, flanked by a group of other men in similar military attire, was a dark-haired man with the jawline of a mythical hero and cheeks that dimpled when he smiled. He looked, Rosa decided, as if he ought to have formed part of the parade. He was certainly holding himself with the kind of air that suggested he believed that, wherever he went, he ought to be the centre of attention. Rosa had known men like that before.

'Monty Matheson,' he said, '1st Canadian Infantry. I couldn't help overhearing – you might be in need of assistance.'

Rosa was quite flabbergasted at the man's sense of confidence and grandeur.

'That's as may be,' she said, 'but I'm not jumping on some stranger's shoulders just to catch a sight of this parade. I'll do fine with my two feet on the ground.'

The Canadian infantryman stepped back, holding his hands up as if to calm a raging bull.

'Ma'am, with a spirit like that, you could just command the crowd to open!'

Rosa glared at him fiercely. Then, something changed in her heart, and she relented. She grinned.

'Be off with you, I want to catch a sight of this.'

'You've a better chance further up the road,' Monty said. 'Stick with me, and I might even get you into the square on Horse Guards Parade. You *might* catch a sight of the king.'

Though he had had no way of knowing it, this was one of the only things bound to tempt Rosa. She glanced over her shoulder. Mary-Louise and the others had been swallowed up by the crowd. She planted her hands firmly on her hips.

'How?' she asked.

Monty Matheson's answer was to simply tug on his navy lapels.

'I'm a servant of the king, ma'am. A proud soldier of the Commonwealth. Trust me – stick with us, and you'll be in the thick of the action.'

Rosa looked around once more. It was too late to ask the girls in any case; they'd already gone. She fancied she could hear them whooping. The parade was perilously close now.

'Go on, then,' she said, 'but I haven't got long. We've been given grace for an hour. We've got to get back.'

'Trust me,' said Monty, 'you won't miss a thing.'

The parade was almost on top of them. Rosa heard the tramping of feet, heard the hullabaloo as she followed Monty and the other Canadian infantrymen along the pavement. At least Monty hadn't been lying; the way he scythed his way through the crowds was like an icebreaker carving its way through the floes. Keeping pace with the march, they reached the entrance to the square of Horse Guards Parade – and there they remained as the column finally reached them.

'I can't see!' Rosa cursed.

'Ma'am?' Monty Matheson grinned.

A ripple of irritation – threaded through, perhaps, with a little glee – ran up and down Rosa's body.

'Oh, go on, then!' she sighed. 'But just for a second, mark you. I'm not a married woman, but I intend to be. And my Frank would . . . Well, he'd do nothing. He's too gentle a sort. But . . . Oh, just get on with it! I'm missing it!'

The pavement was packed, but when light infantryman Monty Matheson put his hands on Rosa's hips and hoisted her skywards, she could see the parade in all its glory. They said that all eight hundred men from the crews of the *Ajax* and the *Exeter* were marching through London today. Mr Chamberlain was proud as a new father, or so the editorials all said. Here were the men who had crippled the *Admiral Graf von Spee*. The men who had proven an adage as timeless as the oceans over which they had sailed: that Britannia rules the waves. The first victory of the war – and how London roared its approval today.

Suspended high, gazing out over the caps and bowler hats in the crowd, Rosa felt something she hadn't been searching for today: a surge of such pride, and such belonging, that it caught her off guard. All those brave young men, off to see the king and reap the rewards of their service. She felt light-headed. Until this moment, war had been blackouts and gas masks, boards in the windows and signs stripped from the streets. The ordinary inconveniences of life. Now that she saw them – these boys who'd been there and done it – she felt something shifting inside her.

She thought about Frank, and how dispirited he'd been. When she heard the applause and cheering from all around Horse Guards Parade, she thought she knew why.

'Put me down,' she said. 'Put me down!'

This Monty Matheson did.

'Not leaving us so soon, surely?'

'I told you,' she told him, 'we've only got an hour's grace.'

One of the other infantrymen drew nearer, some other girl from the crowd on his arm, and opened his jacket. Hanging from his belt was a little flask; he unscrewed the top and breathed in the scent of whatever liquor was inside.

'I'd say this is cause for a little celebration, wouldn't you?' he said.

Rosa looked at the other woman and saw how she was smiling.

'You only live once,' the other girl shrugged. 'If this war's teaching us anything, it's that life's short. You got to take your pleasures where and how you will.'

Rosa looked at the hip flask. There was a moment when she might have said no, but then some other thought seemed to flicker into her mind. *You only live once*, the other girl had said. *You got to take your pleasures . . .*

'Oh, just one!' she grinned. 'But then I've got to be back. They'll murder me if I'm not.'

*Dear Raymond*

*Change is afoot in the Buckingham Hotel. Marcus Arbuthnot has today moved into the suite that you vacated last year. It was the strangest of feelings to step inside there this morning, to perform our ordinary housekeeping services, and to be reminded of those precious moments we spent together there. My memories are full, Raymond. I miss you more than ever.*

*Mr Arbuthnot has brought changes to the ballroom itself. Frank tells me he is a most unexpected kind of gentleman — full of such passion and theatricality that he seems, at times, a music hall performer, and might even be comical, were it not for his tremendous talent and pedigree.*

*Frank reports that he speaks of you often, and always in flattering tones; but, by the Summer Ball, he will surely consider himself King of the Ballroom. Raymond, you are dethroned! But you are dethroned in the service of something the rest of us still marvel at.*

Nancy had received his letter only days before:

*We are billeted with the West Yorkshires and the 14th Battalion outside Armentières. What stories I can tell you are scarce. Today was two reconnaissance patrols, separated by long hours in barracks. But I was fortunate enough to play at cards with Artie, who has won himself some plaudits from our staff sergeant for the fervour with which he has thrown himself into fortifications. There goes my brother: he has found his calling . . .*

Artie had energetically built the barricades along Cable Street in 1936 as well, Nancy remembered with a smile. There seemed something right about Artie and Raymond being out there together. That the brothers patrolled together, or played cards together – that they *existed* together, in a way that they never could in London, where Raymond foxtrotted with princesses while Artie prowled the Whitechapel night. That brought Nancy some pleasure as she spent a quiet hour in the Housekeeping Office, her pencil dancing across the paper.

She was telling him about Vivienne, and how the Daughters of Salvation had finally moved into their new premises in the old H. J. Packer building, when the girls returned from the parade. She could hear them, in the lounge on the other side of the office door.

*You will think us taking a risk too far, Raymond, but Vivienne has determined to meet with Elliott Knave. By chance, Sir George Peel is in correspondence with Knave's equity firm. Well, in the City of London, backs are scratched all of the time — and one man of means inevitably knows another. For my own part, I feel I cannot sit idly by while the men whose cause you are fighting against are quietly celebrated in the very hotel where you should be dancing tonight. And as for Vivienne? Well, her motives are different but no less just. She extricated herself, once upon a time, from Lord Edgerton's control. It is only natural that she should feel herself pulled to the same cause on behalf of others.*

At this point she put her pen down and gravitated to the office door. In the lounge, the girls were taking off their over-coats, changing their shoes, straightening themselves in the mirrored wall.

'How was that, girls?' she asked as she stepped through.

Their faces told it all: the delight of schoolchildren suddenly told that classes had been cancelled for the day, that the May Fair was coming to town.

As they were gabbling, something occurred to Nancy. Her eyes roamed the room, counting the girls.

'Where's Rosa?' she asked.

The girls continued hanging up their coats and fixing themselves in the mirror. Only Mary-Louise looked up to answer.

'We lost her at the parade, Mrs de Guise. Maybe she's back already.'

Nancy tried to picture precisely how Mrs Moffatt would react in this situation.

'Quite so,' she said. 'I'm sure Rosa is on the rooms already – so please don't leave her to it. Five minutes, girls.'

Then, trying not to fall entirely into the sinking feeling in her stomach, she marched past them, and out into the halls.

It took but a cursory march along the third and fourth storeys – where Rosa was supposed to be hard at work – to ascertain that she was not, in fact, being the most diligent of chambermaids; that she had not, in fact, returned early from the parade to get a head start with her afternoon's work. Six months ago, the thought wouldn't have troubled Nancy – but the world hadn't been at war; six months ago, Rosa had just been Rosa, her zealous and happy-go-lucky friend – Frank's sweetheart, who could breathe light into a room purely by the virtue of her infectious laughter. Now, as Nancy hurried down the service stairs and back to the Housekeeping Lounge, she could not ignore the ominous feeling that was rearing up inside her. Lives were built out of moments – and she had started to fear that one such defining moment was almost upon them.

Yet Rosa was her friend, and she would give her the benefit of the doubt. There was always a chance that something ordinary explained away her absence. She'd always worked hard. She'd always been as conscientious and assiduous as Nancy herself.

For the next half an hour, Nancy worked through paperwork in the office. When Mrs Moffatt appeared, instinct told her that she ought to mention what had happened; but some other little voice inside her told her to keep it to herself – and soon Mrs Moffatt, too, had drifted on, off to look over the girls working the fifth-storey suites.

Another half an hour later, Nancy decided something ought to be done. Rosa's absence on the third and fourth storeys would inevitably be slowing the girls down – so she marched up there herself and set about Rosa's duties with gusto. A floor mistress was not excused from hard work in the Buckingham Hotel;

Nancy still got her hands dirty every morning – and she would get them dirtier still today.

The work put her mind at ease. For a time, she stopped thinking about Rosa at all – and found that she enjoyed being back among the girls. For months now she'd worked in the uppermost suites, the ones where the hotel's wealthiest clientele stayed – and there she had worked alone. Now, with the other girls buzzing around her, she was starkly reminded of what she'd given up when she moved out of the Buckingham Hotel. For an hour, two, three, it was like she was day-tripping into her own past. No war to blight it. No dark days ahead. Just the simple, honest endeavour of a girl trying to make her way in the world.

The girls finished later that afternoon – but, when Nancy gathered them by the service lift, she found herself inordinately proud of what they had together achieved. The girls looked tired – Mary-Louise looked positively drawn – and, in twelve hours' time, it would start all over again.

Not one of the girls had breathed Rosa's name – at least not in Nancy's hearing – all afternoon. Now, Mary-Louise looked up and said, 'Do you suppose she's in trouble? Do you suppose something's happened?'

But Nancy didn't know what to say. 'I'm going to ask the kitchens to send up a trolley of whatever they have to spare, girls. You worked incredibly well today. I'll see you at 6 a.m. sharp.'

The lift had opened behind her. She stepped into it, and vanished.

'Is this the place?' asked Monty Matheson.

A group of four Canadian infantrymen appeared between the town houses of Berkeley Square, just as the afternoon started to pale towards evening. Dangling between them – her feet only just scraping the ground – Rosa hiccuped loudly as she caterwauled the words to an old marching song, 'It's a Long Way to Tipperary'.

'My uncle used to sing it to me in my cradle. Said he'd learned it in the Great War. *It's a long waaaay . . .!*' Suddenly, she picked herself up. 'Home,' she repeated, and only now did her eyes seem to focus on the grand white façade of the Buckingham Hotel. '*Home?* What are we . . .? Why did you . . .?'

'Come on, Miss Bright. The carnival is over.'

Rosa suddenly planted her feet firmly on the ground. The taste of every gin rickey she'd drunk in that little club the infantrymen and their sweethearts had found was, in that moment, back on her tongue. She had to concentrate to keep steady, to stop Berkeley Square from spinning around her.

'No,' she said. 'No – not there . . .'

A hundred thoughts seemed to collide in her at once. The memory of those cocktails, which had tasted so sweet, was suddenly bitter. One hour, Nancy had told them. One hour, and then they should be back at their duties.

Time had had so little meaning in that club, with its vaulted ceiling and dark, subterranean air. There were so many places like that in Soho. But she knew she was lying to herself when she insisted she hadn't known how long she'd spent down there. The sky, above, was greying. She'd last seen the sun when it was sailing high.

'Rosa, darling, you've burned brightly – but now you're burning out. Let's get you back safely, and into—'

Rosa strode forwards a little; the fires of indignation were propelling her onwards, but then they died again.

'Anywhere,' she said. 'Anywhere but there.'

The infantrymen had already carried her halfway across the square when the doorman standing by the hotel's colonnade picked them out against the hardening twilight. His eyes lingered, first on the infantrymen, then, longer, on the girl suspended between them. It was then that he loped, two steps at a time, down the sweeping marble stairs, through the taxicabs lined up to accept the gentry flowing out of the hotel's revolving doors, and started waving.

It took the infantrymen too long to realise he was not beckoning them over, but remonstrating to keep them away. At last, when they had grown too close – almost at the taxicabs, where a particularly debonair gentleman in gabardine turned his moustachioed face away in disgust – the doorman rushed down to meet them on the edge of the grass, where the crocuses were in blossom.

'It's Rosa, isn't it? Oh Lord, Rosa, what have you . . .?'

Rosa looked up. The doorman, three times her age and ordinarily as taciturn as a gargoyle, looked suddenly grandfatherly as he held his arms out towards her.

'You bloomin' fools,' he snapped, directing his gaze at the infantrymen. 'What are you doing to her?'

'Rosa, here, was in a celebratory mood.'

'I don't mean that, you clowns – though I dare say you've had a hand in making her this way! I mean – the guests' entrance! What are you thinking? It's more than the girl's job is worth!'

'Then where—'

'You've done enough damage already,' he seethed. 'Get out of here before I summon the police.'

'Now look here,' Monty Matheson began, 'we've done the honourable thing . . .'

242

The doorman had propped Rosa up on his shoulder and was already marching her towards Michaelmas Mews, and the tradesman's entrance that lurked halfway along.

'I was a sailor, lad,' he called back at the soldiers. 'I was a sailor on shore leave, too. You can't fool me. Now, get out of my sight! I'll take her from here.'

Nancy was making tea, waiting for Mrs Moffatt for their end of day natter, when the knock came at the Housekeeping door.

'It's Miss Bright,' said a breathless Johnson, the evening doorman. 'I think you'd better come.'

He'd left Rosa by the tradesman's entrance, with one of the pages for company. By the time Nancy arrived, Rosa was slouched against one of the walls, using a packing crate as a stool. She'd doubled over, her head hanging between her knees; it was the only way she could stop the world from spinning.

'Nancy?' She hiccuped when she heard her voice. 'Oh, Nance, you're a sight for sore . . .'

Rosa lifted her head, only to find the turmoil and anger colouring Nancy's face.

'Housekeeping,' Nancy barked. '*Now.*'

'She can hardly walk in a straight line,' said the doorman. 'If Mr Knave or one of the guests were to see . . .'

Nancy bristled. She got to her knees, drew close to Rosa. Heavens, but her breath smelled of gin. The sorry girl was sozzled.

'You're right.' Nancy looked up. 'Who else saw her?'

'Certainly some guests,' the doorman replied.

Nancy's heart sank.

'They were heading out for the evening, off to one of their clubs. It might be they don't make a report. They might not recognise her as a chambermaid at all. Well, you know what these toffs are like. We're *invisible* to them.'

*That much is true*, thought Nancy.

But a chance encounter out in Berkeley Square was nothing compared to the scandal of being seen staggering through the back halls of the Buckingham Hotel. If Mr Knave were to see her, it would surely be the end. If Mrs Moffatt were to see her – well, Mrs Moffatt would try to understand, but there were moments in life you couldn't take back, and this was surely one of them.

'Johnson,' she said to the doorman, 'you've done me a great favour already, but can I ask one more?'

'Anything for you, Mrs de Guise.'

Nancy fleetingly wondered if this was one of those tough decisions Mrs Moffatt had warned her about: where she had to choose between being one of the girls, or being their mistress, and live with the repercussions of whatever she decided. There was respect to be won, yes, but she wondered, too, about *understanding*, and what that might mean in a leader as well.

'Instruct one of the taxicabs to the bottom of Michaelmas Mews. We'll meet them there shortly.'

Rosa picked her head up. 'Nance, I've got work to do, I can't be—'

'You'll do precisely what I tell you to do, Rosa Bright, or you can march down there, this instant, and explain to Mrs Moffatt that you're leaving the Buckingham Hotel forthwith.' She turned her attention back to Johnson. 'Five minutes?'

'On my honour, Mrs de Guise.'

After the doorman had gone, Nancy and Rosa remained in wretched silence. Rosa slouched; Nancy paced. When, at last, she heard footsteps in Michaelmas Mews, she stepped outside to find the taxi driver, a short, rotund man of some fifty years of age, waddling along to find her.

'Here, Johnson said—'

Nancy had already accosted him. Together – and both ignoring Rosa's muttered complaints – they frogmarched her to the taxicab.

'Maida Vale,' said Nancy, '18 Blomfield Road.'

'Very good, ma'am. Just make sure your young lady there doesn't make a mess of my seats.'

'There's an extra big tip in it for you if she does.'

Nancy braced Rosa as the taxicab took off. It was only when they'd left Berkeley Square behind, to meet the last of the day's traffic coursing along Regent Street, that she breathed a sigh of relief.

'I'm sorry, Rosa. If I'd let you go in there, it would have been curtains for you – and quite likely curtains for me as well. Good Lord, Rosa, what were you thinking? Don't you know we've been worried sick? Didn't you think the girls would have to make up the work you missed? What do you think they're thinking, right now? Up in the kitchenette, nattering about you shirking and . . . Johnson's discreet, but if it gets around that you were in cocktail clubs with infantrymen all afternoon – and on the day of the victory parade, no less!' Nancy's hands had turned to fists. She had to focus to unclench them. She could hardly look at Rosa, face smeared against the window glass. 'Rosa Bright, what's got into you this year? You're . . . you're not yourself! There's no other way of putting it. You're plucky and bright, Rosa. The star of the morning. Frank's besotted with you. He worships the ground you walk on. And I love you for it, but . . . but this has got to stop!'

Rosa straightened up. She turned, suddenly composed, and drawled at Nancy, 'Oh, shut up!'

Nancy gasped.

'I don't need your lectures, Nancy. I don't want to hear a word of it. You think you're so much better than us now, don't you? High and mighty, up on your high horse, telling us all how it's got to be. Well . . . Well . . .' She was losing what little composure she'd gathered now, her words slurring and coming apart. 'You're not Mrs Moffatt! You're still Nancy Nettleton – no matter what ring's on your finger. And . . . and . . . if I want to go out and do something wild, if I want to see the sun and bask in it for an afternoon, if I want to *live* a little when life gives me a chance, well, it's what I'm going to do! It's what we all should do!'

She was still slurring, but Nancy got the feeling it was no longer because of the gin coursing through her veins. Her eyes, bloodshot as they were, had focus now. She felt as if she was seeing into the very core of Rosa's being.

'We could all be dead by summer,' Rosa blurted out. 'Who knows if there'll be another Christmas? Who knows if we'll be together next year? I'm young, Nancy. *You're* young. Frank's young. And Billy and all of the rest. We deserve a little life, too, don't we? I just wanted to *feel* it for a change. To be young and carefree – and, damn it, a little bit wild. Is there anything so bad about that, Nancy? Is there?' All of her resolve had broken. The words were threaded through with tears. She grappled for Nancy's hand and Nancy, taken aback, let her take it. 'It isn't fair, Nance. I'm meant to be living. We're all – *all of us* – meant to be living.'

There was a silence. Into the vacuum, Nancy said, 'Rosa, you've been carrying on all year like none of it mattered, like none of it was real—'

Rosa spluttered, 'I don't want it to be real.'

'Oh, Rosa.'

There and then, Nancy understood everything that had happened in the last six months. She understood the 'stuff and nonsense'. She understood the way Rosa had lashed out beneath the boughs of the Norwegian fir. She understood every cackle and catty comment.

She shuffled closer, as the taxicab soared past Hyde Park and turned north.

'Rosa, it *is* real,' she said. 'Look at me. Look at me, Rosa.'

Rosa did.

'It's real and it's happening. But we're in it together. All of us. Oh, Rosa, you silly, silly girl! You should have talked to me. You should have talked to Frank.'

'I'm frightened, Nancy.'

She had started shivering – and Nancy knew it was not only because of the gin working its way out of her system.

'Me too,' Nancy whispered.

'I could never tell Frank. He's already so ashamed. He shouldn't have to worry – not about me. I hoped I was right. You have to see that, Nancy. I hoped it really was all "stuff and nonsense". Then Frank wouldn't have to be ashamed, and I wouldn't have to be so . . . frightened, all of the time. My father died at Passchendaele. I never did see his face. And now, here it comes again. Thank God for Frank's lungs. Don't you dare tell him I said it – but thank God for his lungs.'

Nancy put her arm around Rosa as the taxicab cruised, at last, into the familiar streets of Maida Vale. She'd got into the vehicle bracing herself for an altogether different challenge from the one she now faced: not, now, showing Rosa the error of her ways, taking her to task, reading her the Riot Act in the hope of saving her future at the Buckingham Hotel – but somehow piecing her back together, seeing through all the months of false bravado and denial, and setting her on her own two feet so that she could look at tomorrow anew. If fortune favoured them, there was a chance that the news of her spectacle would never reach Mr Knave. If they were lucky, there was still a future for Rosa at the hotel. But right now, that was a problem for tomorrow.

'I snapped at Frank,' Rosa said, softly, as the taxicab pulled up and Nancy helped her on to the pavement. Above them both, the little door to number 18 Blomfield Road was waiting. 'When he said he couldn't come to the parade, I snapped at him. I didn't mean to, Nance. I haven't been thinking straight. It's all such a mess. Such a mess in my own mind . . .'

*And that*, thought Nancy, *was where all troubles began*. The mind eating itself up. One little voice saying one thing, one little voice saying another. Poor Rosa had always been a tangle of contradictions. Fiery and vivacious, gregarious and kind – self-sabotaging, too, and filled to the brim with emotion.

But if Rosa would let her, Nancy would help her put one foot in front of the other. She'd help her step forwards.

She thought she knew exactly where to start.

She reached into her apron pocket, and out came a handful of sweets in waxed paper. Mrs Moffatt's barley sugars.

'And a nice pot of tea,' she said. 'Rosa, let's talk this over with a nice pot of tea.'

March 1940

# Chapter Sixteen

ONDON TURNED TOWARDS SPRING. Across the rolling green of the Royal Parks, the daffodils came into bloom. The year's first picnickers spread out their blankets by the edge of the Serpentine and basked beneath the cerulean sky, writing letters to their loved ones who marched and dug and patrolled hundreds of miles away.

It was the peace before the storm. For every man or woman who said 'let it forever be like this', another was counting down the days – because, to them, every day in which the headlines did not scream of battle was another day closer to the battle being joined. The clock was counting down.

And so it went on.

The woman who stepped off the bus at Victoria Coach Station, with barely a suitcase to call her own, was under no false illusions. Tall and lithe, strong and blonde, she had already seen the world upended twice over. Standing there in the station, as a hundred strangers eddied around her, did not elicit the feeling of home-coming she'd anticipated. She'd wanted this city to be *home* – but, she reflected, it was unlikely she'd feel at home here ever again. Better to accept that now than to pretend. Better to live in the real world than to build your own out of falsehoods and lies.

She was at the ticket desk, meaning to buy a ticket for the Underground trains, when she opened her mouth to speak and thought better of it. An accent like hers would be viewed with suspicion now. It would be a mark that followed her round. So she resolved, instead, to keep her words and thoughts to herself – at least for a little while longer. She wouldn't need them where she was going. You did not need words on the ballroom floor.

Dance was a language all to itself.

It was all that she needed.

At the Buckingham Hotel, Frank was waiting outside the House-keeping Office when Rosa emerged from the door. For too long, he'd been holding his body rigidly, in anticipation of what might happen next. But the look in her eyes ceased the panicked, baby-bird beating of his heart. *Not disconsolate*, he thought, *but determined*. She took his hand and drew him along the hall.

'They're docking two weeks' pay,' she whispered, 'and I'm to cover every Sunday next month. It could be a lot worse, Frankie.'

'Who decided that?'

'It was Mrs Moffatt who told me. But I think Nancy had . . . Oh, but does it matter, Frank?' She gripped him tighter. Her overriding emotion was not indignation but relief. 'I'm fortunate I wasn't seen. Fortunate they understand. Fortunate they don't think I'm a dead loss to the hotel.' She stopped. 'I could stand losing this place, Frank, but I couldn't stand not seeing you every day. I've been a dreadful wretch – and there you were, not once being short with me, even when I was being waspish and . . .'

Frank shushed her; it wasn't the first time she'd spiralled into apologies like this. He hadn't wanted to hear it then, and he didn't want to hear it now – not now that he realised the thoughts she'd been bottling up all year.

'We've both got to get on, haven't we?'

Rosa nodded. 'Come on – I want to watch.'

Moments later, they had slipped into the warren of dressing rooms behind the Grand Ballroom. Mid-afternoon, with the demonstrations already finished for the day, there was ordinarily no sound of live music emanating from the Grand – but today the backstage doors stood open and, through them, Frank and Rosa could see Marcus Arbuthnot directing the dance troupe to the strains of a stripped-down Archie Adams Orchestra: just Archie on his grand piano up on stage, with trumpets and drums.

Frank and Rosa stood framed in the ballroom doors. Gene Sheldon and Mathilde Bourchier were gliding from one edge of the dance floor to another, then spiralling back again as Gene launched Mathilde into the air.

'Gene's just standing in for Mr Arbuthnot, of course,' said Frank. 'All so Mr Arbuthnot can *see it* with an onlooker's eye. That's how he operates. He wants to imagine what it's like to be on the outside, looking in. As if seeing the spectacle for the very first time.'

Rosa nudged Frank in the ribs. 'Sounds like Mr Arbuthnot might quite like the idea of watching *himself* dance.'

Frank's eyes goggled. *It's* good, he thought, *to hear Rosa crack a joke again.*

'You should see him getting ready for the ballroom on a Saturday night,' Frank whispered. 'Three times as long in front of a mirror as Mathilde. Five times as long as Karina used to be.'

On the ballroom floor, the dancers came apart.

'Bravo, bravo!' Marcus Arbuthnot was declaring, as he skipped – impossibly lightly, for such a large man – down to the dance floor. 'Now, my dears, let us think about . . . *light!*' He looked up, at the positions of the chandeliers above. 'Know your environment. This is one of the best kept secrets of the ballroom. Champions are made because one competitor knows his chandeliers better than another. My dears, I think we need to dance better, into the light.'

Marcus Arbuthnot was turning on the spot, pirouetting like a ballet dancer with his face upturned to the cascading chandeliers, when his eyes found Frank standing in the dressing room doors.

'Nettleton!' he announced, and spread his arms open wide. 'Young Nettleton, today is your day. Come, come to the dance floor.'

Frank shrugged at Rosa, who squeezed his hand and let him go. Without a word, she slipped around the edge of the dance floor and took a seat at one of the tables above. Strictly speaking, she wasn't supposed to be in the ballroom at all – but the dance troupe had never minded; they knew how she loved to watch Frank dance.

Frank felt Marcus's huge arm fall around his shoulder, then direct him around.

'Mr Sheldon, it's your news – so perhaps you ought to be the one to share it.'

Gene stepped away from Mathilde and said, 'I got my papers, Frank. By the end of April, I'll be in basic training. By summer, in the Low Countries or France.'

'Yes indeed,' Marcus began, with a theatrical shake of his head. 'A star is leaving the ballroom, as it has long been fored friends,

r danc-
ch her.
nglish.

f the
d to
was
ner
she
d

s

ere are yet other stars in the sky –
r which we have been waiting. And
I have already requested an audience
endorsing your appearance at July's
dancer, catapulted to the forefront of
e before his time, perhaps, but this age
at we rise to each occasion. There is a hole
tleton, and I wish you to—'
opened, and a new figure appeared.
not sensed, rather than saw, the new arrival.
his shoulder and gazed the way that Gene,
he rest of the troupe were gazing.
onde, statuesque; an artist's impression of beauty.
nz was as glamorous as a midsummer's night, even
e dress she wore was dowdy and tan. Her hair had been
torily tied back, but that could not disguise its lustre and
ne. When he had been a boy, Marcus Arbuthnot's theatri-
father – a darling of repertory theatre, the finest Coriolanus
ever to tread a provincial stage – had bought him, as a birthday
present, Richardson's *Encyclopaedia of Antiquity*. The images of
old heroes and gods had always filled the young dancer's imagination. Now, he felt as if he was looking at one of those same
images: a Roman goddess, striding into his ballroom.

He'd always been a man who enjoyed a little overindulgence.
This idea appealed to him enormously.

'Miss Kainz?' Frank whispered. Then, a little more loudly,
'Miss Kainz?'

Karina Kainz put down her small suitcase – a cardboard thing
she'd picked up, somewhere along the way – and gazed out
over the ballroom. She'd been holding herself with such fierce

determination – but, when she locked eyes with her o[l]
something crumbled inside her. She opened her arms.

Gene was the first to embrace her. After that, the oth
ers crowded around. Frank had to scrabble through to re[a]

'It's good to be home,' she said, in Viennese-inflected [E]
'I've missed you all, my friends.'

The crowd around Karina came apart. In the middle
ballroom floor, only Marcus and Mathilde hadn't rush[e]
meet her. Now, Mathilde – sensing that some moment
being lost – hurried over and clasped her hand. In the co[r]
of the room, Rosa held back, uncertain about the spectacle
was watching. Then, at last, Marcus cleaved through the cro[w]
to face her.

'The prodigal returns!' he boomed. 'Miss Karina Kainz, it
my pleasure to make your acquaintance.'

Karina watched as the great man bowed, taking her hand like
a suitor, and then returning it to her side.

'My dear, you must have some tales to tell. The ballroom, in
your absence, has some stories of its own.'

'As I can see,' Karina began. Her eyes were still darting around
the place, noting the faces – and one face in particular – missing
from the troupe. 'Raymond's gone,' she whispered. 'What news
of him?'

'Alive and well,' said Frank, 'and serving in France.'

Karina came further into the ballroom. For the first time since
September – though it seemed so much longer, at the start of a
different age – she stepped onto its lacquered sprung floor. The
feel of it beneath her feet. The smell of the varnish. The way their
voices echoed in the acoustics of the cavernous hall. Old feelings
rushed back, restoring every portion of her.

'Oh, my friends,' she said, and turned to see them making a great arc around her, 'it's been . . . too long. I hardly know where to begin.'

September, 1939: the odyssey beginning. Karina Kainz, frog-marched out of the Buckingham Hotel under the watchful guard of the Metropolitan Police – accusing eyes on her all the way.

It wasn't a feeling of shame that smothered her in the back of the black patrol wagon, as it wheeled away across Berkeley Square. It was panic, pure and simple. Karina had known police officers before. They'd put up a resistance when the Nazis first rolled into the streets of Vienna, but it hadn't taken long before they, too, were raiding houses and aping their new command-ers. People said London was the capital of the free world. A place where tyranny was despised and dictatorship forbidden. But not if you were Austrian. Not if you were German. At the holding station where she'd spent the night, it didn't even seem to mat-ter if you were yourself a Jewish refugee, in flight from the same people against whom Great Britain had just taken up arms. If you came from a nation now allied to the Third Reich, you were the enemy. An 'enemy alien', they called it. Teachers and taxi drivers. Doctors and dancers. Karina would meet them all in the months to come.

Two nights in a jail cell, right there in London, and Karina was bundled into the back of a wagon with six other aliens, just like her. There were rumours, said a banker from Berlin, that the old internment camps on the Isle of Man were being brought back into commission. They'd interned 'saboteurs' there during the Great War as well; the old Knockaloe Camp had been waiting twenty-five years for its time to come again. But that was for the

future. For now, there were old racecourses and half-built hous-
ing estates. It was to these nowhere lands that they were bound.

The holding cells in Liverpool: blankets and dry provisions
were handed out, and Karina stayed awake through the long
night, wondering what might happen next. In the women's cells,
she befriended an elderly Berliner, who'd lived in London since
the end of the Roaring Twenties.

'You think of it as an adopted homeland,' the woman told
Karina, 'but it's never really yours. That's what they're telling
us now – when it matters the most, you're not *one of us*. You're
one of *them*.'

Karina could let the same bitterness infect her, if she let it. She
decided, there and then, that it wouldn't come to pass. And the
next day, as they were marched out to the waiting trucks and
ferried to a crescent of half-built houses, surrounded by cordons
of barbed wire – the place that would be both prison and home
for the next six months – she repeated it to herself, a prayer and
petition underneath her breath.

'I can't say it was a brutal camp,' Karina said – as, in the Grand
Ballroom, the dance troupe sat, spellbound – and not a little
scared – by her story. 'A long terrace of requisitioned houses
and bungalows. We slept two to a bed. If you could ignore the
barbed wire and the guards on duty – if you could ignore the
*guns* – you could trick yourself into thinking you were just in
a little seaside resort, where too many guests had been trapped
for the night. But . . .'

The waiting, she told them. The uncertainty. The sense that
not even the guards who marched among you knew when you
might have a hope of getting out. The gnawing, unutterable fear

258

that – though you *knew* you were innocent, though you *knew* you posed no threat to the country you'd come to call home – there was no way of proving it.

'How does one prove the absence of treachery? How do you prove honour? Loyalty is one of those most slippery things – the more you profess it, the less people seem to believe.'

Suspicion in the camp. Suspicion in your own mind.

'It got to you after a while. You had to find ways of filling the time. There was an old upright piano in one of the houses they'd requisitioned. The promise of music – I think that's what got me through.

'They brought me before the first tribunal in January. They quizzed me on my brothers. They pored through my father's life. Most of all, they wanted to know about Matteo – who, for many years, was my lover back home. The man I would have married – if it hadn't transpired that he was already married to somebody else, and lying to me for five long years. I don't believe they were satisfied. Not at first. I was sent back to the camp, then brought before them again at the beginning of March. They wanted to know who I wrote to back home. They wanted to know why I'd fled. It wasn't enough to speak of dance – though, by then, I was teaching ballroom to the old women I lived with. I was waltzing and doing the quickstep with them across the camp lawns. Anything to stave off the boredom of another interminable day. Dance could be a cover, they said. The perfect reason to skip from one country to another, taking secrets with me as I did.'

Frank ventured, 'What changed their minds, Miss Kainz?'

The pain of it was that she didn't know.

'The hand of God,' she shrugged. 'Fate? Chance? Pity? I don't know. But three days ago, they categorised me as a "doubtful case". Enough to set me free of the camp – but not enough that they mightn't sweep in here, at any moment, and take me again.' A smile turned her lips upwards, perhaps for the first time since she'd started telling her story. 'I should like to make the most of the ballroom while I'm here.'

In a second, she had stepped into Gene's arms. With his old instincts resurfacing, he took her in hold – though there was no doubting that it was she, not him, who led them on to the dance floor. Up on the stage, where he remained at his grand piano, Archie Adams hammered out the opening refrains from Jack Jackson's standard, 'Make Those People Sway'.

After a few bars, the music and the dancers came to a stop. Karina stepped out of hold and said, 'I've got catching up to do. I haven't been indolent in the camp, but Gene and I will have to—'

'Not Gene!' announced Marcus Arbuthnot. Like some hero returning from afar to sweep up his lost love, he ducked between the dancers on the ballroom floor and took Karina into hold himself. 'Alas, our fine Mr Sheldon is to leave us soon. To take the king's shilling, and off to do his bit for the war. You will have to entertain a different kind of partner this summer. But I've trained world champions, my dear, and we still have weeks to perfect our art.'

Marcus stepped out of hold and clapped his hands together.

'Let's dance!' he declared.

Just like that, the rehearsal was back in session.

Marcus was arranging the troupe on the ballroom floor when, all of a sudden, the slamming of a door echoed in the ballroom's cavernous interior. He swivelled on the spot, counting the heads of the dancers who remained.

'It was Mathilde, sir,' said Frank. 'I think you may have . . . upset her?'

'Distressed the young starlet?'

'Well,' said Frank, flushing red, 'she *was* to dance the lead at the ball, sir. And now that Miss Kainz is back . . .'

Marcus hung his head in theatrical shame. 'Young hearts. One forgets the passions they have.' He turned to address the troupe at large. 'I must go and mend a broken spirit. Mathilde will shine this summer, as shall we all. But we have our belle of the ballroom back, and the light must shine on her most vibrantly. Please, excuse me. Dance on!'

Frank scampered after him as he marched towards the doors.

'Mr Arbuthnot—'

'She will understand, young Nettleton. I will make her see. Sometimes, setbacks like this can make our stars burn more brightly still. The Grand Ballroom must cling on to each one of its treasures – and Miss Bourchier is certainly one of those. But the ballroom gives and the ballroom takes away. That is but the circle of the dance.'

Frank had wondered if it might be better for him to go and console Mathilde, but Marcus's words were so bewildering that, in only a few seconds, he had lost his own train of thought.

'Leave this to me, young Nettleton. Your job is here – with your troupe. This Summer Ball, boy, could be the defining moment of your fledgling career. Do the ballroom proud. No – dare I say it? – do your *country* proud. Get back among the troupe. And, Nettleton?'

'Yes, sir?'

'*Polish*, boy. Elegance and poise. The ballroom comes naturally to you, young man – but, when I look at you, I still see a hotel page. I still see the lad who turned up on the train from the north of the country. You'll need to be sharper and smarter than that, by the time summer comes around.'

Frank watched him go, then turned back to the ballroom floor. The rest of the dance troupe was still gathered around Karina. He heard her laugh, wild and uproarious, for the first time in months. That sound: an unutterable delight.

Frank sensed Rosa coming near.

'Frankie?' she ventured.

She had her arms open, as if he might fall into them. He wanted to, as well. But the shock of it was still settling over him. He tried to picture the ballroom, filled with guests. The music in full sway. The hotel board, the visiting gentry, the great and the good . . . and there among them, little Frank Nettleton.

'I know what you're thinking, Frank,' said Rosa, threading her arm through his. 'You're thinking it's not right. Mr Sheldon, off to basic training – and you still here. Well, listen to me! Listen to me like I should have listened to you.' She tightened her hold on him. 'To hell with those thoughts. To *hell* with them. We're meant to be living, Frank. And this is your dream. How can it ever diminish a man to embrace his dream?'

Frank nodded. *If there was anything to rush headlong into*, he thought, *it was the dream of a lifetime.*

'Mr Arbuthnot says I have to smarten up. It's what Raymond's been telling me for years. Scrub up, Frank Nettleton. More elegance. More poise.'

'So do it,' said Rosa. 'What's stopping you, Frank?'

Frank was silent.

'We're only living once, aren't we? And . . .' She trembled, as the flood of the last year's thoughts rushed through her again.

'. . . isn't that the lesson this year? We only live *once*, so do it right?'

'Yes,' said Frank, who finally seemed to believe what she was saying. 'Yes. I'll . . . go and see Miss Marchmont,' he declared. 'Start my tuition again. I'll make it count this time. Give it everything I've got.'

*And by summer*, he thought, *I'll be taking my first guest on my arm and leading her out, to the blast of trumpets and stampeding piano of the Archie Adams Orchestra. Frank Nettleton: a star being born.*

April 1940

# Chapter Seventeen

VIVIENNE COHEN HAD PLANNED THE start to her day
down to its finest details – it was what a mother did –
but, as soon as she turned the wireless on and set about
fixing Stan's breakfast, she knew that the world had changed.

'*Reports of last night's air battle over Oslo have been rapidly
followed by the news that King Christian X of Denmark has sur-
rendered to the armies of the Third Reich. Prime Minister Chamberlain, who will make a further address at noon, has promised
that the devastated nations will have the full support of Allied
forces in the battle ahead . . .*'

Stan started wailing when the teacup dropped out of Vivienne's hand and shattered against the hard kitchen floor. He
wailed on, because Vivienne didn't automatically rush to him.
There was a moment's delay before she swept him into her arms,
and in that moment all of her fears about Artie, her fears for
the future, her fears for their son seemed to overcome her. She
tried to focus on the BBC news, but Stan was still sobbing, so she
turned her attention to him instead.

'He'll be OK,' she told him. 'He's in the Low Countries. He
isn't in Denmark. He's nowhere near Norway. He's sunning
himself out there, with nothing to do and nobody to fight.' She

carried Stan through to the sitting room, where the last of Artie's letters were held under a paperweight on the table beside the armchair where he used to sit. 'See?' she said, reading again his lines about the patrol he'd been on – and how, sentimental old fool that he was, he was gazing at the very same stars that looked down upon Vivienne from the skies above Whitechapel. 'Your pa's all right. And we're all right, too.'

She told him the same thing when she arrived at Alma's house later that morning, and put Stan down on the living room rug to play with the old wooden toys Alma had dug out from the cellar – the playthings Raymond and Artie had bickered and fought over when they were small. At a little more than a year old, Stan looked the spit of his father, said Alma; seeing him wrestle with the same wooden train was like being dragged back into the past.

'Let's hope he grows up as big and strong,' said Alma, before Vivienne left. 'And if he can miss out the ne'er-do-well phase along the way, so much the better.' She hovered on the doorstep, Stan playing happily behind, and made sure she took Vivienne's hand. 'You're scared, girl. I'm scared, too. But he's not in the thick of any fighting. He's deployed where he's deployed, and that's that. And there isn't any fighting in a surrender, Viv. Even if he was there . . .'

'He'd just be a prisoner of war,' Vivienne whispered.

'There's lots in this world better than death,' said Alma. 'But, right now, he's neither. Let's hold on to that.'

It was an impossible emotion to shake off. Even as she paid her visit to the H. J. Packer building – where Mary Burdett and the girls already had the Daughters of Salvation in full swing – it kept flurrying up inside her. She would sit down and write to him tonight. She would sign off, as ever, that she loved him; and, this time, there would be more magic in the words than she had ever mustered before.

But first there was the business of the day to attend to.

Vivienne had paid visits to the City of London before – but only ever in the company of her mother and stepfather, and only ever sitting in sullen silence in the back of his motor vehicle, keeping her mouth shut, not looking up unless she was told to do so, nodding and paying deference to all of his cronies and colleagues. She'd known enough older men like that in New York – wealth was wealth the whole world over – but there had always seemed something supremely smug and self-satisfied about the wealth in London, somehow. *Old money*, they called it. The money that had built an empire.

The address given to her by Sir George's secretary was in the centre of Threadneedle Walk. From its apex you could see the imposing stone edifice of the Bank of England. Compared to that, the address on Threadneedle Walk was positively nondescript: just a door between an investment brokers' office and a coffee house redolent of days gone by. Vivienne looked at the gold plaque by the door – where tiny script read KNAVE AND PARTNERS – and knew she was in the right place.

She did not knock. Men in places like this saw deference as weakness – and Vivienne was not weak. She strode in as if she belonged there, refusing to acknowledge the strange regard of the gentleman who was marching in the opposite direction. Inside, at a reception desk, sat a company secretary, her hair tied back in a tight bun.

'Vivienne Cohen,' she announced. 'I have an appointment to see Mr Knave.'

The woman at the desk appraised Vivienne coldly and said, 'Are we expecting another party?'

Vivienne knew what that meant. Inwardly, she fumed; but, outwardly, she was made out of steel.

'There shall be no chaperone, madam. Now, if you could kindly tell Mr Knave I'm here, I should be pleased to be shown through.'

The woman stood primly, vanished through a back door, and reappeared some moments later with a softened expression.

'This way, madam. Mr Knave will see you now.'

Vivienne tried to hold herself proudly as she followed through the doors. She tried not to let the lunacy of what she was doing weigh on her. She had come, she reminded herself, on the recommendation of Sir George Peel. As far as Elliott Knave knew, she had come to petition him for support in financing the Daughters of Salvation through the perilous years to come. She had every right to be here; none of it was a lie.

Not yet.

The receptionist had brought Vivienne up a single flight of stairs to the building's second storey. Here, she opened a heavy oak door and stood back for Vivienne to pass through.

Inside, in an office banked in cabinets and shelves – where a vast window looked out towards the great stone temple that was the Bank of England itself – an enormous figure, with broad shoulders and thick chestnut hair, sat behind a desk as imposing as the man himself. As Vivienne entered, he turned.

There was little resemblance to Walter Knave about the man. He was as big as his great-uncle was small; as imposing as his great-uncle was unassuming. It had been some years since the occasion when Vivienne's mother had warned her to keep away from the man. She'd thought, back then, that the warning did not suit the gentle giant she'd met – the man who'd virtually bowed at everything her stepfather said. Now, she saw immediately that her mother's advice had been right. The Elliott Knave who stood in his own environs was a man of almost supernatural confidence. He filled the room with his spectacle. In a dark, gravelly voice he thanked his secretary and requested that she leave.

Then he said, 'Mrs Cohen, you'll forgive me, I hope, for saying how familiar I find your face.'

Inwardly, Vivienne breathed a sigh of relief – at least, for the moment, he had not truly recognised who she was. She supposed she had changed much in the years since those moments at her stepfather's manor. Grown and matured, in the way that young people do. And, of course, she was known by a different name now; she dressed differently, held herself with a different bearing.

But, by the end of the hour, he would know her for who she was.

'I was grateful that you would meet with me, Mr Knave. Sir George speaks very highly of you. I believe he's given you a little understanding of what we aim to achieve?'

Elliott nodded. When he sank into his chair, inviting Vivienne to sit opposite him, she had the impression of a bear lowering itself onto its haunches. Even the backs of his hands were coarsely furred.

'Mrs Cohen, I'm impressed by what you've achieved, and at such a tentative age in life. This "Daughters of Salvation" that Sir George has told me about appears to be a most admirable endeavour – and I understand that he has thrown his lot in with

271

you for reasons very personal and dear to his heart. I agreed to meet with you, today, because Sir George has done much business through Knave and Partners across the last two decades. We consider him not just an associate, but a close friend. But –' Elliott Knave made a steeple of his enormous forearms, onto which he propped his significant chin – 'what I cannot see is how Knave and Partners could involve ourselves in such an endeavour. As a woman of sound business sense – as Sir George assures me you are – you must know our operations. We are an investment fund, Mrs Cohen. We handle the finances of wealthy men, like Sir George Peel, with the ambition of deepening those resources. You understand?'

How like a man of power it was to assume a young woman needed such simple things spelled out to her.

'You make rich men richer, Mr Knave.'

Elliott Knave paused. Then, with a sudden flourish, he rocked back in his chair and guffawed.

'Your tongue is as smart, Mrs Cohen, as you are beautiful.'

'Mr Knave,' she persisted, ignoring his comment, 'this morning's news only makes what the Daughters of Salvation achieves more pressing. If war is to come to London, as the greatest minds believe it will, there will be more need than ever for organisations like mine. We set out with a specific purpose, Mr Knave – to reform addicts and free them from their curses – but since then our mission has broadened, to encompass the needy from all corners of life. I must broaden it further, if I am to do the job I was put on this earth to do.'

'There is a religious fervour about you, Mrs Cohen.'

'It isn't religion,' she said. 'Just simple, unadulterated humanity. I came from a humble beginning.' This was not strictly true;

Vivienne's true father had been a man of not insignificant means in their native New York – but, for now, the lie was useful. 'I believe, Mr Knave, that you did the same?'

There was a silence. Vivienne feared, for a second, that she had revealed herself too soon. But she had spent too long speaking about the reason she had concocted for coming here. She needed to move past it soon, if she was to uncover what she really wanted to know.

Elliott Knave shifted in his seat. 'My beginnings are more humble, perhaps, than others in the City of London. I freely admit it. My family were never paupers, but I do not come from old money, Mrs Cohen – and I believe that this has given me the drive to succeed. I know the value of a shilling. I know the value of not having one as well.'

'I believe you learned your trade as an underling at the Buckingham Hotel?'

Vivienne saw an old ghost flicker across Elliott Knave's face, but – whatever it was – he was successful at suppressing it.

He said, 'We all begin somewhere, Mrs Cohen.'

'We all need our benefactors as well. We're the same in that, Mr Knave. You had your great-uncle. Walter, is it?'

Now the ghost returned. This time it lingered in Knave's expression a little further. His eyes pinned Vivienne in her seat a little more severely as well.

'You know my family background well, Mrs Cohen. Sir George has prepared you well.'

'Not Sir George, Mr Knave. You see – we've met before.'

Elliott Knave lifted himself – though he did not yet get to his feet. His eyes bored into her.

'I knew your face was familiar, Mrs Cohen.'

'You did not know me by that name, Mr Knave. We met some years ago, when I was just a girl. Back then, I'm afraid I was made – under some duress, I can assure you – to go by my stepfather's name. When you met me, I would have been introduced as Vivienne . . . Edgerton.'

Elliott Knave's face was a rictus. It was as if the mere sound of Lord Edgerton's name had summoned a dark spirit out of him – and now he was possessed. He got to his feet – and Vivienne was struck, suddenly, by his gargantuan size. Beneath the carefully cropped beard, his face was purpling in fury.

'So this is a ruse,' he growled. 'A way of entering my premises undetected. A deceit. Well, well done, Mrs Cohen, well done. You are as full of duplicity as your family. But now I should ask you – no, *instruct you* – to leave.'

Vivienne's heart was beating out some wild fandango, but she remained impassive and in her seat.

'I needed to see you, Mr Knave. I had an inkling that, if I told you the real reason, you might be unwilling to—'

'Unwilling?' he seethed. '*Unwilling?* By God, do you know how hard I've worked to build this? How much of my life has been devoted to building something that can outlast me, that can profit my children and my grandchildren long after I'm gone? It's my entire existence. And there's your family, lurking in the shadows, reaping what I've sown.' His eyes were a fury; his face a blood-red mask. 'I wish, by everything that's holy, that I'd never heard the name Edgerton. I pray, nightly, that the ground should open up and swallow your dynasty whole – that your father should close his eyes and never wake up again. But I see now that, even then, it wouldn't be over – because here *you* are. From one generation to the next.' He stopped. 'Well, go on then. Tell me what it is you want. What is it this time? Favours or money? Information my partners would exile me for, if I was to share it? The secrets of the City, so that your lot can grow more wealthy and powerful yet? Or do you just want me to bleed for you? *Again?*'

The words had rushed over Vivienne like a wild torrent. She was still trying to make some sense of them, to piece together the story in all of the anger, when Knave went on.

'Don't be shy, young lady. If you're here to inherit your stepfather's position, at least do me the honour of being bold about it. There isn't any secret here. You know what I am, and I know what you are. So let's stop dancing and speak straight. Your family have been extorting mine for a generation now – and all because of one little misdemeanour, long ago set straight. But money has never been good enough for your kind, has it? It wasn't only money you wanted. You had enough of that. No – it was *service* you wanted. It was fealty, like some baron of old. Well, you've got my great-uncle back in your clutches now. My poor great-uncle – the best of men. He saw the good in me, even when I slipped up. And I love him for what he did for me. So, go on, take what you want of me. I'll give it to you freely, as always I did—'

'Mr Knave!' Vivienne declared – and the force of her exclamation brought her the second's silence she needed to continue. 'If you would give me a moment, I'll show you that I'm not here at my stepfather's behest. I'll show you that the very last thing I am, on this earth, is my stepfather's servant.'

Elliott Knave was quiet. He looked like a bear contemplating attack – but Vivienne did not intend to play dead.

'Speak your mind now, Mrs Cohen. You have thirty more seconds of my time before you are ejected from these premises.'

Vivienne stood up. She stared the bear in its dark, black eyes.

'On the same New Year when we first met, your great-uncle led me to believe that my stepfather holds some power over him – a weakness he could expose, perhaps. A secret not to be revealed. He let slip that it concerned "his boy" – and Mr Knave, from what you've said today, I believe that he meant you.'

Knave only stared at her.

'I came here today, Elliott, because I was once a woman who made mistakes. I know what it's like to have secrets hanging over you. I know what it's like to be owned by secrets. A few years ago, my friend Nancy came to my rescue. She set me free to be the mistress of my own life.' She took a breath. 'Mr Knave, I should very much like to be that friend to you.'

'Friend?' he barked. 'I have met you but twice in my life. The sum total of our engagements lasts less than an hour. What reason could you possibly have to help me?'

'I owe my stepfather a debt. I should like to repay it.'

'Debt,' Elliott Knave spat. 'The word that has defined me. The word that could undo everything I have accomplished.'

'You misunderstand me, sir. I did not mean a monetary debt.' She hesitated. 'My stepfather took my mother from me. He took my life and left me to fend for myself. He took my confidence, my passions, my love for life, and rendered me an empty husk. Then, when he discovered I was carrying a child, he took the roof from over my head. I am fortunate to be standing here now. *That* is the debt I wish to repay.'

The righteous fire had dimmed around Elliott Knave.

'And I wish to repay it now because, even as we speak, my stepfather is contriving to turn the Buckingham Hotel into a home away from home – not for the foreign dignitaries and royalty who used to frequent its suites, but to the kind of men who once stood shoulder to shoulder with Mr Hitler. The kind of men who, even now, are manoeuvring for peace – the kind of men who would, given a chance, welcome the Third Reich into the streets of London, who see Britain not as an island fortress to withstand the war, but as the natural ally of all that is wrong in the world. I have friends in that hotel. They have families who depend on it. I would not see it ruined. My husband has gone to fight for what's right. I cannot stand idly by while my stepfather propagates all that's wrong on my very doorstep.'

She hesitated. When Elliott Knave said nothing, she knew this was the moment.

'I came here, today, on a false pretext – I'm sorry, but I didn't know how else to barter an hour of your time. Yet I had an idea that, if we were to work together, we could both get what we want.'

Elliott Knave's breath was deep and laboured. He grunted, 'And what is that?'

'Nothing less than the downfall of Lord Bartholomew Edgerton, the ruin of his life's work, and his removal from the board of the Buckingham Hotel.'

Vivienne hesitated, letting the words hang in the air between them. In that silence, she knew she had roped in her man; Elliott Knave's eyes had widened, as if he had just witnessed something unimaginable. A destitute man, who has been offered the hand of an angel.

'I believe,' she said, reaching out across the desk, 'it is customary for a deal to be sealed by shaking hands?'

# Chapter Eighteen

'KING HAAKON SURVIVES,' SAID JOHN Hastings.

The hotel board were arrayed around the table in the Buckingham's Benefactors' Study – the grand conference chamber, banked in portraits of feted guests from times of yore, where the hotel's most critical meetings were always held. The table – perfectly circular in design, so that no one member of the board ever appeared at its head – dominated the room, so vast that it seemed a mathematical impossibility that anyone had ever levered it in here. Around its edges Uriah Bell, Sir Peter Merriweather and Lord Bartholomew Edgerton regarded Hastings's pronouncement with much interest. The lesser members of the board, Francis Lloyd and Dickie Fletcher – whose shares together amounted to a tiny fraction of the hotel's worth – remained mute, as they nearly always did. Walter Knave, who had just slipped into the room, did not know where to sit, and studiously ignored the chair waiting at Lord Edgerton's right-hand side while Hastings went on.

'Resistance in the Drøbak Sound was more than the Nazis had anticipated. Oscarsborg Fortress still stands. The short story, gentlemen, is that King Haakon and his family were able to escape Oslo before they came to harm. But the king has remained true to his word – he has refused to acquiesce in the face of German demands.' John Hastings smiled. 'The man always had honour. He always had grit.'

King Haakon of Norway and his family had used the Buckingham Hotel as their London residence throughout all the thirty-five long years of his reign. Hastings himself had had the honour of speaking to him at Christmas Balls. Raymond de Guise had waltzed his wife, Queen Maud, across the Grand Ballroom. Yet, according to the telegram whose news Hastings was relaying, they had spent the last days and nights in Norway's vast winter woodlands, while Hitler appointed some nasty Norwegian fascist as the head of his new puppet government.

'They're safe at last,' Hastings concluded, 'and on board HMS *Glasgow.*'

'Bound for Great Britain?' asked Uriah Bell.

'That is not yet the indication,' Hastings went on. 'Not while the Allies still slug it out to quickly liberate his nation. But, gentlemen, we are advised that preparations are afoot. Should Norway be lost, King Haakon and his cabinet will form a government in exile, right here in our own city. It is considered likely that the king and queen will ultimately reside in Buckingham Palace.'

Queen Maud, as everybody in the Benefactors' Study was aware, was the grand-daughter of the old Queen Victoria, the daughter of King Edward VII. Family ties still mattered. The palace would take them in.

'But there are many in their extended family,' Hastings continued, 'dignitaries and diplomats and members of the cabinet, who will look for sanctuary alongside them. Gentlemen, I am proposing that we prepare to be nothing less than a seat of government.'

Muttered words and whispered imprecations spread around the table.

'The war has begun, gentlemen. We have existed in limbo for long enough. Now is the time to act. Let us leap to the challenge – because, believe me, gentlemen, Norway will not be the last nation to fall. Not now this has begun. By summer's end, there will be governments sundered and royal families in flight all across the Continent. Let's make the Buckingham their home. Let that be the legacy we leave behind us. Let all of London – all of Great Britain, all of the old world – know that this is what we stand for. You gentlemen have taught me the costs and benefits of reputation. Well, we have an opportunity to seal that reputation now.'

'A home for dethroned governments,' said Lord Edgerton, weighing up the idea.

'Until such a time that their homelands can be restored,' said Hastings. 'Let me make it clear – there is a need in the world, and we must fill it. If we do not, it will be the Savoy, the Imperial and the Ritz who rise up from this war and are remembered. Let's not let that happen, gentlemen.'

'I see no downside to this proposition,' said Uriah Bell. 'Why not profit from national pride?'

'Nor I,' interjected Sir Peter Merriweather, who seemed to have grown more corpulent still since the start of the war. Shifting his enormous belly, he went on, 'Patriotism as policy. Are we agreed?'

Walter Knave could anticipate what was coming next, but even he winced as Lord Edgerton cleared his throat, as if to announce some coming condemnation. It would not matter what Edgerton said, not if the rest of the board was united; but Walter Knave knew, better than any, how a man like Edgerton influenced others' minds. There wasn't a man in the room, Hastings excepted, who didn't owe him in some way. And what Edgerton meant to say was this: *the downside, gentlemen, will come when this island is itself overrun. When our own Royal Family are fleeing into the north of the country. When Mr Hitler has appointed his own government – headed, perhaps, by the Right Honourable Archibald Ramsay – to Downing Street. We shall need a different reputation, when that day dawns. We would be fools to ignore the possibility.*

But Lord Edgerton didn't get the chance to voice that opinion – not quite yet – because, at that moment, the clock on the wall struck 1 p.m. and, as if being directed by the hand of another, Walter Knave got to his feet, said, 'Shall we continue our discussions in the Queen Mary, gentlemen?' and tottered, lamely, towards the study door.

Out in the hallway, he could think straighter. At least, out here, he couldn't feel Lord Edgerton's eyes boring into him. At some point, soon, the man was going to expect Walter to declare his own opinion on the matter. The longer that could be put off, the better.

As they stepped through the doors of the Queen Mary, Walter Knave felt suddenly better. The restaurant was full; waiters, dressed in their pristine white and gold brocade, waltzed between the tables. The air was rich with the scents of roast lamb and mint, the buttery, crisp quails being served on the tables around them. In a place as busy as this, he thought, it would be near impossible to speak of anything that mattered. Certainly, to speak of *politics*. For an hour, at least, there would be a temporary respite from the battles of the board. Walter Knave would take advantage of that.

He quite fancied the beef Wellington, too.

The restaurant manager was approaching across the busy floor, ready to guide them to their designated table – it was always the same, the tall one in the Berkeley Square windows, raised on a stone plinth to separate it from the rest – when the doors opened behind them.

Walter Knave didn't know what happened next. All he heard was the shouting.

A shoulder barged into his own, sending him tumbling into Lord Edgerton – who, despite his imperious size, staggered into Uriah Bell. By the time Walter had picked himself up, more figures were among them. Ten, twenty, thirty figures, all streaming past, dividing one board member from the other.

Across the restaurant, a sudden hush had descended. A hundred faces looked up, trying to decipher this bewildering scene.

Thirty women – not one of them dressed in finery fit enough for the Queen Mary restaurant – had marched brazenly through the doors. Now they were looming over every table, while the discombobulated hotel board could only stare on in perplexity and horror. Half the women were holding up placards, makeshift things made out of garden canes and wooden offcuts. Walter Knave had no need to focus on what the placards said, because the women were shouting it, too.

'*Ration the rich!*' yelled the women from one table.

'*The rich get their fill!*' exclaimed another.

One woman had plucked a quail breast off the plate of some horrified old dowager.

That was when Walter Knave knew something had to be done.

It hadn't been like this in his day. Back then, people knew where they did and did not belong.

THE GOVERNMENT SAYS EAT LESS! one banner screamed out.
BUT THE RICH GROW FAT!

'Do something, Knave!' seethed Lord Edgerton. 'This is your castle, man!'

Yes, thought Walter. A castle. And it was under siege. Under siege by . . .

'Mr Knave,' came a voice. Somebody had taken him by the elbow and now whispered into his ear. 'To the shelters, Mr Knave? Give the order and we'll—'

Knave had been dithering for too long already. A stream of porters and kitchen-hands had erupted from the kitchens to confront the intruders. The junior patissier – responsible for the Queen Mary's famous afternoon fancies – had wrenched a placard out of one woman's arms, while the afternoon sous-chef wrestled her away from the table. Walter looked up, to see the restaurant manager looking earnestly into his eyes, begging for an order.

'Do it, man!' Lord Edgerton barked.

Walter Knave reeled around.

'This way, gentlemen,' the restaurant manager declared. 'The staff shelters aren't far.'

It might have been easier to beat a retreat back towards the hotel reception, but by now the veritable army of Buckingham staff were forming human barricades, driving the interlopers towards those very doors. At least the restaurant manager seemed to have his wits about him. Walter Knave felt himself buffeted and trampled as the hotel board marched around him, but soon they reached the kitchen doors – where one of the restaurant's two head chefs was standing with a cast-iron frying pan in hand.

Through the doors, a staircase plunged down into the hotel's wine cellars. Down there, in flickering darkness, the board gathered.

The air-raid shelters constructed here had little of the opulence of the guest shelters in the old hotel laundry. There were benches and boards aplenty, old trolleys filled with blankets and furs; and, because the restaurant still needed a wine cellar, the dusty shelves were filled with enough Château Haut-Brion and Sempé Armagnac to see the entire staff through whatever battles were to come.

'I'll take a tipple now,' said Uriah Bell, 'to steady the nerves. Pour on!'

The restaurant manager did as he was instructed, then beat a retreat to the kitchen above to ascertain whether the situation was yet under control.

'I warned you,' seethed Lord Edgerton, after he had drained his glass, 'but you wouldn't hear me. Belittle the hotel like we did at Christmas, and it soon comes back to haunt you. Well, look at us *now*! Invite riff-raff in once, and suddenly they presume this is *their* domain. You damned fool, Hastings. You damned—'

John Hastings, who seemed the only man among them not relying on the Château Haut-Brion to calm him, only polished his spectacles; there was still much dust in the wine cellar.

'Christmas was a triumph, Bartholomew,' he said – again ignoring Lord Edgerton's title. 'That you don't see it as such is your embarrassment, not mine. The whole country is proud of the Buckingham Hotel for the show of solidarity and generosity at our Winter Serenade – so let's not reconstitute it as failure, now. I won't hear of it. It was not a lowering of standards, but a proud display of moral vigour. What's happening in the Queen Mary, right now, is a quite separate—'

'I'll hear no more from you,' Lord Edgerton barked. 'You deny the evidence of our own eyes. What would it have taken for one of those ingrates to strike us down? We survive by happenstance, you fool, not by—'

'The Buckingham Hotel is a *part* of the city, gentlemen. It is not an island fortress, to be barricaded up until the war comes to an end. Our reputation, as you have taught me, is our most treasured possession. We enhanced it at Christmas – and we will, when the moment comes, enhance it further by making our halls a home away from home for King Haakon and his exiled ministers. When the next nations of Europe fall, we shall open our halls to their governments as well. Gentlemen . . .' John Hastings had removed his eyes from Lord Edgerton alone and, in the subterranean light, looked at the whole board as one. 'We can prevaricate no longer. There can be no more talk of war as a dangerous illusion. The battle has begun. It's time to stand up.'

In the shadows on the edge of the group, Walter Knave shuddered. As long as he could keep his silence, perhaps it would be all right. But he could already sense that it wasn't only Europe where battle had begun. It was right here, in front of him – right beneath the Buckingham Hotel.

He knew what the staff at the hotel thought of him. He knew he was spent; that the days when he might run the place effectively were long gone; that, without his wife Blythe, he was a shadow of his former self. He knew that the chambermaids tittered and the audit clerks whispered about his suitability for the role. He knew, too, that they were right. The hotel needed a hero, somebody with heart. But his heart was withered. It felt rotten and black. It felt as if it wasn't beating in his own breast, but in the hands of the man looming there in the darkness – Lord

Edgerton. If he had to take a side, there was no answering the calling of his own heart. No – there would only be one thing he could do.

'Gentlemen, I have an alternative solution,' declared Lord Edgerton. 'According to the Articles of Association of this board, the removal of a troublesome member can be enacted by majority consent. I am therefore proposing that we move, at once, to a confidence motion in our colleague, Mr John Hastings – on the basis that a lack of cultural understanding, propagated by his place of origin, has blindsided Mr Hastings to the people this hotel needs most. When we were deprived of foreign dignitaries as guests at our establishment, we should never have indulged foreign riff-raff. We should have focused ourselves, with a marksman's accuracy, on the people we knew needed us – the English dignitaries, the British politicians, the British newspapermen and leaders, who find themselves, suddenly, with no place to go.'

It looked as if John Hastings's heart hadn't skipped a beat. Walter Knave wished he was like that; his own – wherever it was – was hammering dangerously wild.

'Perhaps you might say it more plainly, Bartholomew? Which dignitaries, which politicians, which British leaders can you possibly mean when—'

Footsteps clattered down the shelter stairs – and the restaurant manager reappeared.

'It's finished, gentlemen. The Metropolitan Police are here now. They're already escorting our visitors away.'

Hastings nodded, decisively. Then he turned on his heel, marched to the foot of the stairs, and looked back.

'Convene what meetings you must, gentlemen. But I caution you – without the continued funding of my family trust, the

Buckingham Hotel will quickly need further investors. Which of you is able to guarantee this hotel will not fall?' He stopped, looking over his shoulder at them all. 'I shall wait to hear of your timings. The Articles our colleague speaks of merely permit a process to begin, with no immediate vote to be taken – and no vote at all until a formal meeting is convened. Your secretaries may speak to mine. In the meantime, I suggest we busy our-selves with making certain this spectacle never happens again.' He paused. 'Mr Knave?'

Walter felt the tightening in his chest. He lifted his eyes, to look at John Hastings.

'Y-yes?' he whispered.

'I believe an address ought to be made to the restaurant, should it not? And, I should think, a good number of gratis meals ought to be incorporated into the accounts.'

By instinct, Walter Knave flashed a look at Lord Edgerton. The lord was impassive, so meekly, he said, 'Yes,' and watched as John Hastings vanished up the stairs.

*So*, thought Hastings as he left the wine cellar and re-entered the restaurant through the kitchen doors, *we've reached this moment already.*

It would have taken a man of monumental stupidity not to predict that as Lord Edgerton's next move; it had been in the air ever since the moment John Hastings stepped off the boat and joined the Buckingham Hotel.

The restaurant looked as if it hadn't been touched. Half an hour ago, it was the site of an invasion; now, a place where plates were being re-provisioned and conversations were back in full flow. Only the presence of some unusual members of staff – too many of them – suggested anything untoward had ever happened here.

Mrs Nancy de Guise was waiting by the reception doors. She seemed to be trying to catch his eye as he passed.

John Hastings had always admired Nancy de Guise. It had been her husband who'd first escorted Hastings to English shores. The truth was, it was Raymond who'd convinced him that there was a viable investment in this hotel – and all because of the magic he saw in the Grand Ballroom at night. As he passed, he inclined his head in greeting.

'What news from the front, Mrs de Guise?'

'All quiet,' she said, though her voice was heavy, 'but that was two weeks ago, Mr Hastings. A different world.' Here was the familiar fear: that, by the time her husband's words reached her, they were already obsolete. Time moved either too sluggishly or far too fast; there was no in between. 'Mr Hastings, I wondered if we might talk.'

John Hastings looked over his shoulder, only to see the restaurant manager leading the rest of the board – among them a dishevelled Walter Knave, his head bowed down like a penitent – out of the kitchen doors. No doubt they would discuss his denigration of the hotel over a lovely lamb lunch.

'I have only a narrow window, Mrs de Guise,' he said, tracking the group of men with his eyes as they took to their table. 'There are things I must set in motion.'

And Nancy said, with such sudden force that John Hastings was quite bowled over, 'I think it will be worth your while, sir.'

They were waiting in the Housekeeping Lounge. When Nancy opened the doors, it was to reveal two figures sitting at the long table. Both scrambled to their feet at his approach. The first he knew well: Vivienne Cohen – née Edgerton – had been living in the Ethelred Suite when Hastings first came to the hotel. The second was a stranger to him: a hulking behemoth of a man in middle age, thick beard coiled around his collar, his charcoal suit marking him out as an inhabitant of the City of London. Hastings knew many men like this, on both sides of the Atlantic, but the appearance of one of them in the Housekeeping Lounge was a mystery. John Hastings, though, knew the value of silence. He waited as Nancy closed the door behind them, then made the introductions.

'Mr Hastings, I trust you remember Mrs Vivienne Cohen.'

She'd changed, of course. Not only in her appearance – though she'd matured in this as well – but in her confidence and bearing. When she shook his hand, she was greeting him, he thought, as an equal. Somebody else might have found that impudent; John Hastings was intrigued.

'And this, Mr Hastings, is Mr Elliott Knave.'

As he took the great man's big, furred hand, the first piece of this mystery fell into place.

'Mr … Knave?' He flashed his eyes around the room; the thought came to him that he had walked into some kind of trap, but he quickly dismissed it. He was with Nancy de Guise, and that meant he was among friends. 'Am I to infer some connection to the current director of our hotel?'

'He's my great-uncle,' Elliott replied, 'and my godfather to boot. Please forgive the subterfuge. We came by the tradesman's entrance – because it would not pay for dear Uncle Walter to see me here today. I made him a promise, twenty years ago, that I would never again return to the Buckingham Hotel.'

John Hastings said, 'And yet – here you are.'

Vivienne stood. 'Mr Hastings, give us but a few minutes of your time and everything will make sense.'

Hastings nodded. 'I was supposed to be at lunch. Perhaps . . . a crumpet or two?'

Nancy was happy to oblige. As she lined up the toasters, Vivienne continued, 'Mr Hastings, you will remember how little love there is between my stepfather and me. I'll be plain – I loathe the man with every fibre of my being. But there are people in this hotel to whom I owe my heart, and I'm hoping that what we tell you today might change things for them, for the better. There is a secret at the heart of the hotel that has been left to fester – and my stepfather is using it, right now, to consolidate his control.'

John Hastings had long ago been taught to take three breaths before confronting any accusation, in business or in life. After a pregnant pause, he said, 'Perhaps you'd better explain, Mrs Cohen.'

'No,' interjected Elliott Knave, 'perhaps I should. It is my story, after all. I'm the seed of this rot. Mr Hastings, after you hear what I have to say, I ask you to take into account everything I've told you – the good and the bad of it – and to consider clemency.' He paused. 'Because it's my mistake that's been hanging over the hotel. It's my sin – and my great-uncle's conviction that I could mend the error of my ways – that's been turning this place to rot. Walter Knave is a good man, Mr Hastings. It's just that he's paid for that goodness in the worst of all possible ways. He's been paying for it for the last twenty years of his life. He's out there, in the hotel, paying for it even now.'

The end of 1909, turning into 1910, had been a different age in the Buckingham Hotel.

Elliott Knave was the youngest of five brothers in his corner of the family tree. Errant and overlooked; overshadowed and

290

forgotten. Thank goodness for his great-uncle and godfather Walter. Walter and Blythe Knave had managed the Buckingham Hotel since its grand opening in 1889, and in that time they had raised two beloved daughters. But Walter Knave had always longed for a son. His peculiar fear was that, should he die without having one, he would be the first Knave since time immemorial not to have produced a male heir. That was a lineage, he was often known to remark, that stretched back to the Garden of Eden (or, if the scientists fashionable in the previous century were to be trusted, back to the prehistoric great apes). Walter Knave never did get the son he longed for – but nobody did more to fill that void than his great-nephew Elliott.

Elliott was an unfortunate son. Brothers in the armed services, decorated for their service to the late queen; one brother in industry; another, out on the Cape mining for gold. They'd had leg-ups along the way, as good sons do, but Elliott Knave had never been thought of as much in his family. Last sons went to the priesthood, his father was known to joke, half hoping that such a thing might come to pass. Perhaps it would have done, too – if Elliott's great-uncle Walter hadn't made him an offer.

'Come and work for me,' he'd said that Christmas. 'Opportunities abound in a place like the Buckingham. You'll cross paths with so many people, high-born and low. It might be the making of you.'

In fact, it was to be the making of them both.

Elliott Knave spent four long years working in the audit and accounts office. His mind was naturally suited to numbers. He was one of those who could see them dance. He enjoyed the balance in the profit and loss accounts. He enjoyed making one mirror the other. He learned to enjoy the intricate, and perfectly permissible, deceits with which businessmen danced around the duties of His Majesty's tax collector. He was fast, he was eager – and, most of all, he was hungry. Hungry to make something of himself. Hungry to prove to his father and his riot of brothers that even bad sons came good.

Then came 1914, and all that came after.

Elliott Knave's hunger in the audit office did not translate, easily, into hunger in the fields of Flanders. As an officer, he was largely discontented. He saw the slaughter in those foreign fields as nothing but a profit and loss account in a spiral of terminal decline: all those boys slaughtered for infinitesimal, and ultimately worthless, gains. Were a business run like that, it would certainly flounder. No, far from being a business properly run, Elliott began to see the Great War – the war to end all wars – as a gamblers' den. Whether you were successful or not depended not on your skills and your insight, but on cruel, damnable chance.

Perhaps it was because of this that he started gambling with the officers in the mess at night. Playing for coppers and sticks was better than playing with lives. Soon, he developed a taste for it. Random luck was energising. Those incredible, electric games of pitch and toss were what got him through the long, long months of toil.

When he came home, back into his waiting post at the Buckingham Hotel, he brought that passion with him.

'So much had changed at the hotel,' Elliott explained, as John Hastings sat in careful, considered silence, trying to predict the story to come. 'I wanted it to be my place again, and perhaps it was – or perhaps *I* had changed, too. But when I looked at the ledgers, I didn't get the same satisfaction any longer. No amount of ducking and dodging around the tax inspectors, staying just inside the limits of the law, satisfied me. Some people brought back terrors from the war. Some people brought back shudders, or problems with the demon drink. I came back a gambler. So I started gambling.'

A gamblers' paradise was established in the Candlelight Club: honoured guests invited, after hours, to play at blackjack and cribbage. Then there came a new, more complex game: poker, with all the glamour of the New World.

'I'd go to the clubs. I knew how to find weaker men and prey on them. I just didn't know that, somewhere along the way, I'd turn into a weaker man as well . . .' Elliott faltered. 'One day, I ran out of money.'

The gambler's curse: nobody realises the drought is coming, not until it's already upon you.

'There used to be rumours,' said Nancy, 'that Walter Knave used the Buckingham as his own personal bank account.'

'But it wasn't Uncle Walter,' said Elliott. 'It was me. You see, nobody knows how better to hide money in a place like this than its audit office. If you keep the money moving, nobody notices when a few hundred pounds disappears. As long as it keeps moving, in and out of the ledgers, round and round, nobody will notice when a few thousand disappears either – money is just numbers. That's what I'd been discovering. So, no, my dear uncle didn't use the Buckingham as his bank account. I did.'

Hastings removed his spectacles and wearily polished them on his sleeve. Without commenting on the story or decreeing a judgement, he said, 'How does this connect to your uncle Walter?'

'It was 1920, 1921. My uncle had done his job. He'd shepherded the hotel through the Great War. He kept it alive, even after the outbreak of Spanish influenza on the second storey. A scandal like that might have sunk the hotel. But he'd done it, and he'd earned his right to retire on his own terms. This he was desperate to do. But—'

'Let me see that I understand this correctly,' interjected John Hastings. 'You were in debt to the hotel – by a not insignificant sum. You were able to hide it in the books – that was rudimentary enough – but your great-uncle's departure would mean a new director coming in.'

'Mr Maynard Charles,' said Nancy.

The hotel had missed him every day since he had departed.

'And you feared that, on assuming control of the hotel, Mr Charles would undoubtedly sift forensically through the ledgers of the last years.'

Elliott Knave nodded. 'And uncover the black hole in the centre of them.' He faltered before going on. 'So I confessed everything. I sat with my great-uncle in the Candlelight Club, when I was sure we would not be overheard, and I told him what I'd done. Mr Hastings, I have never felt more ashamed of myself. I have never let a man down as I let down my uncle. I could see it, in the way the lines stretched and deepened on his face. He barely said a word. He just got up and left.'

It wasn't until some time later that Elliott Knave understood what his uncle Walter had done to put things right.

'He went begging. He called on friends and relations – anybody who might lend him the sum we needed to plaster over the cracks in the ledgers. If we had the capital, we could do it. The records existed – we merely needed to make them match reality. Most friends, of course, declined his overtures. That they kept the secret at all was, I think, a good deed too far for many of them.

But there was one man, a frequent guest at the hotel, who promised to lend us the money. His name was Lord Edgar Edgerton, and he was a fine, principled man.'

'It's just a shame,' interjected Vivienne, 'that he'd sired the most reprehensible of sons.'

'The old Lord Edgerton attached various conditions to the loan. The first was repayment in full, across the following five years. This we eagerly agreed to. The second, and more important, was my instant removal from the hotel. I was horrified – but by then, I had made connections and friends in the City. I was lucky to land on my feet, to find a role that suited my talents, and start making the money with which I could repay my uncle for his sacrifice. Leaving the Buckingham Hotel helped me to defeat my addiction to gambling as well – because, as foolish as it might sound, I do believe I was in thrall to it in the same way that a derelict is in thrall to his drink and drugs.'

Vivienne shifted, uneasily, in her seat.

'So the story ends there,' said Hastings. 'All's well that ends well.' He said it with one eyebrow arched – because, of course, he knew it was no such thing.

'Well, it should have been. But Edgar passed on in 1925. The debt passed with him. So did his title. The new Lord Edgerton saw opportunity where his father had only seen kindness to a friend. It wasn't enough for Lord Bartholomew Edgerton to balance his family's estate. We repaid our debt in full, but soon he wanted more. By then, I'd graduated to a position of some influence in the City. I had become the custodian of fortunes far vaster than mine. But Lord Edgerton knew that, if my clients were ever to know what I'd done at the Buckingham, I would be finished.' He took a deep breath. 'Mr Hastings, I've been feeding him secrets and information ever since. When Vivienne, here, first approached me, I thought she was inheriting the mantle. Half the current Lord Edgerton's fortune is built upon the advice I have given him – advice I would be exiled and ostracised for having provided, were it to be found out. But I had no choice. To preserve one lie, I have had to tell a thousand others.'

'And yet you confess all to me, a stranger, today?'

'It is time. There are bigger things in play, Mr Hastings. When Vivienne explained what Bartholomew Edgerton is doing to this hotel – the things my great-uncle has become a party to, and all to maintain his protection of me ... Well, I cannot stand for it to happen. I'll take my chances, Mr Hastings – I've done more good in life than I've done bad. I've come a long way since 1925 – I have enough friends in the City who'd vouch for me, if Lord Edgerton seeks to bring me down. But I'm a proud Englishman, sir. Too old for fighting, but if I can do my bit against men like Bartholomew Edgerton ... I haven't always played by the rules – but I'm no traitor to my country.'

Here, Vivienne took a deep breath and said, 'When the position of hotel director became vacant, my stepfather seized his chance to institute somebody in his thrall to the position. Mr Hastings, it is his gambit to wrest control of the hotel purely for himself. To circumvent the will of the board.'

'Since early summer,' Nancy said, 'he's been using the hotel as a meeting place for men working against the war. I'm sure you know the kind of men I speak of. The British Union of Fascists might be outlawed now, but its spirits and ideals go on. Mr Ramsay has stayed here on multiple occasions. Sir Barry Domvile and Mr Leese took Christmas dinner, right there in the restaurant.' She paused. 'Lord Edgerton brought Mr Knave back because he knows the poor man will put up no protest. He knows he can do nothing but nod and say yes. Some of us here believed Mr Knave was one of them – rotten, in his own heart, and against the principles we're proud of here. But . . . it isn't so.'

'Far from it,' said Elliott, with true conviction.

'We believe he's been trying his best to keep this quiet,' said Nancy. 'Sweeping up that magazine, *Action*, whenever he sees it. Just getting from one day to the next. But it can't go on like this, Mr Hastings. The war's begun. And we're changing the sheets of men who want us to lose it. We're serving them, every day.'

Hastings said, 'I've seen these men. Of course I have. But wheels are in motion now. There may be little I can do.'

'That's why I'm here.' Elliott produced an envelope from his overcoat and slid it along the long breakfasting table. 'A full and frank confession. Mr Hastings, I ask for your forgiveness – and I ask you to petition the rest of the board for the same. With a majority decision, the secret could be undone.'

'You're asking for . . . exposure?'

'In the hope it sets my uncle free from Lord Edgerton's grasp.'

'And,' Nancy added, 'by doing so, it would give us a hope of restoring the Buckingham to the place it ought to be. I'm sorry, Mr Hastings, but we couldn't say nothing. Our husbands are out there. Friends from the hotel. It doesn't seem right that they're out there fighting, and we're at home, serving the enemy breakfast in bed.'

Hastings stood. There was a grave look on his face.

'Perhaps you might accompany me out, Mrs de Guise.' When Nancy nodded, he looked at Vivienne and Elliott, both their faces set in stone. 'Thank you both,' he whispered. 'Let us hope tomorrow brings better tidings.'

In the Housekeeping hall, he walked abreast with Nancy.

'Your part in this must never go detected, Mrs de Guise. I like your family a great deal, but I'm learning that, in England, one must know one's place. I wouldn't want this to reflect on you. You need a home, you need a profession – and I'm told that you are of increasing value to this hotel.' They had reached the edge of the reception hall. Across the chequered black and white tiles, the doors of the Queen Mary were opening up. Through them tottered Walter Knave, dwarfed by Lord Edgerton and the other members of the hotel board. 'I tell you this in the strictest confidence, Mrs de Guise, and only because I value you and your husband dearly. The board plot my removal.'

Nancy exhaled. 'Can they do that, Mr Hastings?'

'If I've learned one thing in business, it is this – never underestimate the power of a disrupted board.'

He watched as the group of men disappeared through the revolving doors, out on to the sunlit pasture of Berkeley Square. Then he marched to the concierge desk, retrieved a pencil and paper from the young man standing there, and, having first scribbled something down, returned to Nancy with the paper folded in his fist.

On giving it to her, he said, 'I must ask you one more favour – something you must keep to yourself, and yourself alone. Can I trust you, Nancy?'

'Yes, of course.'

Nancy opened up the paper. On it was written a name she knew well, and below that an address in Cambridge Circus of which she had no recollection whatsoever.

'I want you to gather together a file. Proof of every instance Lord Edgerton has invited his associates here. Every time they stayed in the suites, or took luncheon in the restaurant – and, if you can, every time they're expected here as well. Commit it to paper, seal it in an envelope, and send it to this address. Can you do that for me?'

Nancy hesitated. 'There's a copy of the guest register in Housekeeping,' she said, 'but as for the Queen Mary . . .'

'It doesn't have to be complete, Nancy – just complete enough.' Hastings braced her by the shoulder. 'The board plan a reckoning. A meeting to decide my future. But perhaps there's a way of cutting the head off this particular hydra, before the fate of the Buckingham Hotel truly is out of my hands.'

As Hastings crossed the reception hall to follow the board out into the sunlight, Nancy looked again at the paper in her hands. The name of that man brought hope back to her heart: the solid, dependable defiance of the man who had last run the Buckingham Hotel, and under whose watch Lord Edgerton would never have been able to transform it into a members' club for the very worst of mankind. She wondered what he was doing now, what Cambridge Circus meant, and why *him*. Then she remembered the very reason he'd tendered his resignation to the board, two Christmases before: the former hotel director hadn't just been in the pay of the Buckingham Hotel; he'd been in the pay of the security services as well. He'd pledged himself to them, for the betterment of Great Britain.

The name 'Mr Maynard Charles' was written on the paper in her hand.

'I'll do it, Mr Hastings,' she said – and Nancy felt, for the first time all year, as if, perhaps, the tide might be about to turn.

May 1940

# Chapter Nineteen

VIVIENNE COHEN HARDLY DARED LOOK at the head-lines. The silence of April, not a single letter back from Artie, had been unnerving enough – but the caval-cade of headlines across early May had, too often, turned her to thoughts that had not entered her head in years: the sweet lure of oblivion, of an overload of cocktails, of the opiates she used to let rush through her system. It was only the endless routine of feeding Stan, bathing Stan, rocking Stan to sleep (and then feeding him again), that kept her sane. The whole world thought Vivienne Cohen was strong: a woman who'd turned her back on the riches of her stepfather and chosen to blaze her own way through life instead; only a precious few would recognise how weak she felt in this moment, how her heartstrings called out for something to take her away from it.

There were still opium dens aplenty in the East End. She knew the location of every one. If it hadn't been for Stan, she'd have been there this weekend, riding on a sweet, hypnotic tide to a place where none of it mattered – not the war, not her stepfather and his minions, and certainly not the fact that, three days ago, the forces of the Third Reich had swarmed into Belgium and France, unleashing battle from both land and sky.

Today, Vivienne ignored the newspaper when it landed on her doorstep. She needed air. Fresh, clean air – which was not, perhaps, possible in the East End of London, but it would have to do. With Stan snugly fitted into his pram, she left home – where all the possessions Artie had collected across his life had started to suffocate her – and picked her way, instead, to the H. J. Packer building and the Daughters of Salvation. Even then, as she walked through the complex, the heartfelt looks she got from Mary Burdett and the other girls – even from some of the destitutes in the mess hall, where soup was being served – unnerved her. She took Stan into the back office, meaning to get some privacy – but there was Warren Peel, at the desk with his head buried in the *Daily Express*.

'Well, it's done,' said Warren. 'It's happened.'

'What's happened?' asked Vivienne.

Warren turned the newspaper around. Vivienne could hardly bear to see it, but there was the headline, big and bold:

CHURCHILL NAMED PRIME MINISTER AS TOTAL WAR BECKONS.

Vivienne shuddered. 'Put it away, Warren.'

'I should be there,' Warren murmured, darkly.

'If you were, there's every chance you'd be dead,' Vivienne snapped.

She hadn't meant to be so vicious, and regretted it immediately. The look on Warren's face was changing. His shame was palpable.

'I'll make myself useful here,' he said – and, as he left the room, he reached down to tickle Stan under the chin. 'He's growing up nicely, Vivienne. He looks so much like his father.'

Another one of Vivienne's weaknesses: she could still be too fierce. Patience was a virtue she'd learned the hard way, but sometimes she bottled up emotion for too long – and the problem with a stoppered bottle was that, sooner or later, it was going to pop. She would make her apologies to Warren later. It would plague her until she did.

The newspaper he'd left behind was still on the desk. Churchill as Prime Minister. Well, a change was bound to come. Mr Chamberlain, good soul that he was, had made a mess of peace. Perhaps Mr Churchill could make a triumph of war. He certainly looked dogged enough.

Vivienne couldn't help it any longer. She roamed over the story, whispering out snippets to Stan as she read.

'"An ordeal of the most grievous kind",' she breathed. '"Many, many long months of struggle and of suffering."' She looked up. 'Oh, Stan . . .' But her eyes were drawn inexorably back to the words. '"You ask, what is our policy? I can say: it is to wage war – by sea, land and air, with all our might and with all the strength that God can give us; to wage war against a monstrous tyranny, never surpassed in the dark, lamentable catalogue of human crime."' She slammed the newspaper down. 'And your father in the middle of it, Stan.'

There was a telephone sitting on the desk – just another symbol of how far the Daughters of Salvation had come from its humble beginnings in a disused chapel. Her fingers dialled a number she knew by heart, then listened to the rumbling tones of one of the office clerks at the Buckingham Hotel. She did not hope for much when she asked to be put through to the Housekeeping Office – it was the wrong time of day, she thought, for the girls to be doing anything but marching through the guest

305

rooms – so her heart skipped a little when the very voice she'd been desperate to hear picked up.

'Housekeeping,' said Nancy de Guise.

'Oh, Nance,' Vivienne brokenly replied. 'Nancy, I don't know what to think. When . . .? When did you last hear from Raymond?'

Nancy, whose mind had been occupied with the same thoughts all morning, seemed to have more resolve than Vivienne. She always had. Even so, she faltered for too long before replying – and Vivienne understood, then, that Nancy, too, had barely snatched an hour of sleep during the long weekend; that she had been plagued by pictures of Raymond and Artie, cut off from the rest of the British Expeditionary Force, encircled or ensnared – or, though neither of them dared say it, eviscerated in some foreign field.

'It was weeks ago, before Norway,' said Nancy. 'But we're not alone in that, Viv. Nobody's heard from anybody. Nothing's getting through. It's—'

'Where are they, Nancy?'

Vivienne's voice had risen to such a pitch that, in the background, Nancy could hear Stan starting to cry.

'Where are they?' she repeated.

'I don't know,' said Nancy. 'Trapped behind the lines, stranded on a farm . . . I don't know, Vivienne. I'm sorry.' She paused. 'I suppose they could be anywhere at all . . .'

Gunfire sputtered across the rooftops, shattering tiles and brick.

Private Raymond de Guise threw himself to the ground. He could hear the sound of two dozen other soldiers crashing down at his side. In that moment, his face buried in the cobbles of a

French market square – where, mere months ago, citizens had sat, peacefully drinking wine and enjoying the long summer evenings – all he knew was that he had not been hit. The countless bodies around him might have either been taking shelter, or disgorging their life's blood onto the stones.

'Artie?' he called out, when he dared. 'Artie, are you there?'

'You're damn right I am,' Artie replied. Raymond felt a hand grapple for his, wrenching his wrist. 'There are barricades at the end of the row. French manned. You see them?'

Raymond dared to lift his head. Artie, who had shuffled stealthily to his side, was directing his gaze along the long barrel of the road. At its apex, a makeshift barricade of sandbags and packing crates blocked the route ahead. There was a flash of light from one of the sandbag turrets, and then the air was alive with gunfire once again.

Artie spread himself flat against the ground.

'That's the French, returning fire,' Raymond realised. 'Boys!' he called out. 'At the first break in the fire, we run for it!'

Raymond only hoped they'd listen. They'd lost their sergeant somewhere further back. Two dozen of them had been scythed apart from the rest some miles before reaching Dunkirk. It ought to have been easier here, among the streets – but there were too many hiding places, and too many unknowns. Raymond thought they were as likely to be cut down by French fire as by Nazis. From here to the beaches it was pot luck. A gambler's chance.

The gunfire stopped.

'Go!' ordered Raymond.

Halfway down the row, one of the privates plunged to his feet at Raymond's side. Raymond stopped to help him up – but the boy hadn't tripped over his shoelaces; he was dead, and would never see England again. Even so, Raymond wanted to bend down, hoist him over his shoulder and continue his charge – and would have done exactly that if, at the last moment, another hand hadn't flailed for his own, heaving him along the row.

'No heroics, Ray!' thundered Artie. 'Just get to the barricade alive. I don't want to be turning up at the Buckingham, telling them I left you behind!'

Suddenly, the gunfire from behind was met by gunfire from ahead.

'English!' Artie Cohen yelled, diving to the wall with the rest of the troop.

'*Anglais!*' cried Raymond.

Artie threw him one of his wolfish grins. 'There's you with your *learning*. They'll let you over the barricades, de Guise – you're practically one of them!'

There was a lull: a moment of simple, pure peace.

'Now,' said Raymond – and the brothers threw themselves at the sandbags and crashed together, in a tangle of arms and legs, on the other side.

The French soldiers manning the barricade barely saw them. The sandbags trembled every time the enemy's bullets cut into them; just another day, standing at the edge of Hell.

Artie had barely broken stride. Raymond rushed to catch him up. Beyond the barricade, what was left of the division was reassembling. They came down another narrow row, which turned suddenly into an incline. Raymond looked at Artie. Artie looked at Raymond. The Cohen brothers had played, as boys, down by the Limehouse docks. They knew the smell of the sea.

And there it was.

The division reeled out of the cobbled row and saw, for the first time, the beaches stretched out in front of them – the infinity of grey water that separated them from home. Scarcely thirty miles of water, but still an infinity.

The beaches were a swarming mass of soldiers.

Three days had passed since the evacuation order, and here was what remained of the British Expeditionary Force. Artie looked one way along the beach – up to the promontory where a single vast jetty, leading out to sea, was thronged with soldiers lining up to board the destroyer at its end. Raymond looked the other way – where, at low tide, fishing boats were left listing in the sand. Everywhere, the surviving divisions were gathered in groups – some on drills, most crashed out, sprawled across the sand.

An explosion tore across the beach. Raymond ducked by instinct; Artie turned his shoulder against the blast. It had been too far away to deal them any damage – but, further down the beaches, one of the divisions was in disarray. There came roars from up above as three Stukas – the gleaming new attack aircraft of the Luftwaffe – soared out from their inland base and unleashed their shells. A wall of sea spray, a hundred feet high, eclipsed the jetty for long enough to make Raymond think it was destroyed. Then it reappeared through the settling sea – minus half of its soldiers, who had crashed into the unforgiving waters.

'Come on.' Raymond marched down, onto the sands, his eyes on the heavens above. 'Look,' he said, 'one of ours . . .'

Three RAF Spitfires had appeared, in formation, from the furthest skies. They ripped overhead, then disappeared into the artillery fire above Dunkirk.

*A year ago*, thought Raymond as he led the survivors into the throng, *I'd never held a gun, never truly feared for my life.*

His world had been populated by sidesteps and oversways, fleckerls and open promenades; now it was the Spitfire and the Messerschmitt, the forced march and bayonet. Sometimes, he still marvelled at the madness of it.

He turned on the spot. The task seemed too vast. On the horizon, waiting in the water, he saw two other destroyers. But it would never be enough. There were nearly half a million who needed rescue – and nobody, yet, dared wonder what would become of the French.

Four months of empty patrols and fortifications. Now this. Was a war really lost as easily?

'Mr de Guise!'

The voice had come from somewhere in the crowds. He tried to pick it out, but all his attempts were futile.

'Mr de Guise, it's you!' cried a beanpole of a boy, a young private with his face smeared in ash and blood, who lifted himself from the sand where he'd been sitting, and reeled towards Raymond. 'Mr de Guise, it's me – Billy!'

At first, Raymond had only seen the dirt. It was so difficult to think of anyone, here on this beach, as an individual. They were but ants, and about to be destroyed.

Then he focused on the boy's eyes. He'd have recognised those eager, earnest eyes anywhere.

'Billy Brogan,' he whispered.

The boy threw himself at Raymond, and Raymond held him fast. In the corner of his vision, he saw Artie and the rest of the division scouting the beach, trying to judge their place, trying to make contact with a commanding officer.

'What happened to you?' Raymond asked.

'I was the last one, Mr de Guise. We were at Lille. The rest of my unit died or scattered.'

Raymond gazed up and down the beach. 'Two weeks since the invasion,' he whispered.

'What will they think of us, back home?'

Raymond recognised that fear; somewhere along the way, he'd let go of all the rhetoric about returning a hero.

'Let's just get there first, Billy.'

'But . . . how, Mr de Guise? Look at us. Look how many there are. And—'

Billy was cut off as the roar of another Stuka split the skies over the water. This time, though the soldiers all threw themselves into the sand, its shells exploded in the water. A raging maelstrom reared up, then died again.

'Where's the RAF?' Billy asked.

'They're up there,' said Artie, who had reappeared at Raymond's side. 'They won't let you down, boy.'

Raymond took a deep breath. 'Stick with us, Billy. We'll find a way, do you hear me?'

'Across the wild blue sea,' sighed Artie – though even he lacked conviction now.

'Billy,' said Raymond, 'I promise you I'll stick with you. That's my oath – do you hear me? But if there's anything you want to say – anything you want to tell your ma and your pa, and all those brothers and sisters of yours – now's the time to say it. Have you got any paper in your pack? An old envelope?'

Billy's pack was still on his shoulder. He hoisted it up.

'Then write to them, Billy. Artie, you too. I'm going to write to Nancy right now.' He looked upwards. 'If the skies let me.'

311

The other boys in the division were drawing nearer, too. Some of them, Raymond noted, were barely half his age – and yet, they all had become veterans in the last two weeks.

'Look to the ocean, boys. You can almost see the cliffs. On a sunny day they'd be there, a blur on the horizon. That's where we're going. That's where we're headed together – every man among us. I'll raise a glass with you on the other side. You can bring your sweethearts to my ballroom.' He summoned up a smile – he did not know how, for there hardly seemed one within him – and finished, 'Just one more day, boys. Just a few more hours. Gather your wits and gather your guns. We're going back home.'

To Nancy de Guise, the days had become interminable.

She'd slept in the Housekeeping Lounge last night. She hadn't meant to – though she'd thought of it too many times, trudging back to the empty house in Maida Vale and eating alone, with only the echo of Raymond's voice for company. Last night, she'd simply sunk into one of the armchairs in the lounge and closed her eyes. She hadn't known it was morning until Mrs Moffatt's hands were upon her, gently waking her up. The tea was already brewed, which meant the older woman had come in some time before.

'It won't be the last time you sleep here, Nancy, my girl, but there are beds aplenty in this hotel.'

'I'm sorry, Emmeline.'

Mrs Moffatt smiled, sadly. 'There's no need to be.' Then, without any warm-up or warning, she folded her arms around her in a deep hug. Nancy, who hadn't known a mother since she was eight years old, took a moment to lean into it. Only then did she allow herself to feel the older woman's embrace. 'You don't know anything yet. None of us do.'

The morning's newspapers were on the trolley by the door, those few that were not designated for deliveries to the guests. Mrs Moffatt waddled over and lifted up a copy of the *Daily Mail*. ARCHBISHOP LEADS PRAYERS FOR OUR SOLDIERS IN PERIL, read the headline – but Nancy didn't want to hear it.

'I've read too much,' she said. 'I just need to work.'

Mrs Moffatt understood that need more than most.

'History repeats itself in this Housekeeping hall,' she smiled sadly. 'My Jack used to send letters here, for me, during the Great War. Me and the girls would pore over them at breakfast. He was quite a romantic soul. And then, suddenly, he didn't write anymore. And that was the end of that.' Mrs Moffatt realised she had wandered into a memory of her own, and stopped when she saw Nancy's crestfallen face. 'It doesn't mean it's like that for you. Raymond's a brave man. One of the best. He's coming home for you, Nancy.'

*Random chance*, thought Nancy. *The hand of fate.*

There were so many things out of her control – but at least, now, the doors were opening for breakfast, her girls were flocking through, and she could throw herself into her work.

By the time evening came around, and Nancy was ready to go home, the discomfort of the night was catching up with her. At least, for a time, the Housekeeping Lounge was empty. She retired there again, studiously avoiding the newspapers still lurking there – with their news, out of date in the moment it was printed, now like ancient history – and sank into the armchair she'd slept in, promising herself she would not do so again. She realised, then, that it was the idea of the empty bed at home that was troubling her the most. She hadn't thought about it, not until the Low Countries were overrun, not until the British Expeditionary Force was routed; but now, the prospect of the emptiness felt like some sort of omen, a promise for the future. The longer she could put it off, the better.

The Housekeeping door opened, and there stood Rosa.

'Mrs Moffatt thought I'd find you here, Nance,' she said gently, coming to sit by her side. 'You fancy some company? Some crumpets? Some tea? Me and the girls upstairs, we wondered if you might want to join us. Mary-Lou has got the backgammon board out.' Rosa paused. 'Now, I know what you're thinking – and no, you're not *one of the girls* anymore. Well, we don't care about that. You're our friend. You're *my* friend. You've been good enough to me this year, Nance. Let me be good to you back?'

Nancy felt blown open. Even Rosa's gentle affection was like a gale tearing through her. Everything felt so intense.

'Come on, Nance. I don't have Frank to keep me company tonight. He trotted off down to Rye after lunch. Two days of tuition with Miss Marchmont – Marcus Arbuthnot practically ordered it. "Smarten yourself up, Nettleton. Elegance and poise." Now, I don't understand why Frank can't go in the ballroom just the way he is – but, well, I've never had the same kind of tastes as those whose beds we change, have I, Nance? But he's there now – and, if I can't have one Nettleton, another will have to do. You coming?'

Rosa had reached out her hand. Nancy was grateful for it; she was too dog-tired to consider standing herself.

'Thank you, Rosa,' she said – and, together, they left the lounge behind.

They were almost at the service stairs when one of the pages scuttled past.

'Metropolitan Police again,' he grinned. 'They've swarmed all over reception. I'm off to fetch the lads. They've got Mr Ashworth escorting them to the Candlelight Club.'

The young man was as full of joy as a schoolboy seeing one of his masters getting into trouble. Nancy and Rosa watched as he hurtled off.

They were about to climb the stairs when a deep, heavy voice sailed around the corner.

'The back stairs please, sirs. I'm sure you'll appreciate the need for decorum.'

'Decorum's one thing,' returned another voice, 'but this is police business.'

'This way please, sirs.'

Rosa seemed rooted to the spot. Nancy had to draw her away as Mr Ashworth, from the reception desks, strode purposefully into view, trailing four police officers in his wake. From the strident fury in his steps, Nancy knew that he was only marching forwards with such force to maintain the pretence that he was the one leading the procession; had he broken stride for just a second, the police officers would have surged on alone.

Mr Ashworth fixed Nancy with a look as he passed.

'Fetch Mr Knave – at once!' he commanded.

Nancy said, 'But where—?'

'There was no answer at his office door,' Mr Ashworth called over his shoulder, as he reached the landing above. The police officers were parallel with Nancy and Rosa now; her eyes were drawn to the handcuffs hanging from the first officer's belt. 'Perhaps his rooms? Please, Mrs de Guise.'

As the policemen passed out of sight, their heavy footsteps sounding on the stairs above, Rosa's eyes goggled. She was about to take flight, up to the Buckingham's uppermost storey – where the hotel director kept his own quarters – when Nancy grabbed her by the hand.

'No answer at his door doesn't mean he isn't there,' she said. Some strange instinct had told her it was the better bet. 'Come on, Rosa, quickly now!'

Some moments later, gasping for breath, they reached the end of the hall where the hotel director's office lay. The door was shut fast – but, just as Nancy had predicted, light glimmered from underneath. She knocked gently; then, when there was no response, she knocked more firmly still. After the third time, she reached for the handle and tentatively pushed open the door.

There was Walter Knave, sleeping at his desk as he did so many evenings, his breast rising raggedly up and down and his fingers twitching as if in some fever dream.

Nancy was rooted to the spot, Rosa clamouring at her back. For the very first time, she felt all her sympathies rushing out to the man. She had a fleeting image of the demons that troubled him as he slept: Lord Edgerton's hands closing around him; Lord Edgerton's words, whispered into his ear. He'd done what any godfather would have done; he'd protected his family, in the only way he knew how. And he'd been paying the price for it ever since. How many times had she heard the cruel whispers about him in this hotel? His age. His infirmity. How unfit he was to lead. None of it seemed right, tonight. If he was weak at all, it was a weakness in his heart, that he'd been blind to the consequences and needed to protect the people he loved. In a world full of untrustworthy blackguards, there was such a thing as too much trust.

'Mr Knave?' she ventured. The man slept on, turning fitfully. 'Mr Knave, are you there?'

'Oh, for heaven's sake,' said Rosa. 'We're missing all the action!'

She took Nancy by the elbow, hoisted her backwards, then scurried forwards to rap her knuckles on the desk with such force that Mr Knave erupted out of sleep in a wild panic.

By the time he'd come to his senses, Rosa was back at the door, making it seem as if they'd simply knocked.

'Mrs ... Mrs de Guise?' Walter Knave stammered. 'What's the—?'

'It's the Candlelight Club,' said Nancy, before he could go on. The fewer questions she received about his rude awakening, the better. 'I think you'd better come.'

It took them an age. Mr Knave was too frail for the stairs, so they stepped into the golden cage of the guest lift together and ascended slowly.

On the third storey, the Candlelight Club was lit up, according to its name, with the flames of a hundred flickering candlesticks. The blackout boards were already in the windows, the guests taking cocktails there cocooned from whatever was happening in London tonight – but the boards could not protect them from what was happening within. By the time Nancy led Mr Knave – still scouring the sleep from his eyes – to the door, the voices were already thundering inside. Diego, the cocktail waiter, had shepherded various guests away to the relative sanctuary of the bar – while, in the centre of the club, the clot of police officers had arranged themselves, in a circle, around one of the tables.

The voice admonishing the police officers was unmistakable to Nancy. It was unmistakable to Mr Knave, too. It was the voice that had been whispering to him for years. The devil's voice issuing him every command.

'Should you try to put a hand on me one more time, gentlemen,' declared Lord Edgerton, 'your positions in this city will be forfeit. Under whose authority do you dare to suggest—?'

'It's the authority of His Majesty's government,' the lead officer replied, with the air of a man who has doggedly said the same thing, over and over, to a truculent child. 'In full accordance with Defence Regulation 18B, sir.'

'Eighteen B?' repeated the man at Lord Edgerton's side – the weaselly little writer Adalbert Grice. 'It's designed for the Irish, you fool – the dirty little saboteurs! Enemies of the state, you fool! You can't come for us. I'm a mere writer. *This* man has a title!'

'Nevertheless, sir.'

Nancy had never heard such gravity imported to two such insignificant words.

*Nevertheless, sir*, she thought.

Walter Knave hovered on the threshold of the Candlelight Club. He had the appearance of a man at the circus, the spectator to a marvellous illusion he was quite unable to figure out. He turned, feverishly, to Nancy and said, 'Who summoned them?'

Nancy replied, 'I don't know, sir,' – but, no sooner had the words left her lips, then all the pieces fell into place and, at last, she understood.

*I summoned them*, she thought. *Or rather – John Hastings summoned them, and I gave him the powers to do it. The names from the guest list, the times and dates of their soirées in the Candlelight Club.*

And . . .

*Maynard Charles*, she smiled, keeping the thought to herself. *Still championing the Buckingham, still fighting for its survival as a force of good, all these months after he left.*

Walter Knave reeled forwards into the Candlelight Club, reached for the rack of newspapers by the bar, and pulled one out.

'They arrested Mosley last week,' he said, thumbing through the pages in search of a story. 'They took Archibald Ramsay the same day. Well, Mr Churchill hasn't been messing around, has he? No more tolerating the dissenters. No more room for other voices at the table. We're at war, girls. It's us or it's them.'

He looked up from the newspaper, across the darkened club, and saw Lord Edgerton and Adalbert Grice rising from their seats. Lord Edgerton might have towered above the police officers around him, but there was no doubt, now, who was corralling who.

'But Lord Edgerton – why him . . .?'

*Because of the sanctuary he was giving them*, thought Nancy.

*Because of the dinners and the gatherings; the suppers and cocktails and quiet ententes.*

*Because the Buckingham Hotel is a nexus, where people meet and alliances are built, where decisions are made, where wealth can be wielded to wreak changes in the world.*

Though Lord Edgerton might not have stood on a podium and pronounced his fascist ideals like Oswald Mosley and the Right Honourable Archibald Ramsay, he was as guilty as the rest of them; he wanted this hotel to be the oil in the machine.

The police officers had started marching towards the doors now. Nancy and Rosa scrabbled backwards, leaving Walter Knave to stand alone.

At least Lord Edgerton had ceased his diatribe. Too late, he had decided that dignity was the best defence. He was holding his head high as he came to the entrance. The same, however, could not be said of Adalbert Grice; the man fidgeted and muttered, cursed and spat as the police officers shepherded them on.

'Mr Knave,' Lord Edgerton declared as they left the club, 'I'll have this sorted by midnight. Prepare me a suite for next Saturday night. My wife Madeleine and I should like to take a turn around the Grand Ballroom. This little situation will blow over by then. I assume, of course, that you will testify as to my character at whatever tribunal these fools hold.'

Walter Knave didn't get the chance to answer. Nancy was not sure he even had the words.

One of the officers said, 'I'm afraid this is more grave than you've acknowledged, my lord. Defence Regulation 18B demands your immediate incarceration as a person of hostile associations. You're to spend tonight at His Majesty's pleasure in Wandsworth. You'll be there for some days, my lord.'

They had already marched him past Walter Knave, rounding the corner towards the head of the service stairs.

'Preposterous!' Lord Edgerton railed. 'I shall have to inform my wife!'

'Oh, that won't be necessary,' one of the officers said. 'I believe she herself was arrested some hours ago.'

Nancy had not mistaken the way Walter Knave's face had paled. To wake from a nightmare, and find yourself in a dream – nothing, it seemed, was real anymore.

She and Rosa followed him back to the guest lifts, and rode down to the hotel reception – just in time to see the officers of the Metropolitan Police emerging from the back hall.

Faces watched from every corner. Too many hotel pages had gathered by the obelisk for it to have been mere coincidence. Marcus Arbuthnot and Karina Kainz were standing at the ornate archway that led down to the doors of the Grand. Concierges and clerks manned the check-in desks in unnecessary numbers.

Nancy was still standing at Walter's side when Mr Ashworth reappeared and marched over.

'Mr Knave, we're at risk of making the newspapers ourselves. Oughtn't we order them to leave by the tradesman's entrance?'

Walter Knave was lost in a reverie. Nancy was not mistaken – the corners of his lips had twitched upwards in a smile.

'The tradesman's entrance?' he idly wondered. 'Oh no, not at all. Let them sally out the front. Well, they're about their business now, aren't they? It would seem awfully rude to disrupt them.'

The police officers had to stop marching when they reached the revolving doors, because a flurry of guests, dressed for the ballroom, were arriving. Even from across the reception hall, Nancy could see Lord Edgerton's face purple with a rage he could do nothing about.

'Yes,' said Walter Knave softly, 'I should think we really will make the newspapers – but there's nothing to be done now, is there? No.' He smiled. 'Absolutely nothing at all.'

# Chapter Twenty

FRANK NETTLETON WOKE IN A bed that was not his own.
At least, this morning, he was not in the Brogan house,
number 62 Albert Yard. Yesterday, he'd woken before
dawn – only to hear the bitter words and screaming in the living
room below. Mr and Mrs Brogan had never fought, not in all the
time Frank had spent lodging there, but there had been so much
emotion in the air that he feared the very walls of the house were
trembling with the forcefulness of it. He'd tried not to listen – he
really had – but it was difficult not to hear the anger: Mrs Brogan
screaming at her husband that he didn't care; Mr Brogan, trying to quell her – but, in saying that she cared too much, only
opening the wounds even further. It had taken some time before
Frank realised they were not truly warring with each other; they
were simply scared, and rudderless, their minds spent with the
exhaustion of weeks of increasingly broken sleep. The torment
and fear of not knowing if Billy still lived; the agony of wondering if he'd ever return; the hazy thought, pieced together from
what little the newspapers were reporting, of him stranded on
the beaches at Dunkirk.

It had taken Mr and Mrs Brogan even longer to realise they
were not truly at odds. It was only as Frank stole down the stairs

and out of the back door, determined to climb over the fences and escape that way rather than sneak through the room where they were fighting, that they reached some oasis of calm. The last thing Frank had heard, before he slipped out, was Mr Brogan tenderly saying, 'He'll come home, sweetheart. I promise. He's our Billy. Our invincible Billy . . .'

Frank only hoped it was a promise Mr Brogan wouldn't live to regret.

Mr and Mrs Brogan's fear had surfaced, too, in Frank's nightmares. It had been some months since he'd last lain awake at night, his mind dominated by the guilt of not being out there, but all of the headlines about the BEF's race to the sea, the abandonment of Lille and the battles at Calais, had been preying on him for days. Not even two days away from the Buckingham Hotel, where the hallways throbbed with talk of so little else, were enough to whisk him away from it. Not even waking up here, in one of the many guest rooms at the estate of Miss Hélène Marchmont, could change the pattern of his thoughts.

He lifted himself from the covers. Miss Marchmont was an admirable tutor – she'd been one of the very best, her face gracing the covers of *Vogue* and *Harper's Bazaar*, her sophistication a legend of the Grand Ballroom in all the years she'd danced there. The benediction of Hélène Marchmont would make even the most unpolished dancer seem like a star. That had been her gift in the ballroom – to make the hotel guests, whether they were adept at the foxtrot or could barely put one foot in front of the other, feel like champions. Frank ought to have woken, thrilling for the day ahead.

But instead his mind was miles away, out across the ocean.

He lingered at the bedroom window, before venturing downstairs. You could not see the ocean from here, but Frank knew it was there. Seabirds arced and wheeled overhead, oblivious to the conflagration happening over the horizon. Rye Harbour itself was only a half-hour walk away. The long, rolling expanse of Camber Sands. Step into the water on one side, and it was just a sunny day at the beach; but on the other side, battle and death reigned supreme.

How was he meant to dance, in a world like this?

Hélène was waiting when Frank reached the bottom of the stairs. Until last year, when the estate had belonged to her late father, the manor house had carried with it the air of the nineteenth century. Since then, Hélène had set about its transformation. Still grand and palatial, now it seemed homely and inviting. All of the old family portraits had been taken from the walls, replaced, in part, by photographs of Hélène and her daughter Sybil – who, at five years old, was turning into an enthusiastic ballroom dancer herself. A single portrait of Sir Derek Marchmont remained, as a testament to the family that had been – but, dominating the hallway, was a coloured photograph of Hélène and Sybil, with Hélène's mother and aunt, both of whom now lived at the manor, and Sybil's other grandparents, Maurice and Noelle Archer. They'd been living in the old cottage in the grounds since the outbreak of war, having escaped their South London home.

Hélène was waiting in the drawing room – or, as she liked to call it, the Baby Grand. It was her little joke; Frank was the only person she'd tutored since leaving the Buckingham Hotel nearly two years ago. For Hélène, the ballroom belonged in the past. They had once called her the Ice Queen of the Grand, but that description had never quite made sense to Frank; yes, she had a kind of glacial beauty – with short cropped hair, so blonde it was almost white, and pale blue eyes that looked like winter all year round – but, to him, she was as warm and comforting as any mother could be.

'Breakfast, Frank,' Hélène began, when she saw him appear. 'Some light ballast to see us through the morning. Come on – Aunt Lucy's prepared something in the breakfast room.'

Frank wasn't sure he could touch a thing, so it was only his good manners that made him follow his host. Inside the room, Hélène's middle-aged aunt was already feeding Sybil a breakfast of the year's first strawberries, small and sweet, and porridge oats. Sybil's looks favoured her father – a talented trumpeter with the Archie Adams Orchestra, now sadly deceased – with coils of black hair and rich brown eyes; but every wrinkle and expression on her face seemed performed in perfect imitation of her mother.

'Mama,' she said, with a face smeared in strawberry, 'why can't *I* dance today?'

'Because, my dear,' said Hélène, pinching her by the cheek, 'today it's Frank's turn.'

'Frank doesn't *look* like he wants to dance, Mama.'

At least this made Frank grin. He knew from spending so much time with the Brogan children that, sometimes, the most perceptive things came from the mouths of the young.

'I do,' he declared, trying to summon up the hunger for it. 'It's just . . . dark days, isn't it?'

Aunt Lucy clucked around Sybil, determined that she hear nothing of it – but Frank had no intention to speak further. He let a small bowl of porridge oats and stewed apple settle in his stomach and then repaired to the Baby Grand, where Hélène had set up the studio for that day's tuition.

*Put your heart in it*, Frank told himself. *There's nothing you can do. It's your chance – and Rosa was right, there's nothing to be ashamed of in seizing your chance.*

He tried to keep that in mind as Hélène had him take her in hold and perform simple waltz steps up and down the studio, moving from the bay windows in the front of the manor to the bay windows in the rear. From time to time, he was able to get swept up in it – to imagine that he was dancing with Hélène in the real Grand, and that all of London was gazing in admiration at how gracefully his body flowed. But it was a mirage that never lasted long. One moment, he was gliding across the imaginary Grand while the Archie Adams Orchestra played; the next, he was listening to Mr and Mrs Brogan fight, or being a pallbearer at Billy's funeral – all the while slowly dying inside.

'Frank,' Hélène said, at last.

They had reached the middle of the afternoon and, after a short lunchtime break, they were back in the Baby Grand – but Frank barely seemed able to hold his poise. And that, after all, was what he was here for: he already knew the steps, he was already familiar with the *feeling*; it was the elegance he lacked. He'd thought he could soak it up; let the grace scintillating off Hélène and find its way into him. But, by the look of her, even Hélène knew it was hopeless.

'When Raymond told me about you, it was with the sparkle of discovery in his eyes. "Yes," he said, "Frank's a little rough around the edges. But that's nothing that won't polish out of the boy." Raymond said he knew you'd be a star one day – he could see it in you. *You had heart.*' Hélène paused. 'But Frank – there's no heart today.'

Frank knew it. It was as if, no matter how much he *heard* the music, he wasn't truly *listening* to it. He was starting to make his apologies when Hélène said, 'You can't rely on sudden inspiration, Frank. If we waited for inspiration, dance would be a very rare thing. Do you imagine Archie Adams is *inspired* every time he sits at his grand piano? Do you imagine our old friend Louis Kildare is *inspired* every time he brings his lips at the saxophone reed? Was *I* inspired every day I stepped into the ballroom, to let some lecherous lord take me in his arms?'

Frank's mind coursed back through Hélène's history. Her last years at the Buckingham Hotel had been ripe with secrecy and lies. She'd had Sybil in secret, fearing for her place in the ballroom – and all because Sybil's father was black. She'd kept the secret bottled up, lived it every day – and every night her love for the ballroom had withered. Such was the cost.

'But I still put on a show, Frank,' she said, sensing what he was thinking. 'Every evening. Every demonstration. Every summer and Christmas ball. New Year's night. I wasn't pulsing with love and inspiration – though, Lord knows, there's enough to inspire you, the moment you step out into the Grand. But I summoned it up from somewhere deep inside. Elegance and poise have to be worked for, Frank. You have to reach for them. But hunger and inspiration can be fleeting things. They'll rear up inside you here and there, but you can't sustain that kind of passion all day and night. If you don't learn to summon it from somewhere deep within, you won't last long in the ballroom. That's the cold and brutal truth of it.'

'Do you mean I should just . . . fake it, Miss Marchmont?'

'If you must. Oh, Frank, I was faking it for most of my career. But there's a funny thing that happens, after that first dance. Sometimes, I'd go into the Grand feeling bitter and dejected with the world – feeling *tired* to my very soul … and then the lights would go up, and the music would play and, more often than not, I'd start to feel some flicker of it again. Then I had something to latch on to. Then I wasn't really faking.' She paused. 'Frank, there's more emotion in the world than there's ever been. If you want a career in the ballroom, you have to find a way to harness it – to channel the goodness in the world, and leave the rest at the doors.'

Frank had slumped onto Hélène's chaise longue.

'I think I understand, Miss Marchmont.'

'There are still six weeks to the Summer Ball.'

He nodded.

'I'll help you,' she told him, 'but I can't carry you the whole way. Frank, whatever's plaguing you right now, you're going to have to find a way.'

There was no more dancing after that. Frank was certain Hélène would have waltzed on if he had wanted, but the feeling in the air was much the same as when the lights went down in the Grand Ballroom – so he made his farewells, thanked Hélène for the promise she'd made to see him again soon, and tramped out across the manor house grounds.

The fresh air was a tonic. So were Hélène's words. If what she was saying was true, Frank reflected, then it gave a man control: he didn't have to ride his luck, *hoping* that tonight he would feel the emotion necessary to make an impression in the ballroom; he could reach, somehow, for the passion. Almost …

328

manufacture it. He could set aside what was happening in the world beyond the ballroom doors, and just inhabit a simple, perfect moment in time.

The bus that would take him back into Rye was a long time in coming. The afternoon had grown pale by the time it arrived. On one of its seats there was a copy of that day's *Daily Express*.

### BEF FIGHTS DOWN NARROW
### CORRIDOR TO DUNKIRK
### MARINES ENTRENCHED ALONG THE COAST

'Down a rapidly dwindling corridor,' Frank read, 'thirty miles at its widest, the BEF and its French allies are smashing a way to the sea in the most glorious rearguard action of any war.'

He had to stop; his heart was beating too wild a percussion. His eyes roamed further down the page.

### HEROISM WORTHY OF TRADITIONS!

*Heroism*, he thought – and here was he, learning elegance and poise.

The bus came to a stop. Frank knew he ought to jump out here, with the station nearby. In a few hours, he'd be back at the Buckingham Hotel. He'd scavenge something from the kitchens to take home to Mr and Mrs Brogan and tell them that everything was going to be all right. *Heroism . . . worthy . . . of . . . traditions.*

*But it wouldn't do*, he thought.

So he rode the bus onwards.

Rye Harbour was the end of the line, only fifteen minutes further on. At least, here, he could see the sea. The late afternoon sun had broken through the clouds – and Frank tramped through the cobbled village until he reached the long, golden stretch of Camber Sands. On the water's edge, he stood and stared. Frank didn't often pray, but he did so now. He prayed for Billy and Raymond de Guise. He prayed for the rest of them, all the untold thousands, stranded across the water. And he prayed, too, for his own spirit and soul. *Let it all not be in vain*, he thought. *Let Billy come back to his parents. Let Raymond come back to Nancy. Let the world keep on turning, from the dark and back to the light.*

If only there was some way he could help. Some way better than prayers . . .

Frank left the water's edge only when his stomach started putting up a protest. Tramping back into the village, seeking a place to find something to eat – seaside chips would always take him back to his childhood, and that time Nancy had taken him all the way out to Blackpool to see the illuminations – he felt adrift, cut off, as if he was walking in some other world altogether.

At first he did not see the men in uniform – not until he was walking towards the jetties, and almost upon them. A burly man shouldered past, sending Frank spinning – and when Frank picked himself up, they had already marched on, halloing an elderly fisherman prising the barnacles off his boat. Frank watched them with a strange detachment: *they're Royal Navy*, he thought, *and yet miles away from the battle.* Miles away – just like Frank Nettleton himself.

There was activity on the jetties. Frank looked up, to see one fishing boat already out past the jetty's end and taking to open water. *Too late in the day to fish*, Frank thought, but he scrambled on, past the jetty and reaching the outskirts of the town.

The fish and chip shop had its door propped open, and out of it rolled the divine smells of cod and scallop, whiting and hake. Frank had some coppers weighing down his pockets, and didn't realise how famished he was until he was holding a newspaper cone filled with chips, drenched in salt and vinegar.

He was still at the counter, sorting out his coins, when a fisherman obviously familiar to the shop barrelled in and put in an order.

'For me and the lads,' he said. 'We're setting out.'

The man at the fryer shook his head in what Frank thought was a kind of weary admiration.

'Are you sure, Harry?'

'Too bloody right I am,' the man named Harry replied. 'Seeing as what we've been summoned. And those navy sods aren't getting a hold of the *Camber Queen*. If I leave it any longer, they'll have her requisitioned. If she's going to risk being scuttled in the Channel ... Well, let's just say, I'd rather take that risk myself than let somebody else take it for me.' He stopped. 'I was in France for the last war, Ralph – just the same as you. I won't leave those poor bastards on those beaches if I can help it.'

'Harry, these are on me,' the shop owner said, and started filling yet more newspaper cones.

'Best last meal on earth, mate.'

'Well, best of luck then, Harry.'

And the old fisherman left.

Frank was still counting out his coppers. His eyes flashed around.

'What's happening?' he asked.

'Where've you been, boy? Got that head in the sand, have you?'

Frank remained dumb.

'They're getting our boys off the beaches. It's all hands on deck. Navy's been up and down the coast today, snaffling up every boat they can. They've already got them sailing out of Ramsgate and Dover. There's not many've handed their boats over so easily, though. A fisherman's boat is his soul. You don't let somebody else sail your soul into battle.'

Frank whispered, 'They're going . . . to France?'

'Every man of them,' said the shop owner, 'and may the Lord be with them. Hey!' he called out – because Frank had hurtled out of the shop. 'I owe you a ha'penny!'

Frank was scattering chips behind him as he cantered after the fisherman the shop-owner had called Harry. By the time he caught up with him, the older man had already reached the jetty and swung aboard his boat, a small vessel painted in royal blue and with the legend CAMBER QUEEN stencilled on her sides in glossy white paint. To Frank, who knew little about fishing boats – except for those day trips out to Morecambe – she looked an ancient vessel, lovingly cared for by her owner's hands.

Harry had a trapdoor open at the boat's stern – by the scent of it, checking the fuel left in the tank. Inside the covered wheelhouse, a younger man – Harry's son, perhaps? – was heaving crates into place. Every one of them was filled with orange life jackets. Yet more crates were piled on the jetty.

'You heading out?' Frank cried.

He had to say it twice and had to place his foot on the *Camber Queen* itself before the grizzled captain, Harry, looked at him with an inscrutable expression.

'Get your foot off her, boy. Haven't you any sense?'

'You're going out there,' Frank breathed. 'You're going to Dunkirk.'

'That's right, we are,' said the younger man, who'd stuck his head out of the wheelhouse, 'so you'd better get yourself back on the jetty. There's men in need out there – they're waiting for us.'

Nine months of tortured thoughts were tumbling through Frank. Nine months of distraction and disappointment. Nine months of incandescent doubt.

And yet, here he was, standing on the brink of something – as ordinary people, people just like him, were about to play their part. Fishermen didn't get conscripted. Fishing was reserved. But now the chance was upon them. The moment was here. And they were seizing it.

He looked out at the sea and felt a plunging in his stomach; he'd never so much as swum a stroke in his life. But he had a dancer's legs. He had balance. He was . . . brave.

Wasn't he?

'I want to come.'

'Get out of here, boy! We've got to cast off!'

'You're not listening to me,' said Frank. The words poured out of him; the lies, too, because he knew it was what he needed to say. He wasn't sure where any of it came from. He just felt the conviction, possessing him like a religious fervour. 'I'm a fisherman's son. Morecambe Bay. Grew up on the boats all my life. Look, you could use an extra pair of hands out there. If it gets rough, you'll need somebody who can . . .'

The captain looked at the younger man; the younger man, seeing the sense in it, shrugged. And that, it seemed, was agreement enough.

'You do as I say, understand?' Harry said.

Frank nodded.

'What's your name?'

'Nettleton,' Frank replied. 'Frank Nettleton.'

The captain had cast off. Moments later, the roar of an engine announced the boat coming to life.

Frank felt the world judder underneath him as they moved away from the jetty. The first swell of the water was gentle; it was the second that caught him unawares. Only balance and poise kept him on his feet.'

'Well, Frank Nettleton,' the captain said, 'grab yourself a jacket. You're going to war.'

# *Chapter Twenty-one*

# EVENING STANDARD

31ˢᵗ May 1940

~

TENS OF THOUSANDS SAFELY HOME ALREADY!

THROUGH AN INFERNO OF BOMBS AND SHELLS, THE
BEF IS CROSSING THE CHANNEL FROM DUNKIRK – IN
HISTORY'S STRANGEST ARMADA

Under the guidance of the British fleet, under the protection of the Royal Air Force, a large proportion of the
British Expeditionary Force are returning from the
beaches of Dunkirk, as hundreds of south coast fishermen lend their vessels to the crusade to bring our boys
home. Tens of thousands of His Majesty's loyal forces
have already been ferried home to Ramsgate in Kent,
after long days of fighting their way back to the coast.
Tired, dirty and hungry – they are nevertheless our
unbeatable boys . . .

*Unbeatable*, thought Vivienne Cohen as the black cab she was riding in sailed into Berkeley Square.

'Do you hear that, Stan? *Unbeatable*.' Stan looked at her from her arms, his big, wide eyes unable to comprehend the import in the words. 'Your father's unbeatable, Stan. You'll be seeing him soon.'

She stepped out into late spring sunshine, but could hardly feel the warmth as she looked up at the hotel. The scene of so many of her past disgraces had haunted her throughout the last year. Every time she saw it, she felt herself tugged back in time to a Vivienne she hardly recognised. But today the feeling of seeing the Buckingham was different, somehow. As she hurried along Michaelmas Mews, pushing Stan's pram in front of her, it was not a chaos of old memories that stole up on her, but a sense of freedom – a sense of victory, perhaps.

Her stepfather's shadow no longer haunted this place, and it had changed everything.

*The Times*, of course, had been more interested in Oswald Mosley being marched into the back of a police vehicle and remanded at His Majesty's pleasure. *The Daily Telegraph* and the *Daily Mail* had led with stories of the Right Honourable Archibald Ramsay, Great Britain's only MP – *so far*, thought Vivienne, darkly – to have found himself put under arrest as a traitor to his nation. But among the reports, listed with only the briefest of mentions, had been the name Lord Bartholomew Edgerton. According to the report, he was incarcerated in HM Prison Brixton. *And there he could rot*, thought Vivienne. They'd arrested his lickspittle Adalbert Grice at the same time. Some reports said that a warrant had been served on that delightful fellow Arnold Leese. All across the United Kingdom, they were being plucked off, one at a time – and Vivienne could not have been more proud of the small role she had played in directing their attentions towards her stepfather. She'd been free of his control for more than a year now; but it was only when she stepped into a Buckingham Hotel that had been similarly freed that she felt the enormity of it. How the world kept changing.

She was savouring that triumph as she wended her way through the back halls and approached the Housekeeping Lounge. But she was feeling the mounting dread as well. She'd tried to keep it at bay over the last few days. She'd tried to focus on what was happening directly in front of her: changing Stan; feeding Stan; filling in the ledgers at the Daughters of Salvation; talking to Warren Peel, Mary Burdett and all of her girls. But a mind could not be tricked as easily as that. The more she turned away from the newspaper headlines, the more they seemed to scream at her from every news-stand and corner shop she passed. The more she ignored the wireless sitting in the corner, the more her hands gravitated towards it, to hear the rich, rounded vowels of the BBC news.

She hadn't visited Alma or the rest of Artie's family in days. She'd wanted to, but she just couldn't bear it. Being in anyone's company was a danger. She felt she might crack. Even standing here, at the door to the Housekeeping Lounge, seemed a risk too far. She opened it – and there were Nancy, and Mrs Moffatt, just as they'd promised. Both strong women, Vivienne reflected, who had picked her up when she was at her lowest and put her back on her feet. Vivienne only prayed she wouldn't need that today.

Some of the other girls were here, too. Rosa, and some of the chambermaids, were coming off shift. Vivienne tried not to catch their eyes as she followed Nancy and Mrs Moffatt through to the office.

In Mrs Moffatt's office, the wireless was crackling. The steadfast voice of the BBC – preternaturally calm in the chaos.

'*First to return have been the wounded, but the able-bodied men of the British Expeditionary Force are at last being welcomed back to England. And yet the cost of an operation carried out in an inferno of bombs and shells is vast. The Royal Navy reports the loss of three destroyers in the Channel, along with auxiliary craft and a small steamer. The numbers of French and British personnel lost to the conflagration escalates daily. And, though the weather today turns foul, this is as much help as hindrance to the armada of tiny boats that have answered the king's calling and have, over the past days, been taking our boys off the beaches, one by one . . .*'

Mrs Moffatt turned the dial so that the newsreader's voice crackled into static, and then silence. She shuffled over to her desk – and, just when Nancy thought she was about to draw out a handful of barley sugars, she lifted three cognac glasses from the trolley instead. There was a half bottle at the bottom of her drawer.

'If ever a moment in life demanded more than barley sugars, girls, here it is.'

Glasses were poured. Vivienne, who had barely touched a drop since her Buckingham days, thought twice before she put it to her lips. But she did it all the same. Mid-afternoon, and she needed something to dampen her fears. So did Nancy.

'If the weather's foul, Emmeline, it might mean Malcolm isn't flying.'

Mrs Moffatt nodded. The girls in this room were two of the only people in the world who had heard the true story of Mrs Moffatt's lost son. She was grateful, now, that they knew – for too many airmen had already been lost over the Channel, and if anything was to happen to Malcolm, to grieve in silence would have been unbearable.

Vivienne whispered, 'You've heard nothing?'

Nancy shook her head. 'If he was home, he'd have been in touch. Or somebody would.'

'I keep telling myself, it doesn't mean bad things. There are tens of thousands home, but there are tens of thousands still on the beaches. It doesn't mean—' Vivienne broke off; Stan had started whimpering, and she went to lift him out of his pram. 'I wish they'd *say* something. But you listen to the BBC or read the newspapers and it's all just Lille and Boulogne and . . .' Vivienne snorted at herself. 'It isn't Artie or Raymond.'

There was silence.

'The stars might shine on you yet, girls,' said Mrs Moffatt – and, in her head, she was twenty-three years back in time, standing grief-stricken in the Housekeeping Lounge, her heart filled with the knowledge that her Jack wasn't coming home. 'It isn't over by a long chalk. You'll hear a knock one day soon, and go to the door – and there they'll be.'

As if in answer to Mrs Moffatt's words, there came a rapping on the office door – and, when it inched open, there stood Rosa.

'Come in, dear,' said Mrs Moffatt, 'come in.'

Vivienne was not sure why, but Rosa looked as frazzled as Nancy.

'No word?' Nancy began.

'Miss Marchmont left a message at the front desk. She's saying Frank visited, took his tuition, and left exactly on time . . . He just didn't catch his train.'

'And the Brogans?' said Nancy. 'Still nothing?'

'He hasn't been home, Nance.' Rosa hesitated. 'Nancy, I'm scared.'

Vivienne's eyes flashed around the room, taking in all the steely, unfaltering faces. There was a story here – something she'd missed.

She asked, 'What happened to Frank?'

Rosa and Nancy had drawn closer together.

'Frank went for tutoring this week, with Miss Marchmont. He didn't come home.' Nancy shook her head fiercely, as if denying some inner thought. 'But he'll be OK, Rosa. Whatever he's doing, wherever he is, he'll—'

'Oh, Nancy, *stop*!' The words tore out of Rosa; then, realising how she'd snapped, she brought a hand suddenly to her mouth. 'You know what's been going through his head all year. You know he thinks he's letting everybody down. He's down on the coast. I don't care that he went there for dancing – it's not what he's doing now! All he's wanted all year has been to prove himself, to stand up alongside Billy and Raymond and the rest.' She paused to take a deep breath. 'So that's what he's doing, isn't it? He's found his way to play his part. He's a dancer and a hotel page – and he's out there now, going to rescue his friends from the beaches. I know it, Nancy. I can feel it in my heart!'

The waves crashed and rolled.

*Dancing legs*, Frank told himself. *Dancing feet. You've got balance. You've got poise. Doesn't matter that your music isn't being played by the Archie Adams Orchestra. Doesn't matter that your real music, today, is crashing waves and roaring engines, the occasional Hurricane or Spitfire blasting overhead. You're here – and you're dancing, all the way to Dunkirk . . .*

340

The *Camber Queen* was a powerful little vessel. Its captain, Harry Reardon, was proud of the pluck she'd always shown; he'd just never imagined she'd have to show it in a situation quite like this. Still, his father had manned the lifeboat out of Rye harbour when he was a lad. Harry had always thought he'd do the same, when the time came to hand the *Camber Queen* down to his son Neville, now standing anxiously at the prow. Saving lives was in the Reardon blood. To ignore the calling would have been to ignore history. To ignore everything that was good and right in the world.

Frank didn't have a sailor's heart, but he knew how to do what he was told, and – so far, at least – his stomach hadn't betrayed him. They'd clung to the shore for miles, the coast peppered with other boats as they rounded Dungeness and, twenty miles later, reached the seas around Dover. Frank had never seen a collection of boats like this. Speedboats and fishing skiffs, pleasure yachts and sailing barges like he'd seen on the Thames. At Dover they set ashore, to refuel and take orders – but the Royal Navy were here, marching from boat to boat, sending crews packing (with train tickets home) and putting their own men on board. Requisitioned boats were being corralled into small flotillas, roped up to tugboats to save fuel for the crossing. Harry Reardon wanted none of this.

'Back on board,' he told his son, and Frank as well. 'We'll take no orders. If I've said it once, I've said it a hundred times – the *Camber Queen* needs us. There's not another who'll sail her.'

Boats were setting out from Dover. Boats were setting out from Ramsgate. Calais, directly across the strait, was under siege and constant bombardment – but now was the moment to set sail. Harry Reardon avoided the requisition officers for a second time and steered the *Camber Queen* away from the coast, as Frank Nettleton watched England diminish behind him.

*Keep your eyes forward*, Frank told himself. *Don't look back.*

Wise words, but he wished there was somebody else here to whisper them to him. He wished he didn't have to say them to himself. It was awfully hard to be brave, especially when the boat kept rising and pitching. Frank had never really thought about it before. Being brave took practice – just like dancing – and he'd never had the chance.

It wasn't until the white cliffs of Dover shrank to a stark white line behind him that he was gripped by the sudden fear that he might not be coming back; that, if he did not return, Nancy and Rosa would never know what had happened in his final hours. Those fears were almost too mountainous to conquer. The only way he could battle them back was by looking forwards and pretending those cliffs just didn't exist.

That worked – for a time.

The sea seemed vast. To a boy who had grown up in valleys and hills – and as a young man grown used to the small, dark spaces of the underground world – it seemed unnatural that such emptiness should go on forever. But, of course, it did not. It wasn't long before the sea was pockmarked with other boats. Wreckage, too. Silent and smoking, the fuselage of a downed aircraft stuck out of the water, its great hulk somewhere underneath. The *Camber Queen* sailed past it, but Frank's eyes would not leave it alone, even as they sailed.

'One of theirs, son,' Harry said gruffly, as he lifted himself from the wheelhouse. 'Something to be thankful for.'

'How far away are we?' asked Frank.

The captain looked at the sky, where the clouds were drawing in and the afternoon had started paling towards evening.

'I expect we're an hour from the beaches, boy. But, chances are, we'll be seeing something long before then.'

From that moment on, it was not the water that made Frank wary. The fear he'd been burying faded away – those nightmarish images of the boat upturned, and Frank flailing uselessly through the water, crying out that he wasn't really a fisherman's son, that he'd lied, that he didn't want to die here, so far away from the people he loved. Now his fears focused on what lay ahead. He started counting the minutes, then the seconds until they reached Dunkirk.

He needn't have bothered. They were still a distance away, too far to see anything but a smudge of land on the horizon, when the cacophony of the bombardment reached Frank's ears. Noises like that – like the earth being opened up, like the sky being racked apart – were unlike anything he had heard in his life. It was a cavalcade of thunder, relentless and fierce. There had been nights he'd woken, as a boy, to hear the storms breaking over the Lancashire hills. Back then, even ordinary thunder had seemed unearthly. So vast and unknowable. Now it was the same. Frank felt as small as he had ever felt. His knuckles whitened as he held on to the gunwale against the wild, urgent rolling of the sea.

The closer they got, the more boats appeared in the Channel around them. They were coming in convoy, not only from Dover but from Deal and Ramsgate and Margate, too – and here they converged, forming one raggedy armada as they approached the beaches.

'Captain!' Neville Reardon cried. 'Wreckage!'

The detritus of boats that had been here first was pockmarking the water – and, everywhere Frank looked, the sea roiled black where the oil pumping out of a vanquished naval vessel coloured the surface. The wreck of a destroyer was cresting out of the water like a mythical beast.

Some of the other boats had already heaved to, fishing men out of the water. The *Camber Queen* sailed on.

By now, Frank fancied he had started making out shapes on the beach. At one end of the harbour, a vast promontory stretched deep into the water – and on it huddled hundreds of men. Sometimes, great waves arced out of the ocean to swamp them – only to reveal them again, moments later. Up and down the beach: a black, milling mass, barely visible in the fading light.

Guttering engines roared up above. Frank looked up, to see three planes banking in from over the Channel. *English boys*, he thought. *The Royal Air Force.* They vanished again, somewhere over the beaches, and the cavalcade of thunder resumed.

'We've got to get down there,' Harry said, sticking his head out of the wheelhouse. 'Neville, take the wheel. Nettleton – start sorting out these life jackets. We'll need to move fast.'

'What's the plan?' Frank asked, heaving one of the crates away from the gunwale.

'No plan,' said the captain. 'We'll do what everyone else is doing. Just the very best we can.'

Harry was scanning the waters in the failing light. Frank followed his eyes. There were already boats bobbing close to the beaches. Frank saw men being heaved aboard. What he had taken for dark crests in the waves were actually the heads and shoulders of men standing chest-deep in the sea, steadfastly resisting each swell until it was their turn to come aboard.

'That way,' the captain said, and his son started bringing the boat around.

Frank gagged at the stench of oil in the air. Sometimes, as the boat drew nearer to the beaches – other small tugs and pleasure craft now looming up on either side – he looked up from his work and saw the silhouetted figures crowding the water's edge. The wreck of a fallen aircraft still burned somewhere up the beach. Flames danced around it like a funeral pyre.

Three hundred yards from the shore. Two hundred. One. Men were swimming out to meet them now. Frank heard the roar of mortar fire, plunged down to the deck, then scrambled back to his feet. There was no breath in his breast. There was only one thought in his mind. How was it possible that a world of fire and destruction existed only a short day's travel away from the Grand Ballroom? How did the beautiful and the terrible persist in the very same world?

'Take the rope, Nettleton – heave! These men need help!' Harry was at the gunwale, unspooling a great coil of rope. 'Heave to, Neville! No further! *No further!*'

The engines put up a guttering complaint, and Frank felt the boat judder and resist the waters underneath them. He scrambled up, took the end of the rope in his hands, and braced his feet against the deck. At least his body was built for this. *Balance*, he told himself. *Strength and poise.* Was it such a fancy to believe that all the years of his life had been building to this? Not the Grand Ballroom – but this moment, right here, on a foreign beach as far from home as he had ever been.

'Heave!' the captain thundered.

So Frank heaved.

One after another, half-drowned soldiers rolled over the gun-wale and onto the deck. Frank rushed to their sides, covering them in life jackets, pressing tin cups of hot, dark tea into their hands. Five men came aboard. Then ten. Then fifteen.

'Below!' the captain was roaring. 'Nettleton, get them below!'

There came the sudden scream of a banshee. Frank looked up – too late to see the German planes banking overhead. One second, he was standing there, cajoling the sodden soldiers down the narrow wooden stairs into the darkness of the *Camber Queen*'s hold. The next, a bomb had torn a hole in the ocean, and a great eruption of water rose up, monstrous and inhuman. Frank reeled. There was a second of perfect stillness, in which the torrent seemed frozen above. Then it came crashing down, a frothing, icy cascade over the top of the *Camber Queen*.

Frank was lifted from his feet.

He was drowning. Drowning in mid-air. His hands wind-milled, grappling for anything – and, in front of his eyes, all the years of his life rushed by. Nancy, leading him by the hand when he was small. Rosa, dancing in his arms across the spotlit floor of the Midnight Rooms. His first afternoon, demonstrating in the gilded world of the Grand . . .

Frank smashed up against the gunwale. All of the wind was driven from his lungs. He picked himself up, retching out the salt water he'd inhaled, only to find himself – by some miracle he did not understand – still on the deck of the *Camber Queen*. One of the soldiers had been swept over the other side. Frank lunged for a coil of rope, threw it down to him in the deeps. Then, with every muscle straining, he set about heaving him back on board.

The *Camber Queen* was already arcing around. When the sol-dier was almost at the gunwale, Frank reached out and took his hand. Pitching backwards, he pulled him to safety, then stood up and surveyed the seascape ahead.

The sea was on fire.

Somewhere beyond the *Camber Queen*, the waves themselves were turned to rippling flames. The falling incendiaries, the oil on the surface – all of it had come together and transformed the water. Against the encroaching blackness, it looked like a nightmare given form.

Frank turned to Harry Reardon, who was forcefully bustling through the rescued soldiers to fight his way into the wheelhouse.

'There's a clear way to the west!' Frank shouted. 'Captain, that way!'

Harry looked back, and followed Frank's gaze. Between the fields of frothing fire, there was a single channel of blackness. A pleasure yacht was sailing into it now. It looked as if it was entering a gate ringed in flames.

*But that . . .* thought Frank. *That was the way home.*

Nancy opened her eyes.

She hadn't meant to sleep here – but she had to admit that it felt good. Part of her had intended to go home with Vivienne, if only to sit and help her with Stan through this, the longest night of their lives – but Vivienne had decided to go to the old Cohen house instead, and perhaps that was right. Nancy herself, too afraid of what the emptiness of her home might portend, had awoken in the chambermaids' kitchenette. When she opened her eyes, she could hear the girls clucking around her.

'We thought we'd leave you sleeping, Mrs de Guise,' said Mary-Louise. 'What with everything that's been going on, we reckon you deserved it.'

Nancy wasn't sure what Mrs Moffatt would have made of this; probably it contravened all sorts of wisdom about how to lead their group of girls. But something about the smell of the place, something about the touch of the old sofa she'd slept on, made Nancy feel safe – as if, for one night, she belonged in a completely different time. Before war. Before loss. Before Raymond.

Rosa clattered into the room.

'Nance!' she cried out. And then, catching the looks from the other girls, 'Mrs de Guise, you've got to come.'

'What is it?'

Rosa stepped aside. Loitering, uneasily, behind her was one of the hotel's newest pages, a tousle-haired sixteen-year-old lad named Clarence.

'He's on the telephone, miss.' The boy swallowed. 'They're holding it at the desk.'

Nancy was on her feet in a second. 'Who?' she gasped.

'It's Frank, Nancy,' Rosa exhaled. 'It's Frank.'

Nancy sent Clarence ahead with an instruction to send the call through to the Housekeeping Office. By the time she got there, still feeling dishevelled, the telephone was already ringing. Nancy staggered into the darkness of the ill-lit office, Rosa on her heels all the way. She fumbled the receiver to her ear.

'Frank?'

His voice crackled down the line.

'Oh, Frank!' Nancy gasped. 'Frank, where are you?'

Rosa couldn't stand still. She was bouncing so feverishly from wall to wall that Nancy opened her arms and beckoned her down to the telephone, too.

'Frankie?' she trembled into the receiver.

Frank's words were frothing out of him. Nancy fancied she could only understand half of them.

'I'm in Ramsgate,' he was saying. 'Ramsgate in Kent. Oh, Nancy, you won't believe . . . but he's here and I'm here with him.'

'Who, Frank?' Nancy beseeched him. 'Who?'

'It's Billy,' Frank said.

There was silence in the Housekeeping Office.

'Billy?' Rosa whispered. 'Frank Nettleton, where have you been? What's going on? Is he . . .? Are you . . .?'

'I'm sorry, Rosa,' he said. 'I'll explain everything. But I'm all right. I promise – I'm all right. And Billy . . .' Frank tailed off. His voice seemed suddenly far away. The office door opened and there, in its light, stood Mrs Moffatt, her face etched with confusion and concern. 'He's hurt, he's in a bad way. But he's going to survive. There's too many didn't – but our Billy's going to be all right. He's going to be all right – and I'm bringing him home.'

June 1940

# Chapter Twenty-two

THE FIRST DAY OF JUNE. Summer in the air. The evenings were growing long and lazy in the heart of Mayfair. For those who stood on the balconies of their Berkeley Square town houses and took in the sight of a fading summer night, it was easy to forget that there were still a hundred thousand souls stranded on the beaches at Dunkirk; that the misfit armada of Royal Navy auxiliary craft, leisure yachts and Thames river steamers still ran the gauntlet of torpedo and air attack to rescue those who were left behind. Nightingales warbled and the first fledglings of the year were already taking flight.

The balmy summer night was showing the first intimations of dusk when the olive-green Rolls-Royce entered the square from Piccadilly and drew up outside the Buckingham Hotel's white marble colonnade. The first figure that stepped out of it had scrubbed himself clean but wore clothes dishevelled and torn; the second could hardly stand. His left trouser leg was cut open around the long wooden pole strapped as a splint to his bandaged shin – and he wore only one boot, for one of his feet was swaddled and braced in bandages too. This second man looked up at the hotel with an expression that spoke of homecoming. A yearning he'd had for nearly a year. He had to brace himself against the first young man as they stepped away from the colonnade. The driver of the Rolls-Royce hurried out of the front of the vehicle to take the wounded young man on his shoulder.

In this way, Frank Nettleton and Maurice Archer – father-in-law to Hélène Marchmont, and dispatched on this errand at her request – helped Billy Brogan along the edge of the hotel, and along Michaelmas Mews.

Nancy was waiting at the tradesman's entrance. Rosa was waiting too. The moment they saw Frank, they rushed to him with such force that, had it not been for Billy Brogan himself, they would have knocked him clean off his feet. As it was, they fell short, their eyes harbouring tears, and smothered him in kisses instead.

'Get off, get off!' Frank cried, battling them back. 'Oughtn't you to be saving your kisses for Billy here? Genuine war hero Billy Brogan, reporting for service?'

It was the sort of comment, filled with bolshiness and bravado, that the young Billy Brogan might once have made himself. But now he just stood there, hanging between Frank and Maurice, as the girls turned to look at him. *Their* Billy Brogan. Long-standing page and latter-day concierge. Loyal stalwart of the Buckingham Hotel. He looked, Nancy thought, five years older than when she'd last seen him. His hair, ordinarily wild, was cropped short and he seemed broader in the shoulder, fuller in the face. But it was his eyes that were truly different. They used to twinkle; now they just stared. Even when his lips twitched into a familiar smile, and he said – with the same roguish Irish brogue of old – 'Missed me, girls?' his eyes could barely muster a glimmer.

'Billy . . .' Rosa said, and her voice cracked in just the same way as it had when she saw Frank, 'Billy, you silly sod! Billy, look at you.'

Billy looked first at Maurice, and then at Frank.

'"Silly sod", she says. "*Silly sod.*" Ain't that a hero's welcome?'

'I'll show you a hero's welcome, Billy.' Rosa was trying to take him by the hand. 'You too, Frank – though I've words for you, once the hero stuff's out of the way. Going off to sea, Frank Nettleton! What were you thinking? What did you—'

'It's just as well he did,' said Billy. 'It was your gentleman dancer here who fished me out of the water. If he hadn't—' Now it was Billy's turn for his voice to crack. 'Ah, damn it, look at me. I've had enough salt water for a lifetime, girls – and here it is, leaking out of my blinkin' eyes.' He shook his head fiercely, like a dog determined to get dry. 'I could murder a cuppa. Could you girls get an invalid soldier a cup filled with sugar?'

'Well,' said Nancy, 'sugar's been on the ration books since January, Billy.' She smiled. 'But I reckon the Buckingham Hotel can spare a few spoonfuls for one of their own. Come on – you too, Mr Archer – we've got a bit of a spread.'

They had. At night, the Housekeeping Lounge ordinarily lay in a quiet slumber. This evening, however, its table was laid with jam and scones, fresh cream and stewed apples; a treacle pudding, spirited out of the Queen Mary kitchens when the head chef learned Billy Brogan was coming home. They'd all want to see him soon, Billy supposed – but, for now, this was enough. The smells of the Buckingham Hotel made him feel more like himself than he had since September. The sound of the footsteps ringing in the hall – or even the music softly drifting up from the Grand Ballroom, where the Archie Adams Orchestra was in full swing, and a dance troupe Billy would hardly recognise was on display for the guests.

*Home*, thought Billy. He'd go to his other home soon, of course. Show up on the doorstep, with Frank in tow, and fall into his mother's arms, just like any of the other younger Brogan children she was currently missing. Who knows, perhaps he'd even put his arms around his father and (Heaven forfend!) tell him that he loved him. Well, all of those old conventions could go to hell. Billy had tasted death in the water and—

*Death in the water.* No sooner had the words entered his mind, then he hardened. He'd been about to put a currant bun to his lips and savour its taste – it had been such a long time since he'd had a delicacy like this – but, suddenly, he was back there, in the roiling dark.

He put it down. He'd come home and the divine, heavenly honest-to-goodness *pleasure* of it was rushing through him. But he'd come out of Hell, and people he knew and loved were still out there, weren't coming back. There was a reason he'd come here first, before Maurice took him down to Lambeth and the comfort of his mother's arms. Because there were things he needed to say, while he still had the courage. Things he needed to tell them, before he finally crumbled. Now he looked from one face to another and wondered if he could do it at all. He looked, lastly, at Frank – and the thought entered his mind that he might let his friend tell it all, because Frank already knew. But that was cowardice speaking. So he drained his cup of tea (the sugar touched corners of him he'd forgotten existed) and said, 'Nancy, there's something you have to know.'

She must have been preparing for it, he thought, because her face did not blanch as she reached across the table for his hand.

He let her hold it, but only for the most fleeting of seconds. Then he ripped it away.

He was here to break her heart. He ought to be quicker about it.

'Nancy, I found Raymond on the beaches. Raymond and his brother, too. The rest of my unit was gone, wiped out before we reached the town. But there was Raymond. It was like a bloody . . .' His voice fractured, then knitted itself back together again. '. . . omen. I was going to be all right – because there was Raymond. We were all coming home. Buckingham boys together.'

Nancy's face was ghostly white. Billy looked at her and found he could hardly go on.

'Please,' he said, 'just hear me out. I'll answer everything, everything I can. But I've got to . . .'

*Purge myself of it*, he thought. *Rid myself of the terrible knowledge.*

'It was wild on the beaches, Nance. You wouldn't believe the noise. Out there, in the open, playing for time. Just, please. Let me explain . . .'

The Stukas roared over the beaches again.

Billy was still writing his letter home, messages for his mother and father, for Patrick and Roisin and Grace, all of the Brogan brood. He'd even sneaked in a message for Frank Nettleton – who was, no doubt, keeping his bed warm at home, helping his mother and father with all the little titbits Billy used to pilfer for them from the Buckingham kitchens.

Then the Stukas banked over the beaches, their terrible wailing sirens tearing holes in the sky. A hundred yards from where Billy sat, the ground erupted in a violent explosion, flinging one poor soldier up into the air and smearing him, in pieces, across the sand. Billy picked up his packs and staggered backwards.

'Mr de Guise . . .' He'd never get used to calling him 'Private', nor even just 'Raymond', not even out here. 'Where to?'

Raymond had been sitting on his pack, Artie beside him, all the rest of the unit spread out across the sand. The beaches were a milling blackness. Out on the mole – the breakwater at the harbour's edge – a thousand soldiers had formed lines, waiting to board the destroyer out in the water. But they were prioritising the wounded, the battle-scarred, the ones in desperate need of the Red Cross nurses on board the vessel. For the rest of them, the wait was interminable.

Night came on. Billy slept in snatches – something about seeing Raymond again had given him comfort enough to think he might risk it – but Raymond himself remained awake into the blackest hours. There was mist enough coming in off the sea, and enough cloud cover above to hope that the Nazi dive-bombers might give them a few hours' reprieve; but, in the town of Dunkirk, the rattle of machine-gun fire at the barricades still went on. Raymond didn't dare to think about what would happen if the German infantry overcame the town. His only scant comfort was in believing that there wouldn't be a full assault on the beaches from inland. The Nazis would never risk their infantry and ordnance like that – not when it was easier to simply take their time and pulverise the beaches from above.

He looked out, over the dark Channel waters. From here it was only fifty miles to the white cliffs of Dover. He'd marched further in the last few days and he was still standing. He'd march right now, if he could. It was the waiting that killed you.

Billy was awake before dawn, and begged Raymond that he, too, get some sleep. In the eerie pre-dawn light, the beach was a hive of activity. Out on the mole, auxiliary craft were still being loaded. Cheers rippled along the beach at the sight of RAF planes banking above. But there hadn't been enough of them for Billy's liking. The emptiness of the skies could be unnerving.

'Where do you think they are?' he asked Artie, after Raymond had finally acquiesced and, drawing a length of tarpaulin over him, dared to close his eyes.

Artie, eyes silently fixed on the horizon, took a moment before he answered.

'They won't be throwing the full might of the RAF at us, Billy. They're smarter than that.'

'Smarter?'

'You can bet on it. That's generals for you, Bill. They make the calculations they have to make. For them, it's better to lose us than decimate the air force.'

'Not a chance, Artie,' Billy said, with passion. 'They'll do everything they can to bring us home.'

'I'm not saying they don't care,' said Artie. 'There's hearts breaking on the other side of that water. There are voices raised in righteousness and fury. I can almost hear 'em. But, Bill, they can't risk the air force. They need to keep 'em safe for what happens next.'

Billy's eyes narrowed. 'What *does* happen next, Artie?'

To which Artie, with a kind of resigned defiance that Billy did not yet understand, said, 'The Battle for France is over, Bill. It's lost.' He paused. 'Our boys over there, they're getting ready for the Battle for Britain.'

'The Battle for Britain,' Billy whispered. The very idea chilled him – that Blighty might need battling over. It didn't seem real – and yet, here he was.

'I only hope we'll be there to fight it,' said Artie.

He clapped Billy on the shoulder.

'We'll get there, Artie. All of us.'

Artie nodded. 'I'll swim it myself, if I have to.'

An hour passed. Then two. Mid-morning came, and Billy took what dry rations he had in his pack and shared them around. Somebody was boiling water over a camping stove and handing out tea. Billy took a tin cup gratefully; good old English tea would always restore him. He just longed for the coarse brown sugar cubes they kept at the Buckingham Hotel.

He was draining his cup when his eyes caught something, out on the horizon. He wasn't the only one to have seen it. Soldiers were already clamouring at the water's edge, either ditching or hoisting their packs onto their shoulders.

It was happening up and down the beach. Billy scrambled to his feet, took three loping strides, then turned back to rip the tarpaulin off Raymond.

'Mr de Guise,' he said, rousing him with his foot, 'Mr de Guise – look!'

In his dreams, Raymond had waltzed across a Grand Ballroom ringed in fire. The stage had burned. The bar had burned. But, across the interlocked wooden boards of the sprung dance floor, he'd pivoted and turned with Nancy in his arms. What a strange melange, dreams were. And then there was Billy Brogan, reaching out a hand to hoist him to his feet.

Officers were rounding up soldiers, trying to form lines and ranks at the water – but many had already started wading out, with their packs held high. Raymond looked beyond them and understood why: the sea was dotted with a multitude of ships of different shapes and sizes. *Little fishing skiffs*, he thought. *Leisure yachts.* Part of him thought he might still be dreaming. He reeled a few paces down the sand. Artie was already hoisting his pack and tumbling forward. Because this was no mirage. This was . . . *An armada*, thought Raymond, *but quite unlike any armada I've ever seen.*

By the time he got to the water's edge, Billy striding into the water ahead of him, whistles were sounding up and down the beach, all the NCOs trying to impose order on a hundred thousand men who'd just caught their first glimpses of rescue. Raymond could see the outlines of two vast Royal Navy vessels out in the Channel. The smaller boats had been dragged along in their wake – but now they were cut free, and riding the waves towards land. Others, which had never been tethered to the greater ships, were coming in, higgledy-piggledy, from all sides. A fishermen's flotilla. A navy of boys and old men.

'Let's go home, Ray.' Artie grinned.

They would have charged into the sea there and then, but some semblance of order was finally forming at the water's edge. For hours they waited, as teams of men were dispatched into the waves to reach the incoming boats.

The first boats came as close to the shore as they could risk without being beached. In the first hour, two skiffs found themselves stranded on the sand, waiting for the tide to turn and send them back to sea – but most hung out there, where the waters remained deep, so that thousands of desperate soldiers swam out to meet them, dragging their companions along in their wake. Half the day had passed before Billy, Artie and Raymond reached the head of the line and received their orders to march into the waves. Billy Brogan, who hadn't swum a stroke since he was a boy, thrashed as he made his way out, afloat only because Raymond and Artie flanked him, geeing him along as the waters coursed around him.

'Tide's going out,' Raymond cried. 'Just stay afloat, Bill, just keep kicking!'

Kicking wasn't enough to make the first boats. They were already full, and turning back towards the destroyers out on the horizon. Billy, Raymond and Artie had to brace themselves in the water, each taking turns to hold the others up, until the boats sallied back for a second run at the beaches. By then, the sun was already high. The roar of mortar fire was like a wall of thunder beyond the streets of Dunkirk behind them. An RAF plane scythed overhead, opening fire somewhere above the townscape – and vanishing, in a plume of fire, into the French countryside beyond.

A leisure yacht was almost upon them. Twenty feet long, manned by Royal Navy cadets, it heaved to, its crew casting out coils of rope to the men in the water. Raymond urged Billy – already tired and flailing – towards one of the ropes, then braced him as the young man scrambled aboard. Then Billy, suddenly rediscovering the fire he'd lost in the water, turned back and, bustling the Royal Navy cadet out of the way, reached down for Raymond.

'Thank you, Mr de Guise,' he said – and felt the triumph of escape rising in his breast. 'Thank you!'

Then, when Raymond was aboard, both men reached back to draw the sodden Artie out of the water. Artie was laughing, wild and uproarious, as he crashed onto the deck of the yacht. He had the appearance of a drowned sewer rat.

'Well, you don't look like a handsome gentleman dancer yourself, Ray,' he laughed. 'Just get us home. We'll scrub up all right. Then it's up and back at them. Take these beaches if they want, but they'll never take *ours*.' Artie paused. One of the Royal Navy cadets was handing out life jackets, and he forced one over his head. 'By God, I could murder a smoke.'

The screech of Stukas rent holes in the sky above the beach. Bombs plunged into the frothing sea, sending eruptions of water fifty feet high. Raymond reached out, grabbing Billy by the arm as the great wave crashed over them, the yacht listing so that Artie plummeted backwards. Only the iron bow pulpit stopped Artie crashing back into the water. When the boat righted itself, he was lying there, winded. Raymond rushed to him. His brother's eyes were open, sparkling with the insanity of it all – but he was still here; he was still alive.

'On your feet, Artie.'

'Oh, right,' said Artie, 'I'll die on my feet.'

'You won't die at all,' said Raymond. 'We're nearly there.'

The destroyer waiting for them was called HMS *Othello*. Raymond urged Billy to go first, up the scaling ladders and onto the deck. By the time he rose over the side himself, the younger man had already been taken below – where the warmth of the boiler room permeated the hold and volunteers were waiting with tea. To Billy's delight, they even had sugar with which to lace it.

The hold of the destroyer was a bustle of six hundred soldiers. More were piling aboard. Raymond weaved his way between the press of men, the stink of sweat and seawater – and the acrid taste of fear – coating him, until finally he reached Billy's side.

'Private Brogan?' he said.

'I want to go home, Mr de Guise.'

Through the steel walls of the vessel, there came the roar of engines given new fuel. Seconds later, it was matched by the roar of the boys packed into the hold. Now, it wasn't just sugary tea, sweat and seawater they could taste. It was *home*. They were going back home.

In the Housekeeping Lounge, Nancy had started to shake. She knew to breathe through the panic, to let it wash over her and fade away – but that only made her think of the waves that had crashed over Raymond, Artie and Billy; and, when she looked into Billy's eyes, she saw that they were filled with tears. He'd broken off telling the story, because he couldn't go on.

'If you all got onto the destroyer, Billy, why is it you're the only one here?'

Billy's eyes darted into the corners of the room. Billy Brogan: lost for words. Frank gripped him by the hand. He supposed he ought to take over, to tell them about how, having sailed through fire and darkness, the little *Camber Queen* had come upon yet more wreckage strewn across the water – and, how, clinging to that wreckage, had been the ragged soul of his friend. But Billy's part was not finished yet. He whispered, 'It's all right, Bill. You're home now. You're—'

*Yes*, thought Billy, I'm *home*. Me. *Only me*.

He took a deep breath.

'I'd barely finished my tea when it happened. A few minutes, feeling like everything was going to be fine, like we were already out of there. And then . . .'

The roar of the engines had been filling the hold – but now a different reverberation seized the ship.

Later, Billy Brogan would look back and think about the moment of pure stillness that had preceded the chaos. He would wonder if, somehow, everybody had *known*. But that was just his mind playing tricks. Trying to make order out of chaos. Because the only thing he really knew was that, one moment, he had been putting a tin cup of tea to his lips – and, the next, an explosion rocked the vessel, smoke and churning blackness filled his eyes, and the sound of raging water was all around.

Somehow, Billy lost his footing. He crashed backwards, colliding with one of the steel pillars that lined the edges of the hold. He was still grappling for purchase, desperate to stay upright, when the screaming started. There was smoke in his eyes; the hold had become a dark blur. Bodies buffeted past him. Arms clawed out and barrelled him out of the way. A stream of other soldiers were racing for the stairs to take them up to the deck, heaving at the door and erupting back to the light.

Billy's eyes cleared.

*A torpedo*, he thought. *HMS* Othello *has been hit by a torpedo.*

'Mr de Guise!' he started shouting. 'Artie! Raymond!'

He couldn't see them anywhere, but he'd already waited too long. He lost his footing again; the destroyer was listing, and by the sounds of it taking on water too quickly. He looked back, across the stampeding crowd, and saw the flicker of flames where steel panels had been forced apart by the blast. Fire and water – somehow existing together.

He released his grip on the pillar, tried to keep his balance, and threw himself into the stampede of people pouring up the stairs.

With the terrifying screech of metal against metal, the *Othello* listed again. Billy had barely put one foot on the stairs when he heard the roar of water coming through the opening above.

'Go!' somebody was screaming. 'Go!'

Panic took Billy in its fist and squeezed him tight. He clawed his way up the stairs, through the press of other bodies, felt the rage of wind and water from above. He was almost there when a wave broke over him, forcing him – and countless others – backward. It took mere seconds for water to start filling the hold. Past his ankles it came; past his knees. He picked himself up, felt an elbow crunch into his jaw as some other desperate soldier edged his way past – and would have darted back for the stairs, if he hadn't caught a glimpse of the silhouette of Raymond de Guise on the other side of the hold.

Raymond wasn't moving. He was down on his knees – and now Billy saw why. One of the pillars bracing the roof had come loose – and, pinned beneath it, was Artie Cohen.

There are moments that change us, define us forever. Choices, made in the heat of panic and fear, that will stay with us the rest of our lives. Billy's eyes darted between the water pouring through the head of the staircase, and Raymond, heaving to free Artie from the crumpled metal. There was still a chance he could force his way through the water. There were other boats in the sea. Surely he could reach one . . .

But he turned back, and flailed his way to Raymond's side.

'It's his leg,' said Raymond.

On the cold metal floor, the water already churning over him, Artie scoffed, 'And I've told you to get out of here, Ray. I've told you to do the proper thing and get up above before—'

'I'm not leaving you!' roared Raymond.

*I left him behind once before*, he remembered. *Went off to pursue my dream of becoming a ballroom dancer, to see the glittering courts and dance halls of Europe, while Artie stayed in the East*

*End, staggering from scrape to scrape and ending up in Penton-*
*ville Prison. But not again.*

He bowed down, into the water, and heaved on the metal
holding Artie in place.

'Get your arms around it, Billy. Heave!'

'You never listen!' Artie choked; the water had reached his
chin now and, no matter how he picked himself up, it sloshed
into his mouth, cutting him off. 'You can't dance your way out
of this one. So, I'll say this – I have a son back there. You're to
look after him, Ray. *You* are. So don't you dare risk it now. Let's
one of us go back, Ray. One of us has to.' When Raymond did
not reply, Artie choked out, 'Billy Brogan, get him out of here!
Get him out of here *now* – or, so help me, I'll haunt the pair
of you. I'll make your lives a misery. Every waking moment of
every waking day. I'll be there and I'll—'

The metal shifted. The pillar rolled. Artie Cohen let out an
agonised howl as his leg was freed.

'You don't know when to give up, do you, Ray?' he scoffed,
with wild wonder in his eyes.

'Shut up, Artie. This is going to hurt . . .'

Raymond hoisted Artie up, out of the water, heaved him onto
his shoulder, with Billy Brogan bracing the other side.

The hold was half-full now. The water reached Billy's waist.
But the last of the soldiers were still hoisting themselves, against
the torrent, up the metal stairs and into the open. There was still
some modicum of hope.

Between them, they dragged Artie to the bottom of the stairs.
From here, it was too narrow to continue two abreast. Billy
looked up at Raymond, with panic in his eyes.

'Just breathe, Billy. Go on up. I've got him. He's my brother.'

Billy nodded and, taking hold of the iron rail, heaved himself up the first step. Ahead of him, the last soldier was fighting the torrent to force his way through the doorway. He looked back, the water raging around him, and extended his hand towards Billy.

Billy took it.

He needed it, too. Up above, a fresh wave must have crashed over the listing HMS *Othello*, for a fresh deluge broke over the door. Billy braced himself against it. The soldier's hand was already slipping through his when the waters broke, allowing Billy to take great gulps of air again. He tightened his grasp on the other man's fingers and felt himself being dragged, bodily, into the open air.

The lacerating cold of the wind raked across him. The HMS *Othello* was already lost, half-drowned in the water. The seas around it were foul with black oil, and through the dreadful mire swam all the survivors. Boys were still throwing themselves off the listing deck, vanishing into the inky blackness.

'Come on!' roared the soldier who'd dragged him through. 'While we still can!'

Billy resisted the pull of the other man. He looked back, down the opening, into the hold.

He couldn't see Raymond.

He couldn't see Artie.

He screamed for them. Screamed both their names. But, at that moment, the demonic siren of one of the enemy fighters wailed overhead. Bombs plunged from the sky. The wreck of the *Othello* rocked and erupted once again – and Billy felt himself being dragged over the edge of the railing, being consumed by the roiling sea.

After that, there was only the cold. There was only the feeling of the water as it rushed into his lungs. Only the terror as he reared up, coated in black effluent, and started hawking up his guts.

There wasn't any Artie Cohen.

There wasn't any Raymond de Guise.

There was only Billy Brogan and the terrible moment he was trapped in, as the *Othello* vanished into the sea behind him and he grappled to take hold of whatever flotsam he could find.

In the Housekeeping Lounge, Billy could hardly go on. The room was a blur, just like his memories of surviving in the water – but at least he could not see the lines that agony was carving into Nancy's face. She'd hate him forever now, he thought. He'd hate himself too.

A chair clattered as Nancy stood up, unable to contain the emotions coursing through her. She prowled in circles, one hand over her mouth, her other repeatedly curling into a fist.

'No,' she said. 'Billy . . . no . . . it can't be real. There's hope, isn't there? There's . . .'

Billy's sobbing rose up, and Rosa rushed around the table to brace him.

Frank, whose own eyes were shimmering, crossed the room to take hold of Nancy – but she could not stand still. She backed herself into a corner, tried to stop the shaking that were moving through her. The whole world was listing, just like HMS *Othello*. She felt the oceans opening up to drag her down, down, down.

'We got there some time after,' Frank explained, in breathless fits and starts. 'Who knows how long Billy had been in the water?' Not Billy, for sure, because his memories were such a wild kaleidoscope of frigid cold and unearthly fire, of waking up dead only to realise he was still alive. 'We'd filled the *Camber Queen* by the time we saw him. Just some poor soul, floating there in the water. But he was alive. We could see he was alive. And, when we heaved him overboard, it was Bill . . .'

Rosa looked up, from where she still clasped Billy.

'What were you even doing out there, Frank?' Her voice was tinged with sudden rage – Frank Nettleton, *her* Frank Nettleton, being a hero and leaving her behind. It was such a confusing cocktail of emotions – to be both proud and angry at the very same time.

'I don't know,' Frank whispered, 'but I know I had to. It was there, right in front of me, and I just *had* to. And if I didn't . . .'

Billy snorted away the last torrent of tears. He lifted himself, Rosa still draped over his shoulder, and looked squarely at Nancy in the corner of the room.

'I'm sorry,' he said – and in those two words was loaded all the emotion of the world that had been, and the world he was bringing into being. 'I lost them, Nancy. I thought we'd done it. I thought Artie was saved, that me and Raymond were heading to the light. But then there was just me and the ocean. When Frank found me, I thought there was still hope. Maybe they got out, too. Maybe they were picked up by some other boat. Lord knows how long I was waiting. It feels like the whole of my life. But then we got to England and there was no sign of them. No record of them ever making it back. And . . .'

He took one last breath, and made sure that he was looking into Nancy's harrowed eyes. It did not do to shy away from the truth. She deserved to hear it from him as clearly as he could muster.

'Raymond's gone, Nancy. He and Artie went down with the *Othello*. They're not ever coming back.'

# Chapter Twenty-three

I N THE HOTEL DIRECTOR'S OFFICE, Walter Knave put down his copy of the morning's *Daily Mail*. His heart was beating like a baby bird's as he read the headlines. The last soldiers, plucked from the beaches at Dunkirk, had arrived to a fanfare two evenings ago, and every column was filled with some other testimony or tale of derring-do. It stirred even Walter's ancient heart. It made him feel old, as well. He'd felt old the last time he'd seen the hotel through a world-devouring war. That it had come again seemed to beggar belief; that he was here, in this office chair, was stranger still.

But strangest of all was the feeling of freedom he'd had in the last two weeks. The feeling of waking, in the morning, certain in the knowledge that he would not be hearing Lord Bartholomew Edgerton's sibilant voice dictating to him down a telephone line. It was a light feeling, a buoyant feeling, and it kept him hopeful, even as he read about the rout on the Continent, the destroyers lost to the Channel, the lives squandered for a battle that was already lost. There was something about snatching not-quite-victory from the jaws of defeat that appealed to an Englishman. Something about holding your head up high, proud of the knowledge that you had lived to fight another day.

He'd have to gather the hotel staff together soon. He knew what many thought of him – in their eyes he was a weak-willed and reluctant leader, hardly the man they would choose to follow into battle. He supposed they had not been wrong in their assertions. Now, without the sword of Lord Edgerton hanging over him, he could set about putting things right. He should like it if his staff came to have faith in him.

*If*, of course, he was permitted to remain – because, though Lord Edgerton had been his captor, he had been Walter Knave's benefactor well. Walter was not certain what the other members of the board thought of him at all.

On the other side of the desk, John Hastings was perusing his copy of the same newspaper. As he read, he pinched the bridge of his nose, as a gentleman does when he is overcome with emotion.

'We are at a turning point, Mr Knave.' Hastings put the paper down. 'For the nation – but for the Buckingham Hotel as well. The events of the last few days – they must be a rallying point for us. The beginning, not the end.'

The story of Lord Edgerton's removal, at the hands of the Metropolitan Police, had ricocheted around the hotel in the past few days. From hotel page to audit manager, from prized guest to doorman, the story was told and told again.

Walter Knave had settled on a particularly apposite portion of the newspaper's front page. He began to read out loud. '"We have found it necessary to take measures of increasing stringency, not only against enemy aliens and suspicious characters of other nationalities, but also against British subjects who may become a danger or a nuisance should the war be transported to the United Kingdom."' He looked up. 'Mr Churchill's own words.'

The speech had been delivered in the House of Commons yesterday afternoon. The BBC had broadcast it on the radio, repeating tranches of it on the evening news. Out of all the wonder and majesty of that speech, it was this section that Walter Knave lingered over today – for it had been the key to his salvation.

John Hastings said, 'The unfortunate arrest in the Candlelight Club leaves us with certain challenges to overcome. It nullifies the need, of course, for the confidence vote Bartholomew sought to hold against me. That, I must admit, is a quite welcome *side effect* of our board member's regrettable flirtation with Defence Regulation 18B. And yet . . .'

Was Walter Knave hearing him right? Was there some element of pleasure – of victory, even – in John Hastings's tone? Surely it could not have been that Lord Edgerton's arrest was part of the scheming and machinations that always went on at board level? How could it be that something as momentous as this was part of a gambit Hastings had played?

'Mr Knave, you will know that I did not support your reappointment as director at this hotel. I believed the job required a man of finer fettle, somebody with more passion and vigour than I have seen in you this year. It was Lord Edgerton, of course, who manoeuvred the board toward your appointment. And now that he has gone . . .'

Walter Knave rose, at once, to his feet.

'I will tender my resignation this afternoon, Mr Hastings.'

Hastings looked sharply at the hotel director. 'That was not the intention behind our discussion today, Mr Knave.' He stood. 'It seems, to me, that this hotel has seen enough disruption in the past twelve months – and that to lose another director, so quickly after the last, might prove detrimental to our survival.

Order and serenity in the eye of the storm, Mr Knave. That's what we need. That is, I believe, what all the good souls out there, toiling to make a success of the Buckingham Hotel, deserve.'

Walter Knave was silent. The last pieces of a jigsaw seemed to be sliding into place in the back of his mind. Was it possible, he wondered, that John Hastings had somehow *known* Lord Edgerton was to be arrested in advance? Could it really have been part of a *design*? At last he ventured, 'Are you asking me to stay?'

Hastings directed his attention back to the newspaper.

'The tide is turning, Mr Knave. War is coming to the United Kingdom. By summer's end, it might be that we are overrun.' He read, '"Turning again to the question of invasion. We are assured that novel methods will be adopted . . . every kind of brutal and treacherous manoeuvre . . ."'

It sounded hopeless.

'Or perhaps,' John Hastings went on, reading further, 'this island can . . . ride out the storm of war . . .'

Walter Knave said, 'Outlive the menace of tyranny.'

'"We shall not flag or fail,"' John Hastings read. '"We shall go on to the end. We shall fight in France. We shall fight on the seas and oceans . . ."'

'"We shall fight on the beaches . . ."' said Walter Knave, and felt a tiny tear pricking the corner of his eye.

'"We shall fight on the landing grounds, we shall fight in the fields and in the streets . . ."'

Walter Knave straightened his hunched back, beset by something he had not felt in decades. Readiness. Being fit for the fight.

'And, by God, we'll fight in the hotel if we have to. We'll fight them out on Berkeley Square. We'll fight them in the ballroom. We'll fight them across the Queen Mary and the guest suites and . . .' His voice cracked. 'I'm sorry, Mr Hastings. I should have fought him sooner. Lord Edgerton, I mean – and all of his ilk.'

'They're gone now,' pronounced Hastings, 'and never to return to our hotel – not them, and not a man like them. The hotel has to survive, Mr Knave – but what use are we, if we've sold our very souls in order to do it? No, we must fight with tooth and nail – but we must not sacrifice ourselves along the way. So there'll be no more genuflecting to apologists and sympathisers in our hotel, Mr Knave. We are to be a beacon on a dark night. Not an embassy for our enemies. We will stand for what's right. And should you agree to be my hands on the tiller, then I should very much like that. You won't have to do it alone. I shall build a new team around you, to shepherd this hotel through its darkest days. But we have to begin today.'

Walter Knave looked, one last time, at the newspaper where Mr Churchill's words were spelled out in black and white – and nodded his head.

'So then,' said John Hastings, 'where to begin?'

'Well,' said Walter Knave, 'the Buckingham Hotel is a very different place now than it was when I first ran the show here. But if there's one thing I know about the new Buckingham, it's that occasions like these need marking. And there's only one way to make declaration of intent like this. Mr Hastings, let's look to the Summer Ball . . .'

One broken day turned into the next.

Mrs Moffatt had suggested Nancy take a few days of compassionate leave – and, when Nancy appeared in the Housekeeping Lounge for the breakfast service the very next morning, she quietly transmuted that suggestion into an outright order, and banished Nancy from the hotel until the next week began. Exile: it was the only thing that could stop Nancy de Guise from rolling up her sleeves and getting on with the job at hand. But Mrs Moffatt remembered the feeling of loss that had gripped her during the Great War when the news of her Jack came, and the sense of history repeating itself hung heavy in the air.

'Just hold yourself together, Nancy,' she told her. 'And, if you can't, why, let the rest of us hold you until you can.'

Yet it felt, to Nancy, as if there was nothing to hold. Not even Frank, who appeared religiously on her doorstep in Maida Vale, and sat with her at night, listening to Raymond's records on the gramophone and trying to engage her in memories of back home, could keep her from coming apart. She felt like a water-colour painting left out in the rain: the colours that made her were all washing away. They smudged and smeared until she could hardly recognise herself any longer.

'I need the work,' she said to Mrs Moffatt on the fifth day. 'I don't feel like myself.'

*Nothing to anchor me*, she thought.

'I need the girls and I need the guest suites and I need . . . you,' she said, trying not to sob. 'I need to sit with you after shift and talk about the next day, and the day after that. I need to be . . . sorting out other people's problems, not my own.'

'Oh, Nancy.' In the evening light of the Housekeeping office, the older woman wrapped the younger in her arms. 'If there's a time in your life to think of yourself, it's now. Of course, I'll bring you back to work, if that's what you want. You can lead the breakfast service tomorrow and lead the girls out into the halls. Maybe you're right – maybe it would numb the pain, if just for a little while. There are worse things than that. But, Nancy—'

'I know,' she said, 'they need to see me strong. I'm meant to be their leader. Not breaking down sobbing outside the Continental Suite and . . .'

Mrs Moffatt gave her a sad, crumpled sort of look. 'I didn't mean that. Those girls' hearts are breaking for you right now. I just meant – there are other people grieving right now, and grieving for the very same man. Perhaps a few days more, Nancy – and perhaps you might think about another journey out east?'

She was right, of course, as always. Nancy had made the journey into Whitechapel the day after Billy Brogan's return, crossing the city by omnibus and Underground in a spectral daze – but, of course, Vivienne already knew. Nancy hadn't needed to breathe a word. She just appeared on the doorstep, took Vivienne in her arms, and drank tea with her through the long afternoon, neither of them voicing more than a few words at a time.

It was different this time. In the days since, Vivienne had decamped to the Cohen house – where the young girl Leah played nanny to baby Stan, and Alma had rallied Vivienne into a flurry of activity. It was the way, Nancy reflected, of the Cohen women from time immemorial: roll your sleeves up, and get on with the job at hand. She supposed she was more like them than she knew.

The house was spotless. The chicken coop in the yard had been mucked out and patched up, so that it almost looked like new. The smell of carbolic and coal tar in the air, the scrubbed carpets and rugs hanging out to dry – all of it made Nancy think that she had been right; she ought to have been marching up and down the Buckingham halls. But she was here now – and somehow she detected the faint taste of hope in the air.

'Here you go, Nancy. See – Mr Churchill himself says as much.'

Alma passed her the newspaper from a few days before and planted a thumb firmly on the page. That speech: it had rallied a nation. 'We shall fight on the beaches,' Churchill had said – but Raymond and Artie had already fought on the beaches, and given their lives in the endeavour. Nancy had seen the soldiers standing at Oxford Circus. She'd wandered around Maida Vale on Sunday and seen the pubs open and the bunting flying – because even the Lord didn't mind giving up his day of rest to celebrate those who had returned. But all of that existed in another world.

'Read it,' Alma said.

When Nancy could not, it was Vivienne who gave voice to the words.

'"There may be very many reported missing who will come back home, some day, in one way or another. In the confusions of this fight it is inevitable . . ."'

Nancy hardly knew what to say. *Mr Churchill was only giving hope to those who needed it*, she thought. In his speech he imagined those soldiers who had fled, or not been on the beaches, who had abandoned their positions where honour did not require them to stay. He was not speaking of two brothers, one of whom carried a mortal wound, trapped in the hold of a sinking ship. There was little hope there that Nancy could muster. But she looked at Vivienne and decided that, if hope was what she needed, then that would be what she should have.

'There's always a hope,' she whispered, pretending to believe it, and took Vivienne's hand. 'It's Raymond. It's Artie. If there's a way, they'll find it.'

*But if there is any hope*, thought Nancy, *it is that they'd been washed up back on the beaches – and what sort of hope is that?*

'There are others,' said Vivienne.

Rather than finding her friend's belief comforting, Nancy started to think that it was frenzied somehow, that there was a maniacal glint in Vivienne's eye as she sifted through the recent newspapers and unearthed the story of forty French soldiers who had made it across the Channel, long after the evacuation's end. Nancy had not seen that mania in Vivienne for a long time; not since her days of raising hell and drunkenly reeling around the Grand Ballroom and the Ethelred Suite.

'You'll see,' she insisted. 'Artie's been down and out before. People have given up on him in the past. But not me. He wouldn't let go that easily – not when he's got Stan . . .'

Nancy hadn't intended to stay the night, but something about Alma's stubborn resilience and Vivienne's manic belief made her feel it was the right thing to do. Besides, it was probably good that Leah got a break from looking after Stan; Nancy remembered what it was like to be a young girl, in charge of a little boy much younger still, how all-consuming that could be. So she resolved to spend the evening among the Cohen women – and though she did not, at first, admit that she was doing it for herself as much as them, as night came on and the smells of a pot roast chicken filled the little terrace kitchen, she was overcome with such a feeling of family, such a feeling of *home*, that for the first time she gave in to the full brutality of the emotions coursing through her. She went to bed that night and sobbed until sleep came to take her away.

Some time later, when she woke – the rippling curtains revealing the moonlit street outside – she thought she heard Stan crying. She rolled over, her eyes still raw from the night before; Vivienne would certainly stir and go to him soon. But, when the crying went on, Nancy picked herself out of bed, ventured into the corridor and the room next door. There, Stan was crying in his crib – and the bed where Vivienne slept was empty, its bedsheets a tangle on the floor.

Nancy cradled Stan as she crept to the top of the stairs, cooing at him to keep him from waking the rest of the house. There was no sign of Vivienne in the living room. No sign of Vivienne in the kitchen or back yard. An empty foreboding was opening up inside Nancy, pulling on her coat and shoes, she stepped out in the front step and breathed in the ripe tang of the Whitechapel night.

'Vivienne?' she called out. 'Vivienne?'

She did not want to venture out there, not after midnight with a babe in arms, but something compelled her – because she was certain, now, that Vivienne had gone off, into the night; and she had a ghastly inkling of where she had gone. Because that manic glint in Vivienne's eyes today had been too bright to ignore. The frenzied, harrowed look of somebody who needed help. The look of an old addiction, rearing its ugly head.

It was the same with drunks, Nancy knew. Ten years of sobriety could be undone in a moment of grief. And yet – Nancy hardly knew where to turn. There were opium dens that she knew of from her dealings with the Daughters of Salvation – but surely she could not brave them, not with Stanley to take care of, and not alone. She needed Artie. She needed Raymond, more than ever.

Then she thought of the Peels. Warren Peel, whose life had followed such a similar path to Vivienne's. Perhaps he would know where to start.

She could brave it to Limehouse, at least. She could do that for Vivienne.

She turned, meaning to make haste to the river. It was then that she heard her name.

'Nancy?'

And there was Vivienne, a shadow beneath one of the shop awnings.

They looked at each other, across a dark divide.

'Vivienne,' Nancy trembled, 'I was so worried. I thought you'd—'

'Thought I'd what?'

The words hung unspoken. Then Nancy said, 'Given in, Vivienne. I thought you'd . . . given in.'

As Vivienne dared to draw near, Stan recognised her – and, reaching out, gurgling, he tumbled into his mother's arms.

'I want to,' Vivienne said, with simple and brutal honesty. 'I don't want to be myself tonight. I thought – if I could just go back, just once, just taste the smoke and feel the touch of it, just sail away for a few small hours, then perhaps I'd be all right. Just *once*, Nancy.' She breathed. 'But I didn't do it. I couldn't do it. I . . .'

Nancy didn't know she was holding her breath until she exhaled. The feeling of a fresh disaster that had been averted filled her, like one of the barrage balloons strung up above.

'You did it, Vivienne. You survived it.'

Because that was what it was: *survival*. Just putting one foot in front of the other, from now until the end of your days.

'I know you don't believe it,' said Vivienne. 'That they might be alive. I can see it in your eyes – and that's OK, Nancy, it really is. But I *need* to believe it. It's like – that hope's my opium now. If I keep hoping and I keep believing, then I don't have to crumble. Because the moment the hope's taken away . . .'

Vivienne buried her face in Stan's wild, black hair and started to cry.

'I know,' said Nancy. 'I know.'

Then there was silence, just the skittering paws of a stray dog, up and down that Whitechapel street.

'Come and stay with me,' Nancy said. 'At least for a time. Alma needs you, too, but . . .' She faltered. 'It's like sleeping with their ghosts every night, isn't it? I sit down to dinner, and there's Raymond, in an empty chair.'

'I keep hearing Artie whistling at me.'

'Raymond's records, on the gramophone player.'

'Artie's betting slips, all over my kitchen table.' Vivienne stopped, held Stan tighter still. 'Oh God, Nancy, it's so empty. The *world's* so empty. That's why I have to believe.' She paused, took great gulps of air. 'I'll come out west soon, I promise. But I need to . . . I'm not going to give in to it, Nancy. You don't need to fear for me. I'm stronger than that. If I was going to do it, it would have been tonight.'

Nancy nodded. She almost believed it as well. But then she thought: *what happens when the hope truly dies? When weeks have passed, and months, and there's still no sign of them – and, worse yet, no certainty in their fate? What will hold Vivienne together when all her belief in miracles has drained away?*

The thought would plague her in the days to come – but, for now, there were only Nancy and Vivienne with Stan in her arms, wending their way home through the Whitechapel night.

Nancy returned to the Buckingham three days later, determined that she would roll up her sleeves and muck in with the girls again. The moment she stepped into the tradesman's entrance, she knew it was the right thing to do. She wended her way to the Housekeeping Lounge, where Mrs Moffatt received her like a returning daughter and said, 'You're just in time, Nancy. It's all hands in the ballroom. Come with me.'

Mid-afternoon, and in the Grand Ballroom, the staff of the hotel were gathered. It was like stepping into the Grand for the very first time – because the world was different now. Nancy followed Mrs Moffatt through the backstage doors and looked out upon all the familiar faces – Frank, among his gaggle of pages (and, beside him, Billy Brogan himself, propped up on crutches); Rosa, Mary-Louise and all the chambermaids; the concierges and desk clerks, the kitchen porters, the dance troupe – or what was left of it, because this was certainly not the troupe that Nancy held in mind whenever she thought of the ballroom. It struck Nancy, suddenly, how already time was slipping through her fingers. Day was still turning to night; lives were still being lived; the world had lost something it could not replace, but people still slept and woke up and went about their days, hardly noticing the dark, empty shape in the centre of her life. That was death.

Mrs Moffatt had taken her by the hand. Together, they joined the crowd – just in time for Walter Knave to enter the ballroom.

'I remember standing here once before . . .' Mr Knave began – and Mrs Moffatt remembered it, too, that day when war had been declared and the hotel had last gathered. He'd tried to bolster them then, hiccoughed and slurred his way through the rallying of his troops, and not a man in the ballroom had been filled with the confidence they needed. Today, though, Mr Knave seemed sharper. He was steadier, and did not slur. Only Nancy knew the truth of the burden of which he'd been relieved – but, by his tone, every man and woman in the ballroom knew to listen to him more keenly today.

'I told you, then, that we would get through this together. That we would look to our Winter Serenade and rally as one. Well, I come to you, now, in perhaps our nation's darkest hour. But you will all have heard Mr Churchill's words on the matter. That, though we face bombardment from above – and though we face invasion from over the sea – we indomitable people of this island have never before given in to tyranny. And nor will we now. I am standing in front of you to make you a solemn promise – that the Buckingham will, by virtue of all of us, survive the battles to come. This will, from this day forth, be a beacon of what is good and right in this country we love. That the Buckingham Hotel – *my* Buckingham Hotel, *our* Buckingham Hotel – will survive with its soul intact, and its arms wrapped tightly around all who help her through the storm.

'My friends, some of us here, in this room, have already lost people we love. Should terror come from the skies, it is inevitable that more will perish. By the war's end, it may be that we are not standing together, all of us, as we are now. I've known war before. I know how it recasts worlds. But if we hold to that one, inalienable truth – that, together, we are stronger than apart; that an army of women and men, alike in their ambitions and objectives, can accomplish anything to which they set their minds, there is every hope for us here. We have built our defences. We have dug deep. Divided, we will fall; but together, we will see the light again.

'I am announcing, today, that the Summer Ball set to brighten Society's calendar in three weeks' time, will be held in honour of those who returned from the beaches at Dunkirk – and those who, sadly, will not waltz with us again. I speak of our principal, Raymond de Guise, presumed to have perished in the Channel crossing. The best of dancers, and the best of men. But I speak of all the others too. The board convened last night to extend invitations to the veterans associations, so that a number of those men who survived the Battle of France might dance with us here on a sparkling summer night. And let this be a message to the world – like Britain, the Buckingham is not bowed. Come what may, we will prevail . . .'

In the crowd, Nancy could listen no longer. She realised then that she, too, had picked up a little bit of the belief from Vivienne. The hope that things were not as they seemed had burrowed into her, planting its seeds. But what had been sustaining Vivienne had become like a parasite to Nancy. It only made it harder to hear it when others said Raymond was never to return. And the thought of a ball that commemorated his death – while celebrating the survival of so many others – was too much to bear. Quietly, she broke away from Mrs Moffatt and gravitated back towards the stage doors.

In the dressing room, she lingered by the mirror where he used to get changed. She went to the closet and ran her fingers up and down the weave of his midnight blue dinner jacket. She wondered if somebody else would wear it now. The dance troupe, after all, had been preparing for his absence for months already.

A year ago, it had been Raymond's ballroom. Now: Marcus Arbuthnot and Karina Kainz, Mathilde Bourchier – and her own brother Frank. They'd dance for the heroes. They'd dance in celebration and defiance. They'd dance because the world demanded it, because the world needed to find its joy wherever it could.

But for now and ever more, she thought, they'd be dancing with Raymond's ghost.

July 1940

# Chapter Twenty-four

**N**ANCY AWOKE, FROM A DREAM of wild, frothing waters and a wilder, strident tango.

Music was playing in the sitting room downstairs.

She hurried there, half in this world and half not, only to find Vivienne sitting on the sheepskin with Stan on his tiptoes in front of her, clinging onto her fingers for balance.

Vivienne, who had been staying with her the past few nights, looked up and said, 'It's the only way he'll stand. Look at him, Nance, a natural dancer. I suppose – I suppose it's in his blood . . .'

The dream stayed with her all through the day. Up and down the Buckingham halls, round the rooms and guest suites, inspections and inventories and time-sheets for the girls. Let one day wash over you, Mrs Moffatt had said; then let the next, and the next after that. One day, you'll find you're not drowning any more and you're on solid land.

Solid land, thought Nancy.

Well, not today.

In the fishing villages and harbours along the south coast of England, stories would forever be told. The village pubs would stand free pints for the old boys who'd gone out into the mael-strom. New names were chipped into the memorials and market crosses for those brave few who had not returned.

On the beaches, only a short distance from the white cliffs that would forever signify the return home of Great Britain's vanquished soldiers, a father and his young son were out walk-ing the dog, hunting through rock pools, climbing on stones. Too old to serve in this war, the father had assumed a role of leadership in the local civil defence brigade. The 'Home Guard' they called it, and he had brought his son here, today, to show him the waters across which so many had been ferried home. For three nights now, his son had woken from a nightmare of German boats landing on these beaches. Probably he ought to be sent to the countryside soon. But, for now, his father wanted him to feel the power of that sea – for he felt, in his heart, that though they might try, the Nazis would never land an invasion force here.

'Just think, my boy, of what Mr Churchill says.' That speech – they were talking about it in every pub, too. 'There has never been a time, in all the hundreds of years of history of this island, when we could have said, for certain, that invaders wouldn't come. Countless times they've tried. The Spanish and their Armada. Napoleon, and his hordes. They all tried, son, but none of them made it. Because we're the people we are. This is our island, and it isn't going to fall, not while there's breath left in our—'

'Then what's that, Daddy?'

The little boy had lifted his finger and was pointing it out to sea. In the same moment, their dog started yapping wildly, into the wind.

The father followed his son's direction. A black smudge was sitting on the horizon. A boat. But there was only one, he realised, not an invasion. Just a tiny fishing vessel, alone on the wild blue sea.

A man was standing in its prow, wearing the proud khaki battledress of the British Expeditionary Force.

Rosa had told him it was right to be excited. She'd sat him down at night and drilled it into him – that he, Frank Nettleton, had nothing to be ashamed of.

'I know,' Frank had said – and, for the first time, he had the conviction of those words. 'But it isn't right, is it? To think of the Grand Ballroom without Raymond?'

He'd been thinking that he ought to forsake his place in the ballroom – at least for the Summer Ball. Part of him had wanted to ask Nancy – but, every time he saw her, the idea of relying on her for direction seemed crass, somehow. He'd stayed with her two nights before – he was grateful that Vivienne was there too – and realised that the very best thing was companionable silence. Lancashire hotpot. To talk of other things, and happier times. Now, he stood backstage at the Grand, on the eve of the Ball itself, and wondered at what the right thing was.

At least he had Billy Brogan here, to direct him.

'You're a madman, Frank, to think he'd want anything else. Crikey, you weren't just a brother-in-law to Mr de Guise. You were practically a *brother*. Look me in the eye and tell me that, if he was here, he'd want you walking away from the ballroom?'

There was a hubbub of activity backstage. Tonight, the ballroom would be silent – there was a team working in there right now, raising the chandeliers, hanging the wreaths, hoisting the flags that would ripple in an artificial breeze above the dance floor itself – but, tomorrow, the doors would open in a riot of music and colour, and out the dancers would stream. Archie Adams was about to put the orchestra through its paces, along with the guest singers who were performing – and being housed, at not inconsiderable expense, in the hotel's suites. Marcus Arbuthnot was in the studio, leading Karina Kainz through the finer points of the spectacular that would open events. Frank himself was due to be the first out of the doors, leading Mathilde in a wild foxtrot that, Marcus had explained, symbolised the mad dash across the Channel. There were going to be veterans swarming the ballroom, from high and low. An invitation had been extended to the retired Admiral Bedbrook, and there was even a rumour that the Right Honourable Albert Alexander, no less than the Earl of Hillsborough, was to attend in his new capacity as First Lord of the Admiralty – a rare night of leisure, for a man who now sat at Mr Churchill's right-hand side.

'You're nervous, Frank.'

That was only a part of it – though Frank would admit that, the closer the night came, the bigger a part it was. The rest was the ghostly feeling he would get, dancing across the sprung dance floor where Raymond had made his name. A dream he'd once had, of being led out by Mr de Guise – and now, in some small way, he felt as if he was being asked to supplant him.

'Frank Nettleton,' said Billy, brandishing his crutches, 'you tie yourself into knots with all this talking. You ought to be proud, you daft sod.' His voice broke; it had been crackling too much in the days since he'd returned, and increasingly he didn't even care about disguising it. 'You're going to dance tomorrow night, and be proud of it. You're going to do it for all those lads who come to see you. And you're going to do it for Mr de Guise . . .'

*Yes*, Frank thought, *yes I am.*

'I'm going to do it for you too, Bill.'

Seeing Billy hobble around on his crutches could sometimes provoke terrible sadness. He wasn't much use as a concierge anymore – and, of course, there was little hope of him returning to his unit, not with his ribs cracked and his foot crushed like it had been, somewhere in the water. But Mr Knave had said there was always a place for a man of Billy Brogan's mettle at the Buckingham Hotel – and a place had been found for him in the hotel post room, where Billy had assisted the elderly Mrs Farrier once before. All the talk was that Mrs Farrier wasn't long for the Buckingham anyway; she spoke of a sister in the country, and getting out before the invasion began. Perhaps there was a future for Billy there.

'Ah,' said Billy, getting dewy-eyed for the second time that day, 'I think you've done enough for me, Private Nettleton.'

Then he limped off, out of the dance studio.

Nancy was crossing the reception hall when Billy emerged. She caught his eye across the black and white chequered tiles, and he followed her into the Housekeeping hall.

'Billy,' she ventured.

He nodded, if only to acknowledge the unspoken emotion between them.

'You going to look in on the ball, Nance?'

She'd been torn, during the past few days – the pride she would feel for Frank and all he'd accomplished was doing battle, in her heart, with the emptiness she expected upon seeing the ballroom devoid of Raymond. The truth was, she still wasn't certain if she could do it. The ballroom held too many memories. It was the place she'd first locked eyes with Raymond – she just a chambermaid, risking her livelihood by stepping into that gilded world.

'You're on the list,' Billy said. 'I seen it.'

'So are you, Billy.'

He reached into a pocket and pulled out his invitation card, signed personally by John Hastings and all the other members of the Board.

THE BUCKINGHAM HOTEL IS PROUD TO INVITE YOU,

MR WILLIAM BROGAN, TO THIS YEAR'S SUMMER BALL.

'I reckon I won't be doing much dancing,' said Billy. 'But, then again, I never was much good.' He twirled his crutch so that he almost toppled, and had to brace himself against Nancy just to stay upright. 'But when else will I get an invitation to the Grand? They don't let any old concierges in there, you know.'

'Well, you're a veteran now, Billy.'

Nancy and Billy stared at each other, neither one acknowledging the gulf of sadness between them. 'He was the best of men, Nancy,' Billy finally croaked. 'And Artie too. Is Vivienne . . .?'

He couldn't say anymore. Neither could she. Somehow, it was easier to talk about the bigger aspects of a war – the sieges that had been broken, Italy's declaration that they would now join the conflict as staunch allies of the Third Reich – than it was to dwell on the little part they themselves played.

Billy let his hand linger on Nancy's shoulder, and then he limped on. She could hear him trilling one of his little tunes as he left. There wasn't much music in it. Nancy wondered if there would be, ever again.

At least the sun was shining on the day of the Summer Ball. Berkeley Square was bathed in glorious sunshine from dawn until late afternoon – and, even when the sun started sinking below the horizons of the city, it left behind a rosy glow. Backstage at the Grand Ballroom, Marcus Arbuthnot had gathered his troupe to give them a rousing speech he was certain was comparable to anything Churchill had said in the weeks just past – and, though Frank Nettleton wasn't sure it *quite* reached those heights, there was certainly something inspiring about the way the older dancer spoke. Frank moved nervously from foot to foot, as Marcus told them about the sanctity of the occasion, the glory of the first dance, the duty they all held – not only to their feted guests, not only to the veterans whose deeds they were commemorating, but to music and dance itself.

'And I would be remiss, in this moment, were I not to breathe a word about the Grand ballroom's own champion, missing in action. I never danced with Raymond de Guise, but I shall dance in his shadow tonight. I will imagine it is he who will be leading us out . . .'

Frank was stilled by the idea – because, by Mr Arbuthnot's own design, it was Frank himself who would lead the charge onto the ballroom tonight. In his wake would come all the other dancers of the troupe, until, at the last, Marcus and Karina themselves spun out, to the adulation and applause of the crowd. Fleetingly, he allowed his nerves and doubts to prey on him again. Then Archie Adams, who was marshalling his orchestra to go through the doors, took him by the shoulder and said, 'You'll be brilliant tonight, Frank. You'll make the whole Grand proud.'

And Frank thought: *I know I will – because I'm doing it for Mr de Guise.*

At Victoria Station, the locomotive ground to a halt halfway along the platform, and shrill whistles filled the air. When the doors opened, an unusual collection of passengers flooded out to fill the concourse. Among the rush of clerks and daytrippers there walked a group of five men in the khaki battledress of the British Expeditionary Force, their uniforms threadbare, torn, rimed in the salt of the seas and the dark brown stains of their comrades' blood.

One of those men stalled at the concourse's end. He ran his hand over hair that had once been thick and black, now shorn down to a charcoal stubble, matched today by the dishevelled beard that lined his jaw. He'd take a razor blade to it soon – and perhaps that would restore him. For now, though, he only needed to breathe in the world that had once been his. He'd have to be at barracks soon – but there was time first. Time to make sense of it all. Time to find out what was to become of him, and all the people he loved.

Time to grieve.

He bade farewell to his fellows at the station's entrance. Watched as they fanned out into the London streets, seeking their own answers, their own loves, their own reprieves from the madness across the water. Then, he joined the queue of people snaking out of the taxicab rank. One or two of the old dears stepped out of his path, in deference to his uniform – but he quietly ushered them back. He needed a little longer, he supposed.

Just a few moments more, so that he might make sense of the city he was coming back to. It was London, he thought – home of the honourable, the valiant, the free. But it felt so different now. He lingered, for a moment too long, over the thought of how far he'd come. From his childhood, scrambling around the streets of Whitechapel, to the battle-strewn fields of France, to a month and more trapped behind enemy lines. Derelict farmsteads, the cellars of some defiant haberdasher, a final, desperate scramble back to the sea.

He thought of the woman he loved.

He thought of baby Stan.

Hearts were going to break. He was going to have to be the one to break them.

The stage doors opened, and a hush fell across the Grand ballroom.

It was the moment Walter Knave had been waiting for. He stood at the dance floor's edge, with John Hastings on his right-hand side, and watched as Archie Adams, bedecked in his classic white dinner jacket, led out the orchestra. Spotlights found them from above, tracking them up the steps to the stage where Archie's grand piano was waiting. He lowered himself, statesmanlike, onto his stool, and allowed his fingers to dance up and down the ivories while the rest of the musicians assumed their positions. In the ballroom, the expectation was high. Walter Knave allowed himself to survey the evening's guests. In one corner, hidden from the outside world by the tall blackouts in the windows, groups of Dunkirk's survivors were standing in their full battledress. In another, King Haakon of Norway and Crown Prince Olav stood among members of their government-in-exile. They had made the crossing to English shores only weeks before. From one side of the room to the other, London's industrialists and gentry trained their eyes on the dance floor doors.

The music struck up. It was Archie Adams who would lead them into the song. The melody that came from his piano started soft but soon started swelling. When the wall of trombones and drums joined in, there was such anticipation in the air that Walter Knave felt like he could touch it. It was strange, how something as simple as music could play with your feelings. He felt full of hope. He felt fit to burst.

The dance-floor doors opened. A single spotlight picked out the young Frank Nettleton – and, hanging in his arms, the stunning Mathilde Bourchier. Out they spun, onto the dance floor alone, to be met by rolling waves of applause.

'Well, there's a true Buckingham hero,' said John Hastings. Rumour of Frank's journey across the Channel had ricocheted from one corner of the hotel to another.

'And one more,' said Walter – for Billy Brogan was standing among the other veterans of Dunkirk, looking as out of place – with his woolly hair now growing back, and the crutches still at his side – in the Grand Ballroom as any of them did.

'Look,' said Hastings, 'here the rest of them come . . .'

Frank was dancing on air. It got so that he hardly noticed the people watching him. He'd soared out of the doors, Mathilde in his arms, and the wild foxtrot on which he carried her kept growing and growing in intensity as the spotlight followed them around the floor. Then, in a crashing of piano, the music changed; the orchestra played a more ghostly number now, quieter and softer, and all across the Grand the lights went up. The dance floor doors opened once again – and out turned the other dancers, one pair after another, until, at the very apex of the song, Marcus and Karina made their appearance.

It was, Frank realised, the singular wonder of his lifetime. As soon as he had stepped through those doors, all the doubts and guilts that had been plaguing him simply sloughed from his shoulders; he cast them off, like a snake does the skin it no longer needs, and threw himself headlong into the music. He had tried to keep in mind all of the things Marcus told the troupe – about drama, and passion and love – but, in the end, it was so much simpler than that: he just had to exist, in the same moment as the music, and let it flow through him. All of the lessons Miss Marchmont had been keen to impart were built into him now. He held his postures and poises to perfection; he knew his steps and his pivots. But all of that was secondary to the *feeling* of it. You had to step through the sadness of the days just past. You had to acknowledge that the grief and death were real, and reach for the transcendent joy that existed on the other side.

The music burst open around him. He felt, for a second, as if he was being showered in starlight. Marcus and Karina were in the centre of the dance floor now, Karina soaring high above Marcus's head and balanced on the flats of his palms. Round they turned, and in their orbit spun all the other dancers.

*Summer is here*, thought Frank – *and all around me is love.*

The music came to its titanic conclusion; the song announced its end in a final flurry of horns. And then the air was filled with the applause of the Dunkirk veterans, the exiled kings, the parliamentarians and gentry and officers – and all of the many others who had turned out tonight, in defiance of the threat of invasion, to prove that there was still space for joy in the world.

Frank turned around, breathless. Billy Brogan was cheering him from the sidelines. He felt filled up.

In Maida Vale, Nancy stood in the sitting room doorway and looked at Vivienne, who was changing Stan into clean clothes on the sheepskin rug. She supposed Frank was taking to the dance floor about now. She felt a little pang in her side at the thought of him stepping into the ballroom in the company of such greats, the image of all those eyes trained on him as he turned Mathilde Bourchier round and round. It would not, ordinarily, have been the done thing for Nancy to attend the occasion – but Mr Knave's invitation had been extended to both Vivienne and herself. For long days she'd agonised about going; in the end, it was the thought of Raymond's ghost that had kept her away.

And yet, now, the sense that she was missing something would not leave her alone. She'd cooked and cleaned the house, if only to try and rid herself of the feeling she was letting Frank down. She'd gone for a long walk, after her shift ended, around the green expanse of Hyde Park, where she and Raymond had picnicked every summer since she came to London.

'But his ghost's everywhere,' she said to Vivienne, now. 'It's not just the ballroom. It's here, in this house. It's out there, on those streets. It's in *here*.' She folded her hand over her breast. 'So . . .'

Vivienne looked up. 'It isn't too late, you know.'

The clock on the wall had not yet reached 8 p.m.

There was silence.

At last, Vivienne said, 'Put your gown on, Nancy. Perhaps you could find me something too? I'll find us a taxicab.'

Upstairs, Nancy opened her wardrobe. She didn't own the most ostentatious ball gowns. The thought of a wardrobe filled with chiffon and lace didn't appeal to her as it did many others. But she lifted out a simple satin gown, the ivory one she'd worn to dance with Raymond on their wedding night, and felt its touch against her cheek. Yes, she thought, this would do. No more talk about ghosts. Memories did not have to haunt you; they could be celebrated, too.

It was almost nine o'clock by the time the taxicab dropped Vivienne, in a borrowed sky blue gown, Nancy and baby Stan on Berkeley Square. By rights, they could have come through the revolving doors at the main entrance, but the blackouts were up in the front of the hotel and they slipped in through the tradesman's entrance on Michaelmas Mews. Moments later, they were in the Housekeeping Lounge – where Mrs Moffatt, up late writing a letter to Malcolm, was only too happy to take Stan in her arms.

'He wrote to me this week,' said Mrs Moffatt, 'he's got two weeks' leave coming up. We thought we might see some of the country together, before he has to go back to . . .' She faltered before saying more. Malcolm had flown two excursions over the Channel during the retreat from Dunkirk; two of his fellow airmen had vanished, somewhere over France. The hope was they were in one of the PoW camps the Nazis were rumoured to have constructed in the French countryside. The whisperers said that that was where all of the French and British soldiers who didn't make it to the beaches had gone, too.

Vivienne and Nancy drifted back to the hotel reception together. The sound of wild music and wilder applause was flowing up out of the Grand Ballroom. A great Union Jack flag had been strung up above the ornate archway leading down to the ballroom doors. They followed it together, drawn down by the lure of the music.

On the threshold of the ballroom, before they opened the doors, Nancy stopped and took Vivienne by the hand.

'Do you remember the first time?' she said.

Vivienne wasn't sure that she did. 'I was always so loaded, back then.'

'We shouldn't have been in there, really. Neither of us. Little country mouse that I was – all I wanted to do was take a look inside. I had no idea that the gown I'd stitched wouldn't suit the occasion. I had so little idea of what it was really like in the Grand Ballroom. I don't think I really understood what wealth there was in the world, back then. But I'd slipped inside and—'

Vivienne remembered now. 'I was already in there. I was in there every night. Out of my own body, out of my own head – but, every night, down to the ballroom. You crashed into me. I tried to rat you out, for having sneaked in . . .'

'It's how I met Raymond.'

The two women – war widows, they supposed now – turned to face each other.

'Let's go in there together,' said Vivienne.

So that was what they did.

The dance floor was alive, the ballroom bedecked in bunting and flags. Nancy and Vivienne picked their way through the crowd to the balustrade that ran around the edge of the dance floor – just in time for the energetic waltz the dancers were performing, now having taken the ball's many guests in their arms. On the dance floor, Frank – who had a young debutante in his arms – looked up to see Nancy smiling back down, dressed like an angel, radiant in the chandelier's light. His heart felt as if it was overflowing.

'Ladies and gentlemen,' Archie Adams announced, his voice filling the ballroom, 'please put your hands together for Mr John Hastings, the head of the Buckingham board.'

John Hastings cut an unassuming figure as he took to the stage. Once he'd frowned on fripperies like the ballroom, but now the pride was evident on his face as he weaved between the dancers – patting Frank on the shoulder, and taking Marcus by the hand – before he reached the stage.

'Ladies and gentlemen, let me begin by telling you how proud I am to be standing among you today – not only because the Buckingham ballroom values you, each and every one, as its patrons. Not only because we are gathered here, today, to celebrate a summer like no other. But because we do so in commemoration of our brothers who have lost their lives in this great British endeavour to rid the world of aggression and hatred – to deny the worst of men their dominion over a world we hold dear. We have, all of us here, followed the news of the Continent closely across the past weeks. Great Britain finds herself on a precipice. Alone, perhaps, but not defeated. Defiant, and not diminished. And it is in that spirit that we dance tonight. Survival is our strategy – but nights like these remind us what we are surviving for. They remind us why we fight.' John Hastings paused. A smattering of applause had met his words, but he was not finished yet. 'It is the privilege of my lifetime, tonight, to bestow the thanks of the Buckingham upon those veterans of the Battle of France who have done us the honour of joining us in the ballroom.'

He opened his arms, so that every face in the ballroom turned to greet the group of servicemen who occupied the tables at the back of the Grand. Some of them stood on the dance floor – but, among those who remained at the back, Billy Brogan tried to hide his face. He'd never been much of a dancer, Nancy remembered – but the blushes he was hiding were so much more than that tonight.

'And among them,' Hastings continued, 'I should like to pay special mention to our own Mr William Brogan, who fought valiantly since the declaration of September the third, and has returned to us, now, the very pride of the Buckingham himself. Mr Brogan, and all you others, you have our eternal thanks. The Grand ballroom is yours tonight!'

Applause took the ballroom in its hands – and Nancy watched as Billy, shaking, leaned into his crutches to back out across the ballroom floor. As he passed her, she reached for his arms.

'Billy, are you all right?'

'It's nothing, Nance,' he said, unable to meet her eyes. 'I just . . . I can't be here. Not tonight.'

Out on Berkeley Square, a black taxicab entered by the southern avenue, coming up from Piccadilly. Ordinarily, the driver would have deposited his fare at the bottom of the hotel's sweeping marble stairs, but tonight the passenger had other ideas.

'Here is just right,' he said – and, having tipped the driver, made to march across the square himself.

He wanted one last chance to look at the Buckingham's gleaming white façade – how dark and unknowable it appeared, with the blackouts strung up in the windows – before he stepped inside and destroyed a life.

The doorman didn't recognise him – perhaps that was just as well – so he climbed the marble stairs without being stopped, and entered through the revolving doors. For a moment, neither in nor out, he was cocooned in perfect blackness. Then he stepped into the familiar light of the reception hall.

There was music flowing out of the Grand Ballroom. A figure had just hurried through the ornate arched entrance, levering his way forward on a wooden crutch.

'Billy?'

Billy Brogan turned around. He hadn't meant to give in to the tears that overwhelmed him when Mr Hastings made his speech, but his eyes had welled up just the same and nothing he could see was very clear at all. All of this emotion – it was quite unseemly. It didn't become him. He was Billy Brogan, champion of the Buckingham Hotel. A stoic, stalwart lad.

And now he couldn't believe what he was seeing.

'I went back to the old house,' the serviceman explained, 'but she wasn't there. Billy, is she here?'

Billy didn't know where to begin. He stuttered forward, clasped the newcomer's hand; his body cried out to drag him into an embrace – but he was a soldier, a solid, reliable soldier, and somehow he reined himself back in. He opened his mouth to speak, but all he could do was choke out the words, 'But I saw you go down. I saw you—'

'I'm here, Bill.'

Billy's shaking subsided. 'She's here too. She's in the Grand.'

He breathed, long and low. 'I'll tell you everything – but I need to tell her first. Billy, my brother is dead.'

War threw up such a multitude of emotions. It robbed and it gave back, and then it took away again. Only moments ago, Billy

Brogan had believed he'd seen both men swallowed up by the water as HMS *Othello* went down. Now, along with the knowledge that one of them survived, came the cruel blow of death once again.

'Follow me,' Billy said, finally in control of the wavering of his own voice. 'I'll show you.'

The doors of the Grand Ballroom opened again. Inside, the speeches were all over. The Archie Adams Orchestra had welcomed another guest singer to the stage, and already they were crooning out one of Archie's own numbers, 'Sweetheart, Stay With Me'.

Down on the dance floor, Nancy was dancing a simple quickstep with Frank, while Vivienne – unwilling to take to the floor with anybody but Artie in her arms – watched from the balustrade above.

Billy Brogan limped towards her. He tapped Vivienne on the shoulder.

At first she did not recognise the serviceman who was standing beside Billy. Seeing him standing there scarcely seemed credible, even in a ballroom that had served up so many miracles in the years since she'd first come here. But, down on the dance floor, Nancy saw. She was turning in Frank's arms, and the blur of khaki battledress strobed past her in such a rush that she, too, refused to believe her eyes.

At last, she broke from Frank's arms and stood there, an oasis of stillness in the spiralling dance floor.

'Oh,' said Vivienne. She gripped the man's hand.

Nancy had been thinking about ghosts for weeks now. What was it she'd thought, earlier this evening? Haunted by memories, she remembered. And here was one right now.

She left Frank behind, hurried from the dance floor, picked her way through the crowd to reach the place where Vivienne and Billy were standing.

She looked at the serviceman. She looked at Vivienne.

Worlds could be destroyed – but she realised, now, that there really had been a chance they could be built back again. She threw herself forward – and this time her leg put up no protest as she launched herself up and into his arms.

'You're late,' she said softly, her head falling against his breast as he put her arms around him.

And then, in an echo of words he'd said long ago, Raymond de Guise replied, 'But I got here in the end.'

# Chapter Twenty-five

IN THE HOUSEKEEPING LOUNGE, RAYMOND de Guise took his nephew Stan in his arms and kissed him on the brow. Of all the eyes peering at him now – needing answers, begging for his story to be told – these ones meant more than any. He pressed his lips to the little boy's shell-like ear and whispered, 'Your father loved you, Stan, more than I can say' – and, as he breathed out the words, he fancied he could hear Archie echoing in them. It was a promise fulfilled.

He looked up and around him. Nancy was still at his side. Vivienne, feeling the terrible certainty of Artie's death, sat at the breakfasting table – while Mrs Moffatt, mindful that this, perhaps, wasn't her place, hovered uncertainly in the office door. The last of them, Billy Brogan, had propped himself against the wall – his crutch at his side, his broken body held rigid and straight, like a soldier on parade.

Raymond cradled Stan in one arm, trailed his hand across the small of Nancy's back, and went to grasp Billy by the shoulder.

'Billy, you can stand down now. We're not in France anymore. We're here, where we belong, at the Buckingham Hotel.'

Vivienne had started sobbing. Her tears came in silence, her body wracked by spasms so great that Stan squirmed uncomfortably on her lap. As Mrs Moffatt came to comfort him, Nancy rushed to Vivienne's side. There she crouched, with her arms draped around her.

'But how?' Vivienne finally asked. 'Billy said you were in the hold of the ship when it went down ...'

Raymond seemed to be staring straight through her. Six weeks had passed since that fateful moment when a torpedo had torn through the hull of HMS *Othello*; six weeks, but it may as well have been a lifetime.

'I'll tell you everything,' he said. 'But before I do, there's one thing I want to make clear.' Raymond cleared his throat; he had a part to play this evening, perhaps the finest role of his career, and he intended to do it justice. 'My brother saved my life, in every possible way. And he died a hero. He died in my arms, and he died for this country he loved. He died for every one of us in this room, and I intend to honour that for the rest of my life.' He turned back to Vivienne; he would do this thing properly, and say it to her face. 'We made it out of the *Othello*, Vivienne. We made it out – but that was only the beginning ...'

Raymond put a boot upon the first step, the dead weight of Artie against one shoulder. It wasn't going to be easy getting up those steps, but Artie still had the use of his hands; he was already grasping the rail, to hoist himself along.

'It's not far, Artie. This is the hard bit. If we make it through this bit then—'

'Oh, *this* is the hard bit, is it, Ray?' scoffed Artie; quite how he could be cracking jokes and making that wolfish smile in this situation, Raymond did not know. 'I rather hoped that drowning in the dark with a metal pillar pinning me down might have been the *hardest* part – but now you tell me that was a doddle.'

'Just hold on, Artie, we've got to—'

The terrible shriek of metal grating against metal filled the hold. Too late, Raymond realised that, somewhere at the back of the hold, the damage done to the structure of the *Othello* had been too much for the vessel to bear; now, the ship was being scythed apart by the pressures. The water they had thought was rushing into the hold had, it transpired, been a mere trickle. Now came the deluge.

'Artie . . .' Raymond gasped – but that was all he could say.

One moment, they were readying to go up the steps, tightly bound to each other, two bodies moving as one; the next, they were being cleaved apart, ripped into churning waters, smashed against steel and railings, just flotsam made out of flesh and bones.

Darkness. Darkness everywhere. Sometimes, Raymond opened his lips and breathed in air. Sometimes, he breathed in salt water. He didn't know up from down. Forward from back. All he knew was that he was trapped in some formidable current, being pounded from all sides.

He reached out. What he was reaching for, he did not know. And yet, somehow, his fingers brushed Artie's own outstretched hand. After that, they were being tossed and turned together.

Until they saw light.

It was nothing – just a small portal of brightness. Raymond tried to angle himself towards it, but all his attempts were in vain; the pressure in his lungs was too vast, and he felt heavy, heavier than he had ever felt in his life. He kicked feebly. He threw his body forward.

He blacked out.

Time: vast and meaningless.

'Wake up, Ray! Ray Cohen, you ol' dog, wake up!'

He opened his eyes. Somehow, he was still alive.

It took Raymond some time to ascertain where he was. The darkness was so absolute that the only way he knew he was above water was by the wind that raked across his face, and the salt spray of the sea that coated him. He was lying, half spread-eagled, across some piece of wreckage – and clinging to the other end of it was Artie.

Artie heaved himself around to Raymond's side, slapping him until he was sure he was conscious.

'You got to wake up, Ray. We can't stay here.'

The horizon was pitch black all around – except in one direction. Lights were gleaming, somewhere in the south: great pyres of fire on the coast. Raymond dared not dream it was England he was looking at; he already knew it was not. Those fires were what was left of the supplies and ammunition caches the British were being compelled to leave behind as they abandoned France.

Raymond thrashed in the freezing water, if only to prove to himself he was still alive. It was only then that he realised how swollen his face had become; he could only see through one eye. Minor wounds, he supposed. He gripped Artie's arm.

'Your leg?'

'Hanging on by a thread,' scoffed Artie. 'You might have to do the kicking, Ray – but we have to get back to the beach. Tide's taking us that way anyway, if I'm any judge. It just needs a helping hand.'

Raymond nodded. He strained against the agonies of his body and arranged himself so that, using the wreckage as a float, he might propel them forwards. He supposed it was only by some strange miracle that he was here at all. But if one miracle had happened, well, he supposed he might as well hope for another.

'They'll be taking more off the beaches tomorrow. We can still get home, Artie.'

'One problem at a time, Ray. Let's just get out of this water first . . .'

Two bedraggled soldiers, tossed up on a beach to the west of Dunkirk.

'You can do this, Artie.'

'I keep telling you, Ray, I'll be dancing by midsummer's night . . .'

Picture them: each hanging from the other's shoulder as they staggered up, out of the surf, onto a stretch of wild, abandoned beach. Cold and exhausted – and suddenly exposed – they reeled away from the water's edge, not stopping – even in spite of the pain eviscerating their bodies – until they'd reached the semi-shelter of the rocks and scrub above the beach. Here, Raymond lowered Artie off his shoulder – and then collapsed, into the thistles and thorns.

In the Housekeeping Lounge, Raymond took hold of Nancy's hand – as if to say that he needed her guidance, if he was to keep on telling the story. Her touch brought him the comfort he had needed – because, for a split second, it had felt as if he was back on that midnight beach, just him and his brother in the middle of a swirling vortex.

He looked at Vivienne and said, 'I went to scout the area. I needed to know where we'd washed up. I suppose it was the first morning of June. Summer in the air. But all I could smell was smoke. The smell of artillery fire, blowing in on the wind.'

They'd come ashore somewhere west of Dunkirk, a hike away from the beaches where the BEF was assembled.

'How far?' Artie gasped, when Raymond crashed back into the scrub to join him.

'Too far for that leg,' said Raymond. 'We're outside the perimeter, if I've got it right. Artie, you're going to have to let me see it.'

It was a swollen, blistered mess. Raymond, remembering his basic training, hoped the salt water had sterilised the wound – and the chill of the ocean must have numbed the pain, because only now did Artie seem to be suffering with it. Perhaps adrenaline and sheer grit had been carrying him through. It was broken – it didn't need a medic to tell that – but in how many places, Raymond could not say.

'You're going to have to go without me, Ray.'

Artie reached into the inside of his sodden uniform and pulled out the wax pouch he kept in the inner lining. Inside was the letter he'd written for Vivienne, before they boarded the boat.

'Artie, I'll carry you all the way if I have to. We're going to get back to the beach and we'll get you up onto the mole. You're walking wounded now – they'll give you priority. Onto some trawler and away. And this time we'll make the crossing, plain sailing all the way. Well, lightning can't strike twice.' Raymond threw himself onto the ground. 'I just need to catch my breath, Artie. Then we'll set off.'

'You can't carry me all that way, Ray . . .'

'I dragged you out of the water, didn't I?'

Artie laughed. 'You're forgetting – you'd still be bobbing around in a daze out there, if I hadn't knocked some sense back into you.' He paused. Then, more gently, he said, 'One of us has got to get there, Ray. Look at me—'

'Then I might as well have left you in the water!' Raymond snapped.

'Fat chance!' Artie laughed. 'You needed somebody geeing you along. Performing artistes like you can't do anything without an audience!'

*Even now*, thought Raymond – *in the middle of Hell, on the brink of death, in the edgeland between what was real and what was not – Artie can't waste an opportunity to bait me.* The insanity of it made him laugh.

'Up you get, old boy,' Raymond said. 'Let's see how far we can go.'

They didn't get far.

In faltering fits and starts, they picked their way along the beach, but it wasn't long before they sensed movement in the road above them – a convoy of blacked-out vehicles, moving through the night. They hunkered down until the convoy had passed, but scarcely two hundred yards further on, it became clear they were not alone. The roads were filled with Nazi patrols. Raymond and Artie watched, from a gorse thicket on the road's edge, as part of an armoured division roared towards the Dunkirk perimeter.

'It's only two miles until the perimeter, Artie. We get over that, and we can get you some help. That's if the French don't shoot us on the spot . . .'

*Two miles*, thought Raymond – walking in the wake of the German advance. Well, they hadn't been spared a death at sea, just to capitulate on land. He waited until there was nothing moving on the road, and made to heave Artie out of their hiding.

But this time Artie wouldn't be moved.

'I can't,' he said – and Raymond knew, by the agony that clouded his features, that this was his final word. 'You have to go, Ray.'

Raymond shook his head. 'I'm not going home without you. Just think of what our mother would say, Artie.'

Artie seemed to know what Raymond was thinking. He put up his arms in protest – but, once Raymond had stopped holding him up, it was all that he could do not to topple over into the scrub. In the next moment, Raymond had hoisted him over his shoulder. He'd made more delicate, refined lifts in his time in the ballroom – but Raymond didn't suppose anybody was judging his technique out here. Of course, he'd never had to carry Karina Kainz or Hélène Marchmont for two miles through a nightscape teeming with enemy soldiers. That, he supposed, was the major point of difference. But he was going to give it everything he had.

One foot in front of the other. One foot in front of the other again. Four times, Raymond barrelled Artie into the shadows on the edge of the road when he heard the guttering roar of vehicles approaching; twice he left the road altogether, fearful of the roadblocks that marred the way ahead.

'But there wasn't a way,' said Raymond, softly, in the silence of the Housekeeping Lounge. 'The night was teeming. The sky itself seemed to be crashing around us. We got close to the perimeter. I could hear the sputtering fire of the Bren guns, keeping the perimeter safe. But there wasn't a way through – not without being seen. Not without being strafed down as we dared the approach. And then, suddenly, daylight was pouring back into the world. I knew we couldn't stay out in the open, not without risking capture. So I found us a barn, and I barrelled us inside it – and we stayed there, hidden in the hay, until the darkness returned. All through the day, they were taking them off the beaches. The harbour was so close. I fancied I could hear the waves crashing. I could hear the crash of the artillery. At one point, I dared peek out – I could see them dogfighting in the air above Dunkirk. But, as close as they were, they might as well have been on the other side of the world.'

When darkness returned, Raymond was determined to try again. By then it had been thirty-six hours and more since he'd last eaten. A gnawing hunger and exhaustion had taken hold of him, but he kept it at bay, drinking water from a puddle that had formed in the corner of the barn.

'But Artie couldn't go anywhere,' Raymond said – and, this time, he let go of Nancy's hand and crouched at Vivienne's side, daring to take hers instead. 'It had turned to fever. He kept slipping away from me, into dreams – and it got so that that was better for him. So I sat with him – and, though I knew he'd think me a sentimental old fool, I took his hand, tried to talk him back to consciousness. When he was lucid at all, he told me to get out of there. I got sick of hearing those words. But daylight came again – and, Vivienne, I'm so sorry, but that was the last day he'd ever see.' Raymond's voice broke. 'I buried him there in the barn, myself. An old shovel had been propped up by the bails. I lay him down in the hole I'd dug and promised him I'd come home.'

Raymond paused; the doors of the Housekeeping Lounge were inching open, and in their frame stood Frank Nettleton and Rosa – and, behind them, Karina Kainz. There was an intermission in the ballroom – and now, here they all stood, staring in consternation at their returning hero.

'And here I am,' said Raymond.

Raymond didn't expect to feel Frank Nettleton's arms around him. The younger dancer had barrelled over and wrapped himself around his brother-in-law, while yet more figures filed into the Housekeeping Lounge. Raymond did not recognise the gentleman dancer at Karina's side – and he hardly recognised Walter Knave as well; the elderly man seemed more sprightly somehow, and certainly less inebriated than when Raymond had seen him last. At his side stood John Hastings, who inclined his head in a nod of such reverence that Raymond felt as if all the countless sacrifices he'd seen made in France were being honoured.

Vivienne was silently quaking in her seat. Nancy went to wrap her in arms.

'I never did make it to the harbour in time,' said Raymond, and though his story was for Vivienne and Nancy, he found that he was speaking to the room at large. 'I meant to set out, the moment I buried Artie – but I couldn't bring myself to leave him. My only brother. So I lingered a little. It's fortuitous I did. That night, three others who'd been left behind came to take shelter in that barn. After that, they were my unit. The coast was overrun, and all the French armies – and what British didn't make it to Dunkirk in time – were being taken as prisoners of war. But we found a cellar to take sanctuary in. We didn't know what the next thing was. We only knew the nights bled into the days, over and over again. But then there was hope – a little fishing skiff, tossed back onto the beaches after it was abandoned out at sea, one of that little armada the English sent over to get their boys back. The very last boat. Chances like that don't come around very often, so by cover of night we took it. Had to bail water all the crossing, and Lord knows how we ran the gauntlet of mines left out in the Channel, but we made it back.'

Raymond looked up and across the room.

'So here we stand,' he said, softly. 'The miracle of Dunkirk – over. The Battle for France – lost. Empty holes in our lives, where the ones we loved used to stand. But . . .'

Raymond faltered and, into the silence, John Hastings said, 'Mr de Guise, I think, perhaps, you should come this way.'

Raymond could hardly bring himself to leave Nancy – but, in the end, he didn't have to; in the end, they all followed after, Nancy and Vivienne and Billy and Frank, Karina Kainz and Marcus Arbuthnot, back across the hotel reception, through the dressing rooms at the rear of the Grand, and into the open dance floor doors. Through them, with baby Stan cradled in his arms, Raymond saw the great and good of London hobnobbing with men in the uniform of the British Expeditionary Force. He saw the ballroom strung up in Union Jacks and summer bunting. An explosion of colour. A riot of light and noise to celebrate the miracle of Dunkirk. His heart filled when he saw the Norwegian king and crown prince beyond the dance floor balustrade – noble figures in exile.

He took Nancy's hand. She, in turn, held Vivienne's.

'So here we stand,' he said. 'Broken, yes – but defeated? Not yet. Not while my brother's memory burns so fiercely in my mind.'

*Look at them out there*, he thought. *Dancers and soldiers and dethroned kings. People driven out of their homelands. People running scared from war. People for whom the world will never be the same again.* At this, he looked sidelong at Vivienne and felt the burning in his heart. *But they're still dancing*, he thought. *They're still coming together, in music and song. They haven't stopped living. And neither will we.*

'We've been knocked down,' said Raymond at last, as the Archie Adams Orchestra reassembled in anticipation of the next number to come, 'but Great Britain still stands. And we don't stand alone – not really. Not when all of the Continent's toppled governments make their way to us. To London. To the Buckingham Hotel.'

Raymond wanted nothing more than to step on to the ballroom floor, but it was not his place – not any longer. He stood back as the dancers – led by Marcus and Karina, with Frank and Mathilde cantering behind – returned to the floor, and the waves of applause that greeted them. Then, as the stage doors closed and the music began, he passed baby Stan to Nancy – and, reaching into the folds of his jacket, he produced a single envelope, which he handed to Vivienne. Her name was written across the front, in Artie's spidery scrawl.

'He had it on him, when the *Othello* went down. He had it on him, when we were washed back on to the beaches. Safe in its little wax pouch. Even his tobacco stayed dry.' Raymond hesitated. 'He had it with him when he died, Vivienne. He's up there now, asking you to open it up.'

Vivienne trembled. 'Not now.' She fingered its creases obsessively before hiding it in her house dress.

'What now?' asked Nancy.

'I must go to Whitechapel,' said Raymond. 'Would you come with me? My mother believes both her sons have perished. I have to give her the truth – and break her heart all over again.'

Frank Nettleton woke late and rolled over to find the mid-morning sunlight already lancing through the curtains. It had been many months since there were sounds of voices raised in cheer at number 62 Albert Yard, and at first the sound was discombobulating. Then, his face opened in a wild, unbidden smile. Pulling on his clothes, he staggered to the doorway – he'd been sleeping in one of the younger Brogans' bedrooms, ever since Billy came back home – and listened to the voices from below.

Rosa was already here. He hurried down the stairs and found her at the dining table with Billy and his parents.

'Postman's been, Frank!' Billy cried out. 'Letters from Patrick and Conor and Roisin and all the rest. They all heard I'm back. Now *they're* clamouring to come home, too!'

Frank hurried to the table. Breakfast was still spread all around, and Rosa immediately started fussing around him, covering a crumpet with greengage preserve.

'So tell us, young Frank,' said Mr Brogan, 'what does it feel like, finally a ballroom professional?'

Frank's first instinct was to dismiss the words – but, the moment he opened his lips, Rosa (who, naturally, knew what he was thinking) chastised him with her eyes, and instead he said, 'Like it was a dream, I suppose. Like it never happened at all. What, with Raymond appearing in the middle of it and . . .'

422

'You showed 'em you can dance, Frank Nettleton,' said Billy. 'Whatever else happened last night, don't forget your part in it. You're a natural in that ballroom, Frank. It's where you're going to stay. And . . . well, it's where I'll be staying as well. I might not have dancing legs anymore –' he patted his crippled leg – 'but it's not going to stop me doing my bit. You and me, Frank, back at the Buckingham. Well, somebody's got to keep that place safe in whatever's coming. Cometh the hour, cometh the man.'

Billy took a big slurp of tea and sat back. There was something about his bravado that filled Frank's heart with cheer – it was as if he was watching the old Billy resurgent; the Billy Brogan who had sashayed so freely through the Buckingham halls in those years before war came down. The Buckingham would be a better place for having him there; perhaps Frank would not feel quite as left behind and alone. And, besides, if what they were saying was true, not a woman or man – whether he'd been conscripted or not – was going to escape the next battle. It was going to rage all around them.

Mr Brogan turned round the edition of the morning's *Daily Express* he was reading and showed them the headlines. During the night, German bombers had targeted coastal radar stations and warehouses up and down the south coast.

'They already know they've got us on the back foot. But they know something else as well – or they ought to, if they've been paying attention.'

'What's that?' asked Rosa.

'I reckon your Frank can explain. And our Bill. Well, boys?'

Frank and Billy exchanged a look – and, in the fractional silence that passed between them, there was a story of the surging waters of the English Channel, and one friend who had dragged the other out of the brine.

'The resilience of Great Britain,' said Billy.

'That we might have danced with disaster,' said Frank, 'but we kept on dancing.'

'That we didn't give up, not when all the odds in the world were stacked against us.'

All those fishermen and fishermen's sons, the riverboats and pleasure craft, rallying to the defence of the nation. They were going to have to do it again, Frank supposed. Up and down the land, in countryside and city, in farmers' fields and town squares, everybody was going to have to arm themselves and fight. One of the newspaper headlines was even asking for people to turn in any old metal they had lying around. 'Give us your pots and pans!' an advert declared. 'We'll turn them into Spitfires and Hurricanes! Protect your country!'

*That was the British way*, thought Frank. Beaten but not broken, down on their knees but not knocked out, using every last piece of ingenuity they could to pick a path to victory. The Battle for France could have been a massacre – but, by digging deep and doggedly working together, it had turned into a triumph. The battle to save Britain was only just beginning, but already Frank could sense the country rolling its sleeves up. And this time there would be no crippling doubt from him. You didn't need a medical certificate when the battle was on your own doorstep. He'd be right there, ready and willing to defend the people and place he loved most in all of the world – the Buckingham Hotel, with his best friend Billy at his side.

'How long do you think we have?' Frank wondered, staring at the advert.

'Oh, not long, son,' said Mr Brogan, sadly. 'So enjoy these long summer days while you can. The world's about to change, for every last one of us.'

In the same moment that Billy, Frank and Rosa stepped out into the summer sunshine to take a long perambulation along the river, Vivienne Cohen pushed Stan's pram into the shadow of the old H. J. Packer Building and looked up at the new 'Daughters of Salvation' sign hanging above the entrance. Her mind raked back to all those long nights at the old red-brick chapel, Artie standing sentry outside while she worked within. She liked to think of him here, on the doorstep now – but, no matter how hard she focused, she couldn't summon his ghost, so instead she pushed Stan inside and crossed the great warehouse floor.

Work hadn't stopped at the Daughters of Salvation. That, she reflected as she kept her head down and bustled towards the office doors, was the cruellest thing. The sun still rose in the morning. The London buses still weaved their routes across the city. Seabirds still wheeled over the river, shoppers still queued up with their ration-books beneath the awnings on the Whitechapel Road – and she, Vivienne Cohen, still took laboured breath after laboured breath. Artie was gone from the world, but the world barely reeled.

'Vivienne,' said Warren Peel, looking up from his work at the desk as she entered. 'My God, Vivienne, what are you doing here? We've got everything covered. You didn't need to worry. You should be taking your time. Resting and—'

Vivienne ignored him as she manoeuvred the pram into the corner and, checking that Stan was still soundly sleeping, began taking off her coat.

'It's really no fuss, Warren, I'm quite—'

At that moment, the office door burst open and Mary Burdett tumbled in, her doughy face etched in lines of incomprehension and concern.

'Mrs Cohen. Vivienne. As I live and breathe! What are you—?'

Vivienne took her arm out of a resistant sleeve, hung up her coat, and turned on the spot.

'Warren,' she said. 'Mary. I appreciate your concern. I do. But you're my friends – and as my friends I ask that you . . .'

*Don't speak of it*, she wanted to say. *Don't question me. Don't go fussing around me like I'm the widowed mother I am. As if life hasn't knocked me down and repeatedly kicked me, while I'm lying there in the gutter, looking up at the stars.*

'I was due to be here, and here I am. That's the end of it.' She bustled around to take the seat Warren had just vacated at the table. 'If you want to help me, I should enjoy a pot of tea. And some sugar, if we've any to spare.'

She was taking hold of the ledger Warren had been working through, perusing the columns of figures, when she realised they were still there – just staring at her.

She looked up.

'Vivienne,' Mary ventured, 'we all had a talk last night. We rather thought that you . . . Well, what with Stan and Artie and everything that's happened, we rather thought you might be taking a little absence from . . . Some time, to get things straight for you and your boy.'

Warren added, 'We can cover everything, Vivienne. We don't want you thinking that—'

'Thinking that . . . you might need me? No, I won't be going anywhere. I'm to stay, right here, where it matters. Or else . . .'

426

She steeled herself so that she did not crack. 'What was it all for? What am *I* for, if I'm not here, right here where I belong?'

There was a long, lingering silence.

'Tea, then,' said Mary. 'I think we can just about manage that.'

She and Warren slipped, quietly, out of the office door.

After they were gone, Vivienne laid out the envelope on the ledger in front of her and stared, again, at Artie's handwriting. He'd never had much of a hand for writing. Vivienne had known him to sign his name in block capital letters, and the only way she could really picture him with a pencil in his hand at all was if he was using it to fill in a betting slip, or to annotate the racing tips in the newspaper. Those images brought her a strange, wistful cheer. It seemed incredible that he'd penned her an actual letter.

Until she opened it, it could have said anything. That, she supposed, was why she hadn't opened it yet. Right now, it either contained all of Artie's heart, or a list of the things he was looking forward to having for dinner. Perhaps there was more value in leaving it forever unopened; more value in the anticipation, than in knowing, with every certainty, that she'd read the last words he ever wrote for her. Not opening the envelope was like keeping him alive.

But her finger was already sliding under the lip and gently teasing it open. She needed to hear from him one final time.

*Dear Viv*

*Well, things have got tricky out here. If you're reading this letter, I'm either sitting there with you and we're toasting it over a nice cup of tea — or I'm not, and Billy or Ray have brought it back to you, to see me off. We reached the beaches yesterday afternoon, but what hope there is of us being lifted off, I daren't say. Still, where there's a will, there's a way. The British Expeditionary Force is full of ingenious minds, and among them I am certain there is at least one stage magician who can orchestrate the illusion of his lifetime: how to make 300,000 honest British Tommies walk on water?*

*Viv, you know me better than anyone who ever lived, and you know I'm not much for emotions or big words. But it seems to me that, if ever there was an occasion in my life where I ought to say the things I feel, it's right now — right now with the Stukas just rolled overhead, and the bodies piled up on the beach behind me. Vivienne, I love you.*

Vivienne let out an involuntary whimper. Her hand was shaking. She had to avert her eyes from the letter, if only to catch her breath – and, when she returned them to the page, the words were still there, staring at her. Real words, she thought. Genuine words, unfiltered, unread, uncensored by anyone in the armed forces – words, directly from his heart, into hers. His last gift for her, and her alone.

*I've told you before that I never expected to find someone to share my life with. Not outside of a Pentonville cell. I'm not like my brother. I didn't grow up with my head filled of grand romantic ideals. But then, three years ago, there you were — and, since that day, my life has been better for it. I am a better man for having known you, Vivienne. I am a better man that you asked me into your life. And I am standing here on the beaches at Dunkirk, trying to get home to you, because of that. I am standing up for what is good and right in the world, because, in you, I have something that's worth fighting for. If these days are to be my last, well, I will die knowing that I did what was right. I will die knowing that we stood up against the darkness — and that, one day, you will tell our beautiful son Stanley that that was the kind of man his father was. A man who, though he might have erred along the way, never wavered in the face of evil; never looked away when the world came asking.*

*I'm hungry, Viv. I bet you can imagine this of me! I could eat a horse.*

*I suppose I should leave you here with all my hopes and dreams for the future. I'll wager it's what Ray is writing to Nancy, even now. But I have only one dream, and I know it will come true, whether I make it across the water or not. I dream that one day, in this world or the next, I'm standing next to you, with the sun shining on our faces – and our family all around. I dream that we'll meet again. And, one way or another, I know it will come true.*

*Eternally yours*

*Artie*

For a long time after that, Vivienne simply sat and stared at the letter. She was sitting and staring at it still, when Mary Burdett returned with the pot of tea, and bowl of sugar lumps she'd managed to procure.

As she laid them down, she said, 'Vivienne, if there's anything else I can do, anything at all . . .'

Vivienne looked up, through eyes filled with tears that seemed to make the whole world shimmer. It was those three words that had done it: *we'll meet again*. Words filled with such infinite sadness – and yet, somehow, such hope as well.

'Mary,' she said, 'let's keep at it. I'm not going anywhere, I promise. Not now, and not ever – not until all our work is done.'

Well, she reflected as Mary beat a retreat out onto the warehouse floor, if there was one thing she'd learned from Artie, that was it: every time you were on your knees, you picked yourself up, dusted yourself off and got on with it.

It was the Cohen way.

Let us fly now, across the rooftops of London, past the spires of Westminster and the emerald expanses of St James's, and into the heart of Mayfair. Down over Berkeley Square we go, down through the revolving brass doors of the Buckingham Hotel, across a reception hall where Archie Adams is making small-talk with guests and concierges, past the office doors where the hotel director Walter Knave, freshly restored to his own good graces, contends with the scandals of the day; down the long Housekeeping Hall where Rosa, Mary-Louise and the other chambermaids gather for the direction of their stalwart Mrs Moffatt – and round, past the service stairs and lift, through the network of dressing rooms and studios at the back of the Grand Ballroom, and into the ballroom itself, where Raymond de Guise dances quietly, with only Nancy in his arms.

The ballroom was still strung with garlands from the night before. The flags still rippled and the bunting still streamed. But the only sound on that dance floor was the gentle foot-work of Raymond as he led his wife in a dance that nobody had designed – the simple, everyday dance that flowed out of him whenever they were near one another. Apart from that, all he could hear was the music of his own heart: the gentle, rhythmic percussion that came whenever he held her near.

After some time, Raymond drew back and, reaching into his own pocket, produced the letter he had written for Nancy on the beaches at Dunkirk. She watched, with curious eyes, as he lifted it in front of her and shredded it to pieces.

'What did it say, Raymond?'

Raymond smiled. There had been only six words in that letter, and yet they encompassed the entire world.

'I will always love you, Nancy.'

The ballroom around them was empty. Soon, Raymond would have to depart. Three days' leave, and then he would have to rejoin his unit for whatever came next. If the lesson of the last weeks had been anything at all, it was this: that every day might be the last one now, every farewell the final one. There wasn't enough time in the world to say all the things you wanted to say. There weren't the hours to do justice to the things a man felt. All you could really do was live, right now, in the moment you were given. They'd go to Vivienne, soon. The family would rally round, and Raymond would uphold every promise he'd made his brother: that his son would never go without, that his family would never forget – nor diminish – the sacrifice he'd made. But first there was this moment in time, one to live in, one to treasure.

'Raymond,' whispered Nancy, as they turned across the dance floor, waltzing to the silence, 'have you ever thought . . .'

She faltered, and Raymond did not press her. They danced on, until at last she said again, 'I know it's not the time to think about the future, not with Artie, but you're back and I can't—'

'Artie would want us to think about the future,' Raymond said, and believed it as well. 'It's why he died – for the future we all should have.'

So Nancy stepped out of his hold and she and Raymond stood, cocooned together, in a perfect stillness.

'I should like it if we were to have a child. I'm not saying right now, when the world's on fire – and, Lord knows, perhaps we won't be here by summer's end. Perhaps it's all going to be over, or very different, and none of us know how that might look. But I can feel it now, that need, deep inside me – that life should go on.'

Raymond folded his arms back around her.

'Nancy,' he said, 'I've been dreaming about it, too.'

But that was for another day – and, for now, while they were together and the world, for the most fleeting of moments, was holding its breath, they did the only thing that truly felt right.

They danced.

# *Acknowledgements*

From *Strictly* group dances, to choreographing my shows and recording my album, I've always loved working in a team and collaborating on my projects and my writing is no different. The Buckingham and all the characters within represent people I've met and places I've visited throughout my life, so recreating them as a work of fiction has been a joy, but I wouldn't have been able to bring them to life without the support of my amazing publishing team.

My incredible editor, Sarah Bauer, has worked with me from the beginning and whilst I've missed doing edits in person with her, I've not missed trying to park near the Bonnier office! Thanks for the Zoom calls and for reigning me in when I get a bit too 'creative' on who to kill off, and how. Thanks also to the rest of my marvellous editorial team – Katie Meegan, Katie Lumsden and Kate Parkin – who have been there every step of the way. I'm very lucky to have worked on all of my novels with a wonderful – and so *sympatico* – writing collaborator; thank you for all your input and assistance over the last few years.

Thanks also to Steve O'Gorman and Jon Appleton for their thorough copyediting and proofreading – such unwavering eyes for detail, and tenacious fact-checking!

I have the best team of publicists, working all year round to promote my books. Thank you to Francesca Russell, Clare Kelly, Karen Stretch and Jenna Petts for all you do, and here's hoping we can get back out on the road again soon. And a special congratulations to Francesca on the new addition to the family – I'm sure she won't mind me mentioning it.

When I write the books, I visualise everything. So, I'm incredibly impressed that not only are the covers beautiful, but match exactly what's in my mind's eye. I'm so grateful to Jenny Richards for all her stunning artwork, bringing the Buckingham to life.

So many people are involved in marketing and selling a book, so my heartfelt thanks go to Vicky Joss (and welcome to team Buckingham!), Jess Tackie, Stephen Dumughn, Felice McKeown, Elise Burns, Mark Williams, Stuart Finglass, Andrea Tome, Stacey Hamilton, Maddie Hanson, Amanda Percival, Jearl Boatswain, Vincent Kelleher, Sophie Hamilton and Kate Griffiths. They all work tirelessly to sell my books around the world.

To Alex May, Ella Holden and Eloise Angeline and the whole production department, I never cease to marvel at how you turn my many word documents into actual, real-life books! Yours is a very special magic for which I can't thank you enough!

Thanks also to Laura Makela, Jon Watt and Alexandra Schmidt who organised and created the audiobook, and for letting me sneak into the studio to record some bits, too. Being such a fan of audiobooks (they're the perfect driving companion between shows), it's thrilling to think that others will be listening to my stories read aloud in the same manner. Vocal thanks to Thomas Judd for bringing the members of the Buckingham Hotel to life in the audiobook . . . and my apologies for the vast range of accents you have to do!

Thanks go to everyone else at Bonnier Books UK, including Ruth Logan, Stella Giatrakou, Ilaria Tarasconi, Nick Ash, Amy Smith and Shane Hegarty. I'm sorry I've not been able to visit your offices this year, but hope to see you all again soon.

I am indebted to Melissa Chappell for her guidance, insight, and support as my agent, but more importantly, as a true friend. Your talents are endlessly invaluable in bringing so many of my ideas and projects so wonderfully to life. Thank you also to Hollie Paton Pratt whose skills know no bounds in keeping me organised, up to date, and at the right place at the right time – no mean feat, I'm sure! Thanks, too, to Kerr MacRae, my literary agent, for opening the door to this wondrous world of publishing, but also for your continued belief in me as an author.

Thank you to Scott Mycock – ten years now on 'Team Anton', and so fabulously diligent on all things digital.

A very special thank you must be reserved for you, my readers, for without your tremendous support and encouragement there would be no novels. It never ceases to thrill me when I hear how the Buckingham and its characters have connected with you when we chat on my book tours or after shows. Dare I say, I'm a performer at heart – having an audience is my lifeblood – so to widen this with a readership with whom I can share my stories brings me an unforetold joy. Thank you, once again, for opening these pages and stepping into the world of the Buckingham Hotel with me.

My loves,

I've been so looking forward to writing this personal note to you – excitingly if you've reached this page, it means you've very likely just finished reading my new book, *We'll Meet Again*, I so hope you've enjoyed it!

*We'll Meet Again* is the fourth instalment in my series of novels. If you've been following the lives of Raymond, Nancy and all their friends and families in and around the Buckingham Hotel, my heartfelt thanks to you. Your readership really does mean the world to me. If this is your first step into what's now the wartime world of the Buckingham Hotel – may I extend the very warmest of welcomes . . . and invite you to fill in the preceding years with *One Enchanted Evening*, *Moonlight Over Mayfair* and *A Christmas to Remember* – there is much to catch up on!

The past year has been eventful for us all, though more a case of event-less for so many of us in the entertainment industry with theatres closed and tours cancelled due to the restrictions. Finding myself with a little more time on my hands, I'll readily admit that reading gave me such comfort in those quiet months, so wonderful to lose oneself in the pages of a good book – I hope you've been able to find this, too. Much of my reading was to prove invaluable as background research for *We'll Meet Again*, swotting up on the timings and events around the onset of war – all so important to building up a picture of how it would effect the Buckingham, our characters' day-to-day lives, and how their stories might then weave between the threads of history.

Set at such a tumultuous time with the blackouts, rationing and the call to arms, this always promised to be a challenging book – scenes of war and conflict being such a departure from the gentility of the Grand Ballroom. Great changes would take place with emotions running high for all: in those who went away to fight, and those unable to; in those who were left behind; in newlyweds pulled apart; in all the children evacuated away from their homes and parents; even in those who couldn't accept that war was being waged – until it eventually touched them all personally. How would our characters fare, brought together and bonded over the course of three previous books, but now facing so many kinds of separation?

I was also tasked with ensuring the magnificent Buckingham could keep its doors open and stay alive, large and central to our story. Neither you nor I would have been happy if there wasn't the usual chitchat in the chambermaids' kitchen or demonstration dancers quick-stepping across the Grand Ballroom to Archie Adams's latest tune – there simply had to be dancing! But with conscription for the menfolk, and clarion calls for so many of the women determined to play their role in the war effort, could our hotel stay afloat?

As it happened, those challenges all helped to shape the story: out of this time of crisis came new opportunities to seize, new directions to take, new roles to fill. Thrillingly, the characters stepped up so vividly in my mind, each driven to help the national effort in their own individual way, to find their own front line. Even the Buckingham, with windows blackened to the street but becoming a beacon of hope and light within, proudly hosting celebrations to boost morale, reminding all of happier times before – and promising of those to come.

There were of course difficult, dark scenes of conflict – and I hope so very much that I have sensitively portrayed the incredible bravery of those men and boys on the front line. Much inspiration has come from the privilege of speaking to war veterans at commemorative and Remembrance events over the years – so many remarkable men and women. Their stories of bravery and heroism made such an impression and I felt duty bound to do them justice and write as truthfully as I possibly could. I hope I've succeeded in that.

As for the title, I'm sure you'll agree, it couldn't be more perfect: that simple line which lifted the hearts of those who felt a world away in wartime, giving them hope of returning safely home to their loved ones. And with the passing of Dame Vera Lynn just last year, her song of hope spoke once again so timely to the nation, to all those on today's front lines, to families separated by the new enemy in this pandemic.

I mustn't give any more away just in case you haven't yet read *We'll Meet Again* – I've done very well in avoiding any major plot spoilers so far! What I can say is that the characters are already willing me on to begin the next chapters in their lives – after all, there's a war to be won. So, my loves, if you'd like to keep reading, please stay tuned for the next instalment – there are more stories to be told, and it would be my very great pleasure to keep writing!

Until next time, and with much love,

Anton
XX

If you loved *We'll Meet Again*, find out where it all began
with the previous books in the Buckingham Hotel series . . .

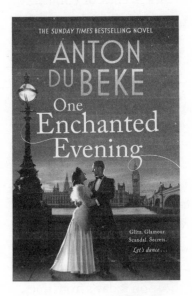

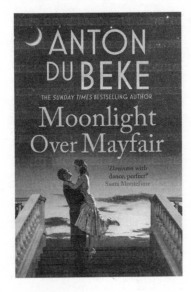

**Available now**